# SHATTERED COVENANTS BOOK III

## The Consultant

### By

### Dwight E. Foster

Credit for cover art by Brian Kappel

This book is a work of fiction. Places, events, and situations in this story are purely fictional. Any resemblance to actual persons, living or dead, is coincidental.

ISBN: 1-4033-0303-7

This book is printed on acid free paper.

1stBooks - rev. 3/22/02

# Dedication

TO: Russell F. Peppet, a man who favorably influenced many lives and consulting careers, including that of the author.

# The Consultant

Joe Baxter's management consulting career with McKenzie Barber began on the Tuesday after Labor Day in 1968. He spent a restless Monday night in the house on Palmer Street and bolted up from his bed at the sound of the electric buzz from the alarm clock. Jennifer stirred slightly, but returned to sleep. It was five-thirty in the morning and Baxter estimated that the drive to the Chicago Loop would take an hour and twenty minutes.

He had made the trip from Racine to Chicago twice during the two week interval following his acceptance of McKenzie Barber's offer of employment. Baxter used the two week period as a "get ready" period. He had talked once by telephone to Bill Dwyer who informed Baxter that he should report to the Chicago office on Tuesday and fill out the firm's "bloody papers" and "play Nickerson's game of orientation charades". You will be assigned a file case in the consultant's pool and a place to sit. But don't get too comfy." Dwyer's voice rose over the din from a crowded airport. "Pack a bag and pick up some airplane tickets for a late afternoon flight to Toledo. I've got you on a production scheduling assignment at a hydraulic component manufacturer. Nickerson's secretary, the lovely Lorna, will have tickets and some briefing documents for you. I'll meet your flight. They're calling my flight, Joe. I have to run. Glad to have you with us." The line went dead.

Baxter bought a new blue suit at J.C. Penney and visited the Racine public library to research hydraulics, review production scheduling texts and learn about Toledo. He read every piece of business magazine material with articles concerning McKenzie Barber. He was cramming for his new career with an elite world class firm. His career experience to date included the US Army and Washburn Manufacturing. Had it prepared Baxter to compete and survive in the world of McKenzie Barber?

He visited the barber shop on Saturday and purchased a carry-on suitcase from the luggage department of Sears Roebuck. Agnes, the housekeeper, was waiting in the kitchen for Baxter.

"I'll have breakfast in Chicago, Agnes," Baxter said accepting a cup of black coffee.

"You look very nice today, Joe. I know that you're going to make a very nice impression on your first day."

"I will be going to Toledo this evening and won't be back until late Friday evening."

"I'll keep things under control here, Joe, and I'll have a hot supper waiting for you on Friday night."

Baxter drained the coffee mug in rapid sips and paused to observe his reflection in the hall mirror. His red hair was neatly combed. His large frame was very comfortably presented in a blue suit, white shirt and red tie, and his shoes were highly shined. "McKenzie Barber, here I come!" He proclaimed to the mirror.

Baxter found himself in the McKenzie Barber reception area on the Tuesday after Labor Day waiting with three attractive young women. There was a tall, reserved woman from Cornell named Andrea, a heavily tanned woman from Cal-Berkley named Sandy, and a short, dark haired, energetic Jewish woman from the University of Chicago named Naomi. Naomi, who chose a blue linen suit to wear on the first day of her career with McKenzie Barber, looked familiar to Baxter. She wore dark rimmed plastic glasses, smoked two cigarettes as they waited for Nickerson's secretary, Lorna, to gather them up.

Baxter made the connection when the group was placed in the pool to fill out their forms. Naomi was Naomi Schwartz from his University of Minnesota days. She recognized Baxter at the same time.

"You're Joe Baxter, who went off to Wisconsin to install a Scanlon Plan at a small company," Naomi observed during a coffee break. "I didn't recognize you with a suit on."

"I barely recognized you, Naomi."

"Lose two to three hundred pounds and your best friends won't recognize you," Naomi explained with a sharp smile and Baxter remembered her waddle.

"I thought you were going to be a GS-9."

"I tried it and decided I'd go off to the U of Chicago on a Jewish Virgin scholarship. I finished my MBA and decided to come here."

"I'm glad you're here," Baxter said.

"So am I. You and I should have a drink one night and get caught up."

Baxter recognized invitation in Naomi's dark eyes and round face. "Let's get our bearings around this place first," he suggested.

Baxter was immediately assigned to an engagement with a manufacturer of hydraulic components headquartered in Toledo, Ohio. The engagement was the development of a materials management system for the client and was led by an Associate named Russell, with Baxter serving as the "grunt consultant".

Baxter was charged with all the detail and basic information gathering. Each Sunday evening, Baxter was expected to fly to Toledo, check in at the Holiday Inn, and meet with Russell for breakfast at six-thirty a.m. the next morning to go over the week's work plan. Following their breakfast meeting, they would drive together to the client in a rental car, timing their arrival for ten minutes ahead of the first shift. They would generally work until 6 PM and return to the motel. After freshening up, Baxter would meet Russell for dinner and they would review the day's progress. Russell would excuse himself at nine o'clock to go to his room and call his wife. Baxter would try to call Jennifer, but she was consistently out for the evening.

The project lasted three months and was succeeded by a four month project for a large physical distribution company in Cleveland where Baxter worked for an Associate named Dave. This was followed by a month long stint reviewing purchasing practices for a farm equipment manufacturer in Des Moines, Iowa, working with Russell again. Baxter would pick up his airplane tickets for the coming week at his cubicle in the pool on late Sunday afternoon and catch a cab to O'Hare to leave for the next week's work. He would also leave off his time and expense sheet which were required every two weeks by McKenzie Barber.

There were always consultants in the pool on Sunday afternoon. They drank coffee, smoked cigarettes in spite of the No Smoking signs, ate pizza and poured over data charts, while operating Friden calculators. One Spring Sunday afternoon, Baxter found Naomi and Andrea working feverishly on a project with papers strewn over the long table at the back of the room. "Hi stranger," Naomi greeted Baxter. He hadn't seen her since the Pool Consultants Christmas cocktail party in December. "You remember Andrea from our morning of filling out insurance forms? She goes by Andy."

Andy stood up to shake hands. She was quite tall, arranged her hair in a bun and wore a turtleneck and slacks. Naomi had her black hair cut short, was dressed in a black sweater and slacks with a single strand of pearls. She was still large breasted, but now her waist was narrow. Her legs appeared shapely, although Naomi still showed heavy thighs in her black slacks. She noted Baxter's eyes moving over her body.

"Joe knew me when I was as fat as two hogs. That's why he always gives me the once-over, Andy."

"And what are you ladies up to?" Baxter asked.

"We've been given a very interesting special project for the firm," Andy announced proudly. "We are completing a study that was launched many years ago. It is concerned with the feasibility of opening new practices in emerging markets. We have carte blanche to use all of the resources of the firm and computer time on the IBM 7070. We have been traveling around to meet the Managing Partners of different offices and we have a half-hour with Ernie Grey when he's here next week."

"This is the old satellite office study," Baxter observed remembering a long ago discussion with Lee Heller on Pool projects.

"They put a new face on it, Joe," Naomi explained. "Besides they've never had well motivated, non-chargeable women to work on this project before."

3

"I believe the firm is very serious about this project," Andy said defensively.

"So where are you off to, Joey?" Naomi asked.

"Des Moines. I'm on the third week of a four week study."

"Oh for the life of a traveling man visiting faraway places with romantic names. When's your flight?"

"6:10," Baxter said looking at his watch. It was 4:45. Naomi picked up the tattered copy of the pool airline guide and began to leaf through it. "There's an 8:55 flight. If I can get you on it, will you have supper with Andy and me?" We rarely can get a male consultant to talk to us."

Baxter shrugged his shoulders. "Just get me there so that I can make breakfast promptly with Russell, the Associate on the job."

They had supper at a Chinese restaurant in Rosemont near O'Hare driving out in Andy's car. After two bottles of Chinese beer, Andy began to relax. Naomi drank white wine by the glass and maintained the conversation at a lively pace.

"What happened to that girl with the tan from California?" Baxter asked after they had returned to Andy's car.

"Sandy? She quit in January," Naomi announced. "Every time she was assigned to a job they just wanted to use her for maintaining the workpapers during the day and for evil purposes in the evening. She spent a lot of time in the pool room doing her nails, and a lot of Associates used to hang around her desk. No one ever wanted her on their jobs. Then she was invited to the real Christmas party. The one the Partners, Managers, and Associates are invited to. The Pool party is for pool people and condescending Associates. But our little Sandy was invited up to the big time by one of the Associates. I think his name is Jeff or something. Anyway, Jeff invited Sandy to the big party at the Drake. It's all she could talk about for two weeks. Bought a new cocktail dress, had her hair done, and went off like Cinderella to the ball! Then at the Drake, she was swept off her feet by this Southern gentleman who was a manager. She dropped Jeff like a stone and glommed on to this guy. Jeff got drunk and went home without her. This other guy, the manager from the South, took her off to his suite in the Drake, ravished her and in between ravishes promised to do a little for her career. Sandy came back on the Monday after the party convinced that she would be promoted to Associate in January. Except the Manager didn't call. Comes mid-January, Sandy is getting tired of doing her nails and flirting with Associates in the pool room. So she takes the initiative and calls the Manager. It seems that Prince Charming was all done in the Chicago office after the night of the Christmas party and had transferred to Barber-Paris. She calls him up in Paris and he can barely remember their fateful evening. Sandy then went to Nickerson, resigned, and went back to California to regain her tan."

4

"Seduced and abandoned! A tale of high voltage relationships in big business," Andy offered. "It would make a great Beth Gold story."

"Who's Beth Gold?" Baxter asked.

"She writes novels that women like to read. She's also big in the anti-war movement and shows up on talk shows," Naomi explained. "She's just published a book about the 1968 Chicago Democratic Convention. Where have you been, Baxter?"

"Toledo, Cleveland, and Des Moines."

They talked at length about Beth Gold. Baxter was positive it was his old friend. Apparently she had a book of short stories published which was well read on college campuses, and had written two novels which were regarded as readable, entertaining, and trashy. For the past two years, Beth had been highly visible in the anti-war movement speaking out from platforms in the company of folk singers and film stars.

"I used to know a Beth Gold fifteen years ago," Baxter commented. "She was a Jewish girl from Philadelphia who was determined to be a famous writer. I even have a couple of letters from her someplace."

"Joey, you never cease to amaze me," Naomi said, placing her hand on Baxter's thigh. She continued to touch him from time to time. McKenzie Barber was the primary subject for them. Baxter's view of the firm was far different from that of Naomi and Andy. He was simply instructed to visit engagement sites and work under Associates. His only exposure to the pool was to pick up his air tickets on Sunday afternoon and turn in his time and expense reports on a bi-weekly basis. He had seen Bill Dwyer twice in his eight months with McKenzie Barber. Both times were at engagement wrap-up meetings with the client. They would strategize the evening before relative to the add-on work opportunities with the client. Dwyer would present the findings in a series of flip charts to the client and script out comments for the Associate and Baxter to make.

"If you don't say anything lads, the client will wonder why we're charging them to have you there. The catch is that you can't say anything that I don't approve. If you do talk out of turn, you will never work on another of my engagements, which could limit your careers with McKenzie Barber."

"How have your appraisals been on your engagement?" Andy asked.

"I've never been formally appraised," Baxter answered. "Bill usually critiques us the night before and slaps us on the back after the presentation. That's based on a sample of two completed engagements."

"Firm policy dictates that every consultant be reviewed by the Associates and the Partner at the conclusion of each client engagement," Andy recited.

"I suspect that firm administrative policy is not strictly observed in the Manufacturing practice," Baxter responded.

"Well, they're chicken-shit as hell in the Chicago office," Naomi added. "Most of the pool is paranoid over appraisals. I suspect that Andy and I are a protected species because we're token women."

Andy and Naomi described the pool as a politically charged sweat shop. Andy likened it to being a plebe at West Point where her brother had gone. "An Associate is like an upper class man and the hazing can be debilitating. Clyde Nickerson is a kind of chaplain. You can go to him and talk. He's very nice, but he doesn't seem to be respected by the partners. I found out that he came to Chicago as a Manager and was supposed to build a practice in organization planning and failed. Now he's some kind of personnel manager. I rather like him."

"The problem is, Joey," Naomi interjected, "That no one wants women on their engagements. Nickerson tries to make them take us and evokes the name of Ernie Grey. The Managers and the Associates pay a little lip service and the Partners wash their hands of the whole matter. Frank Alvardi is the only exception."

"But he's like Dwyer. He didn't come up through this culture," Andy pointed out. "He has no hesitation in having us work on his engagements. But you never meet a client. You simply research data and grind numbers on his engagements. The man is very patient and quite charming. It's a pleasure to work for him. He does expect you to work long hours and he does see that you're rated after each engagement."

"He looks just like Joe DiMaggio," Naomi added. "I think he's divorced or separated and I've seen him out a couple of times for drinks with Nickerson's secretary, Lorna. That's the closest I've come to see socializing of any kind around this place. That is outside of tonight."

"I must say, Joe," Andy commented, "This has been a fun evening."

"Which should be repeated periodically," Naomi recommended. Baxter looked at his watch. It was time to catch his plane to Des Moines. "I have one last question before we break," Baxter said. "That Southern man whom Sandy met and went on to transfer to Barber-Paris, do you remember his name?"

They both looked at Baxter with blank stares. "We have met so few managers," Andy explained. "They just send Associates to the pool."

"I've got it!" Naomi announced triumphantly. "It's a very impressive name. Hamilton Burke III."

"I've met him," Baxter acknowledged, and that was how he learned that Burke had transferred to Paris.

# Jennifer and Baxter

Jennifer had achieved a life of her own. She had her projects with the Gellhorn Institute, graduate school, the anti-war movement and Agnes as her live-in baby-sitter on pension. Jennifer left the house on Palmer Street before eight each morning and returned after dinner usually in time to tuck in Joel. Jennifer customarily had an evening meeting which usually kept her out until 11:30. Her friends marveled at her energy level.

A line was drawn between Jennifer and Agnes which was not crossed. Jennifer made no demands on her to prepare meals other than Joel's. Agnes had her own income from the pension established by Tom Washburn and ran the household expenses frugally. She lived in the kitchen and ventured outside the kitchen only for periodic cleaning ventures.

Baxter left on Sunday after lunch for Chicago to pick up his tickets at the McKenzie Barber office and did not return until eight o'clock Racine time on Friday evening. Jennifer was usually out for the evening by the time Baxter arrived home. Joel had his bath and waited up with Agnes for Baxter to return. Agnes would pour Baxter a drink and he would hold Joel on his lap and they would listen to the classical station together. At nine o'clock, Joel would be placed his crib and Agnes would make Baxter a sandwich provided he was hungry. They would always have a few drinks together. Agnes would fill Baxter in on the events of the week on Palmer Street, and Baxter would tell Agnes about his work. Agnes would ask about places like Cleveland and Des Moines. Baxter would send postcards during the week addressed to Agnes and Joel. At eleven-thirty, Agnes would head out to the carriage house and Baxter would pour one final Canadian Club which he would carry to the upstairs sitting room.

On Saturday morning, Baxter and Jennifer slept in. They usually read the papers, talked, and drank coffee in the upstairs sitting room until late morning, and then went out for lunch. After lunch, Baxter would drive Agnes around grocery shopping and handle chores. Jennifer would remain behind with Joel, but then would go out for the evening after Baxter returned. Baxter would play with Joel, read, and have a drink or two with Agnes on Saturday night while they awaited Jennifer's return. On Sunday, Jennifer slept late while Baxter drove Agnes off to church and picked her up an hour later. They had a family lunch that Jennifer prepared, and Baxter was off for another week at McKenzie Barber.

Occasionally Baxter accompanied Jennifer on Saturday night to a party or a dinner. Once a month they would have dinner with Chuck and Didi and every six or eight weeks there would be a family dinner hosted by Nelson and Martha Washburn. Jennifer was very affectionate to Baxter in front of her family and very cold when they were together. While they slept in the same bed, there was no affection between them. "Please don't paw me, Joe!" Jennifer would plead. "I'm not into sex right now."

Baxter broached the subject several times over Saturday morning coffee. "Do you really want to be married to me?"

"Joe, I could have done better and I could have done worse. We have a lovely son and you have your life and I have my life. There is no reason for us to separate. If you want to have sex with someone, you have my permission. Just don't bring any diseases home to Palmer Street."

Some evenings were late nights for Jennifer. She would not return until midnight or two in the morning. The anti-war meetings usually ran late. Baxter was invited to join her but declined. "You're a bit like a mushroom, Joe," Jennifer condemned him. "The world is coming apart unjustly before your very eyes and you're too lethargic and complacent to take any action!"

"Say hello to Joan Baez!" Baxter would say as she went out the door.

One Sunday morning in June 1969, Baxter went to bed at midnight. Jennifer had been out at a rally in Madison and had warned him that she would be late. Baxter turned in the bed once with the morning light and saw Jennifer sitting in the rocking chair across the room. She was naked and smoking a cigarette. Baxter sat up in bed. "When did you get in?" he asked.

"Just now. The rally lasted until 3:30. It was really powerful!" Jennifer's body had remained attractive. She was firm with high pointed breasts, and graceful legs. Jennifer sat in the rocking chair smoking in the nude watching Baxter. Then she stamped out the cigarette, stood up from the rocking chair, and padded her way across the carpet to the bed.

Jennifer sat on the edge of the bed and pulled the covers away from Baxter. He lay there in J.C. Penney underwear looking up at her. Jennifer brought her hand down to the opening of his shorts and began to touch Baxter. They had not had sex in a year. Her hand touched his member and Baxter erected quickly. Baxter started to reach for her, but Jennifer pushed him back. She climbed in bed on top of him and Baxter slipped in easily. He noted that she had applied some kind of cold lubricant jelly before joining him. There was ten minutes of coupling and substantial ejaculation.

"That should be a baby," Jennifer said as she unstraddled. She kissed him lightly on the mouth and went on to the bathroom. Baxter could hear Jennifer brushing her teeth and humming. Perhaps this morning would mark a change in their marital relationship.

Jennifer announced her pregnancy in August of 1969. There was no sex after that time. This time a girl was born to the Baxters in March 1970. She was named Martha after Jennifer's mother, but came to be known as Muffin when Agnes saw her for the first time in the hospital and proclaimed that she looked like a little muffin in the incubator.

"Now Joel has a sister and we have completed our family, Joe," Jennifer announced from her hospital bed.

Baxter continued to work on engagements around the country under Associates. He never had a formal appraisal, but there was encouragement from Dwyer. As a pool member, Baxter was reviewed by Clyde Nickerson who expressed his concern about never receiving a completed appraisal form from Dwyer other than the following informal memorandum:

To: C. Nickerson
Chicago
From: W. Dwyer
Chicago
Subject: Annual Appraisal-Joseph Baxter Jr.

I am in receipt of your memorandum requesting form 116 relative to the subject consultant's performance on the following engagements:

- Morgan Hydraulics
- BBB Companies
- Des Moines Tractor Services Inc.
- Muscatine Heat Exchange

The subject consultant had performed ably on each assignment carrying out his work within the highest quality standards of McKenzie Barber. I request that Mr. Baxter be granted an increase equal to the 50th percentile of the firm's salary increase plan and a bonus equal to the 50th percentile of the firm's bonus allocations for the first year consultants.

"Dwyer really hasn't done much for you, Joe," Nickerson explained. "We can comply with his recommendation, but he may be shortchanging you, and there is nothing I can do about it."

Bill Dwyer collapsed in the Spring of 1970 and was hospitalized. Little new work was developed for the manufacturing practice, and Baxter remained unassigned in the pool. He experienced the Wednesday afternoon cattle call for the first time in his consulting career. Alvardi asked for him and Baxter reported to him on Thursday morning.

"How are you, kid?"

"How's Bill? I tried to call the hospital and they said he had been released," Baxter reported.

"Bill's doing fine, kid. But he'll be out another two or three weeks. He specifically asked me to keep you busy. Do you know anything about compensation?"

Baxter shared with Alvardi about the University of Minnesota Industrial Relations program experience and the Scanlon Plan he had been doing to install at Washburn Manufacturing.

"Looks like we're starting at ground zero, kid!" Alvardi ruled.

Baxter liked working for Alvardi, but found it was office work. He no longer traveled. Baxter commuted in each morning from Racine and worked in his cubicle in the pool. Baxter drove back each evening arriving about eight o'clock.

Andy and Naomi were still in the pool, and they would periodically go out for drinks. Andy cut her hair short and began to wear make-up. Naomi looked better to Baxter every time he saw her.

"So you're the father of two and working for Alvardi now," Naomi summarized. "What else is new with you, Joey?"

"You've said it all, Naomi. What's new with you guys?"

"I'm being transferred to New York," Andy announced.

"Ernie Grey fell in love with her. Andy's going to be one of his executive assistants and go on to be chairman," Naomi predicted.

"We had a very good meeting with Ernie on the satellite office program and I was invited to transfer to New York," Andy was ebullient.

"This makes me the senior woman in the pool, Joey, with the three new debutantes in place," Naomi reported.

"I hope that you will look me up when you come to New York, Joe," Andy invited Baxter.

"They say that Dwyer will be out six months, Joe. What in hell will the manufacturing guys do? Who's going to bring in the work?" Naomi queried.

Baxter worked well with Alvardi. He came to love compensation issues and he learned the tax and accounting conventions of stock option plans. Alvardi took him aside in June 1970. "Look, kid, Dwyer will be back after Labor Day, but I need an Associate right now in my practice. Commit and I'll have you out of the pool on Monday. But there's no going back to manufacturing right away. You might be stuck in Executive Compensation for the rest of your career at McKenzie Barber."

"Give me the weekend," Baxter requested.

Baxter took the weekend and really didn't know which way to direct his loyalties. Alvardi, however, represented a way out of the pool. Effective July 1970, Baxter moved out of the pool to the compensation practice as an Associate.

Jennifer wasn't very excited about Baxter's advancement. Naomi was. Baxter announced at Palmer Street that he would have to be out of town and invited Naomi Schwartz out for a celebration dinner.

Naomi wore a black dress with a V neckline and they ate at an Italian restaurant with a great piano player on the North side. "How's everything at home?" Naomi asked two sips into their martinis.

"I am now the father of a son, age four, and a new baby. My wife is active in stopping the war in Vietnam and other social causes."

"Somehow, Joe, you don't sound happy to me"

"What was your first clue?" Baxter asked.

"When you asked me out to dinner to celebrate, Joey," Naomi proclaimed after their second martini. "I've always dug your act. Back at Minnesota when I weighed 200 pounds, I used to fantasize about you. If you're looking for someone to sleep with, I'm here!"

Naomi's hand reached across the table and Baxter accepted it.

Naomi lived in an efficiency apartment in a high rise off Division Street. She poured Baxter a brandy, piled the pillows on the floor and opened the couch while Baxter watched. Placing her glasses on the kitchen divider, Naomi smiled shyly at Baxter. "Shall we take off our clothes, Joey?"

Naomi was self conscious about her thighs, but proud of her well toned body. She climaxed thirty seconds after he entered her. "Don't worry, Joey. I usually have a ton of small ones on a good night," Naomi explained.

They sat up in bed, listened to a soft music station, and talked through the night. Baxter told Naomi about the Washburn family and Jennifer.

"My God, Joey, that woman must be as crazy as a bedbug. Are you going to stay with her?"

"Naomi, I once abandoned a daughter back in Iron Creek. I have paid child support for the past seventeen years, but she regards her stepfather and her mother as her real parents. Joel and Muffin represent my last chance to be a father. I'm going to stay married to Jennifer until they're out of high school and into college.."

"That's a lot of one night stands, Joey," Naomi forecast.

"You're my first indiscretion," Baxter confessed.

"I'm not always available, Joe. But when I am, there will always be a space for you in my sofa bed."

They took separate transportation to the office. Naomi took the bus and Baxter took a taxi. He was now officed in a windowless green walled interior office cubicle within twenty yards of Alvardi's window office with the LaSalle Street view.

Baxter learned that Frank Alvardi was all business and managed every minute of his day either in or out of the office. He traveled a good deal, brought back a lot of work and expected that his Associates would work night and day around Alvardi's 9 to 5 day. Staff meetings were held at 9 AM on Monday mornings and each engagement was reviewed in front of his five Associates.

Baxter was the oldest of the Associates by at least five years. The others were MBAs in their late twenties and graduates from the pool. They were smart, upbeat, and hard workers competing with each other for Alvardi's favor and sponsorship. They were named Robbie, Carl, Lance, and Win and they had come to the Executive Compensation practice to gain Associate's stripes and escape the pool. They openly plotted to move laterally to an Industry practice. Of the four, only Carl saw Executive Compensation as a career track. Alvardi, in turn, worked his associates hard and actively marketed them to other practices. "Everything here is a two way street, gentleman," Alvardi would explain periodically in the Monday morning staff meetings. "You do right by me and I'll do right by you. If you don't want to be in this practice, I'll open up other doors for you either inside or outside McKenzie Barber. If we have a problem in this practice, it stays in the practice. It is not included in the gossip talk with other Associates and pool consultants."

Lorna, Clyde Nickerson's secretary, would periodically stand in Alvardi's doorway making light banter. They had running jokes between them, but Alvardi was close to no one with the exception of Bill Dwyer. He was clearly worried about Dwyer's recovery. Baxter and Alvardi started to visit Dwyer together on Saturdays. Dwyer had an apartment in Lincoln Park and was apparently recovering from some kind of surgery.

"The Doctor told me to take the summer off," Dwyer looked heavier and was dressed in pajamas covered by a bathrobe. He was attended by a large black woman who wore a white nurse's uniform. Dwyer called her Aunt Jemima when she served them tea.

"No booze, no coffee, no sex, and no clients! It's a terrible life, lads." Baxter knew it was not his place to ask Dwyer exactly what had gone wrong.

"Have you talked to Ernie?" Alvardi asked.

"Ernie Grey is a regular caller, Frankie. He even sent me a get well Grey-gram. That goddam Nickerson sent me flowers. Do you think he'll want to take me to a candlelight dinner when I'm better?"

"What did Ernie say?" Alvardi asked.

"He's been inspiring, Francis. Regaining my health is the most important objective. I'm to stay out until September and then work half-days until January. I am to receive no information on my practice, because Ernie wants my mind free from worry. Meanwhile Rolf Bauer, from the bloody IE practice, is mucking up Manufacturing beyond repair. That's why I parked you with Frank, Joe."

It was the first time Baxter realized that he had been parked in Executive Compensation and that it was Dwyer's plan for him to return to Manufacturing. "You come back to me in January, Joe. I'll have to rebuild the whole bloody practice," Dwyer went to pour some tea and found the pot empty. "Aunt Jemima!" He shouted at the top of his lungs.

"Get another pot of bloody tea in here! Please!"

"I can hear you, Mr. Dwyer," the nurse said stomping into the room.

"Be a good little dear and fix us some more tea——and maybe bring in a tray of biscuits. You're such a comfort to an unwell man."

She grumbled out of the room and they continued to talk. Dwyer wanted to know the gossip and Alvardi accommodated him pleading ignorance when pushed for operating data.

"So Hamilton Burke went off to Barber-Paris," Dwyer mused. "What do you make of it, Frank?"

"I think his string in the Emerging Companies Practice has played out. They're folding up the practice and Bahlman is going to work in Lovejoy's group. I think the boy wonder got himself a little exposed in his M&A venture with Joe's old company. There was a lot of bitching from some of the Chicago investment bankers to Brimmer. This is our business, not yours, they told Brimmer. If he wouldn't have done that deal with Wiggins in the manner it was done, the boy wonder could have been in deep trouble and Nickerson would have been dancing in the streets."

"Speaking of Clyde Nickerson, Francis, how is his secretary, the lovely Lorna?"

"She appears to be working very efficiently, Bill," Alvardi answered with a straight face. "Now back to Burke. My theory is that Ernie will float Burke through Barber-Paris, then to London and then he will bring him in due time to New York. Our Chairman has plans for Mr. Burke."

Dwyer sipped his tea and nodded his head in agreement. "We're well rid of him here in Chicago and we're well out of the Emerging Companies Practice. Joe, I almost walked away from that first job at Washburn Manufacturing. Of course that wasn't Burke's referral. Mark Lovejoy was to blame for that one."

"But you showed us how to save the company," Baxter protested.

"Joe, my time, Frank's time and your time is better spent with clients of substance. Emerging Companies indeed! Another hair-brained scheme of our beloved Chairman," Dwyer ruled.

"Frank what's the news on Nickerson? Is Ernie bringing him back to New York?"

"A source I cannot disclose," Alvardi replied, "told me that Clyde and Mavis are house hunting in Connecticut this weekend. Clyde will be back on Ernie's payroll effective October 1 with the new fiscal year."

"Who will handle all of the man's critical duties?" Dwyer asked.

"They will be divided up among several people. Brimmer is going to appoint someone from the pool, make them an Associate, and put them in charge of scheduling and administration and I believe Lorna is going to handle the personnel stuff and report to the Associate. Brimmer is going to ask that Jewish girl to handle recruiting and report directly to him. He'll promote her to Associate."

"Naomi Schwartz?" Baxter asked.

"That's the one, kid. Ernie wants to recruit a bunch of women for the pool and he wants to visit all the big schools. We got five coming in after Labor Day, Bill."

"I'll be back to greet the little dears," Dwyer promised.

Frank Alvardi only opened up his personality to Baxter when he was with Dwyer. In the office they were Partner and Associate. Alvardi proved to be a taskmaster. He was pleasant enough, but he had a way of shredding conclusions, reforming them and making them better. Baxter concluded after two months that Frank Alvardi was the most brilliant man he had ever met, with the possible exception of Dwyer.

Clyde Nickerson was transferred back to New York and a two year pool resident from Harvard named Chris was promoted to Associate and placed in charge of the pool. Lorna was named personnel administrator and Naomi was promoted to Associate and given the title of Manager of Recruiting and an internal office down the hallway from Paul Brimmer.

Clyde Nickerson was given two going-away parties. One was held at the Drake and hosted by the Chicago office Partners. Managers were invited to mandatory attendance at the party. The second party was given by the pool consultants and the Associates and was held in the backroom of a near Northside place called Lefty's. The hat was passed for a gift and Clyde was presented with an expensive golf bag. Informal signals were sent from Brimmer's office that there would be no "roast" of Clyde Nickerson. One or two Managers came including Lee Heller.

Clyde gave a speech extolling the talent level of the pool consultants and reminded them that one day the firm would be theirs to run. He said that he had hoped to remain in Chicago another couple of years, but Ernie wanted him back in New York, and who was Clyde to argue with a chairman. "When McKenzie Barber wants you to go someplace, you go. You're going to be among friends where ever you go in the world!"

Lee Heller stood next to Baxter during Nickerson's speech. "Thank God!" he whispered to Baxter during the polite applause after the speech. "I thought we were going to have to give Clyde the hook. I'd like to talk to you, Joe. But I better have my say with Clyde before he goes out the door. He appears to be back in Ernie's good graces again." Lee started his way across the room to Nickerson, who now had the golf bag under one arm.

Naomi came to Baxter's side and stood next to him with a scotch in her hand. She was wearing a white blouse, black skirt and black pumps with very high heels. "I know you all dislike him, but he was okay to me, Joey."

"He goes and we have promotions. I hear you're an Associate and have a Manager's title."

"Now I have to find someone to manage. I'm sharing Brimmer's secretary. How well do you know him? He looks like a Nazi to me."

"I spent twenty minutes with him one day two years ago and haven't seen him since."

Naomi was standing close to Baxter and he could smell her perfume.

"Do you remember what we did when you were promoted to Associate?" she asked.

"We went to dinner and then had an after dinner program," Baxter replied.

"Well I've had enough hors d'oeuvres already to skip dinner. How about moving on to the after dinner program?"

"We better not leave together," Baxter cautioned.

"We need a plan," Naomi said brightly, "It's 7:15. I will work the room about ten minutes and be out the door at 7:30. You will leave at 7:45. Do you remember where I live?" Baxter recited her address. "Should I bring anything?" he asked.

"Just your hot body. Plan to stay all night!"

"I've got to get back to Racine tonight. I have a client presentation in the morning."

"So be it, Joey. You should keep some stuff at my place. You know, just in case. If you have to go back, I'm leaving right now. You get out of here at 7:30. Now let's shake hands now and I'll shake something else of yours later."

Naomi's hands locked with Baxter's. There was a squeeze and their hands parted. Lee Heller was back. "Not going already, Naomi?"

"I have to make a meeting," she smiled.

"Boy, she's happy about something," Lee observed.

"What's it like being a Manager, anyway?" Baxter asked noting that the time was 7:17.

"This is my second year as Manager," Lee was pleased to be placed in the role of a mentor and statesman. "I was very excited in October two years ago. You can make Associate at any time at McKenzie Barber. It's like making PFC in the Army. Being a Manager seems very special in the beginning. You've left the Associates behind you. Then you come to realize that you have very little authority and won't until you're a partner. Next week it will be October 1970, and my second anniversary as a Manager. I believe I was slow in making Associate. I found out this year that I may not be technically strong enough to become a Partner in the Computer Systems Practice. I knew I'd never make it under Dwyer in the Manufacturing Practice. I'm interviewing next week with a new practice. Have you heard of Dr. Barry Keller?"

"He's the guy who has written all the books about strategic planning," Baxter acknowledged. "He's been a professor at a couple of the big B schools."

"In between the big B schools, he's been senior planning officer for a couple of major corporations. He's been brought in as a direct admission partner. Paul Brimmer recruited him in a unique manner. He engaged Keller to do a mini-strategy for the Chicago practice, had him present the findings to Ernie Grey and they recruited Keller to start the Business Strategy practice. He's going to be in the Chicago office and he's bringing a couple of his faculty with him. They want an experienced McKenzie Barber Manager in the new practice. I'll be very excited if I'm selected. Clyde said it was wired for me. He presumably has talked to Ernie about it."

Baxter looked at his watch. It was 7:25. Almost time to leave in order to get laid.

"Do you have time for a bite, Joe?" It was the first time Lee had taken time to talk to Baxter during his two years at McKenzie Barber.

"Jennifer and I have a new baby at home. She likes to have me in before 9:30."

"How many does this make, Joe?" Lee asked.

"Two," Baxter answered. "I have a boy named Joel, age 4, and the new baby's name is Martha. How about you, Lee?"

Lee shook his head. "No little pitter-patter of little feet at our house. Margo and I still talk about that wedding. I take it that Jennifer's stable now."

Baxter nodded and openly looked at his watch. "I better get going."

"Come up the bar with me, Joe and have a nightcap. There are some things you should know about." It was an invitation worded in a manner that was impossible to decline. Baxter felt like the lower classman following the direction of the upper classman.

Lee Heller had a scotch while Baxter had a Canadian Club. "I know you're with Alvardi now as an Associate," Lee said as they stood in the corner of the room filled with Associates and pool consultants who had been drinking since six. They were now off their good behavior with Nickerson's departure.

"Stay with Alvardi. Dwyer's Chicago practice is going to be chopped up and Dwyer's going to New York. The last six months have seriously set back his career with McKenzie Barber. Alvardi's practice it as good as any for you to be in until you've decided what you're going to do when you grow up."

"What does that mean?" Baxter asked, baffled with the comment.

"Getting ahead around here, Joe, is more than just doing good work and bringing in an occasional client. You need to find a critical mass practice

16

with leadership and high growth momentum. That's the way to become a partner around here. I believed that Dwyer was going to do that, but he just lost critical months. Executive Compensation will never be a critical mass practice. At best it will be one partner in Chicago and one Partner in New York ten years from now. Strategic Planning has a chance to be the major practice of McKenzie Barber over the next twenty years and will have mucho partners world-wide. How old are you, now, Joe?"

"I'm 35," Baxter answered.

"You may not make it. You're old to be at the Associate level at McKenzie Barber. You should spend another year here and then do something else. McKenzie Barber will look good on your resume. The only people who know you're around are Dwyer and Alvardi, and they are not main stream partners. You've got to get Nickerson on your side. He's close to Ernie and he can help you."

"Wouldn't I help myself if I went out and sold a lot of business to clients and successfully and profitably delivered the services?" Baxter asked.

"Joe, you're with McKenzie Barber. Business is sold by the Partners and the Managers if they want to become Partners. Associates see to it that the work gets done the way the Partners and Managers want it. An Associate is nothing without a Partner telling him what to do and where to do it. That's the culture of the firm."

Baxter knew at that point he had enough of Lee Heller for one evening. "This conversation has been a big help in seeing the firm more clearly," Baxter said sincerely in his insincerity.

"Don't be a stranger, Joe," Lee said in his condescending McKenzie Barber second year Manager's manner.

It was 7:52 and time for an early evening of love making. Baxter wondered what Naomi knew about Dr. Barry Keller.

While there were four Associates in the Chicago Executive Compensation practice, Alvardi grew to favor Baxter that Fall. They began to travel together and Baxter quickly acquired the reputation as Frank Alvardi's favorite bag man. As a national practice partner, Alvardi called on all the operating offices of McKenzie Barber U.S. practice and visited with clients at the Chief Executive Officer and senior staff level. Alvardi believed that air travel was best observed from the front of the airplane. Baxter found himself flying in the first class section for the first time in his life. They were flying to Los Angeles following an afternoon meeting with a large bank in San Francisco when Alvardi first addressed Baxter's wardrobe.

"Kid, where do you buy your suits? J.C. Penney?" Baxter had been wearing a blue suit that he purchased two years ago at Caribou Street Men's and Boy's wear. "We were in the goddam Board room of the bank! They

17

were in Brooks Brothers and Hart Shaffner and you were in Sears Roebuck or what ever the hell you're wearing. There you were, well prepared, glib, and self confident in a cheap suit. Kid! I want you to open up an account at Brooks Brothers and buy four suits, dark colors, a bunch of club ties, two pairs of black wingtips, and some shirts with your initials on the breast pocket. In the right wardrobe, I may be able to make something out of you. You're not going into the plants and warehouses that you used to visit for Dwyer. You're off plant floors now, kid, and onto carpeting."

They traveled to all of the offices of McKenzie Barber. Atlanta, Cleveland, Dallas, Los Angeles, New York, and San Francisco. "Now, kid," Alvardi would coach him. "The only thing these offices have in common is their letterhead. The man in the corner office sets the tempo according to the way the Chairman wants it. Remember kid, every office is a Chinese puzzle."

Baxter learned executive compensation the way he had learned everything else in his life. He studied it and lived it. He read annual reports and proxy statements the way children read comic books. He learned the ratios, folklore, accounting conventions and craft from Alvardi. In the beginning, Baxter sought to achieve economic legitimacy in the short and long term incentive plans they developed for senior management.

Alvardi took Baxter aside one evening and explained the ways of the corporate world. "Look, kid! These plans have to pay off! If they don't, the clients will engage someone else. The principal thing is to watch onerous compensation. Incentive compensation should not impact shareholder earnings by more than 10%. If management performance substantially enhances shareholder value, 10% is a modest incentive. Now kid, if the market goes down and all of those Performance Shares plans installed by Art Perrin, my old mentor at RAH, go in the tank, we will have a real marketing opportunity. And kid, the Dow Jones is going to sink like a stone in 1971 and we are going to play that drop like a fiddle. The answer is Restricted Stock. Remember kid, everything that comes around, goes around. We're going to make a bundle installing restricted stock and book value plans to replace the market driven performance share and appreciation plans."

Baxter carefully recorded everything that Alvardi said into his memory and played it back over time. To the outsider, executive compensation seemed an esoteric complex subject. Baxter quickly mastered the accounting and tax conventions and the basic plan constructs. He became accepted as the second banana in the Chicago Executive Compensation practice. Robbie and Win transferred to other practices after a year, leaving Carl and Lance to work with Baxter. Baxter's relationship with Alvardi grew to the point where Baxter made the presentations and Alvardi commented. "You drive the stage, kid and I'll pick off the Indians." Periodically they would make presentations at Associate's roundtables and to other operating offices. Baxter would make the presentations. He also began to do independent research and co-published with Alvardi. He was invited to speak and started to bring in client work. The Executive Compensation practice did well in the crunch years of 1971 and 1972 and Baxter emerged as a Manager effective October 1, 1971.

Advancement to Manager required endorsement from the office Managing Partner. This required a meeting with Paul Brimmer. It marked their first meeting since Baxter's hurried interview in August 1968. Naomi, who now worked for Brimmer, prepped Baxter one evening in bed.

"He barks a lot and bites a lot, but he doesn't seem to bite the people he barks at. The ones he bites never seem to see it coming and his bite is lethal. I get along with him fine, but I only see him for thirty minutes a month. He grills the hell out of me for that thirty minutes and it is the longest half-hour of my life. Just make sure you're prepared."

Alvardi took a different view. "Brimmer's okay. He never bothers me and he stood behind Bill when he was sick. Firm policy says that he must approve all recommendations for promotion to Manager and he doesn't know you. Just be your usual charming self, kid."

Baxter met Paul Brimmer at the Chicago City Club for lunch on a Friday. He had never been in the Chicago City Club which was located in a four story stone building on Hampshire Avenue one block south of Michigan Avenue. The club had a gentle intimidation about it. Uniformed attendants greeted you at the door and immediately asked visitors what business they had at the club.

Baxter announced he was waiting for Mr. Brimmer and was sent to the second floor library to wait. He sat in a stuffed chair and read the Wall Street Journal while he waited for Brimmer.

Brimmer arrived at 12:40 looking fierce with his bald head and handlebar mustache. "You must be Baxter. You're big and you have red hair," was Brimmer's greeting. Baxter was careful to calmly fold the Wall Street Journal neatly and place it back in the news rack and slowly rise to his feet. He was five inches taller than Brimmer on his feet.

"Joe Baxter, Mr. Brimmer!" He said extending his hand which Brimmer accepted and gripped.

"I like a consultant with size. That's good!" Brimmer observed.

"I'm late. Let's go to lunch."

Lunch was on the third floor where they were greeted by a tuxedo clad maitre d' who fawned over Brimmer.

"Andre," Brimmer announced to the maitre d', "I'm going to break the house rules again. I've brought some papers to lunch that I'll need to refer to during my discussions with this young man."

"I'll put you in a corner table, Mr. Brimmer, and instruct your waiter to look in another direction," Andre replied, and they were seated in the far corner in a half-filled room of luncheoners. Brimmer produced a manila folder from the breast pocket of his suit. It had been doubled over and he folded it out in front of him. "It's excerpts from your personnel file. I was trying to figure out who the hell I was having lunch with today."

The waiter approached them with a drink order request. "Want to wet your whistle, Joe?" Brimmer asked.

"I'll have a tomato juice," Baxter ordered.

"I'll have a martini," Brimmer ordered.

"I'll have some vodka in that tomato juice," Baxter added. Brimmer opened up the papers. "Have we met before?" Brimmer asked.

"You interviewed me in August 1968. It was between calls to Mr. Grey."

"My God, man! That was four years ago! Where have you been hiding yourself?" Brimmer looked over Baxter's personnel file. "You haven't attended any staff training sessions according to your file. Is there some mistake here? It's blank!"

"I've always been busy on client work. I missed Consultant's Roundtables because I was out of town on major assignments. The same is true for the Associate's Roundtable."

"Your chargeability is sensational. An amazing combination; highly chargeable and untrained." The drinks arrived and Brimmer raised his glass. "Getting acquainted!" he toasted.

"Getting acquainted!" Baxter repeated while raising his glass. "I take it you think a great deal of the firm's training programs."

"I think they are a bullshit waste of time. They are an example of the Nickerson peanut butter behaviorism that he brought with him from Pennsylvania Steel. Ernie Grey likes all that cheerleader-hurrah-for-the-firm stuff. I'm into serving clients and making money, myself," Brimmer leaned across the table and stared into Baxter's eyes. Baxter decided to remain quiet until his host spoke.

"You worked for Dwyer for two years and now two years for Alvardi. Is that it?"

"It's close. I was hired into the pool, but to work exclusively on Bill Dwyer's engagements, which I did until he got sick. Then I was picked up by Frank Alvardi and he eventually invited me into his practice as an Associate. I believe I prefer working in the Executive Compensation practice to the Manufacturing practice."

20

"And you worked for Washburn Manufacturing——Oh hell, I know who you are. You were with that company that Ham Burke decided he was going to sell. We had Dwyer in there first and somebody died. Burke recommended that the company be sold and then took on the job himself. God, did we have a tempest in a teapot over that one."

"I wasn't aware there was a controversy about McKenzie Barber selling the company. We just assumed that McKenzie Barber could do anything they said they could do," Baxter commented.

"McKenzie Barber is not in the business of selling companies. Burke believed he could do anything. Another man who was never in the pool and probably didn't attend the training roundtables." Brimmer took a long sip from his martini. "I like Burke. Give me five Hamilton Burkes and I can take on the world in the field of management consulting. Ernie likes Burke."

"I like Burke, too," Baxter agreed.

"There's a long letter of recommendation for you from Burke in your personnel file. He obviously thought a lot of you and normally Burke doesn't have a lot of professional respect for client personnel. They elected Burke a Partner at Barber-Paris this year. Fastest rise of any man since Ernie Grey. The two have a lot in common. Both Harvard B School, both war veterans, and both started their business careers late. Burke took to the French practice like a duck to water. He speaks fluent French, you know. He was once married to a French speaking woman he met in Saigon. I guess she's dead." Brimmer sipped the rest of his martini. "I miss Burke. I used to pal around a little with him. I'm not that close to the Partners in this office, but I developed a real fondness for the guy. Now! Tell me about yourself, Joe."

They ordered and consumed lunch over the story of Baxter's career.

"Where do you live?" Brimmer asked.

"In Racine, Wisconsin."

"Racine? Why would anyone live in Racine who didn't have to?" Brimmer asked. Baxter explained about Jennifer, the young children, and the house on Palmer Street. He made it sound like a lifestyle issue.

Brimmer shook his head. "Maybe we just ought to pay you a little more and you can keep an apartment in Chicago."

"I have a friend who does that." Baxter now kept clothes in Naomi's apartment along with a shaving kit.

"Joe, you have a future in the Chicago office, but you had better move to Chicago to be part of it. McKenzie Barber is a New York centered firm. Chicago has been open since 1936. We had our 35th anniversary last year. We're regarded as the office where practices are tested before they are brought to New York where the firm has its primary platform. Good people are developed here and the great ones go off to New York. Chicago is the feeder office for the West, Southwest, Southeast, and sometimes even Canada. Consultants come here and launch new practices. Some succeed and some fail. The successful practice leaders will be called off to New York and it's critical for them to train successors. Dwyer moved out to New York two years ago and left Russell Holt behind to run the Manufacturing practice. Russ is no Dwyer, but he's doing a very creditable job in leading the Midwest Manufacturing practice and he's on track to become a partner. Then we have Frank Alvardi. Frank's done a marvelous job of putting McKenzie Barber into the Executive Compensation consulting business. Ernie will want him out in New York in a year or so. Someone will have to step in and run the Midwest practice. Frank thinks you could be the one, Joe. Now what's this I hear about you working so closely with Barry Keller's Business Strategy practice?"

Baxter began to talk about executive compensation plans tailored to support and reinforce strategic business plans. He had remained close to Lee Heller after Lee had been selected as the McKenzie Barber Manager in the newly formed Business Strategy practice. Dr. Barry Keller had an electric and highly charged personality. Baxter recognized early in his first meeting that Dr. Keller was a salesman at heart and Baxter knew that every salesman could be sold. He then cited compensation as the critical tool to link the achievement of strategic objectives to pay rewards and evoked the behavioral theories of Skinner and Maslow. Dr. Keller smelled hot stuff and suddenly there was a review of executive pay practices module built into every Strategy workplan and proposal. The only stumbling block was Lee Heller who wanted Baxter to discount his practice's rates to provide additional margin for the Business Strategy practice. "You're getting a free ride, Joe," Lee had explained. "You're gaining access to clients and we're absorbing the marketing costs. We need a discount on your rates to catch up."

"Don't we all eat from the same trough?" Baxter questioned.

"The trough is uneven, Joe," Lee explained.

"And that is how the giraffe got his long neck," Baxter quipped.

"Shall we say a 20% discount from standard rates?" Lee had proposed.

"15% is more realistic, Lee," Baxter counter proposed.

They settled at 18% and the next day Baxter talked Alvardi into raising their rates 18% and discounting the rates 18% to clients outside the Business Strategy portfolio.

"Good pricing strategy, kid," Alvardi had concluded.

The pricing discussions did not represent the kind of details that Paul Brimmer wanted to hear. He wanted to hear about practices working together to attract and serve clients. Baxter carefully edited his narration of the relationship between the Business Strategy practice and the Executive Compensation practice. Brimmer was delighted.

"That's fantastic! That's the way it should be! You worked with Heller when he was the Associate on an engagement with your company. You come to McKenzie Barber, stay in contact, bond with him in his new practice, and co-generate new business avenues for the firm. Joe, I want you to get together with Heller and co-author a memorandum to me that I can send to Ernie." They were on coffee now.

"Let's have a brandy," Brimmer offered. "You know, Joe," Brimmer began again. "The example of the teamwork between the two practices is really heartening to me. Ernie Grey has made McKenzie Barber into a highly competitive firm. The firm he took over from John McKenzie was very collegial, well meaning, and virtually the only game in town, provided there was a game. When Ernie came to the firm after the war, the economy was taking off, and McKenzie Barber was the dominant management consulting firm, but the competition was coming fast. That's why John McKenzie picked out Ernie Grey. Ernie Grey brought a sense of competition to this firm. It's a damned shame, Joe, that you missed those roundtables. You would have had the opportunity to see Ernie in action. The man is electric in front of a group of people. Ernie loves to stir things up and he values competition. Sometimes, and too often I think, that is carried inside the firm. We compete with each other rather than the competition. We have practices making war on other practices and offices making war on other offices. Ernie Grey accepts this. He doesn't believe that breaking up the competition between practices and offices is worthwhile. He'll never say this publicly, but I'm willing to say this to you as counsel to a bright young man trying to advance through McKenzie Barber. The competition will continue under Ernie because he believes that only the most market-ready will survive. Example. The Industrial Engineering practice represents the roots of this firm. They are no longer dominant. But this firm was built around the tenets of efficiency, cost reduction, and work measurement. Now it's fifty some years later and the clients require different services. Ernie Grey recognized this and he brought in Bill Dwyer as a direct admission Partner, with the vision of providing clients consulting perspectives beyond the traditional measurement disciplines. I'm talking to you out of school now, Joe. The IEs went after Bill from the first day. Bill Dwyer is an exceptional person and nothing would stop him from his goals. Place a hurdle in front of him and Bill will jump right over it. But like many a good race horse, Bill missed a hurdle and was unable to finish a race. Luckily we didn't have to shoot him. That's why he went out to New York where he had a fresh start and is doing very well. The tensions between the IE and the Manufacturing practices are often vicious and contentious. Bill's practice should eventually outlast the IE practice, but it won't be easy. Alvardi's another story. He came in as a new practice. The IEs have done some salary administration over the years, but Alvardi brought something new to the party. There was no competition for him. He played his peers very carefully and your story about the working relationship between Business Strategy and Executive Compensation is sensational! Joe, I'd like you to talk to Alvardi about rolling out this linkage nationally."

"We've talked about this already," Baxter explained. "Frank is a superior strategist."

Brimmer glared at Baxter. "You're a one-up guy, aren't you? You've played me like a fiddle in this luncheon, haven't you?"

"No," Baxter disagreed. "I can't believe that anyone has ever played you like a fiddle."

Brimmer's eyes softened. "I've enjoyed this luncheon. You've got to get out to more functions so people can get a look at you. You had better get an apartment in town. You need to develop a presence around town, and you're not going to have time to do that driving back and forth to Racine on your days in the city. Alvardi has recommended that we get you into a luncheon club." Baxter looked around the room. "Forget about this one, Joe. You need a starter club. Ask around. The firm will pick up the initiation and you handle the dues. You become a Partner, and I'll get you in here and you can buy me lunch." Brimmer refolded Baxter's papers and returned them in his breast pocket. "What do you say we go back to work and make some money?"

Baxter rose from the table and Baxter followed suit. Baxter felt ten feet tall when they parted in front of the club. The door was open for him to become a McKenzie Barber Partner. All he had to do was to produce, improve his visibility, join a luncheon club, and get an apartment in Chicago. Baxter had survived his luncheon with Paul Brimmer.

Baxter knew his marriage to Jennifer was dead in October 1972. Jennifer went her way, Baxter went his way, and Agnes took care of the children. Joel was now six years old and had been in the Racine Montessori School for two years. Muffin was two years old and the darling of Agnes. Baxter spent all day Saturday with the children and Jennifer was simply gone. She was always present for Sunday lunch which was served promptly at 1:30 PM. Baxter usually headed for Chicago around 5 PM on Sunday to his efficiency apartment on the near Northside. Jennifer accepted Baxter's decision to live in Chicago during the week grudgingly.

"You're going to abandon these children just as you abandoned that little girl in Iron Creek. I understand why you're doing it and recognize that you probably couldn't get anyone in Racine or Milwaukee to pay you as well as these people do. If you must do it, go ahead and do it. You just had better be back Friday night at a reasonable hour and be prepared to spend a full day with the children on Saturday," Jennifer lectured him.

Baxter had a drink with Agnes in the kitchen and explained his Chicago arrangements as they listened to Smetna's Ma Vlast. "It's not good," she said shaking her head. "You should be here in the evening whenever you can. You should find work here. Any kind of work! You should be here with these children!" Tears were forming in Agnes's eyes. "Those little dears need their father. The Missus only pays attention to them when she thinks someone is watching. You know that she sees other men."

"Which men?" Baxter demanded.

"I don't know who they are. They call her and leave messages. She'll be real happy now that she can plan on you not being home during the week. I'm worried about the children." Baxter put his arms around Agnes and kissed her on the forehead and then on the cheeks. "Agnes, thank God I have you!" Agnes wrapped her arms around Baxter's neck and wept. "You're a good man, Joe," she said. "You and those children are my whole life. You go to Chicago during the week and I'll take good care of the little darlings."

The relationship between Baxter and Jennifer had reached it's nadir three years earlier in 1969. It had started with a Saturday morning opening of the mail. There was a letter from Ganski. Baxter hadn't heard from him since the annual Christmas card and it was now May.

The letter read:

Dear Joe:

This is a tough letter to write. Mort's dead. He got killed in Vietnam. He was a first sergeant with a rifle company and the Vietcong lobbed in a mortar shell, looking for no one in particular, and blew him apart at his desk. He died instantly according to a letter his folks got from his CO.

Mort had extended one tour in Vietnam, but was scheduled to come home in three more weeks. He made E-7 and had fifteen years in when he was killed. Mort wrote me regularly but wrote me one time that he had sent you a letter once that he wished he hadn't and felt funny about writing you again. He always asked about you in his letters and seemed real pleased when I told him how well you were doing. Mort and I have always looked up to you as someone very smart and special. They are shipping what's left of Mort back in a box and there will be a funeral service next Saturday in Iron Creek. It would really mean a lot to Mort's folks if you could show up. It

25

would also mean a lot to Diane and me. I tried to call you on the phone a couple of times, but got this woman who said you were out of town. Diane said this letter should reach you in three days maximum. I've written to Tweetman also, Joe. I feel very badly about Mort. I hope you can come for the service.

Your friend,
Edward Ganski
1953 Cougars

Baxter read the letter twice. They had been in the upstairs sitting room, and Jennifer had been sipping tea and reading through Peace Movement tracts.

"Do you remember Mort Himmelman?"

"The big Marine," Jennifer acknowledged.

"He's dead. Killed by a mortar shell in Vietnam."

"Another senseless death."

"There's a funeral service next Saturday. I'm going to go," Baxter announced.

"I'll go with you. It would be a great opportunity to organize a demonstration in that part of the country," Jennifer proposed.

"To demonstrate what?" Baxter asked.

"To demonstrate against that stupid war that's brutally killing innocent people each day. It's got to be stopped and it only can be stopped from this country!"

"Mort was a professional Marine. His country ordered him to Vietnam. He was doing his job and he was killed. All he needs is some respect. I'll go alone, thank you."

"You're such a close-minded fool, Joe. Your whole life is wrapped around your business career. The rest of the world and its injustices make no impression on you. You're a self-centered lout. I will call our Minnesota contingent and organize some kind of demonstration. I believe we have an active chapter in Duluth."

"You will stay the hell out of Iron Creek! If I see any of those shaggy haired twirps at the funeral service or the gravesite, I will personally start busting heads and I know I will have company. They're a pretty patriotic bunch in Iron Creek. It's not your Madison, Wisconsin liberal set," Baxter was angry.

"It's a stupid group of crude, primitive people of which you are a product. I'm sick of you, Joe Baxter! I wish to hell you would get out of my house and my life!"

Baxter folded the letter, placed it back in the envelope, and left the sitting room. He knew it was only a matter of time before the marriage ended and that love was gone forever.

Baxter felt strange and out of place at the funeral. He hadn't been back since the Christmas before his wedding to Jennifer. Iron Creek had not changed. Broadway Avenue was still Broadway Avenue, although Baxter learned from Rose Anne that Mr. Albright had died and both the Iron Creek Department Store and Miss Marshall's had been sold to the Katzmans from Duluth. Mrs. Albright had moved in with Tommy and Lucy. Gordy had a steady job in Duluth as a driver for a man who operated a number of small businesses. Lenore had grown into a fine young woman with an interest in nursing. She worked part-time as a volunteer at the Iron Creek Clinic.

Maggie and Karl came to the funeral and stood next to Baxter at the gravesite. The Himmelmans were obviously grieved, but maintained a stoic exterior. The Marine reserve unit played taps, a salute was fired, and the flag was neatly folded and presented to Mrs. Himmelman. Baxter lingered by the grave and talked with Maggie and Karl. Maggie had gained weight. She was wearing a dark pants suit that fit tightly. Karl was greying now and wore a white shirt and blue tie under his zipper jacket. "Mort was a good person, Joey," Maggie said while trying to subdue sniffling. "I remember when you guys used to hang around the Greeks and everyone remembers the basketball team."

"I guess Rychek died," Karl offered. "He was living down in Florida and had a heart attack or something."

Baxter thought back to his old coach who dressed a lot like Karl.

"Gordy's working in Duluth, but Karl thinks the guy he works for is on the shady side."

"He's been in trouble a lot over the years," Karl explained. "Gordy is driving around delivering things from one business to another. This guy calls himself Miller, but his real name is Amunchek. At least he's working and not a burden on Rose Anne."

"Are you going to see Lenore this trip, Joey?" Maggie asked and Baxter knew he was obliged to visit the daughter he hardly knew.

Lenore was working in Iron Creek Clinic and wore a white uniform with a striped apron. She was tall for 16, standing nearly 5'9" with short red hair in a pixie cut and fading freckles. She smiled sadly at the sight of her father as they sat together in the coffee shop.

"Dr. Tweetman asks about you," she said sipping on her coke. "I heard his son is doing real well with IBM. Mrs. Albright is living with them in Toledo. Gordy is working in Duluth." Lenore apparently felt obliged to recite all the local news to her father.

"And how are you, Lenore?" Baxter asked.

27

"I'm doing OK in school and I want to become a nurse. I joined the Baptist Church and I'm going to devote my life to our savior, Jesus Christ. I believe I can best serve him through nursing. Mother told me to ask you if you can help me through nurse's training after I get out of high school. She said that you were very good about child support. I don't think it's fair to ask Karl to do it." She talked in verbal spurts, Baxter decided.

"Of course, Lenore. Count on me," Baxter agreed.

"Mother said you would but said I should ask. You're quite famous around here. They talk about Grandpa and how he used to fight in the bars and was killed in the strike, and they talk about you and the basketball team that almost went to the State Tournament. You took the last shot of the game and it went in and out. If it would have gone in, the Cougars would have gone to the State, but it came out. I play girl's basketball and I'm good. Sometimes I look through Mother's Cougar yearbook and look at your pictures and the team pictures. You must be very sad today about Mort Himmelman's death. But you must remember, Father, he's with the Lord now. He may have been a sinner like you, but he will be forgiven. The Lord is very wise, but you and I must pray to the Lord for his forgiveness." Baxter was overwhelmed.

Lenore talked in a monotone and the words spurted out of her mouth. "They say you married a rich woman. I remember when she came to the house with you. She was beautiful and her family's company made all of the utensils and the blenders you see at K-Mart. I hope that she's a Christian and bringing up my half-brother and half-sister in a Christian home. They say you work for a famous company and travel all over the country. Do you have pictures of your children?"

They talked for another ten minutes with Lenore doing most of the talking. When they broke off, Lenore promised to pray for Baxter. Baxter felt relieved when he was safe in his car driving away from the clinic.

Dinner at the Ganski's was gloomy and they lingered around the table drinking coffee after the children had been dispersed. They went through their inventory of Iron Creek friends and acquaintances, and Baxter described his discussion with Lenore. "Maggie said it isn't hurting her any," Diane commented. "I was brought up Baptist before I met Ed and turned Lutheran. She's been going over to the Baptist Church about three years now, works volunteer at the clinic, passes her school work, and keeps her room neat. I don't know what more you could ask for."

They talked about Gordy in Duluth and Diane commented, "We hear he's a drug dealer."

"We don't know that for sure," Ganski commented firmly. "Tweetman didn't make it."

"He's the new Branch Manager in Toledo. He and Lucy have two children and Mrs. Albright now. It's tough to get here from Toledo. He always calls when he's in Chicago." It had been apparent to Baxter since Washburn Manufacturing that Tom Tweetman was hustling Baxter for business. He had finally sold a 360 model 20 system to the Henry Wiggins people following four years of persistent selling efforts. Recently he had been trying to use his relationship with Baxter to become better acquainted with the Computer Systems consulting practice at McKenzie Barber.

"Joe," Tommy had said, "I believe it would be mutually beneficial for our two world class firms to have close contact."

"Tommy," Baxter had explained, "Ernie Grey, our Chairman, had lunch with Tom Watson two weeks ago in Armonk. Marching orders are probably being issued now."

Ganski was now a Drafting Supervisor at Penn-Mine. "They've talked to me about moving to Duluth. Diane and I went up there on Friday to look around. It was just too big for us."

"It's a good place to visit," Diane ruled. "But I wouldn't want to live there. This is our home. Tell Joe your news, Ed."

"Joe, this is not official and very confidential," Ganski cautioned. "The DFL has felt me out about running for City Council. I might do it. I love Iron Creek and this is where Diane and I have chosen to build our life. I was looking forward to Mort coming back. He wrote me about settling back on his folk's farm after he retired from the Marine Corps. He had seen a whole bunch of the world, and he knew that Iron Creek was probably as good a place to live as he could find."

Baxter looked at his watch. It was time to go if he was going to make Duluth by eleven o'clock in order to break up the drive back to Racine. He had been asked several times as to what McKenzie Barber was and what he did there, but the answers didn't seem to take with the Ganski's. They thought Baxter did some kind of payroll work. They were more interested in Washburn Manufacturing. Diane used her blender constantly. Ganski knew what a plant manager did, but was at sea with the concept of an executive compensation consultant. No one he knew intimately had ever participated in an incentive bonus plan or ever had been granted a stock option.

Baxter drove up to the top of Pine Hill on his way out of town. He paused in front of the Albright house. Other people lived there now, and he could see them through the big picture window in the upstairs family room. Baxter parked the car at the top of the hill and looked down at the town of Iron Creek. The view from Pine Hill held so many memories for Baxter. He had stood there in the fall afternoon sun with Maggie Sadowski when she had the best body in Iron Creek. He had kissed Beth Gold and proposed to Jennifer on a cold winter night. Tom and Lucy Tweetman and Baxter had escaped, Mort had died, and the rest were trapped in a time warp called Iron Creek, Minnesota.

The fiscal year of McKenzie Barber ran from October 1st through September 30th. Promotions and changes were universally announced during the last week in September and implemented October 1st. The year that commenced October 1, 1972, was referred to within the firm as FY 73. FY 73 marked a year of great change for Baxter. Alvardi invited Baxter out for breakfast on the last Friday in September. It was the first time Alvardi had ever asked Baxter to meet him for breakfast in a meeting that did not involve a client.

"Breakfast on Friday, kid?" Alvardi asked on a Monday morning.

"Sure. Who are we meeting with?" Baxter asked.

"Just you and me, kid," Alvardi replied. "I thought we'd talk."

"About what?" Baxter questioned.

"We don't talk enough, kid," Alvardi said enigmatically.

They breakfasted at the Drake at a corner table and Alvardi started talking in earnest after their eggs were served.

"Well, kid. Things are happening. I think this kind of meeting is best held outside the office. First, I'm going to New York. I have been in Chicago about two years longer than I was supposed to be. The Executive Compensation Practice is being placed under the Business Strategy practice. I am to report to a Group Partner named Roger Dirks who is going to be responsible for the New York Business Strategy Practice. I have recommended that you take charge of the Chicago Office Executive Compensation Practice. This was an idea which Brimmer rejected until he had lunch with you. You will report functionally to me in New York and administratively to Dr. Keller. Prior to this, I reported directly to Brimmer so I regard my new reporting relationship a bit of a comedown. Ernie explained to me that New York is three times the size of the Chicago office. Now get this——Dirks reports functionally to Dr. Barry Keller. So you and I kind of have the same job. This is so confusing that only one man could have provided Ernie this kind of organizational advice."

"Nickerson?" Baxter guessed.

"Bingo, kid. Ernie's had him working on a reorganization project for a year. Not even Brimmer knew about it. Bruce Dinsmore, the Managing Partner for New York, has maybe five years before he retires and Ernie has some kind of succession management plan that only Clyde knows the details. We're not parting company, kid. Just think of me moving down the block. Carl will resent your promotion to manager, but you've got a good way with people and you should be able to rally the people around you. Be careful of your little buddy, Lee Heller. He's looking for something to Partner and I guarantee he'll make a run at you."

"Wow," Baxter observed. His safe fun little world with Alvardi was about to be shaken up.

"Hey, kid. It's too soon to Wow. There's a lot more I've got to tell you this morning. That was just the weather. Let me take you onto the real news. I have volunteered you to work on a special new project for our friend Clyde. It will be funded by Executive Office and it will be an internal consulting assignment in the Federal Systems Practice in McLean, Virginia. You're to call Clyde and make an appointment for a Washington briefing. The practice is all screwed up and your official mission will be to install a uniform system of pay grades, but Clyde's real agenda is for someone to do an organization study. The Federal Systems practice is leaking money, unlike any other office of McKenzie Barber. It will be a political football, but it will also be high visibility. You will probably get a chance to get in front of Ernie. Nickerson will be dangerous, and he was a little skeptical when I recommended you. You'll draw on New York staff and maybe someone from Nickerson's Executive Office staff. For a guy who flopped in Chicago, our boy Clyde is right back in business." Alvardi sipped his coffee and stared at Baxter. He did look like Joe DiMaggio. "Now, more news kid. Do you remember Bob Friedman from LA?" Baxter shook his head.

"Do you remember the big, good looking Jewish guy we met in the LA Airport who was doing all the work for the Thrifts?" Baxter placed a conversation in the Ambassador's Club with a tall, handsome, tanned man in his early thirties who he remembered as very funny.

"Yeah. I can place him," Baxter acknowledged.

"Well kid, Friedman has been doing strategic planning with the West Coast Thrifts since 1969. He started out by selling them management-by-objectives systems and then linked them with forward planning. Now he wants to tie short and long term incentives to reinforce the strategic planning objectives. He heard from Barry Keller about the wonderful things you have done in Chicago and wants you to begin visiting Los Angeles on a regular basis. Near as I see it, you're going to have to add some people and train them. If the next two years won't kill you, people will be singing your praises to the sky. Now, the third piece of news. I don't know whether it's going to seem good or bad to you. McKenzie Barber, in the firm's infinite wisdom, has created a new organizational level. They call it Director. It's going to be placed between Manager and Partner. The Partnership hill has just become a little steeper, kid. Clyde's been promoted to Director and a number of the heavier managers have been promoted to Director. Your friend Lee Heller will be promoted to Director. A Director, presumably, is a Partner in waiting. The wait will be two to three years. If a Director hasn't made it in three years, I assume that he will be counseled out."

"When will you go to New York?" Baxter asked Alvardi.

31

"January 2nd is the magic date, kid. But I won't be around much after the end of October. Just remember, I'm only a phone call and a two hour plane ride away. It isn't like I'm going off to Afghanistan."

Baxter sipped his coffee and processed all of the information Alvardi had provided him. It was tricky, but it could be accomplished. He had always been under someone's wing at McKenzie Barber. Now he was being provided an opportunity to make his mark. Baxter was now 37 years old. If he didn't move ahead in the next few years at McKenzie Barber, he could wind-up as one of Nickerson's 'counsel-outs'. The challenge and the opportunity were there. Baxter would have to step up to it.

"I like it, Frank. I will handle it."

"I know you will, kid. Now I'm leaving town and I tried to get them to give you my office, but they wouldn't do it. They're saving it for another Partner. You'll get a decent manager's office. But I will leave one nice opportunity behind for you." Alvardi was quiet and looked at Baxter with his Yankee Clipper eyes. "I suspect kid, that you're not happy at home. I also suspect that you have been occasionally fraternizing with Naomi Schwartz. I'm leaving you another alternative. Why don't you get to know Lorna better, kid? She knows how to handle a delicate relationship, and she may want some company after I leave town. Understand?"

Friedman called Baxter that afternoon, and Baxter's California adventures began. Nickerson called mid-week, and Baxter's participation in Washington intrigues commenced. It became quickly apparent to Baxter that he could not be home every weekend.

Bob Friedman was a delight from the beginning. He charmed Baxter from their first telephone conversation. They both laughed a lot and Baxter concluded that it was going to be fun to consult in California. The first trip was one week later with Baxter landing late on a Monday night. Bob Friedman met Baxter for breakfast at 7 AM the next morning at his hotel. He was waiting for Baxter at the maitre d's station. Taller than Baxter, Friedman was easily 6'4" with a slender build. He wore a lightweight three piece tan suit and brown wingtips. Friedman's face was handsome with high cheek bones and a Roman nose, and he could brighten the room with his broad smile.

"Well, Joe," he greeted Baxter, "Ready to go to work California style?"

They called on five Savings and Loans on that October, Tuesday and issued three confirmation letters and two proposals. All five meetings led to work for McKenzie Barber. Friedman and Baxter worked well together. In a meeting they responded intuitively to one another. Friedman would brief Baxter in the car as they drove to each meeting and Baxter would quickly digest the financial statements. Their last meeting was in Santa Barbara, where they left a silver haired Savings & Loan Chairman in the parking lot at 6 PM with a handshake on the development of a long term incentive plan. They settled into Friedman's Jaguar with Friedman tallying the day's kill.

"We probably have sold $180,000 worth of work today. Now we can drive back to Los Angeles or hang around here and probably get laid."

"I have a hotel room in Los Angeles with my clothes in it," Baxter explained.

"And it will wait for you. I happen to know a few places where we can stop on the way back which will be filled with friendly California ladies. My goodness Joe, we deserve a reward for our accomplishment today."

They visited two oceanside bars and conversed with a number of California women. They settled for two beauticians named Daphne and Felice. They were tall, long legged girls who wore brightly colored blouses, tight white pants, dangling earrings, and white pumps. They smiled with straight white teeth and accompanied Friedman and Baxter down Highway 101 to a seafood place called Nick's that overlooked the ocean. Traveling in separate cars, Baxter rode in Daphne's Volkswagen.

"Are you married?" she asked Baxter when he was in the car.

"Yes. But I'm very unhappy," Baxter responded honestly.

"I am too, and my husband's a cop," Daphne informed Baxter.

"It's a wonderful line of work," Baxter commented. "It's critical for the community."

"He gets off at midnight," Daphne explained. "We've got to split up by eleven at the latest. Do you get out here a lot?"

"I'll be coming out periodically from now on," Baxter predicted.

"Then why don't we just be good friends tonight," Daphne suggested. "I'll give you the number of the beauty shop and we'll work out something for next trip. I really like you, Joe and I don't like to rush things. Suppose we just have fun tonight and I sleep with you next time you come?"

"That sounds fair," Baxter concluded.

There was some difficulty in separating Friedman from Felice in the other car. Baxter finally rapped on the window. Friedman emerged from the car and indignantly whispered to Baxter, "Really Joe, my tongue just reached Felice's tonsils." They sat in a corner booth drinking white wine and looking at the ocean, while consuming fried food.

"Now who works for who?" Felice questioned the relationship between Baxter and Friedman.

"We work for each other," Friedman announced firmly.

"And we plan to be married in the spring!" Baxter added. Daphne placed her hand on Baxter's thigh and ran it up his fly.

"You guys don't look gay to me," Felice concluded.

So this is what California is like, Baxter concluded. You sell a heap of business to simple thinking thrifts and then frolic with movie star attractive women with smooth complexions, bleached hair, and long legs.

Over dinner, Baxter and Friedman told lies to Daphne and Felice, but assumed that they were receiving an exchange of falsehoods. Beautiful blonde women were within their grasp with quick tongues and shallow minds. Daphne watched her watch, and at ten thirty excused herself and asked Baxter to accompany her back to her car. When they reached the Volkswagen, Daphne asked Baxter to get in. They kissed for a few minutes and then she unzipped his fly and placed her mouth on Baxter's member. It was all over in ninety seconds.

"Call me," she requested and turned the handle of his door. Friedman was with Felice when Baxter returned and a motel was suggested. "Did Daphne take care of you, Joe? Felice asked.

"Yes, she certainly did," Baxter answered.

"Good! One down and one to go!" Friedman observed.

Baxter was back in his room at 3 AM and they met again at 7 AM for breakfast. Baxter was exhausted, while Friedman appeared fresh in a blue three piece suit. "Today, Joe," Friedman greeted Baxter, "We work greater Los Angeles. In fact, we will walk to our first meeting. I assume you're taking the "Red Eye" so that we can get a full day in."

None of the Thrifts had capital accumulation plans. They were depositor held institutions primarily making mortgage loans for single family residences. They were regarded as awkward country cousins by the bankers, and Friedman had discovered them as a client service segment when he had been an ambitious Associate. His entree had been colorful slide show on Management-by-Objectives at a State Savings League meeting in 1967. Friedman had sold his first MBO to one of the largest Thrifts in the State, and written a speech for the client's Chairman to present at a national convention. Friedman entitled the speech, "Managing the Savings Enterprise in the 1970s."

There had been a restless skepticism within the firm. Why was McKenzie Barber cultivating the Savings & Loan Industry? Who was this hotshot Jew Boy out in California who had gone after this work as a lone wolf? Friedman, had dinner with Ernie Grey in August, 1968, during one of the McKenzie Barber Chairman's West Coast visits and was pronounced a winner. The Los Angeles office which focused on the Aerospace, Banking, and Food Processing Industries had about 35 professionals in 1967. In 1973 there were 65 professionals and 15 worked for Friedman, who was elected a Partner in 1971.

Baxter's visit had been carefully orchestrated by Friedman, and each client meeting had a scripted agenda and it appeared they had booked another $200,000 in fees by the time Friedman drove Baxter to the airport. They arrived early for Baxter's flight and settled in a corner of the Admiral's Club to work out the engagement and follow-up details. By that time Baxter knew Friedman's life story.

Robert David Friedman was the youngest son of a swimsuit manufacturer. His older brother had gone into the family business and Bob had gone to UCLA on a tennis scholarship. Friedman had been accepted by Harvard Business School, but found that he didn't like Boston. He completed his MBA at UCLA, which he acknowledged as an easy school, and married a girl named Becky, whose father was a major real estate developer. Friedman had met Becky when he was an assistant tennis pro at an exclusive club. They now lived in Beverly Hills and Friedman was the father of two daughters.

Friedman had interviewed McKenzie Barber on a dare.

"McKenzie Barber doesn't hire Jews, Bob," Dr. Goldman, Friedman's marketing professor, had counseled him.

"They are a waspish, blue blood management consulting firm that is content to hire establishment MBAs. I'd say you're just wasting your time."

Friedman borrowed some money from his father-in-law, assembled a team of graduate students, and developed a study entitled <u>Management Consulting Opportunities in California 1964 to 1974</u>. He brought the study to his interview.

Bob Friedman was the first Jew and the first UCLA MBA to be hired by McKenzie Barber. Being hired was one thing. Getting someone to use Friedman on their engagements was another. He quickly learned that only the scut jobs were going to him. The high profile engagements were staffed with Stanford and Harvard graduates. After two years, Friedman concluded that he would have to bring in his own work. McKenzie Barber's fees were high for the entrepreneurial companies known to his father-in-law and father. But his father-in-law had a wealth of contacts within the Savings & Loan Industry. Friedman had identified his strategic strikepoint to be a success with McKenzie Barber.

Baxter was beginning to get his second wind as they spread their papers out on the table in the Admiral's Club. "Did you go home last night?" he asked Friedman.

"No. It was a work night. I have an understanding with Becky that I will not come home on certain work nights and I have an understanding with the Sheraton that they will always have a room for me when I need it. Night or day." Friedman formed a slight self-satisfied smile. "I would say that you and I, Joe, are a real Butch & Sundance Act. You should think about transferring out here to La-La Land. Based on your performance with

Daphne last night, I would say that you will catch on to the lifestyle quickly."

Friedman, the Los Angeles Partner, then went on to explain to Baxter, the visiting Chicago Manager, the ground rules for all of the work they had sold.

"The work will be performed on LA Office engagement numbers, Joe. You will draft the proposal and confirmation letters for my signature. Your time will come in at 80% of standard fee so that LA can have a little margin. I want Los Angeles consultants to be used on the work as much as possible, but you can slip some Chicago consultant time in if it's required to shore up the quality. It's important to do a quality job, but also do a pretty job. I will personally approve all the graphics. Chicago has a reputation of turning out second rate graphics on client reports. I will have none of that. The reports will be printed here and we're better at making slides than you are in Chicago. Every one of those final reports is a selling piece for the firm. I have taken the S&Ls down this road from their first MBO plans. We installed most of these plans and McKenzie Barber has an installed base that we can farm for years. I just love a continuity of work from the same client base, don't you?"

"That will free us up from selling and provide us more time to pursue active sex lives. Oh, one other thing, Joe. I'm very good about expenses. I don't look closely if you have to stay over an extra night in a good hotel, and have to buy a fancy dinner or two for a comfortable lady. We work very hard for our fees and those little extra comforts help us produce the first class work that is expected from us." Friedman began to pack his brief case around six o'clock. "Well, I'm off to my wife and family. Where do you go now, Joe?"

"I fly to New York. I have a nine o'clock meeting with Clyde Nickerson. I'm going to take on an internal assignment for the Federal Systems Practice."

"My goodness, Joe. What gods did you offend that caused you to draw that job?"

"I was volunteered. What do you know about Federal Systems?" Baxter asked. Everyone in Chicago had pleaded ignorance when Baxter inquired.

"I was there once on a planning study in 1966, when I was non-chargeable at the wrong time. I spent three weeks holed up in some Holiday Inn in the bowels of McLean, Virginia. Luckily Washington was close by, and had its social life compensations."

"What is it?" Baxter asked.

"It's something the old man bought. You know, the one with the mustache whose picture hangs in every office. Mr. Mac bought it in 1949 during peacetime for a song. It was a beltway bandit company. The Korean

War came and their business began to boom again. They are basically a contractor to the military services in the development of weapons systems software. They have scads of people who wear beards and jeans to work and when they lose money, they lose big. They all have engineering and mathematics degrees from universities without football teams or business schools. Even the women have beards there. They come out here all the time to chase contracts that nobody else wants. They're called FSO for Federal Systems Operations. Ernie Grey makes them keep the affiliation with McKenzie Barber on their business cards in very small print. They've been trying to get rid of it for years, and nobody's willing to pay what Ernie Grey wants for it. So FSO goes on and on. It makes money some years, and loses money others. Every now and then a consulting team is dropped in to look them over. It sounds as though it's going to be your turn. Say hello to Clyde for me. He's just a fun guy!" Friedman picked up his briefcase. "You know me, family first, then career, and finally the temple. Hurry back, Joe! And don't fuck me up or I'll get you!" Friedman left with a big smile.

Baxter was alone in the Ambassador's Club with a hangover, sickening fatigue, the prospect of a red eye flight to New York and a 9 AM meeting with Clyde Nickerson. Baxter took off his coat and began to draft engagement letters. It was the biggest client sales day he had ever personally seen at McKenzie Barber.

The "Red Eye" boarded at 10 PM and arrived at Kennedy Airport at 6:03 AM. Baxter rode first class, drank a lot of Canadian Club, consumed dinner, and listened in his headset to Schubert's 8th Symphony (Unfinished) and Holst's The Planets before he went to sleep. It was Baxter's maiden "Red Eye" flight form the West Coast to New York. He awoke about 5:15 when the flight attendant awakened him with coffee service and orange juice. Baxter's eyes felt like burning holes and he entered the taxi for the Waldorf in a fog of fatigue. He was inside his room at 7:20 AM, took a shower, and slept until 8:20. He passed through the revolving doors at 311 Park Avenue at 8:57 AM.

It marked Baxter's first visit to the Executive Offices of McKenzie Barber. The building directory showed that the New York office of McKenzie Barber occupied floors 34 to 39. The Operations Services Department were at the Lexington Avenue Level which Baxter later learned was the basement. The world-wide executive offices of McKenzie Barber occupied the 40th floor.

The people in the lobby looked different to Baxter from the ones in Chicago. He wasn't certain what made him feel that way. The men walked quickly and seemed to be filled with nervous energy. The women were either elegantly or poorly dressed. Baxter entered a crowded elevator, moved his way to the rear, and looked around the elevator. He observed the middle-aged forms of the support secretaries contrasted against the hard athletic bodies of their younger counterparts, and the bright, young, well-dressed young men and women who appeared to be this and last year's graduate class of the top business schools. The elevator began to empty at 34 with exits at each floor. A woman in a trench coat had entered the elevator with Baxter and pushed her way to the back. She wore her brown hair in a bun and peered at Baxter through tinted glasses. Finally she said his name at the 35th floor. "Joe?"

"Yes," he responded.

"It's Andy." She beamed and extended her hand. Baxter quickly recalled an afternoon in Rosemont two years earlier with Naomi and Andy. He accepted her hand and squeezed gently.

"You're meeting with Clyde this morning and you're coming in from LA."

"The elevator stopped at 40."

"I'm supposed to sit in on your meeting this morning. Come back with me. I'll take you to Clyde. We were just talking about you yesterday." Baxter followed Andy as she moved confidently past the reception area and the pictures of McKenzie and Barber set against a map of the world."

"I know you want a coffee. We'll start there. The carpeting was rich and thick and each office had a see-through glass door.

Baxter could see a dark haired man in a blue suit talking to a woman at a desk. "That's Ernie," Andy said.

Clyde's office was three cubicles down from the Chairman's corner office and his door was closed. Andy dialed three digits on the secretary's telephone and reached Clyde Nickerson. "Clyde, good morning, Andy here," she announced cheerfully. "I have Joe Baxter with me in from the coast for his FSO briefing. Yes. I've brought him a cup of coffee. I'll take him to my office. Ring us!"

Turning to Baxter, Andy explained. "Clyde's tied up for at least a half hour. Let's go back to my office and I'll brief you on FSO."

Andy had a tiny inside cubicle that was furnished with a desk covered by neatly stacked piles of letter size papers. She had a swivel chair and there was a single side chair cramped between the edge of her desk and the wall. There was a credenza with book shelves half filled with Andy's textbooks from Cornell and half filled with black ring binders with the McKenzie Barber logo. On the wall was a Georgia O'Keefe poster from the Santa Fe Opera. "It's not much, Joe," Andy apologized. "but it is an enclosed office and sure beats the pool back in Chicago. I'll get coffee. I remember you drink it black."

She watched Baxter eased his way into the narrow space between the front of her desk and the armchair. "I'm just visited by small men and medium-sized women in this office. You're the first large one to come by and see me, Joe," Andy explained. Baxter noted that Andy kept her college diplomas from Wheaton and Cornell on the wall. He was looking at them when Andy returned with the coffee in china cups and saucers.

"This is far different from Chicago, Joe. It's important to show your schools out here." Baxter sipped from his coffee and the cup rattled slightly.

"Oh you poor dear," Andy said. "You've come here to meet with Clyde all the way from California. When do you go back?"

"Tomorrow morning, first thing. I'm going back to the room and sleep after my meeting with Clyde."

"Do you have dinner plans?" Andy asked. While she had appeared plain in Chicago, Andy seemed more cosmopolitan in New York with her tinted glasses and dressed in a blue suit with shiny brass buttons.

"None," Baxter replied. "I'm yours."

"Then I'll pick you up in the Waldorf lobby in front of the clock at 6:30. We'll go to a little French place around the corner from the hotel and we can get caught up." Andy's telephone rang. "Andy Bourke," she answered. "I have him right here, Clyde. I'm just pouring some coffee in him. We'll be right in."

"You're going to be in the meeting, Andy?" Baxter asked lifting himself carefully from the narrow space between Andy's desk and the chair.

"I will be working with you on the project," she announced proudly and Baxter followed Andy down the hall. He concluded that Andy had an attractive figure and was no longer the plain girl he had met on his first day at McKenzie Barber.

Clyde Nickerson's office was two doors down from Ernie Grey's corner office. Clyde had been promoted to Director in October with his return to New York, but he had a partner's size office looking out at the GE building. Clyde's jacket was off and he wore black and red braces and a club tie. His hair was continuing to thin and he greeted Baxter with a patronizing crocodile smile.

"Heard you just got in, Joe," he greeted Baxter. "Andy, have Ellen get us some more coffee and let's talk at the table." Clyde's office was large enough to hold a couch, two stuffed chairs and a conference table.

Coffee was served. Baxter slipped his suit jacket over an armchair. Clyde Nickerson began to talk, and Andy began writing on a yellow legal pad.

"Let me start out frankly, Joe. I have real reservations about you being the consultant to do this job," Clyde began and Baxter controlled his need to groan.. "FSO is a troubled organization and the work we're going to do there has a double agenda, and when I have explained what we want to accomplish, I'll give you the option to withdraw from the project. If you take on the project, your accomplishments or lack of accomplishment will be highly visible to Ernie Grey, our Chairman. This assignment could be a career breaker if it's botched or below expectations. I want that clear from the outset. Frank Alvardi told Ernie that you were the one Manager who had the political skills to do what we want done."

Baxter said nothing. He simply stared ahead in his fatigue at Clyde Nickerson and patiently waited for him to tell his story. No wonder no client had wanted to engage him back in Chicago.

Clyde Nickerson began a recitation of the history of Federal Systems Operations from its acquisition in 1949 by John McKenzie to the present day. "They should be a subsidiary, but we've got them as part of the partnership. They're a $10 to $15 million business and in their good years make a million or so, and in their bad years they lose a million or two. It's a totally different operation from the rest of McKenzie Barber. They have a lot of long term contracts with the Air Force and the Navy that have to do with systems. The Army threw them out two years ago and they are trying to bring them back as a customer. They have a cost plus fixed fee accounting system and nobody up here really understands the business. Ernie has tried to sell it a couple of times and it's the kind of business that you can't close down because of the length of the contracts. You have to wind it down. The senior partner is a man named Dr. John Petting and he has a Deputy Senior Partner named Dr. Norman Thayer. Better take note of those names. Petting is in his middle fifties and Thayer is the protégé in his late forties."

"FSO lost money last year for the second year in a row. Ernie hit the ceiling and refused to approve the salary increases for this year. They are now presumably sitting on a bunch of contracts that if landed, will lock in their profit through 1975. Drs. Petting and Thayer were up here in November and warned that there would be major defections if they were unable to get their raises approved. The losses of these key scientists would threaten FSO's ability to honor their existing contracts. Ernie backed off, but wanted to bring in McKenzie Barber resources to review the entire pay system at FSO. Petting and Thayer proposed that they engage Robson Allen to ensure that the study would be objective. Needless to say, our chairman hit the ceiling! Your mission, Joe, is to conduct a complete study of FSO's pay practices relative to internal equity and external competitiveness and more closely link pay to performance. That's your official mission for FSO. You will have an unofficial mission for McKenzie Barber. Ernie believes they are way overstaffed and he wants an organization study and that will produce some recommendations for substantial expense cuts. This means that while you're looking at pay levels, you're going to be reviewing how they can get by with less people."

"What's their headcount?" Baxter asked.

"800 or so. Andy's got all the information."

"When does the work have to be completed?" Baxter asked.

"Ernie would like to see it done by the end of January," Nickerson responded.

"How many people will I have?" Baxter questioned.

"You will have Andy, some New York pool consultants, as many as you like, and a Manager and an Associate from the IE practice," Nickerson replied.

"First year pool consultants or second year pool consultants?" Baxter asked.

"You can have as many first year people as you want. The second year people are pretty well spoken for out of New York."

"March 31st is the report delivery date, not January 31st!" Baxter announced.

"Joe, the Chairman or McKenzie Barber wants the job done by January 31st," Nickerson explained. "Do you get it? When the Chairman wants a January 31st report, you get it for him!"

"If the Chairman wants a quality report by January 31st developed by an engagement team led by me with a team comprised of a first year Manager, an outstanding executive office Associate, two reluctant IE practice people and a mess of first year consultants, he's kidding himself. March 31st is the date and I will see that the project is delivered at expectations or I will tender my resignation," Baxter promised. He looked to Andy and noted that her eyes had widened.

"That's sixty days later than when Ernie wants it," Nickerson cautioned.

"Get me on his calendar and I will explain it personally."

Clyde Nickerson sighed. "I'll talk to Ernie about the dates and explain that you're willing to put your job on the line. I make no promises, Joe."

"Those are my conditions. I am already committed to substantial work on the West Coast with Bob Friedman. If those conditions are unacceptable, I recommend you find someone else or engage RAH."

"If you don't mind, I'll couch your language a little. The Chairman of McKenzie Barber is not accustomed to having Managers throw out ultimatums," Nickerson said. "When do you go back?"

"Tomorrow morning. Call him now. I want to talk to the IEs and begin the engagement plan in the next half-hour. Lastly, what are the financial arrangements on this engagement? Is there a budget?"

"You tell me what it will cost, Joe."

"I will after I have developed the work plan."

"It's 50% of standard fee," Clyde offered as a caveat.

"Then somebody here had better call Paul Brimmer and tell him that I will be tying up a lot of time at 50% of standard."

41

"Brimmer will understand it's for the good of the firm," Nickerson commented.

"I'm certain that he will if he's told."

"Are you sure you're up to this job, Joe?" Nickerson chided Baxter.

"I am with a March 31st report date."

"I'll talk Ernie into it," Nickerson said with a collegial smile. "Get started on your work plan. Andy will work with you."

"She's going to be my chief of staff," Baxter announced, and Andy beamed back at him.

Baxter and Andy staked out a small conference room on the 40th floor and began to develop a draft engagement plan. The IE practice had no volunteers, but conscripts were developed by early afternoon. A manager named Gresham was produced whose total experience was in pre-determined work measurements. Baxter passed. Finally a wiry, heavy eyed Associate named Jeff Long visited the conference room. He greeted Baxter and Andy with a slow smile. "I hear you folks are looking for someone to help out on some kind of big confidential project," he said seating himself after shaking hands.

"How long have you been with the firm?" Baxter asked after the introductions.

"Two years and five months. I was hired presumably to be an Operations Research Analyst, but they never seemed to have any O.R. work for me. I've worked on some methods jobs in the brokerage industry. I've done some work in logistics and warehousing, and I ran a big job on an air frame industry contract overrun."

"What agencies did they serve?" Andy asked.

"All of them, but they were overrun with the Air Force. It was a big cost job, tedious and boring, and I told the firm if they ever put me on a job like that again, I would quit."

"Why?" Baxter asked.

"These assholes, excuse my French, lady," Long said in deference to Andy, "had too many goddam people and they were over applied to the contracts. I felt like a criminal lawyer defending a crook."

Baxter knew he had found his man. It was only necessary to convince him of the existential purpose of their mission.

At four o'clock, Andy concluded that Baxter must be exhausted. "You were going to take a nap this afternoon, Joe. You must be exhausted. Do you want a raincheck on dinner?"

The table was covered with pro-forma workplans and they had scheduled a visitation date during Thanksgiving week with FSO.

"I'm getting my second wind, Andy, and I'll need your company for dinner," Baxter explained. They broke at 5:30 and Baxter shaved and fished

42

for a fresh shirt. One of his California shirts had lipstick on the collar and he buried it in his suitcase. Baxter was clean shaven and in a fresh shirt, when he met Andy by the clock in the Waldorf lobby. She greeted Baxter with a broad smile.

"Hello again, Mr. Sensational," Andy kissed Baxter lightly on the cheek and they walked up to 51st Street to a place called La Chanteclair. "It's run by French racing drivers who came over here to compete in the Indianapolis 500 in 1940 only to have France fall," Andy whispered as they crossed the threshold to the maitre d' stand.

After they were seated, Andy beamed at Baxter. "I hardly know you, Joe, but you were sensational today. I talked to Clyde before I left the office and he was impressed. I don't think anyone had ever talked to him that way before about an Ernie Grey project. I was impressed today about the way your mind works. You're really very quick."

Baxter ordered a bottle of Merlot and the fatigue started to come back. Andy was animated over the project and her role in the assignment.

Andy began to talk about Executive Office and her move to New York. "I'm so glad to be where I am. Clyde is a super boss and you can see everything from Executive Office. The FSO project is so visible and here I am right in the middle of it. So much has happened since that night you and Naomi and I went out to dinner in Rosemont. By the way, Naomi has found someone."

Baxter looked at Andy quizzically. "Just who has she found?" he asked.

"She flew back with an attorney from a California recruiting trip and they got interested in each other. He's Jewish and from Chicago. He's an Associate with one of the big Chicago law firms. I was really worried about her."

"Why's that?" Baxter asked.

"Because for about two years she's been carrying on with this married man. He can't get a divorce and he's not Jewish. I told her to drop the guy. He's got clothes and shaving things in her apartment. Now she's met this Irving, and it's hot and heavy, and she needs to tell this married guy that the game's over."

"Did Naomi predict how her married friend would handle this news?" Baxter asked.

"She thinks he'll be relieved. Married guys are the bane of the single woman. They're always out there flirting, but all of their commitments are part-time. You're a solid citizen married man. You're like Clyde! All you do is work and you have no time for anything outside your job or your marriage, but you would be surprised to know how many men are less committed."

It seemed like a long dinner to Baxter. Andy talked on about Ernie Grey, Clyde Nickerson, and the role of Executive Office at McKenzie Barber, and Baxter became more and more fatigued. Where was all this going? He asked himself.

Baxter returned to the Chicago office of McKenzie Barber on Friday morning. He had departed for California on a Monday evening and arrived in New York on the Thursday AM red eye and returned to Chicago on a 7 AM flight Friday morning, and was at his desk before 9 AM. Baxter felt as though he had been gone a month.

While Executive Compensation had been integrated under Dr. Barry Keller's Business Strategy practice, Baxter rarely saw Dr. Keller. Baxter, as Manager-in-Charge of the Chicago Executive Compensation practice, reported professionally to Alvardi in New York, and administratively to Lee Heller, who served as Dr. Keller's business manager for his practices. Dr. Keller, who knew very little about McKenzie Barber's policy and administrative practices, delegated all these matters to Lee Heller, who had been promoted to the new Director designation in October. Dr. Keller and his two senior associates, Dr. Nestor Kennedy and Dr. Hans Huhlman, ran around the country developing clients, and Lee Heller administered the practice. The addition of the Executive Compensation, practice under Business Strategy expanded Lee Heller's administrative reach.

Baxter was the practice leader for Executive Compensation, and Carl Miller was his number two. Carl had been deeply disappointed when Baxter had been chosen over him to lead the practice. Carl had come up through the pool and developed an interest in Executive Compensation. He was 29, a Michigan MBA, considered himself a better analyst than Baxter, and wrote and spoke well. Baxter judged Carl to be doctrinaire, rigid and mechanical. Alvardi agreed with Baxter and recommended Baxter to Brimmer as his successor. Lee Heller often implied that he had been consulted on the choice and recommended Baxter.

"Jesus, Joe. You must be exhausted!" Carl commented after Baxter narrated the week's travel. Baxter omitted in his narration any mention of Tuesday evening's adventures with Friedman.

"You booked more business in four working days that we develop in three months around here. Bob Friedman and the California Thrifts sound like a gold mine. The engagement construct is simple and you've got it priced to make a ton of money." Carl went on. "Lee will bitch about the margins, but we're going to make plenty of money."

"You and I are running this practice, Carl, not Lee Heller," Baxter said between sips of coffee.

"Damn right, Joe!" Carl agreed. Carl was tall, thin, a little gawky, and often mercurial. "I'd love to work on than FSO assignment. Even if it's only a 50% of standard fee engagement. You're going to have the opportunity to get in front of Ernie Grey! I'd kill for that opportunity!" Carl said.

"We make our real money on standard fee, conventional engagements," Baxter reminded Carl, "Let's get Mindy in here. Mindy!" Baxter bellowed.

Mindy was a short, frenetic Jewish girl whom Alvardi had hired as an administrative secretary in August. In three months, Mindy had aggressively taken charge of practice administration.

"You called, sire?" Short, demure, with a perpetual grin, Mindy entered Baxter's office. He passed her the confirmation letter drafts for the California engagements and the draft of the FSO confirmation memorandum to Clyde Nickerson. "My God! There's 40 to 50 papers worth here. How did you get all this done?"

"I work every minute, Mindy," Baxter responded. "And here is a work plan for a $300,000 engagement which will be performed at 50% of standard." Baxter produced the engagement plan for the FSO engagement. "Make four copies please."

Mindy scanned the four page work plan.

"Wow! Where are you going to get all of these people?"

"I'm going to work on it this morning. We can probably get by with nine consultants, but I'm asking for twelve," Baxter explained. "Now, type as you have never typed before, type fast."

"Have you heard Naomi's news?" Mindy asked.

"Naomi who?" Baxter asked although he suspected which Naomi Mindy meant.

"Naomi Schwartz! She told me that you were both graduate assistants at Minnesota together. Naomi is engaged! She met a guy named Irving Grossman on a plane coming back from the West Coast. They were both traveling in the front of the plane, 4A and 4B, seated together for three and one-half hours, hit it off, they started dating, and he asked her to marry him in five weeks. He's an Associate with Cohen, Greenburg, and Morse, and a sure partner within two years. Fly me someplace so that I can meet someone, guys!"

"We'll take that into consideration," Carl answered.

"I will fly you anywhere in the country, in the front of the plane, wherever Jewish guys go, if you'll get that stuff typed by three o'clock with no errors."

"I'm going guys," Mindy said exiting the office.

"How are we going to handle this, Joe?" Carl asked.

"You're going to have to look after Chicago in the interim and I'll have to get this work done," Baxter said.

"Will you announce it in a memo?" Carl asked.

"A memo to whom?" Baxter asked.

"A memo to the entire Chicago office," Carl suggested.

"No need for that," Baxter concluded. "It would confuse people. I'm running the Chicago Executive Compensation practice with you as my deputy. I have some engagements outside Chicago to attend to. You will run the practice on a day-to-day basis. You will confer with me before you take any action. No surprises, and we'll get along just fine, Carl." Baxter studied Carl's face. "We're in this together, Carl. If I move forward, you will."

Andy called Baxter in a panic at 11 o'clock. "Joe! The second year pool people aren't available. The good ones are all spoken for or protected!"

"Did you invoke the name of Clyde Nickerson?" Baxter asked.

"That didn't help. FSO has a terrible reputation inside the firm. No one wants to work on an internal engagement because they believe it's career limiting. We can get first year pool people, but there are no two year pool people available," Andy declared.

"Let me check out the pool here," Baxter said. "We have an open ended travel budget from Clyde. Let's get out the crew!"

"Andy, lie if you have to. Consider it equivalent to impressing sailors in the late 19th century. Tell them that the food is very good and we have lots of limes," Baxter instructed Andy. "I'll check out Chicago for pool consultants."

In the Chicago office of McKenzie Barber, the pool consultants were now controlled by Lorna King, Clyde Nickerson's former secretary, and now the Personnel Administrator for the pool.

Baxter had a little contact with Lorna King during his five years in the Chicago office. He could remember being picked up in the reception area by Lorna prior to his interview with Clyde Nickerson and later being conducted to Bill Dwyer's office. Her hair had been brown with a reddish tint and she had been wearing a blue dress with black pumps.

Her cheekbones were high and her nose had a slight beak. Baxter had considered her very young and attractive at the time.

Baxter had been out of the office during the two years he had worked in Dwyer's practice. Working for Alvardi had initially been an inside job, but evolved after six months into 40% time outside the office. Baxter began to see Lorna King in the area around Alvardi's office. She seemed to come around once a day. Sometimes it was in the morning, and other times it was in the late afternoon. Baxter would see Lorna standing in the doorway of Alvardi's office talking. The conversations didn't seem very serious and they never lasted long, but they were daily. When Clyde transferred back to New York and Lorna was promoted to personnel administrator, her office was moved two floors down, adjacent to the pool Staff Room and next door to the office manager. She continued to visit Alvardi daily. Occasionally,

Lorna would come by, find Alvardi's office dark, and encounter Baxter in the hallway.

"Is Frank out for the day, Joe?" She would ask and Baxter would answer as to whether and when Alvardi was expected to return.

"Should I have him call you when he comes back?" Baxter would invariably ask.

"No need for that," was Lorna's customary response. "It was nothing important."

Dwyer had always made innuendoes to Alvardi in Baxter's presence to a clandestine relationship with Lorna. Alvardi never acknowledged Dwyer's comments with anything more than a smile. It was only at their breakfast in September that Alvardi had vaguely alluded that he was leaving Lorna behind for Baxter. After Alvardi's departure, Lorna King ceased her visits to the Executive Compensation practice. Baxter dialed her extension after he hung up from Andy.

"Lorna King!" She answered her phone. Baxter observed that she had a wonderful resonant telephone voice. It was well modulated and controlled.

"Joe Baxter here. Can I come by for a minute and talk about staffing a rather large engagement I have?" he requested.

"Today's a little hectic, Joe. Can we do it close to lunch? I just came back to my office to pick up some files for Paul Brimmer and I'm expected to come right back," she explained.

"Want to have a sandwich in the grill?" Baxter asked. He hadn't intended to ask her to lunch when he called and the invitation had just seemed to pop out.

"I can have a sandwich with you if we order in. We could eat in your office or my office, but my files are in my office if it's pool Consultants you want. Also, you missed the Thursday afternoon staffing call, so very little can be done for you until next Thursday." The voice got to Baxter. Each word was delivered with perfect elocution.

"You take care of ordering and I'll pay," Baxter offered. He though he heard a slight sigh on the other end of the phone. "I'll have Margaret, my secretary, order. What shall I order for you?"

"A peanut butter caviar sandwich with milk," Baxter said.

"They don't deliver those anymore. Do you have any other choices?" The voice calmly asked.

"How about a Ham on rye?"

"Splendid. Shall we say 12:20. I have to be in another meeting at 1 PM. And do you have authorization for staffing approved by a Partner?" she asked in closing.

"The project's for the Chairman's office. Your old leader, Clyde Nickerson is involved."

"Oh, this sounds so exciting. Do you know where my office is?"

"On 18, next door to the pool and across the hall from duplicating," Baxter answered.

"I have to run. I'll see you at 12:20," Lorna clicked off.

Baxter cheated. He came to Lorna's office at 12:15 and found two trays containing wrapped lunches in plastic boxes and paper cups sealed by plastic lids. It was an inside office without windows, and it was immaculately neat. On the credenza behind the desk, Baxter observed a color photograph of a man and a piano. The man was seated at the piano and the woman stood in front of it.

Baxter walked behind the desk for a closer look. The man was in a blue dinner jacket. He had dark hair, thick eyebrows, handsome features, and a beaming smile. The woman was in a low cut evening dress with a strand of pearls around her throat. It was Lorna and she was also smiling, but her smile seemed to be forced. In the corner of the picture in white photographic print were the words:

Buddy & Lorna

5-11-65

Next to the picture lying flat on the credenza was a theatre playbill for a place called Sonny's Supper Club, Victory Lake, Illinois. Baxter flipped through the book. The play was "I Do! I Do!" with Buddy Lake and Lorna King. It was dated November 1968. Lorna looked happier in the stills.

"That's been closed for quite a while," Lorna said referencing the playbill in Baxter's hands.

"You played the Mary Martin role?" Baxter asked.

"No. I played ———," Lorna cut herself short and allowed Baxter to make his way around the desk. "You're two minutes early."

"I couldn't wait to get here and talk to you about pool staffing," Baxter said.

"We really should have Jim Bigdon, the Associate-in-Charge of the pool in this meeting. Jim was just appointed October 1st." Lorna seated herself across from Baxter and pried open her plastic container revealing a salad.

"Peanut butter caviar sandwich indeed!" she said. Baxter stood up and closed Lorna's door.

"I need some second year pool people," Baxter began. As he talked, Laura took notes from a stenographer's notebook that she had produced from a desk drawer. Baxter described his meeting with Clyde and the FSO project and broadly outlined the work plan and time required.

"And how is Andy?" Lorna asked when Baxter had completed his story.

"She's excited about working for Clyde in New York. She's also very keen about working on the FSO assignment."

"I think your choices are first year people. No one at the second year level will want to tie up two or three months on an internal assignment working for a manager when they are looking at this year as their promotion year. We now have initiated annual Partner goal setting and appraisal for the Pool Consultants. The Operating Committee believed the pool consultants were too isolated."

Baxter sat back in his chair. All of these things were going on and he didn't know about it. He spent nearly all of his time single-mindedly pursuing and serving clients.

"That sounds almost civilized," Baxter commented.

"Clyde has worked very hard to change the way McKenzie Barber handles and relates to the pool consultants. The firm hires the best and the brightest, pays them well, and then treats them like galley slaves," Lorna went on.

"That's been said before," Baxter said between nibbles of his sandwich. "This is a critical assignment and it's been requested by the Chairman."

Lorna laughed. "I rather suspect that this project is Clyde's idea and he sold it to Ernie Grey."

Baxter tried to glare at her. This ex-secretary, now personnel administrator, was talking down to Baxter, a hotshot manager on his way up.

"I don't think your editorial comments are called for or particularly appropriate. I have a high priority assignment and I need some pool consultants. I have real problems staffing this kind of engagement with pool consultants who joined the firm in August or September and have spent half their time in orientation classes. I need second year people."

"You really should talk to Jim Bigdon about this. He's the Associate-in-Charge of the Pool," Lorna countered. "I work for Jim. It would be his decision."

"You work for Brimmer. Jim Bigdon is a nice young fellow who probably is classified as a "political" who took on that job in June. Bigdon wouldn't be a bad choice to serve on the FSO engagement. Write his name at the top of the list and ask him to come by and see me. He sure as hell wouldn't be missed around here for three months and the travel would do him good."

"Jim spends half of his time on consulting engagements right now," Lorna protested.

"Here's his chance to fill in the rest of his time. Let's talk about who else is available, but we're starting with Bigdon."

Baxter could see Lorna's body stiffen. She got up from her chair, unlocked a file case and produced an arm full of personnel files which she allowed to drop on the desk next to her tray. "We have ten minutes left to review these files. You can make your preliminary choices and I will see that they are approached and arranged for you to interview them," Lorna said coldly.

"No need for that. I'm taking Bigdon for sure and I'll use him to fill in behind him. He can be group leader for the Chicago contingent. Is he in today?" Baxter asked.

"He's at lunch," Lorna replied looking at her watch.

"Then have him call me this afternoon."

Lorna wrote something in large letters on her steno pad and then glared back at Baxter. "Lunch came to $8.87 and Margaret tipped the delivery boy a dollar." Lorna passed a receipt across the desk to Baxter and returned the files to the file case. Baxter placed a ten dollar bill on the desk next to Lorna's tray. She returned to her desk and placed the ten dollars in her change purse. "Now, do we have anything else to discuss today, Joe?" Lorna's eyes were cold, but she forced a little smile.

"What kind of place is Sonny's Supper Club?" Baxter asked.

"It's a supper club and on the weekends it's a dinner theatre."

"Where is it?"

"It's out Highway 12 south of Wauconda. I sing out there on weekends."

"Is the fellow in the picture your husband?" Baxter asked. Lorna looked again at her watch and stood up from her chair. "The fellow in the picture is Buddy Mancini and I have been singing with him since high school. We can always use new customers. It's straight out 12 past Lake Zurich."

Lorna produced a card from her purse. "We won't open a new show until December. Buddy and I are doing a lounge show for the rest of November. Then we open in Brigadoon. You can bring your whole family for the dinner theatre." Lorna started toward her office door. "I have to be back in my meeting. Why don't you just work through Jim in the future?"

She stopped in her doorway and turned back to face Baxter.

"And thank you for the lunch. I'll have a peanut butter caviar sandwich with you another time."

There was a quick mechanical smile and Baxter was alone in her office staring at the picture of Buddy and Lorna. It was Baxter's sense that he was unlikely to enjoy a relationship with Lorna King that would be similar to the one shared with Alvardi.

Alvardi called Baxter back that afternoon. "Heard you were in town, kid. Sorry I missed you," he began the conversation. "Heard from Friedman. He said you sold a bunch of work out in California. Budget me for eight hours review time on each engagement and have Mindy call my secretary with the engagement numbers."

"You're going to be reviewing our reports?" Baxter asked.

"I'll decide that, kid, after I see the engagement letters and the scope of work."

As always, Baxter concluded, Alvardi wanted his cut. "Frank, how did I get selected for this FSO job?"

"That's your Uncle Clyde's doing. Ernie practically blew a gasket when he saw their year end numbers and held up raises and bonuses. They had the IE practice in there three years ago and war was almost declared. They called me, told me what they wanted to accomplish, and asked if I would personally run the job. I pleaded that I was too busy on real work, but said that there was a man named Baxter back in Chicago who was smart and disarming with clients. He wanted to know all about you. So I tidied up your background a little and Ernie said that you sounded like the man who could run this kind of project. I know he called Dwyer to personally check you out and found him sober and expansive in his admiration for you."

"How did you tidy up my background?" Baxter asked suspiciously.

"I made that spatula company you used to work for around a $100 million company and told him how tight you were with his favorite new partner, Hamilton Burke. Then Nickerson chimed in with you having served with the Special Forces or something in Korea. You've never entertained me with your Army career, kid. Ernie just looked off into space and said, 'Baxter sounds like our man to run the FSO job. Get him briefed and get him going.' He said he wanted a report by January 31st. I didn't stay to tell him it was impossible.

"Frank, I want to thank you for your confidence in me," Baxter said sarcastically.

"Better you than me, kid. Besides, you're good on your feet and I suspect that FSO is one big scientist union. You're the only one I can think of in this firm with any union experience. The rest are all Union League."

"Frank, what kind of a place is Sonny's Supper Club?"

There was a laugh on the other end of the telephone. "Have you been out there already?"

"I was considering going there."

"It's very Italian, and Sonny Bucci is the owner. It's out on Lake Victory, north and west of the city. Sonny Bucci has some tie lines to some closely watched Italian business men in Chicago. Sonny's nephew, Buddy, is a regular performer and Lorna sings with him. They have a pretty good dinner theatre show, but the food's lousy. I was always comfortable there and Sonny Bucci is a very hospitable man. Just don't ask him too many questions about where his money came from."

"Is Lorna close to Buddy?"

"I hardly knew the woman, kid. I would recommend that you catch her in the front lounge for the eleven o'clock show. She sings "You Better Go

Now" as well as anyone in the world. You go out there on a Saturday night when Lorna's doing the lounge show with Buddy and you might run into Brimmer. You never can tell who you're going to see at Sonny's. Join the crowd, kid. You can't spend all of your weekends in Racine, Wisconsin. Adios."

Baxter did better with Jim Bigdon. He was tall, thin, and conservatively dressed in the standard McKenzie Barber three piece suit with red tie and white breast pocket handkerchief. He reminded Baxter a little of Bwana.

"Joe, Jim Bigdon," he greeted Baxter extending his hand.

"Lorna King told me you wanted to see me about something quite important."

Baxter started the conversation by asking Jim Bigdon about his background. He suspected him as a political at McKenzie Barber and wanted to confirm it before inviting Bigdon on the engagement.

"Well," Bigdon began, with appropriate modesty. "I grew up in Chicago in Oak Brook, went to Dartmouth for my undergraduate degree, served six months active duty with the Army AG, and went onto Stanford B School and was hired off campus by McKenzie Barber. I came in with the class of '71 and I was asked to take over the pool effective October 1st."

"Your family is from Chicago? What does your father do?" Baxter asked.

"He's President of Mid-Continent Petroleum."

Bingo! Baxter concluded.

"Now tell me about your consulting experience?" Baxter requested.

Jim Bigdon had worked on long soft jobs during his two year consulting career with McKenzie Barber. There was a four month marketing study for a Chicago based division of Hortense Foods, a three month trust operations study of a major Chicago bank, a three month information systems study for a tractor company, a two month review of the bursar's office in a large university, a functional cost study in a large hospital complex, and four month marketing study for a Seattle Bank."

"Jim," Baxter began, "I have heard about your reputation of contribution on these engagements and I would like to invite you on a highly sensitive and confidential engagement personally authorized by the Chairman of McKenzie Barber———"

Baxter knew that Bigdon was his convert seven minutes into his narration. "Now on an engagement of this nature, we can't very well use first year people———"

Bigdon left Baxter's office committed to contributing three second year pool consultants, in addition to himself, on the FSO engagement.

Lee Heller called Baxter late afternoon. "Joe, Lee here. I've just received my copies of your advice of new engagement forms. Can you come by and see me on your way out the door?"

Baxter visited Lee Heller in his window office at 4:45. Lee was also wearing a three piece suit and Baxter made a note that he would have to visit Brooks Brothers and buy some three piece suits.

"Joe, thanks for coming by and close the door," Heller greeted him. "Joe," he began, "I'm a little disturbed over the valuation percentages on these new engagements. You have $250,000 valued at 80% of standard fee for these California engagements and $300,000 valued at 50% for executive office. It's hard to make the kind of return that's expected of us on that valuation basis," Lee lectured Baxter.

"I followed firm policy on inter-office engagements. 80% of standard fee for inter-office engagements and 50% for Executive Office engagements," Baxter replied.

"Joe, those are guidelines, not fixed amounts. You could have negotiated Bob Friedman up to 85%. After all, Chicago will have to do all the work. Why would Friedman have a 20% margin?"

"He brought in the business," Baxter responded.

"10% is plenty for Friedman, and make certain our Chicago people are used and no time for Alvardi in New York. The Executive Office job should be at 65% not 50%. It's a matter of negotiation."

Baxter picked up Lee Heller's phone. "The Executive Office job is for Ernie Grey. Let's call him and you can hold the line. Don't take any shit from him, Lee, and don't forget to tell him you're a Director. Ernie respects Directors and he sure as hell will cave in for you."

Lee placed the telephone back on the receiver "What are you doing for Ernie Grey, Joe?"

"I can't talk about it. It's firm confidential and it's 50% of standard. Just call him up and tell him it's the Baxter job. You just tell him 50% won't do and you have to have 65%. I'm sure that he will understand."

Lee extended his hands. "All right, Joe. Everything stands, but watch your margins."

Baxter left Lee Heller's office with a sense of victory along with the realization that Lee believed that Baxter reported to him.

Jennifer was upset about Baxter's travel commitments. "You must be back Friday nights to be with the children!" Baxter had rented an apartment in Rosemont near O'Hare Airport and pledged he would be back on weekends. Agnes remained stable in the house on Palmer Street. She looked after Joel and the baby, Muffin. Baxter was free to be a bi-coastal consultant.

*Dwight E. Foster*

Baxter, Andy, and Jeff Long visited FSO for the orientation meeting. They were met with initial hostility and suspicion by Drs. Petting and Thayer. Baxter was at his best in the meeting with Andy and Jeff blending into the background of the meeting. There were certain participation points they had pre-rehearsed, which provided contributions to be made by Andy and Jeff, and the meeting overall went well. It was agreed that Baxter would lead a team of consultants into FSO with the objective of a job evaluation and compensation review of FSO's hierarchy of jobs. Petting and Thayer questioned their objectivity and Baxter responded accordingly.

"Jesus," Jeff, commented on their way back to Washington National. "That sure didn't look like anything that resembled McKenzie Barber."

FSO was located in a five story building in the woods south of Alexandria, but short of the Fort Belvoir Proving Ground. There was a guard post at the front gate, and uniformed guards in the reception area. The blue uniformed guards were the only personnel wearing ties at FSO. The offices were spartan with only a single elevator in the lobby. There was wide stairway to the second floor with men and women briskly walking up and down the stairs. They were provided numbered visitors badges and greeted by Dr. Petting's male secretary who wore a beard.

Dr. Petting and Dr. Thayer met with the McKenzie Barber team in a massive second floor conference room that was the size of a small auditorium. There was an audio-visual booth at the rear of the room, a series of blackboards, and a long conference table in the center of an otherwise empty room. Petting and Thayer were wearing white shirts open at the neck with cardigan sweaters. The male secretary was called Marvin. He served coffee in paper cups, closed the doors, and seated himself at the end of the table with a pencil and stenographer's notebook. Petting, and Thayer sat on one side of the table with Petting, a thin gray haired professional man, lighting his pipe while Thayer, a bald, barrel chested man, lit a cigarette. Baxter and Jeff wore the standard McKenzie Barber dark suits, and Andy wore a tweed suit with brown French heels.

"I want to go on record," Dr. Petting began. "That there is no need for a study of this magnitude. Our annual request for salary adjustments and annual bonuses were forwarded in September to my superior, Mr. Grey. Because we had an unfavorable mix of expenses to revenues for the past two years, Mr. Grey took exception to my request. FSO is a business quite alien to the management consulting practice of McKenzie Barber. Mr. Grey and most of his associates don't really understand our business. Mr. Randolph, Mr. Grey's Deputy, has a grasp of our business and recognizes that with our contract backlog and mix that we are going to be quite profitable over the next three years. I have asked Mr. Randolph to intercede on our behalf, but Mr. Grey insists that this study be conducted and completed before he will act on salary and bonus recommendations. It is my understanding that you will complete your work by January 31st so that we can inform our professional staff by mid-February."

Baxter said nothing. Jeff looked at the ceiling and Andy stared straight ahead.

"We had McKenzie Barber consultants in here three years ago," Dr. Thayer said speaking for the first time. His voice was more gruff. "They were supposed to install a financial planning and forecasting system for you. They were a goddam disaster! Their team was led by this tennis playing womanizer from California and all we got was garbage. They didn't have the vaguest grasp of our accounting systems. We discarded all of their recommendations, and someone at McKenzie Barber had the gall to send us a bill. Needless to say, we refused to pay it."

"They slipped it into our allocation, Norm," Dr. Petting said to Dr. Thayer.

Baxter believed he could identify the tennis playing womanizer from California.

"Dr. Petting and Dr. Thayer," Baxter said. "You are not our clients. Our client is the Executive Office of McKenzie Barber. McKenzie Barber owns FSO. This team of consultants has been engaged by McKenzie Barber to review the FSO organization beginning with it's mission and extending through the job hierarchy supporting the mission. Existing compensation plans will be reviewed during the conduct of our work."

"That's not the help we requested," Dr. Petting protested.

"FSO is not the client," Baxter said softly, but firmly. There was a silence around the table. Dr. Thayer lit another cigarette while Dr. Petting puffed on his pipe. Marvin paused in his note taking.

Jeff stared at an equation on the blackboard. "That's Boolean algebra on the blackboard isn't it, Dr. Thayer?" Thayer brightened and talked Boolean algebra and weapon systems. Dr. Petting joined in, Jeff kept them talking and told a little story about the air frame company engagement he worked on earlier in the summer. The villain of the story was the controller and Drs. Petting and Thayer chuckled. The ice seemed broken. Dr. Petting looked across the table at Baxter.

"Do you have a workplan, Mr. Baxter?"

"It's preliminary. We need to finalize that today and will require your cooperation on a complete briefing relative to FSO."

"We are prepared to give you the morning through 1 PM. Marvin will be your liaison. He serves as Executive Assistant to both Norm and me." There was that title again, Baxter observed. Maybe one day he would form an Association of Executive Assistants.

"Is this your entire project team?" Dr. Thayer asked.

"This is the leadership group. We will bring in other consultants to assist us in completing our work on a timely basis."

"How many additional consultants do you plan?" Dr. Petting asked.

"Seven," Baxter answered.

"We are to be descended upon by ten McKenzie Barber consultants at once? To be frank with you, I'd prefer Federal Auditors."

"You're not going to be done by January 31st are you?"

"Our progress will be greatly enhanced by your cooperation," Baxter said.

"Well then, let's begin," Dr. Petting said with quiet resignation.

Baxter, Andy, and Jeff settled into a United Airlines conference room at Washington National Airport around 4:30 PM and finalized the work plan. They had spent the better part of the day being briefed about FSO's business and reviewing organization charts and salary data. Andy personally xeroxed three copies of everything for individual files and Jeff began to refer to Baxter as Cap'un.

"We could do this job quick and dirty, and be out of here by January 31st. If the pool people aren't productive or don't show up, we would be here until June," Jeff warned.

"We've got three committed from Chicago plus a first year Associate named Bigdon and you have three committed from New York, right, Andy?" Baxter queried.

"There's a slight problem, Joe," Andy announced. "I don't think it's a insurmountable problem, but Jeff and you may think differently." Baxter and Jeff waited for Andy to finish.

"There's been some juggling of the Pool Consultants in both offices," she continued. "We're getting Jim Bigdon and one second year consultant from Chicago. But the other two from Chicago are first year people and they're women. From New York, we're getting three first year consultants and they're all women."

"Who's the second year consultant from Chicago?" Baxter asked.

"Roger White, the big negro man who played for the Bears," Andy announced.

"Bigdon allowed this to happen?" Baxter questioned.

"He had other people scheduled, but Lorna King pulled them out, presumably at Paul Brimmer's direction," Andy explained. Baxter signaled the waiter for more beer while Andy declined with a shake of her head. Baxter looked at Jeff.

"Take the engagement roll, first sergeant," Baxter commanded Jeff.

"Well Cap'un, by my count we have:

- One big, redheaded, working fool manager with a silver tongue.

56

- One ex-Marine, reluctant Associate who is really an OR consultant from Georgia Tech.
- One classy lady Associate from executive office and Cornell.
- One political Associate from Chicago office.
- One EEO qualified second year consultant who can't run deep routes any more.
- Five lady Pool Consultants with three to five months experience.

Request permission, Cap'un, to abandon ship," Jeff said taking a long drag from his Budweiser.

"You're prejudging consultants you haven't met. You're not being fair," Andy protested.

"Andy," Baxter began, "Is there any chance of swapping some people?"

"Joe. I tried! Everyone is locked in. I even tried Atlanta and Cleveland. This engagement is not very popular. FSO is viewed as an assignment where there is much to be lost and not much to be gained. Clyde was wrong when he told me that Associates would jump for the chance to be on this engagement."

"No Sheet!" Jeff commented.

"Okay," Baxter said with conviction. "We'll play the game with the hand we've been given. You guys can withdraw right now if you want to."

"In for a penny, in for a bundle, Cap'un. Count on me!"

"I'm with you all the way, Joe," Andy said with tears forming in the corner of her eyes.

"Then goddamit! Let's get the job done!" Baxter said and held his hand out across the table much as he had when he was an Iron Creek Cougar. Jeff laid his hand on top.

"All the way, Cap'un!"

Andy put her hand on last. "Count on me, Captain Baxter."

When Baxter headed out for the 8 PM United flight to LA, Andy and Jeff saw him to the gate. Andy kissed Baxter on the cheek. "You're too ugly to kiss," Jeff said shaking his hand. Baxter waved from the ramp doorway and they waved back. He felt good about the FSO team as he boarded the plane.

The work with the Thrifts was not all that complicated. The industry was twenty-five years behind banking, and Baxter had come to regard banking as fifteen years behind manufacturing. Only one of the Thrifts was public, and the only long term plan that was in place was a qualified stock option plan their attorney had lifted from the Bank of America proxy. The other four thrifts were depositor held and natural phantom stock plan fixes.

57

"I've brought you virgins, Baxter. Lovely, full bodied, simple minded virgins to be deflowered and debauched," Friedman commented as they moved from meeting to meeting.

"Catch the ten o'clock flight in the morning, Joe," Friedman counseled Baxter. "I have an entertainment planned for us this evening."

Entertainment proved to be Chinese twin sisters with the Christian names of Lana and MaryJo Fu. They wore white low cut halters with USC printed around their navals, black skirts and white thigh length boots. They had dinner, four bottles of wine, and talked a lot about Camus and Proust. When they excused themselves for a visit to the Ladies Room, Friedman patted Baxter on the shoulder. "Now Joe, do you see how well I take care of you. They have fine young bodies and minds, and it is rumored that MaryJo carries a can of Redi-Whip in her purse for special purposes. This should demonstrate how highly I think of you. I have never before gone to this level of advance preparation to get a manager laid. Partners? Of course, but managers? No. Why am I doing this, you ask? I believe you should come to California and work for me. I will personally guarantee that you will be a Partner. No one will do that for you in Chicago." Friedman, at this point, was quite drunk. "Come out to California for a social visit. Bring your family! If it's necessary, we'll get your wife laid. Make the San Fernando Valley your home! This is virgin country for what you do. It won't be the executive compensation frontier forever! The window is open now, Baxter. Finish up the FSO job and tell me you want to come to California. I will handle Alvardi, Nickerson, Brimmer, and the rest of them. You can come to the land of sunshine and migrate to banking, aerospace, and consumer packaged goods. High technology awaits our call! There is an empire to be won! New York is dying! Chicago is complacent and bourgeois! California is the future of the US economy! It will be the center of the Pacific Basin. Baxter! You should, by rights, pay me to come out here! But I, in my generosity, invite you out here without recompense and offer you the delights of willing Asian thighs. What more could you ask for?"

Baxter returned to Chicago and called on Lorna King in her office. Her reddish brown hair was pinned up.

She raised her hand in a peace sign. "I know what you're going to say," Lorna greeted Baxter. "Brimmer changed the whole staffing plan for the office. He wants the unapplied people applied. I have the personnel jackets of your consultants for you and I'm sorry we couldn't produce the kind of experience you wanted."

Baxter closed the door. "You have put me at a disadvantage, Ms. King."

"Joe, I tried to help. Brimmer did not think that second year people should be wasted on the FSO engagement. He was really pleased to see Bigdon applied, so you scored there."

"You're telling me that I've got to live with what you gave me?" Baxter said.

"That's it, Joe."

"When does Brigadoon open?" Baxter asked.

"The second Friday in December," Lorna answered.

"If I come alone, can you get me in?"

"See Sal, the maitre'd. He will be expecting you."

"You will be playing Fiona?" Baxter asked.

"I'm getting old for it, but I want to play Fiona."

"Fiona was three hundred years old, but well preserved. The role may be perfect for you," Baxter commented.

Lorna gave him a stone faced glare as he departed from her office.

Baxter began the FSO work during the first week in December with a very solemn meeting with the consulting team. Jeff and Andy had converted the project plan to tasks and sub-tasks with completion action dates. The three had collaborated on the development of the fact-finding questionnaires which they believed first year pool consultants should be able to handle. "These people are McKenzie Barber consultants, Joe. They're from the top business schools in the country. They're intelligent and poised," Andy protested.

Baxter convened the meeting at 7AM in a basement meeting room at the Holiday Inn. The women consultants were dressed conservatively in dark colored business suits. Roger White showed up at 7:10 in a brown three piece suit cutting an immense and foreboding figure. His features seemed chiseled out of licorice, and there were scars on his ebony face.

"Mean looking son-of-a-bitch isn't he, Cap'un?" Jeff Lord whispered to Baxter. "He must scare the shit out of the clients."

Jim Bigdon appeared full of enthusiasm and seated himself next to Baxter. Baxter asked each consultant to introduce themselves and went around the table. The women were named Stacy, Hillary, Anne, and Priscilla, and they had graduated respectively from Harvard, Tuck, Columbia, and the Darden School. Roger White's voice turned out to be high pitched, but his diction was surprising crisp.

"My name is Roger White. I hold an undergraduate degree in Physical Education from the University of Missouri and earned a MBA degree from Northwestern University. I have worked in the banking and industrial engineering practices and I am honored to have been chosen to participate in this very important study."

"Watch your wallet, Cap'un!" Jeff whispered. "That is one very dangerous colored man."

Baxter positioned himself as the last to talk and he stood up from his chair.

"I'm Joe Baxter. I am the manager on this engagement and I work in the Executive Compensation practice of the Chicago office. Our work at FSO is expected to be comprehensive and you will be expected to work very hard over the course of the next six to eight weeks. We will work the week before and after Christmas and you may expect to be an active participant on this study through mid-February unless you are excused early. Our engagement here will involve daily interaction with professional staff senior to you in age and experience, who may not welcome our presence here."

"For that reason you must conduct yourselves in a professional manner at all times. Our work day will be long and we will meet at the end of each day to discuss what each team member has accomplished that day. You will not be excused for dinner until the progress meeting has been completed. Washington D.C., is a city with ample opportunities for an evening social life and it is only thirty minutes north of our location. You, regrettably, will have little opportunity to visit the night life during the week. I want you alert, bright, and on the engagement by 8 AM each morning. Lastly, the nature of our findings and conclusions will not be discussed outside our progress meetings. Any violation of these rules will be treated harshly and will influence your career progression after the completion of our work. We will work on a first name basis. My name is Joe. Andrea, who will serve as the engagement administrator, is called Andy and Jeff is our operations leader. Jeff will now review the engagement plan with you and discuss your first week's tasks and objectives." Baxter was confident that he had the group's attention just as Sergeant Wilson had held the attention of his audience in the days at Fort Gately.

"Jeff," Baxter introduced his associate. Jeff Lord stood up from his chair and flipped on the overhead projector.

"Thank you Mein Fuhrer!" he began, and nervous laughter filled the room.

They had rehearsed it that way. Baxter would be the black hat and Andy and Jeff would wear the white hats.

Jeff Lord ran the FSO engagement on a daily basis, and Baxter was on site two days a week. He was now spending two days in California and one day in Chicago. Each time he visited California, one or two new engagements were acquired, as Baxter delivered the first of his progress reports to the clients they had developed during his December visit.

"Joe," Friedman would say in the early evening when they were only two drinks down. "It makes me cry every time I put you on an airplane to fly back across the company. You belong here, at my side, selling executive compensation work. It's time to move up market to banks. You need to bring your family out here into the California sunshine."

"Bob," Baxter responded. "My marriage is not what it should be. My wife and I are estranged."

"Then put 2000 miles between you! You seem to make new friends quickly. I'm confident that you would be a natural Californian."

"I can't come out right now," Baxter explained.

"Then I may have to hire another like you. Possibly not as gregarious or as able a nocturnal companion, but a solid type who would take his work seriously and prepare reports with good graphics. You have potential to advance, Joe, but you need the mentorship of a partner who will take an active interest in your career. If you're not careful, your career could be made up of one long succession of FSOs. Once the firm locates a masochistic consultant who likes to do internal work, they never let up. They all die as managers and are buried in unmarked graves. Think about it!"

FSO progressed! Baxter would attend the evening review meeting and then they would repair to Baxter's room, order sandwiches from room service, and Jeff and Baxter would drink "sipping whiskey." Andy would drink white wine. "It's going well, Joe," Andy observed.

Andy and Jeff usually came to Baxter's room in sweat clothes. Tonight Andy was wearing white shorts and a Cornell sweat shirt. She displayed long smooth legs that disappeared into her sweat socks and sneakers. Jeff lounged in blue sweatpants with a New York Mets tee shirt.

"Everybody's behaving and you're being used as the bogeyman. We need some more time with Petting and Thayer, and you have to be the one to orchestrate that, Joe," Jeff advised.

Baxter was beginning to like the FSO engagement. He was proud of having organized and strategized the project team and having it function.

"Joe, you need to spend some time this visit one-on-one with Roger and Jim. They expect some status and recognition over the other consultants," Andy said.

"How are they doing?" Baxter asked.

Jeff answered. "Roger is doing better that Jim. He's not the quickest, but he's catching on and he loves the government business. Jim tends to get rattled. The women are doing great! They're good, smart, tight-assed consultants. Andy was right! They aren't going to hurt us. We got good people on this team, Cap'un."

Andy looked at her watch. "Fellows, I have to make a call. Can I come back and talk some more?" Andy said getting up.

"Only if Joe and I can't get some other women in here that want to do more than talk," Jeff responded.

"You're over your heads right now," Andy said getting up for the door. Baxter noted her exit at 8:26 PM.

Jeff poured some more "sipping whiskey" into Baxter's glass.

"She calls him at 8:30 every night," Jeff reported.

"Who's that?" Baxter asked.

"Nickerson. Andy is Clyde's spy on the job. It took me a week or so to figure it out, but I did. She gives him daily reports."

"Why?" Baxter asked.

"Because it's their deal," Jeff said. "Also she's got eyes for you, Joe. She never takes them off you when you're in the room."

"And she's Nickerson's spy?" Baxter asked incredulously. "Why would he need a spy? I've been sending comprehensive two week engagement status reports."

"I retract that statement, Cap'un. Let me rephrase it. Andy is Clyde's independent source of information on this job."

"Why?" Baxter asked refilling their glasses.

"Because I figure there's a thing going on between them," Jeff explained.

"Andy and Clyde?" Baxter was aghast.

"She's in his department and they spend a lot of time together. There's a bunch of New York office Associates who came up through the pool together and we meet once a month in the back room of O'Grady's Bar. It's a fairly salty group of young men and women. There's a lot of gossip that goes back and forth. I was out with the group the week before Christmas and there was talk about Clyde and our friend, Andy. I guess Mrs. Clyde is about the size of a tank."

Baxter took a sip of whiskey. "So be it."

"You can remedy that relationship, Cap'un. Andy's got eyes for you."

Baxter shook his head. "I'm a married man with young children at home, Jeff," Baxter said self-righteously.

"How's your wife take all this travel?" Jeff asked.

"She manages her life around it," Baxter lied. Then, wanting to change the subject, Baxter asked. "Jeff, what's it like working in the New York office?"

"Whoa! What a question, Cap'un! How many times have you been to the New York office?"

"Once," Baxter answered.

"How many times have you been to New York?" Jeff asked.

"Twice," Baxter answered.

"My advice, Cap'un, is to stay in Chicago. New York is a meat grinder! It is a huge office full of pockets of power and smart, ambitious, and vicious people. New York is the showcase office, presumably filled with the most talented people at McKenzie Barber. Then up on 40th floor is Executive Office, the home of the evil empire and Emperor Ernie. They should have a sign when you enter reception. Welcome to McKenzie Barber! Watch your step, please! Banana peels ahead!'"

"If you feel that way, Jeff, why do you stay?" Baxter asked.

"I'm not staying, Cap'un. I'm passing through. While I'm passing through, I'm learning. I don't fit the typical McKenzie Barber mold and you don't either. You and I shouldn't be long term. We should both be passing through. I came here late. I had a BSIE from Georgia Tech and was commissioned in the Marine Corps with a NROTC scholarship. I shipped over for three years and went back to Georgia Tech and finished my MSIE in one year. I had a professor who pushed me toward McKenzie Barber. They interviewed me on campus and told me my maturity would advance me rapidly at McKenzie Barber. They made me an offer for either Atlanta or New York. I did my research and found out that New York was where the action was. I told them New York it was!"

"So this country boy, Marine IE came to 311 Park Avenue to learn the ropes at age 26. Now it's four years later and I made it out of the pool to Associate, but I really haven't found a practice home yet. Either they don't want me or I don't want them. I know the clock is running on me and I was available for FSO because I had floated from practice to practice and was unapplied."

"I want you to know, Cap'un, that I like working on FSO. It's the way you have welded the team together and organized a management group. I'm learning from you, Cap'un. You're one smart fox as an engagement manager. I looked you up and asked about you after that time we met in the New York office talking about FSO. There's a sweet young thing in personnel records with whom I have an occasional dalliance. She got me your file to look at. I know you're from Iron something, Minnesota, and that you did something in the Army you can't talk about. Nickerson's handwriting is on your personnel file. It says: 'classified military service.' Then I saw you finished up at Minnesota, a decent Big 10 school, and you went on to a real company and ran a plant and became an officer. I told myself, there's a guy I can learn from, as opposed to another MBA prick. And I am learning from you. It's nothing technical, but you have a sense for sorting things out and figuring where things ought to be going and how you're going to get people deployed to do what has to be done. You're a good project manager. I think the Executive Compensation practice is bullshit! Your buddy, Alvardi, is slick and smooth, but he's running behind Ernie Grey's schedule on getting the practice up and dominant. McKenzie Barber is still behind RAH."

"All of your information is based on these monthly discussions in O'Grady's Bar with those hard drinking salty Associates?" Baxter interjected.

"I didn't mean to piss you off, Cap'un.. But you're perceived to be operating in a practice with some cachet, but very limited growth," Jeff responded.

"What does your group say about Dwyer?"

"Oh Jesus! You bring up Dwyer's name and the stories start. He's the most brilliant Partner anyone has ever worked with. He also has screwed one third of the New York office professional staff and maybe 10% of the better looking administrative personnel. I couldn't believe the guy when I met him. We were working with a fabric formation company and he knew the looms and material flow better than the client. Then we went off to a cut and sew manufacturing floor of a sportswear company. Dwyer actually repaired a sewing machine that was down." Baxter remembered the drill press that had gone down in the Caribou Street plant.

There was a knock on the door. "That should be Andy," Baxter predicted.

"Remember, Cap'un, little pitchers got big ears," Jeff cautioned.

Baxter had breakfast with Roger White the next morning. He seated himself across the table from Baxter after a smile and a handshake. Roger appeared as a large, mean appearing black man with a tenor voice.

"I appreciate your taking time out to meet with me personally, Joe," Roger started.

"No problem, Roger. I've been meaning to spend some personal time with you to gain your insights into the project," Baxter said. Roger rambled a little in the beginning, but became more focused as he talked more. He had been reviewing FSO's financial organization.

"This isn't a bad business, Joe. FSO will make money this year and should make money next year. 1976 could be a problem. They need to reorganize and bring in two or three new people. This business is so different from the rest of McKenzie Barber. The FSO people are right. People in New York and Chicago just can't grasp this business."

"What are your preliminary findings, Roger?" Baxter asked.

"The chief financial officer is a crafty old accountant who talks in code to Petting and Thayer, and their accounting systems are archaic. We should send in our information systems guys to clean them up. What they really need is a senior budget and financial analysis manager who can dig in and sort out all those programs and keep those program managers honest. They manage and manipulate the financial statements. They need a top marketing guy too, and this Budget and Financial Analysis guy should be positioned to review pricing. You don't want the guy under the thumb of the chief financial officer, so he should report to Thayer. I talked to Thayer about this and he agrees it's needed."

"You're taking recommendations to FSO?" Baxter tried to look mean. "Roger, McKenzie Barber is the client not FSO!" Baxter said strongly.

Roger stared at his eggs for a minute in silence. Baxter observed that Roger's lips moved silently as if he were rehearsing words before he said them. "Joe, I didn't go making no recommendations. Rather I talked to the man about what was needed." Baxter noted that the 'street Roger' was talking, not the Northwestern MBA. "This is what we're supposed to be doing isn't it? I mean help McKenzie Barber understand what must be done to make FSO perform better?"

"Roger!" Baxter solemnly corrected him. "We have been engaged by the executive office of McKenzie Barber to examine the headcount level and overall compensation levels and pay plans of the organization. On the basis of our study we may recommend to McKenzie Barber, our client, certain changes in FSO's organization structure. We are not here to kibitz with FSO relative to changes in their organization."

Roger again stared at his eggs and silently rehearsed what he was about to say. "Joe, let me talk straight to you! I want to transfer here. I could do that Budgets and Financial Analysis job. I really don't have a future in the Chicago office. I like this part of the country and I like the business they're in. I could contribute to FSO. I'm never going to contribute much at Chicago McKenzie Barber. I'm a black man who wants to achieve. My football career is over. I worked my ass off to get through Northwestern and I worked hard at McKenzie Barber and tried to fit in. You know what I am in Chicago? I'm some kind of special teams player sitting way on the edge of the bench and they will put me on the street when the next draft is made. I could have a future with FSO. I pulled whatever strings I could pull to get on this assignment. I got a young child at home and another one coming in May. I know I don't fit into Chicago office plans. Then they will play the transfer game. How many black consultants do you have? We've got one you can have! I don't want a part of that. I like the Washington area and I know I can be a contributor here."

"What do you want from me, Roger?" Baxter asked.

"I want you to talk to Nickerson about transferring me here. I will write him a note when we're done, but I need some support and a campaign. I need your help, Joe. I admire you. You know how to organize and you're mature and different from all these big schools MBAs. I can sense you came up the hard way. Help me, please."

Baxter sipped his coffee and stared back at Roger White. He thought back to Sergeant Wilson, his taskmaster mentor, and his long battle for recognition. This one's for you, Mal, Baxter said silently.

"I once had a black sergeant who changed my life," Baxter said.

"Saved your life? I heard you were in combat, man," Roger jumped to react to Baxter's words.

"Of course, I'll do what I can to help you. In confidence I would have to believe that McKenzie Barber would be very comfortable in putting their own man in here. I've got to make Clyde Nickerson believe it's his idea. We must never talk about this openly again. I give you my word to help you. I would like you to independently share your findings and objectives with Andy. Don't tell her you have shared it with me and polish up the way you present it."

"This is the kind of help I need, Joe," Roger beamed a broad smile at Baxter.

The final report of the FSO engagement was presented in a conference room on the 40th floor of McKenzie Barber on the 31st day of March 1974. The consulting team had been dismissed on Valentine's Day and following a close out de-briefing meeting, they adjourned to a cocktail party in a private room at the Holiday Inn. It was like air coming out of a balloon. The tensions of the assignment were behind them and they were going back to the world that existed outside FSO.

A strawberry blonde named Hillary, who had worn her hair pinned up since the beginning of the FSO work had unpinned her hair and approached Baxter in a corner of the reception room. Her hair brushed her shoulders and her suit jacket was off displaying her shoulders for the first time.

"Joe, I want you to know that this has been the most grueling ten weeks of my life. I've loved every minute of it!"

"And what office are you from again, Hillary?" Baxter asked.

"New York. And you didn't even remember my name until I reminded you three minutes ago." Hillary had good skin and classic features. Why hadn't he noticed her before? Baxter asked himself. Then he remembered that she had worn glasses in every meeting she had been with Baxter before that evening.

"Now you must tell me how you do it?" Hillary continued. "You run off to Chicago and LA every week and never miss a beat."

"I have good consultants working with me. Where will you go from here, Hillary?" Baxter asked conversationally.

"Los Angeles. There's a big financial management information systems engagement for Golden States Federal under Bob Friedman. I'm supposed to be out there for four months. What is Bob Friedman like?"

"Bob's very thoughtful and professional. He's established quite a practice among the California Thrift industry. He really went out of his way for me when I've worked on his engagements. You go up to him and tell him that you worked with Joe Baxter on the FSO engagement. I'm sure he'll take some time out to mentor you accordingly."

"I heard he's young and good looking."

"That he is, but Bob is a strong family man like me. It's his church, his family, and his job in that order," Baxter said, and noticed Andy waving at him from behind Hillary.

Jeff Long rattled a spoon against a glass for attention.

"May I have your attention please?"

The buzz of the room softened to silence. "We have a presentation to make," Jeff called out. "Cap'un Baxter! Will you please step forward!"

"Excuse me, Hillary," Baxter said. "I believe I'm wanted." Hillary pleased her hand on Baxter's shoulder. "Come back and talk to me. I don't believe that church, family, job routine for a minute!"

"Ladies and gentlemen," Jeff began. "We have been laboring under the steady hand of Joseph Baxter, Jr., for some ten to twelve weeks. Andy and I had the privilege of planning the work under Joe's direction. All of you have made critical contributions to the assignment and we have worked together in harmony and intensity consistent with the traditions of McKenzie Barber, our great firm. Now, all that is ended is for Joe, Andy and me to write the final report and present the findings to Ernie Grey and come out alive with our careers intact." There was laughter around the room. Tense people were finding a relief. "Joe, would you please come forward. We have a little remembrance for you!"

"It's probably a Gideon Bible," Hillary said and winked at Baxter.

Andy was beaming and she had a package wrapped in red paper with a large blue bow on it. The room was silent as Baxter opened the box. Under the wrappings was a tee shirt with printing on it and Baxter held it out for the room to see. The tee shirt read:

I SURVIVED FSO!
I THINK!

There was much laughter and it was Baxter's turn to speak. "I will survive FSO as will you! We've done a fantastic job here over the last ten weeks. You have worked very hard and very smart in a difficult sensitive assignment. Many of you are very early in your careers and there was some risk associated with involving you in an internal assignment of this nature. You have, however, performed both professionally and admirably over the duration of this work. Now that it is completed, you will remember this time we've spent together for the rest of your lives. We formed a team, worked well together, and now disband. That's what management consulting is all about. You are part of a historic tradition of excellence at McKenzie Barber and on this engagement you can take your place on the passing parade of excellent assignments. It has been a pleasure and an honor to lead this engagement assisted by such able consultants. Thank you!"

There was applause and the party resumed. Several consultants shook Baxter's hand. Hillary kissed him on the cheek. Andy linked arms with Baxter and pulled him away to a corner of the room. "The hard part comes next," Baxter cautioned her.

"I know that Joe. That was a very nice speech." Andy took his hand and squeezed. "I need to talk to you. I had a very interesting conversation with Roger White a couple of days ago. I need to talk to you privately." Andy was wearing a dark blue dress with pearls and her hand stayed clasped with Baxter's as they talked. The group in the room remained together for approximately one hour and five minutes by Baxter's watch. Hillary attempted to rejoin Baxter twice, but each time Andy joined them.

Jeff, with an arm around each of two women consultants approached Baxter. "Cynthia and Marcy are coming to Washington tonight for a dinner. Want to come along, Joe?"

"No late nights for me," Baxter replied. "I'm going to Chicago first thing."

"How about you, Andy?" Jeff asked.

"No. I need to talk to Joe about a few things."

Hillary came by, and after looking over Andy, decided to go with the group to Washington.

"Nice young lady," Baxter commented.

"If you like them brazen," Andy commented.

Roger White was the last out of the door. "Joe. It's been a real honor to be a part of this. Andy, I really enjoyed our talk." Andy kissed Roger on his ugly scarred face.

They were the last people in the room. "Want to eat in the hotel?" Baxter asked.

"I have a bottle of champagne on ice in my room. Let's have them send dinner up," Andy said. "I need to talk to you."

Baxter visited Andrea Bourke's room confident he could maintain their relationship on a professional basis. Her Holiday Inn room was much like Baxter's. There was a large bed, a short couch, an arm chair, and a small table with two chairs. The small table contained a tray with an ice bucket, two glasses and a champagne bottle. It was the first time Baxter had been in Andy's room.

"I'm going to change," Andy announced after the door had been closed. She punched the play button on a portable cassette player and a Barbara Streisand tape began to play. "Pop this champagne, Joe, and relax. I'll be just a moment," Andy said and disappeared into the bathroom.

Baxter poured two glasses of champagne and sat back on the couch listening to the Streisand tape and looked out into the Northern Virginia night.

Andy emerged from the bathroom in a blue cocktail dress with spaghetti straps. I was going to wear this tonight, but decided it didn't look very business like." Andy picked up her champagne glass and stood before Baxter. She was quite tall with dark hair and high cheek bones. The hem of her dress barely covered Andy's knees and Baxter could make out a hint of her A cup breasts from the bodice.

"You certainly would have caused a stir," Baxter agreed.

Andy sat down on the couch next to Baxter and clinked glasses. "So far so good." She raised her glass in a toast. Baxter could make out a garter belt as Andy crossed her legs. He knew he had to be careful.

"I'm in marriage counseling with my wife," Baxter lied. He produced his wallet. "Have I ever shown you a picture of my children?" Joel and Muffin were on the swing set in the back yard. Joel had been blessed with Jennifer's features. Muffin was a blonde and round faced four.

Andy held the picture antiseptically with one hand and sipped her champagne with the other. "They are nice looking children," she commented, returning the picture to Baxter.

"How is the marriage counseling progressing?"

"It's too soon to tell," Baxter responded. "It's a last try to pull my marriage together."

"I heard you had a troubled marriage, Joe. A lot of the Partners have been through divorces. This is no business for a conventional marriage," Andy observed. Her body seemed to have stiffened. She hadn't appreciated hearing about Baxter's fictitious marriage counseling or being introduced to pictures of his children.

"Here's to good friends," Baxter said raising his glass and holding it until Andy moved her glass forward against his.

"Good friends, Joe," Andy said. "And maybe, Joe, one day we'll be more than good friends."

"To maybe," Baxter said. They clinked glasses again and Andy brightened up.

"Do you realize, Joe, that it's five and one-half years since we showed up together that first day at McKenzie Barber? And you didn't even recognize Naomi."

"She looked different in college," Baxter said.

"She was as fat as a pig. Naomi showed me some pictures from her Minnesota days. Then one day, Naomi decided she would get her body in order and went on a diet and exercise program. She's quite attractive now, wouldn't you say, Joe?"

"I would say so," Baxter agreed and he wondered what confidences had been exchanged between Naomi and Andy,

"Naomi and I were pretty close in Chicago. Ernie Grey dictated that McKenzie Barber should hire women MBAs and there were Naomi, Sandy, and me on that first day in the reception area with this tall handsome red-headed man in a blue suit with a red tie. You didn't wear pocket handkerchiefs in those days. I wanted to fold my handkerchief and put it in your breast suit pocket. You could have been like a knight wearing a lady's colors. Naomi and I really wanted to be successful and Sandy, I suspect, really wanted to find a man or men. We worked like beavers in the Pool on any task we were asked to do. But nobody wanted us. They would request Sandy because she was California pretty and there would be Naomi and me willing to count paperclips in order to be busy and productive. Clyde Nickerson kept our sanity. He found special projects for us and we excelled. Clyde was the one who put Naomi into college recruiting and Clyde was the one who brought me out to New York. I guess Clyde is my mentor. I know he is not popular with some of the other partners, but he has been very special for my career."

Andy filled their glasses again. "Don't worry about running out. I have another two bottles on ice in the bathroom," she advised. And red garters too, thought Baxter.

"I suppose," Andy went on. "I was a lot like Naomi at one time. I wasn't particularly pretty or popular in high school. I grew up in Portland, Maine. My Dad was a doctor and my Mom was a teacher and I was one of those only children you read about. I was very tall for my age and I was valedictorian in my senior year. My Dad had to talk to my cousin into taking me to my high school prom. I went to Cornell, started out in pre-med, and finished in Economics. I dated a little at Cornell, but the boys preferred the bright, pretty, bouncy girls, to the tall, smart ones. I went on to the Business School and suddenly found that the Instructors and the Associate Professors believed that I was attractive. I became popular in graduate school. I lost my virtue! I thought about matriculating for a doctorate, but my Dad told me I'd have to pay for it myself. I had no idea what McKenzie Barber was when I signed up for the interview. They made me my best offer, I accepted, and there I was in the reception room with Naomi, Sandy, and you. Later I found out that the people they really wanted badly started in July and August. We were mandatory hires. I learned a lot from Lorna King. Her real name is Wisnewski. She's a sharp cookie, Joe. I used to have coffee and drinks with Lorna. She told me how the Chicago office really worked." Andy paused to take a long sip of champagne. "I really love being alone with you. Joe. I've decided I wanted you all to myself."

"How does the Chicago office really work?" Baxter asked.

"Poor Joe. You work so hard and do so well, but you really don't know what's happening around you. Let's have some more champagne." Andy got up and returned from the bathroom with a second bottle of champagne. "Want to talk about FSO?" she asked.

"What can we say further about FSO?" Baxter asked while popping the cork.

"I think FSO needs new leadership. They need a swashbuckling general who can represent them to the government agencies. Next they need some marketing leadership, and finally they need a Vice President for Budgets and Financial Analysis. I believe we have a candidate for the job on our consulting team."

"Roger White, I presume," Baxter said.

Andy beamed. "It's amazing how our minds run on the same track, Joe."

Baxter ordered dinner from room service. Andy became tipsy.

"I love working for Clyde in executive office. You can see everything from executive office. It's like being up on a high hill looking down on the operating offices. Clyde is the administrative nerve center for the firm. Ernie is about to reorganize executive office. Clyde will be picking up more responsibility. Betty Ryland will be moved over to benefits and pension administration. I am going to pick up all of the tactical elements of personnel administration."

"What tactical elements are there in personnel administration, Andy?" Baxter challenged her.

"Management development, performance measurement, organization planning, succession planning, compensation," she recited.

"Don't forget recreation!" Baxter reminded her.

"There's plenty of recreation running around the New York office," Andy giggled.

"What kind of recreation?" Baxter asked.

"Everybody's sleeping with each other. In Chicago there were just a few isolated things going on. In New York, everybody seems to be having some kind of relationship with someone else and then, after a month or so, they just move on to other people. I guess I can understand the phenomena. The New York office has amassed a lot of bright and attractive people, and it's small wonder that they get interested in people of the opposite sex in relationships outside their marriages."

"What's Mrs. Nickerson like?" Baxter asked.

"Mavis? I've met her twice. She's very nice and on the heavy side. She's very devoted to Clyde and she has diabetes, the poor dear. Clyde is very caring toward her."

71

"What do they say about Bob Friedman in Executive Office?" Baxter asked.

"Ernie likes him. Clyde's a little skeptical about him. He thinks Friedman is a flash in the pan. Los Angeles is a long way off from New York both intellectually and geographically. There's been some talk about all the compensation work you've been doing with the Savings & Loans. Ernie sent a Grey-gram off to Roger Dirks asking him why Alvardi hadn't positioned himself with the New York Savings Banks yet? Do you know what Dirks wrote back?" Andy giggled.

"Dirks wrote back that Mr. Alvardi had more important things to do than chase Savings Bank business. He went on to say that pursuing a Thrift Industry strategy may be highly acceptable in certain underdeveloped segments of the country, but in the New York and Northeastern US marketplace, there are more attractive industry segments which will generate higher fees and greater margins. Only that arrogant Dirks could write back to Ernie that way and get away with it."

It became clear to Baxter that properly oiled, Andy was a tremendous reservoir of information and gossip. Ernie Grey talked to Clyde and Clyde confided in Andy.

"How can Dirks respond in that manner to Ernie Grey?" Baxter asked.

"Because he's the most powerful partner in the New York office. More powerful than Bruce Dinsmore, the New York office Managing Partner. Dirks is a Group Partner. He has the Strategic Services group. That includes Marketing, Strategic Planning, and Executive Compensation. Roger Dirks is an intimidating bantam rooster who has an enormous client following. Frank Alvardi reports to Dirks."

"Then what's Dirks' relationship with Dr. Barry Keller?" Baxter asked.

"He pretends that Dr. Keller does not exist. Dr. Keller's national role does not extend further East than Pittsburgh. Roger Dirks is a despicable, arrogant, ruthless tyrant who controls more billings of any other partner in the New York office."

"How does Frank get on with him?"

"I guess okay, but I know that Ernie doesn't believe Executive Compensation has grown fast enough. He wants us bigger than RAH." Andy, with bright eyes and drunken enthusiasm, went on to describe the intricate intrigues of the New York office. There were so many names, departments, practices, and sub-practices. Baxter wondered if she ever thought about the clients. He judged that Andy's information was more sophisticated than the chatter from Jeff's crowd at O'Kelley's Bar.

Baxter left Andy shortly after 1:00 AM. There was a mis-aimed kiss and Baxter was safe outside the door and he could hear the chain drawn behind him. That night he dreamed about the whole bunch of them. Ernie, Clyde, Roger Dirks, Andy and Alvardi. He had only met three out of the five.

At 9:00 AM on March 31st, 1974, Baxter, Jeff and Andy entered the conference room where they were going to present the FSO findings to Ernie Grey. The presentation was set for ten o'clock and the previous two days had been spent preparing the report and reviewing the slides and flipcharts with Clyde who viewed himself as the intermediate client and Ernie Grey as the ultimate client. Baxter and Jeff noted that Clyde Nickerson was very well informed on the details of the engagement. With some massaging of information, Clyde had gotten the product he wanted to show to Ernie Grey. The findings and recommendations approximated what Clyde had anticipated, and now he had presumable independent documentation to support his initial intuitive judgment on FSO. He had used the ploy of a compensation study to conduct an operational review. The FSO management was not completely taken in by the compensation study subterfuge, and subtly planted their own recommendations. Baxter had carefully prepared and monitored the consulting team and believed that their report product was factual and objective.

"I don't believe that three presenters are necessary," Nickerson grumbled. "Joe, why don't you present the whole report? Jeff and Andrea will be in the room to comment." Andy was shocked. They had divided up the presentation so that Jeff and Andy would each have a short piece in front of the McKenzie Barber Chairman. They had practiced the presentation three separate times the evening before, and now Andy's friend and mentor wanted to take her time away from her.

"We've carefully rehearsed the presentation. Clyde. It won't be effective without three presenters," Baxter said firmly.

Ernie Grey entered the conference room at 10:07 AM. They had been ready for him since 9:40.

"Good morning!" he greeted them.

The Chairman looked like his pictures. He was a man of medium height with a muscular build and large, dark eyes. His eyebrows were bushy and his chin was square. Baxter knew Ernie Grey was 53 from his biographical data, but the man in front of him appeared to be at least ten years younger, in his early forties. He wore a dark suit with a black and white striped tie.

"Ernie," Clyde began and was cut off.

"I know, Clyde. These are the consultants who led the FSO study. I would have met them at 10 o'clock, but your secretary directed me to the wrong conference room." He held out his hand to Baxter.

"How do you do. I'm Ernest Grey," he repeated the greeting to Andy and Jeff. Ernie Grey was polite, but he was not smiling nor did he seem especially friendly.

"I see I'm going to be subjected to overhead slides this morning. Let's get on with it, please." Jeff pulled the blinds. Andy dimmed the lights. Baxter stood in front of the slide projector, flipped the switch and stood in front of the Chairman of McKenzie Barber.

Baxter was good that morning and the presentation appeared to go well. Ernie interrupted after the fourth slide. "Congratulations Clyde. You've pulled off the old second year consultant's trick. Conducting the study with the hidden agenda. It's a damn good thing they didn't run you off. That's why you picked Baxter. He's bigger than anyone they have!" Ernie then remained quiet for the next five slides. Andy did two and Jeff did three.

"What's your name again?" Ernie called out to Jeff.

"Jeff Long, sir," Jeff barked back.

"Jeff, what would you do with this company? Would you keep it?"

"I believe that issue is covered in our conclusions and recommendations section, Mr. Grey. That's coming up shortly."

"That's nice, Jeff, but the suspense is killing me. Give me your personal opinion. I don't care what Baxter or Andrea think or believe. What do you believe?" Ernie Grey's question was delivered with thunder.

"I'd keep the sucker, Mr. Chairman. This is a good business. It just isn't run very well. Now I'm going to defer to my manager, Cap'un Baxter," Jeff responded and passed the pointer back to Baxter.

"I agree with Jeff, Mr. Grey," Baxter began. "And you're going to agree with us when we've finished our presentation.

"God speed, Mr. Baxter," Ernie Grey commanded. Baxter looked to Clyde Nickerson. He sat quietly motionless in his chair. Ernie Grey challenged every one of their recommendations. Baxter, Jeff, and Andy responded to the challenges from the knowledge base they had developed in their study. Ernie Grey knew the financials by heart, but it was clear that he did not really understand FSO's business. Nor did he understand government contract accounting. Jeff took Ernie Grey quickly through the concept of overhead rates and government accounting standards. Ernie, who had been sitting with his arms folded, slowly opened his arms. "Okay fellows. I accept your report." Turning to Andy, "you were included in the fellows, Andrea." Then it was Clyde's turn. "Clyde, it was a good report and supports everything you told me last November. Any collusion here?"

"Just the conclusions of a team of crack consultants from the best consulting firm in the world, Ernie," Clyde answered confidently.

"And what did all of this cost us?" Ernie Grey asked.

"Around $300,000 including expenses and you got $600,000 worth of work at market value."

"Will I get a report, too?" Ernie asked.

"They're right here, Mr. Grey." Jeff produced a stack of five final reports of a similar size to the Darien telephone directory.

Ernie Grey rose to his feet. "Clyde, drop off one of those final reports and one of those flip charts with my secretary and come by about 6:00 tonight and we'll talk. Joe, Jeff, Andrea, nice job. Jeff, were you in the service?"

"Yes, sir."

"Marines?"

"Yes sir."

"You handle yourself like a Marine. Joe! You were an enlisted man in the Army, right?"

"Yes sir," Baxter responded.

"I reviewed your personnel file this morning. Army confidential and then the University of Minnesota. Burke told me about you. Looks like you've done a damned fine job. I hear you and Friedman have been going to town out in California. Do you want to move out there?"

"Not at this time, sir," Baxter responded.

"If you move anywhere, you come out to New York," Ernie said. He went to Andy and kissed her on the cheek. "A very nice job, dear." Ernie looked at his watch. "Oh my God! I'm due at the Metropolitan Club in five minutes." Ernie departed briskly out the door slapping Clyde on the shoulder as he passed by him. Clyde sighed. "Well, that was our Chairman. I feel safe and satisfied that our report was well received. I hereby dismiss this group and command you to quit charging time and expense to this engagement number after lunch. Andrea, I'm taking you to lunch at the Four Seasons!"

"That would be fine, Clyde," she agreed coldly. "I would like to talk to you about a few things."

Andy kissed Baxter on the cheek. "This is good-bye for a while, but I really learned a lot. You were sensational!" She hugged Jeff and Nickerson commented, "Don't wrinkle his suit!"

Handshakes were exchanged. Clyde and Andy left the conference room. "I guess those two will try to mend their lover's tiff over lunch," Jeff predicted. "Andy was down right pissed-off when old Clyde suggested that we just have one presenter."

"If their love is truly strong and pure, they will survive in this hurly-burly world," Baxter ruled. "Let's you and I have a farewell lunch, Jeff."

"Want to go to O'Grady's?"

"I'll call friends," Baxter said picking up the conference room telephone. He called Alvardi and reached him on the first ring.

"Alvardi!" The voice answered.

"Baxter here. We've left Ernie Grey and we're going to O'Grady's for lunch. You're invited to join us." Baxter said extending his invitation.

"Who's with you, kid? Not Ernie and Clyde?"

"They're off to other activities. I'm with my adjutant, Jeff Long."

"49th between Park and Lex, kid. I'll be there."

Baxter called Dwyer. "Mr. Dwyer's office." A correct British female voice answered.

"Is Mr. Dwyer in?" Baxter asked.

"Mr. Dwyer is out of the country until April 3rd."

"Any special country?" Baxter asked.

"Who's calling?"

"Tell Mr. Dwyer, his protégé, Mr. Baxter called."

Jeff and Baxter encountered Alvardi on the corner of 49th and Lexington. After introductions they strolled into the front bar of O'Grady's to observe Dwyer in a corner booth in the front bar with a dark haired, broad beaked Irish girl.

They were engaged in intimate conversation and Dwyer's hand was on the girl's thigh.

"He's out of the country," Baxter announced while they waited for the hostess to seat them.

"Then don't look, kid. When you're out of town, you're out of town!" Alvardi ruled.

They were seated in the rear of the main dining room in the midst of a post 1PM luncheon crowd. Two men at the next table took note of Alvardi. His hair was jet black, parted in the middle, and neatly groomed against his head. He did look like Joe DiMaggio, Baxter decided.

Jeff and Baxter ordered martinis while Alvardi had a campari and soda.

"FSO is over," Baxter proclaimed.

"And just in the nick of time, kid. The Chicago Exec Comp numbers look terrible. My national numbers look great because of your California work. But Chicago looks like hell because Carl isn't selling any work without you there. Now that you've done your public service routine and got to perform in front of our beloved Chairman, kid, it's time to get back to productive work like serving clients. The first quarter will not look good for your section of the Chicago office Strategic Planning practice," Alvardi said coldly.

The drinks were served. "To the end of FSO!" Jeff said, raising his glass.

"To the rest of your consulting careers!" Alvardi said raising his campari in a second toast. "Jeff, have you ever worked on one of my jobs?" Alvardi asked.

"I pulled money center bank proxies for you and plotted the top three officers on a chart using "least squares" analysis one time," Jeff responded. "I was unapplied and in the Associates IE pool and they sent me off to work in Exec Comp for a day."

"The IEs have two pools out here, kid. They have an Associate level pool so you can draw on seasoned people with high hourly rates to do clerical work."

"You really know how to hurt a guy, don't you, Mr. Alvardi?" Jeff answered.

"Is this man reliable and confidential?" Alvardi asked Baxter referring to Jeff.

"I've been in combat with him, Frank, and I'd go again," Baxter said.

Alvardi smiled. "Look, Jeff, I just asked Joe if we can talk openly or do we have to talk circumspectly? The rules have now been established. We're going to talk openly and no one will repeat to another what is said at this table. Those were the rules when Dwyer and I initiated Baxter into the order."

"What order is that?" Baxter asked.

"The Loyal Order of Right Thinking Consultants," Alvardi replied. "Want to join, kid?" Alvardi looked to Jeff.

"Is there an initiation fee?" Jeff asked.

"You pay for lunch, kid," Alvardi said in his best Italian tough guy voice.

Jeff looked to Joe. "Can I charge this lunch to FSO, Cap'un?"

"Hell, yes," Baxter replied.

"Is this on Ernie and Clyde?" Alvardi asked.

They nodded and Alvardi stopped the waitress. "Miss, would you please bring me a Beefeater martini straight up. In the front bar is a Mr. Dwyer. He is sitting in the second booth beyond the maitre'd station. He is with his black haired niece. Would you invite him back to join us. Tell them that the check will ultimately paid by Mr. Nickerson. Now will you repeat that back to me."

They were moved to a larger table when Dwyer came by with Mary, his companion. She was a coarse featured Irish girl, tall and lanky in a green suit with strap shoes.

"Mary's from Ireland, lads. She went to college with my little brother."

"What's he doing now?" Alvardi asked.

"He's a college educated bartender. Mary's in nursing and illegally working in the States. I'm going to have her stay with me a while until she gets settled."

"Hush, Bill," she chided Dwyer.

77

Jeff looked at Baxter. It was obvious that they were now entrapped in what would be a long, outrageous luncheon. Alvardi stood up from the table. "I must call my office and tell them that I'm out of the country."

Dwyer ordered Irish Whiskey all around. He looked across the table at Jeff.

"Have you worked on my jobs, lad?"

"Several of them," Jeff answered. He recited the engagements and Dwyer closed his eyes as if he were thinking deeply.

"You're an IE from Georgia and have impractical skills in Operations Research. You're a good smart lad, but need some time on the plant floor. Joe, here, has no formal skills, but has a lot of shop floor time. At least he convinced me he had shop floor time. Because he has no formal skills, he has been reduced to working for my friend Alvardi, the compensation shaman. Joe, lad, how have you been spending your time lately and what brings you to New York?"

Baxter explained the FSO engagement and Dwyer shook his head. "Who put you into that bloody tarbaby?"

"Alvardi recommended me," Baxter explained at the same time Frank returned to the table.

"I ordered you an Irish Whiskey, Frank," Dwyer announced.

Alvardi looked at his partially consumed martini and the Irish Whiskey.

"Perhaps they're best combined." Alvardi poured his Irish Whiskey into his martini. Jeff gasped! Mary giggled! Dwyer roared!

"That makes a very uniquely colored drink," Baxter observed.

"Frank," Dwyer asked. "How could you, in good conscience, have recommended Joe to manage that FSO job?"

"They asked me and I told them. It had to be a big body job with a lot of junior people. Baxter is the only consultant I could think of at McKenzie Barber who had ever run a plant. Joe has good leadership skills and mediocre functional skills. He was a natural for Clyde. I wasn't sure how he'd get by Ernie, but apparently he did."

"Whoa! Whoa!" Jeff interrupted. "We had one hell of an engagement in a difficult client scenario. Joe Baxter is the best engagement manager I've ever worked for and that includes you, Mr. Alvardi."

"Call me Frank, kid," Alvardi replied.

"Joe, did you make a favorable impression on Ernie Grey?" Dwyer asked with his hand resting on Mary's long thigh.

"We did just fine," Baxter said throwing down his Irish Whiskey and signaling for a refill. "We pulled together a team and didn't exactly have our pick of the litter and we got the job done. I'm damned proud of our team and I'm especially proud of my senior people. Jeff was one of them and Andrea Bourke was the other."

"Andrea Bourke!" Alvardi protested. "She probably had a walkie-talkie in her purse connected to Clyde Nickerson."

"They're working out their differences right now at the Four Seasons," Jeff commented. "Clyde wanted to have Joe handle the presentation and cut Andy out. Joe wouldn't do it."

"It was an intramural game, Jeff," Alvardi observed. "It wasn't the real thing."

"The hell it wasn't!" Jeff snapped back. "We were asked to review a troubled company on a hidden agenda approach and we did one hell of a job. The quality of the job is directly attributable to the Cap'un here. I won't sit here and listen to that intramural game crap!" Jeff said.

"I believe this lad has properly evaluated the complexity of the engagement, Frank," Dwyer judged. "Let's not refer again at this luncheon to the FSO engagement as an intramural game," he ruled.

"I stand corrected," Alvardi said.

They bantered on through two rounds of Irish Whiskey. "I've worked two weeks now without a day off," Dwyer explained.

"That's why I have my secretary tell callers I'm out of the country. Otherwise people will track me down."

"If Ernie wants you, he'll ask which country?"

"I have a question for you guys," Jeff began. "Are you happy at McKenzie Barber?"

Dwyer looked across the table to Alvardi. Alvardi formed the wisp of a cynical smile. "What's that got to do with the price of bananas, young man?"

"Frank, Frank," Dwyer appealed. "Don't be so hard on the lad. He hasn't had the benefit of a Catholic education. He's living in a state of non-guilt."

"I think you two are terrible," Mary said and placed her hand on Jeff's hand. "This young man asked you a civil question and you should give him something that could pass for an answer."

"I'll have a go at it, Mary," Alvardi said. "The work is challenging and fun most of the time. The pay is good. It's the political bullshit that gets to you."

"Frank got it," Dwyer agreed.

"You were at Robson Allen, Mr. Alvardi?" Jeff continued to probe. "Was it different there?"

"In the beginning it was different. By the time I got there it wasn't a lot different from McKenzie Barber, except there was only one man at the top versus three at RAH. There are some interesting young strategic planning firms developing, the Accounting firms are trying to be consultants, and the actuarial firms are trying to be compensation consultants, but when you get

79

down to it, there are two firms on top and the top talent is fairly evenly distributed. Robson, Allen and Harbridge will probably all retire or go into government in another year. They've been grooming successor management for years. McKenzie Barber has Ernie Grey and Ernie's got to step up to the plate and groom a successor."

"Who will that be?" Baxter asked.

Dwyer looked to Alvardi and they both laughed. "I say Dirks and Bill says Brimmer," Alvardi said.

Dwyer stood up and pulled Mary to her feet. "This conversation is getting weary, lads. Mary and I have more interesting diversions to attend to." Dwyer led Mary off after the good-byes. She wobbled warmly up against Dwyer as they left the dining room.

"Not your average Wellesley lady, gentlemen, but probably very entertaining on a rainy afternoon," Alvardi observed.

"Kid, I've got to get back to work. I will be out next Monday afternoon. Your good friend Lee Heller has been raising a fit about the disappointing performance of the Chicago executive compensation unit. He had Dr. Barry call me and ask me to come out and work with you. Have you considered just going off to California and working for Friedman? Or is that too Faustian to suit you?" Alvardi shook hands with Jeff and Baxter.

"I'll see you Monday afternoon, kid. Try to have a plan ready."

Jeff shook his head after Alvardi left the dining room. "Those two are not the conventional McKenzie Barber partners, Joe. They just don't fit the rest of the firm and I can't believe they've lasted this long," Jeff commented.

"They may have lasted because they know what they're doing," Baxter reasoned.

"When's your plane, Cap'un?"

"I should be on the eight o'clock to Chicago."

"It's only a quarter of three. What do you say we pour you on the plane, Cap'un? I'll find us some sweet young things to drink with. Excuse me while I make a phone call or two."

They wound up in the front bar of the Sherry Netherland with Hillary and Jane from the FSO team.

"I think we're a few drinks behind these gentlemen," Jane, a perky brown haired Yale, School of Industrial Organization graduate, said as they joined Baxter and Jeff at their table.

"I'd say that we're four days behind them," Hillary estimated. Jeff had lured them out under the pretense of briefing Jane and Hillary on their presentation to the Chairman of McKenzie Barber. Away from O'Grady's Bar, the FSO engagement became important again.

80

Jeff went on to tell how Clyde Nickerson had requested a single presenter and Baxter had refused to budge.

"Capital!" Hillary said raising her wine glass.

"The women of McKenzie Barber need more like you, Joe," Jane added.

"Now let me ask you a question," Hillary began. "Do you believe Andy and Nickerson are sleeping together, Joe?"

"I really don't know or care who's sleeping with whom at McKenzie Barber. All I can see about Andy is that she was a first rate consultant on the FSO engagement. The rest really doesn't matter," Baxter said.

Hillary began to fondle his tie. "You are full of platitudes, Mr. Baxter. You are a marvelous engagement manager, but I really wonder what goes on inside you." She leaned forward and placed her mouth close to Baxter's ear. "I'm really curious to know what you're really like. I'd like to wake up with you once in the morning before you start turning on the platitudes." Baxter leaned forward and they shared a brief, soft, bar room kiss.

"They seem to be having a serious conversation over there, Jane," Jeff commented.

"I'll be back in New York one of these days. Shall we have dinner?" Baxter asked.

"I suspect that it's not dinner that you're after. I'm out in California for the next three months. We can get together out there. I've met your nice family man friend, Mr. Friedman. He's probably a strong candidate for lecher of the year. He told me you would be out in April and that you are less conservative in California."

"You know I'm a married man," Baxter cautioned.

"Half the men I date in New York are married. It seems to be a national sport out here."

Baxter was quite drunk by this time in the evening. He was sitting with an attractive young Wharton graduate with good skin and classic features who apparently was disposed to sleeping with him. Across the table, Jeff was making advances to Jane while the piano played Cole Porter tunes. The FSO job was history and Baxter was millions of miles away from Iron Creek, Minnesota, and the house on Palmer Street in Racine, Wisconsin. It was March 31, 1974 and he would be returning to Chicago on the eight o'clock plane to a faltering Chicago exec comp practice and a failed marriage.

Jennifer announced that she was going to Europe at a Sunday dinner in the house on Palmer Street. It was the first weekend in April and Baxter had spent a full Saturday with Joel and Muffin which had included observing Joel's YMCA swimming lesson, a luncheon at the Deer Lake Country Club, and a movie at the Deer Lake Cinema II.

"We missed you, Daddy," Muffin announced at lunch.

"Mother's never at home. We get tired of just Agnes," Joel said. "She just watches television upstairs and listens to the classical radio station at night in the kitchen. You take us out and we do things. Do you still have to go to California and to Washington all the time? Muffy and I miss you." Joel was a thin boy with sensitive eyes and his mother's crafted Gellhorn features.

Muffin resembled neither Baxter nor Jennifer. She was round faced, blonde, jolly, and outspoken. He loved them both, but had come to recognize that Joel did not like games played with balls and that he was not particularly well coordinated. Muffin had bounce, personality, and enormous energy. She was a cheerful, affectionate child in comparison to her older brother who tended to be remote.

They had a good long Saturday and listened to showtunes on the record player in the evening with Baxter. In the morning, Baxter drove them to church with Agnes and they gathered around the table in the main dining room for Sunday dinner at 1:30. Jennifer presided over dinner. She had returned around one o'clock on Sunday morning and Baxter had been in a heavy sleep. Agnes served Sunday dinner, which was the prelude to Baxter's return to Chicago. Baxter carved the roast and they were fifteen minutes into the Sunday dinner when Jennifer made her announcement.

"I have decided to spend the summer in Europe," she said. "I'm leaving in mid-May and I'll come back after Labor Day. I'm going to Paris with our Peace Group and we're going to tour Europe. I'll be a delegate to the World Peace Conference and have the opportunity to meet with politically aware people throughout the continent.

Baxter was caught by surprise. "Who will be with the children besides Agnes? She doesn't drive a car."

"I have engaged an au pair. Her name is Celeste and she's a senior in Political Science at Madison. She will live here this summer and handle groceries and driving."

"She will sleep in the house?" Baxter asked.

"She will sleep in the third floor bedroom. Agnes will continue to handle the cleaning and the cooking. Celeste will handle the children and errands. She's on my payroll, Joe."

"And you're just taking off?" Baxter said. "Just like that."

"Joe, I'm getting bored here. You're running all over the country. The children will be well looked after and you're gone all week as it is. I've worked very hard for the Peace Movement and I need a break. You're too busy with your foolishness at McKenzie Barber to be at home. Celeste is my financial responsibility. I probably should start to charge you room and board for weekends here at Palmer Street."

Baxter knew at the time that the die had been cast. Jennifer had come full circle. She was going back to Europe and it was only a matter of time before they were divorced.

The children looked at their mother with trusting faces. She would be going away for a while and a nice lady would live in the house who would drive them around when their father was traveling.

"You might have discussed this with me first before bringing it up to the children," Baxter reproached Jennifer over coffee after the children had been excused from the table.

"My life and the children are my business. You're really not much of a husband. I've earned a vacation. I have contributed to slowing down an immoral war in Vietnam while you've been running around the country staying in first class hotels and probably involving yourself with trashy women. Celeste is a real find. I'm expecting you to cooperate on this, Joe."

There was really no other option for Baxter, other than to cooperate. They were separated for all practical purposes. They shared the same roof on weekends when the children were Baxter's responsibility. He had his apartment in Rosemont near O'Hare during the week, and traveled from one to two days a week. At age 36, Jennifer was an attractive, striking woman. She wore little make-up and wore her dark hair shoulder length. Her wonderful saucer eyes now seemed to be cold and calculating. Jennifer appeared to enjoy a full life outside Palmer Street that she did not discuss with Baxter. They now slept in separate rooms, with Baxter sleeping on a day bed in Mr. Tom's old study. He had established a weekend office in the study and Baxter had come to enjoy his privacy.

The Washburn family sensed the estrangement. They were polite and distant at the infrequent family gatherings. Nelson Washburn had completed his consultancy contract at Washburn Manufacturing. The Caribou Street plant had been closed and now stood empty and unclaimed by the industrial world. All of the manufacturing had been moved to Mississippi. The state of Wisconsin was conducting an investigation following complaints by the Washburn Manufacturing pensioners. Nelson had provided testimony, but was generally baffled by pension plan compliance issues. He had been taken care of, and it was unfortunate for the others. "You should have stayed on, Joe. You could have protected the workers." Nelson mildly rebuked Baxter during Sunday dinner coffee.

Chuck was the most friendly. He was now a partner with his law firm and respected the name of McKenzie Barber. "I don't know how you do it, Joe. I simply couldn't travel like that month after month." It was when Chuck began to probe about the nature of McKenzie Barber's organization as a legal entity that Baxter realized how little he knew about the organization of his firm. He didn't know how the U.S. and overseas firms were linked legally, or how many partners there were in the U.S. firm, the Canadian firm, the UK firm, the European firm, or the Latin American firm. September represented his sixth anniversary with McKenzie Barber, and he had yet to attend an orientation or a training class. The majority of his work had been performed for two partners who were well outside the culture and value structure of McKenzie Barber. He was certain that no one like Bob Friedman existed anywhere else in the firm. The FSO engagement really had been Baxter's closest link to the firm, and now that was over. He knew executive compensation and could link short term and long term incentive plans to corporate business strategies. Baxter was under the thumb of Lee Heller, whom he had once identified as a friend and Alvardi always seemed to be there when Baxter didn't especially need him. Bob Friedman no longer asked Baxter to transfer to Los Angeles. He had hired a woman named Ruth Ingvold, who had been Vice President for Compensation at one of the large banks and Baxter was to come out the following week and transition all of the work.

Baxter sat across from Chuck at a picnic table in the Washburn backyard on the first weekend in May. There was a contingent of children which included Chuck's daughter who was Muffin's age, and Sam's youngest, a eight year towhead named Tim, who had played three cornered catch with Baxter and Chuck earlier. They now watched Tim Washburn organize a bat and ball game with the children.

"The kid's got a good arm. He throws naturally," Baxter observed.

"I take it Joel's not big on sports," Chuck said. Baxter had put up a basket in the driveway on Palmer Street but Joel had no interest. He preferred to play by himself with toy soldiers involving them in a number of plots and adventures. Agnes had discovered a box of toy soldiers in the attic that may have belonged to Mr. Tom. Joel took them everywhere and sat under a tree playing with his soldiers.

"Maybe he'll come around," Baxter said watching Muffin brandish a plastic bat as young Tim Washburn lobbed a ball to her.

It was perfect Wisconsin spring day with the temperature in the high sixties under a bright sun in a cloudless sky. The Washburns had catered a family barbecue and a side of beef was being turned supplemented by a turkey.

"Joe, how do you feel about Jennifer running off to Europe?" Chuck asked.

"It's what she wants to do and there's no stopping her," Baxter replied sipping his coffee.

"Jennifer's my sister and I love her very much. I like you, Joe. She's changed. You've changed——."

"And Washburn Manufacturing is gone," Baxter completed his sentence. "Those children are the only thing holding the two of us together," Baxter said sadly.

"Have you thought about a separation and possibly a divorce?" Chuck asked.

"I turned down a transfer to California to be close to the children," Baxter replied.

"Joe, there's something you should know," Chuck said. "Jennifer may stay in Europe past September. Don't ask me how I know."

"She's not going over with a peace group then?" Baxter asked.

"Jennifer's met someone. He's a university English professor who's taking a year's sabbatical to write a novel in Europe. If they get along, she won't be back until September of next year. She's leaving you, Joe. I think you had better get a lawyer."

"Are you telling me this because I'm a member of the family?" Baxter asked.

"Joe, you're not a member of this family anymore. You should think of making the right kind of arrangements and moving on. You should move your things out of Palmer Street and visit every weekend as you're doing now. Alimony will be waived, but you will have child support obligations through their college expenses. I can give you the names of three competent attorneys in Racine who handle divorce proceedings." Baxter stood up from the picnic table. "I hope nobody minds if I stay to eat."

Jennifer was talking in a cluster of family when Baxter asked her to talk privately under a large oak tree.

"I heard from your advance man and it's okay by me," he said.

"I have no idea of what you're talking about, Joe," Jennifer replied coldly and returned to her place next to her mother.

The second week of May in 1974 was especially hectic for Baxter. It started with a Monday morning mid-year review of the Chicago Exec Comp practice. The meeting had been scheduled twice during the month of April, only to have Alvardi cancel twice. The purpose of the meeting was to review the first six months profit performance of Baxter's practice. Between the FSO and the California engagements, Baxter's personal time had been highly applied, but the discount in fee from the inter-office engagements, coupled with Carl's inability to generate enough new Chicago office work in Baxter's absence, placed the practice about 7% net to gross versus a plan of 25%.

Baxter had been welcomed back by Dr. Keller and his strategic planning associates. The work began to reappear after Baxter returned to work with Drs. Keller, Kennedy, and Huhlman.

Suddenly Carl and the four practice consultants became quite busy, and Exec Comp had acquired a handsome backlog of work.

The meeting was scheduled for 10 AM on Monday morning and Dr. Keller, Alvardi and Lee Heller were to attend. Alvardi arrived in Chicago the Sunday evening before the meeting, and Baxter met him at O'Hare in the TWA Ambassadors Club to go over his presentation.

"This looks good, kid. Your problems appear to be behind you," Alvardi said after he reviewed Baxter's last chart. "Now, will you tell me again why in the hell we're having this meeting?"

"I'm off plan. As my national practice leader, Dr. Barry wants your input on what can be done to deliver my profit plan on September 30th," Baxter replied.

"That's a crock, kid. Dr. Barry has little idea of what's going on in any of his practices. This meeting is the brainchild of your little buddy, Lee Heller, who thinks he's running the Strategic Services practice in Chicago. Does he do any client work, kid?"

"He spends much of his time in practice administration," Baxter explained.

"A fucking bookkeeper! I know his game. When Ernie hired Dr. Barry and those crack professors, it was concluded that they would get lost in their underwear with all of the McKenzie Barber administrative bullshit. Brimmer gave them Heller and Heller's taking himself seriously. Let's spin that son-of-a-bitch around in the meeting tomorrow!"

"Want dinner, Frank?" Baxter asked.

"No, kid. I have a social engagement at Sonny's Supper Club. Ever been out there?"

Lorna! Baxter concluded. Alvardi was going to see Lorna.

"I understand that Sonny's is out on Highway 12 past Lake Zurich."

"That's too far out of the way for me."

"Have you transitioned all of the California work, kid?" Alvardi asked.

"I'm going out on Wednesday to spend a day or so with Ruth Ingvold, who Friedman hired as practice leader for the West Coast Exec Comp practice. Have you met her, Frank?"

"Friedman flew her out to New York for my endorsement. You were the one he really wanted and you would have been gangbusters in the West Coast market. Ruth Ingvold was a bit of a disappointment between the two of us. I have come to expect a little more from Friedman. I expected a fine looking California lady, full of personality and light on technical skills. I met an ugly, tight-assed lady, with no personality, who is probably a superb technician, but full of herself and consumed with egalitarian ideas about internal equity. She'll fail badly under a Friedman leadership style. Do me a favor when you're out there, kid. Find out why he really hired her."

Baxter saw Alvardi to the Hertz counter. "Where are you staying tonight, Frank?" he asked after Alvardi had checked in.

"Sonny's Motel. It's next door to Sonny's Supper Club and there are special discounts for Italians."

That night Baxter thought long and hard about Lorna King over several shots of Canadian Club. He came to no resolution of his thoughts.

Dr. Barry Keller was a tall, gangly, articulate man with a mane of greying yellow hair. He chainsmoked cigarettes and loved to write on blackboards and flip charts. He was clever and electric in meetings with clients. Baxter regarded him as brilliant, others regarded him as an academic buffoon and another link in the chain of Ernie Grey's risky introductions to McKenzie Barber.

Dr. Barry greeted Alvardi as if he were a long lost disciple. "Welcome! Welcome! Frank, it's so good to see you. Every time I pick up the Wall Street Journal, you're quoted. I'm delighted to see you!"

Lee Heller was seated in Dr. Barry's conference room table waiting for them. He rose to greet Alvardi. "Frank I'm so glad you could finally make it out." He extended his hand which Alvardi accepted after studying if for a few seconds.

"What's your name again, fellow?" Alvardi returned his greeting. The review, which Alvardi later referred to as a non-review, was highly favorable. Alvardi jabbed Lee Heller repeatedly throughout the discussion.

"It's my conclusion that you have a pretty strong practice here when Joe is not off somewhere else. If something happens to Joe, you're out of business. Carl is a very capable technician, but Joe is your lead horse. I would like to have him in New York. Bob Friedman wanted him to move to Los Angeles. I'd advance Joe to the Director level effective October 1."

"Promotion considerations usually aren't discussed in a mid-year review, Frank," Lee commented.

"This is a business, kid, not a bureaucratic art form. We must talk in realities. Joe is leading major engagements and bringing in new work. He needs recognition in the marketplace in addition to within the equity structure of the firm," Alvardi replied.

Lee Heller stared at Alvardi in incredulous horror. Frank Alvardi was proposing that Baxter be elevated to his level. "Well, I've got some recognition for you, Joe." Dr. Barry produced a grey piece of paper about the size of a telegram. "This is one of those Grey-grams that some of us get. It's from Ernie Grey to Joe Baxter and there are copies to Frank, Paul Brimmer and me. I'll read it."

TO: J. Baxter
Chicago
FROM: E. Grey

Executive
CC: P. Brimmer-Chicago
B. Keller-Chicago
F. Alvardi-New York
SUBJECT: FSO Report

Congratulations on a superb engagement! I have read through the report three times and regard it is an outstanding piece of consulting work. Many of your project team's recommendations are being implemented! I look forward to observing your future contributions to the firm. Please pass my compliments and congratulations to the other members of your team.

"When did you receive that?" Baxter asked Dr. Barry.

"It came in Friday's mail. You haven't received your copy yet?" Dr. Barry queried.

"I was in Rockford on Friday with a client," Baxter explained.

"I haven't checked my mail."

"Kid. I call in once a day to check for Grey-grams. I would suggest you begin to do the same. Ernie must have forgot about your copy, Lee," Alvardi said. "Get two like that in one year and it's an automatic promotion to Director."

"What we have here, gentlemen," Dr. Barry stated, "is another example of Compensation strategy linked to reinforce Business strategy. This is what the rest of the 1970's and the 1980's are going to be about." Dr. Barry stood up from the conference room table and went to his blackboard. He began to outline the business planning and strategy cycle. Baxter watched Alvardi roll his eyes.

"Now driving all these initiatives and action plans is the ultimate piece of behavioral influence and motivation, PAY!"

Dr. Barry wrote PAY and a dollar sign on his blackboard in large letters. "Now we at McKenzie Barber work with pay in three forms:

- Base salary plans and systems
- Annual incentive bonus plans
- Long term capital accumulation plans.

Oh my god! Baxter thought. Dr. Barry was going to lecture Alvardi and Baxter on their own practice!

"Now it is time to examine and embrace the fourth component of pay, Replacement Income," Dr. Barry cried out triumphantly. "More commonly known as Employee Benefits. At McKenzie Barber we have in the past developed certain discriminatory benefits for senior executives, but now it is the time to link Employee Benefit plans to Strategic Planning. Joe, do you realize how much of the labor cost in the American automobile represents employee benefit welfare plans?" Dr. Barry was off to the races. A torrent of words introduced electrically. A glimpse of the future! Sky rocketing medical and pension costs! The emergence of savings plans that would replicate Keough plans for larger groups of employees! Louis Kelso's two factor theory and the formation of ESOPs. ERISA! The Pension Benefit Guaranty Corporation! It was all there, bright and beautiful! It was the kind of lecture that would fill an auditorium. Dr. Barry was a truly brilliant visionary, Baxter concluded. His final words had the greatest impact on Alvardi!

"And that gentlemen, is why McKenzie Barber must enter the Employee Benefits consulting business!" Dr. Barry set his chalk down in triumph and returned to the table with a broad smile.

"Barry," Alvardi said slowly. "Did I hear you just say that McKenzie Barber must enter the Employee Benefits consulting business?"

"It must be done! I'm serving on a special planning committee with Ernie and Clyde, Ned Fleming from Cleveland, and of course, Harvey Randolph. We are going to acquire a goodly sized, high quality Employee Benefits consulting firm which will put us into the business. We want a critical mass right away. Ernie believes that we would have been better off by acquiring a firm for critical mass, as opposed to building the practice with internal resources. If we acquire the right firm, Frank, we could fold your practice right under it and the synergies will be sensational."

Baxter looked at Alvardi. He appeared to be a man who had just caught a bullet near his groin. The wound wasn't life threatening, but it had landed close enough for him to recognize that the next shot would be painful and career fatal.

"The Employee Benefits consulting market place is a mature market for services, Barry. We have excellent relationships with most of the actuarial firms who have not chosen to compete with us in Executive Compensation. Actuarial leadership is very quantitatively driven and often rigid. A top flight executive compensation practice will never fit under Actuarial leadership. I would recommend having Benefits report to Compensation and placing any acquisition under the direction of the Executive Compensation practice," Alvardi said.

"Frank, is there a firm with both a compensation practice and an actuarial/employee benefits consulting practice?" Dr. Barry asked.

"I'd have to research that, Barry," Alvardi replied.

Baxter looked to Lee Heller. He stared ahead at Dr. Barry as if he were unaware that a strategic bombshell has just been dropped. McKenzie Barber appeared committed to enter the Employee Benefits consulting segment of the market about twenty years too late. The price for a successful critical mass acquisition would be very high.

There were handshakes and a few questions from Alvardi relative to how long the committee had been meeting. He seemed relieved when Dr. Barry said that their second meeting would be at the end of May.

Lee Heller shook hands all around and publicly congratulated Baxter on his mid-year progress. Alvardi walked calmly with Baxter to his office. He closed the door, looked out at Baxter's view of the Chicago skyline and shouted.

"What mischief is that dumb son-of-a-bitch up to? Acquiring a Benefits firm! That's master stupidity! Let me call Dirks! This is bullshit, kid!" Baxter had never before seen so much emotion from Alvardi.

"Roger Dirks, please. Frank Alvardi calling," Alvardi said into the telephone. "Then interrupt him!" Alvardi instructed the secretary.

"Roger, I didn't want to bother you, but I heard something very personally disturbing in a meeting this morning. Your good friend, Dr. Barry, announced in a meeting that the firm is entertaining the acquisition of an Employee Benefits consulting firm. Dr. Barry stated that they are looking at a critical mass firm and if they acquire such a firm, I want to go on record that I am history with McKenzie Barber. I know everything I want to know about Actuarial/Employee Benefits consulting firms. Roger, reporting to a fucking actuary is a resignation issue with me! I did not leave Robson Allen to come to McKenzie Barber to run a second class practice!"

Alvardi cradled the phone and listened. Baxter looked on. "Yeah! Yeah! No he didn't give me a date! Chicago is great! We've got a good guy running the practice out here. Ernie just sent him a laudatory Grey-gram. Yes, Baxter, our man in Chicago, is of above average intelligence. Look, Roger, I get disturbed when discussions about long term strategy concerning my practice are carried out without my input or participation. Yeah, I'll be back tomorrow. I'll make dinner on Wednesday night. Seven o'clock, Le Cygne! I'll be there. Thanks for taking my call, Roger."

Alvardi appeared mollified after he had hung up the phone. "I'll talk this over with Dirks and keep you posted, kid." It seemed like a minor matter to Baxter. He had only brushes with actuarial firms during his time in the Chicago practice and customarily recommended that they could use their established resources in Benefits matters or McKenzie Barber could contract for services in their behalf. Baxter could see some synergies between Executive Compensation and Employee Benefits consulting. Apparently Alvardi saw other things.

Lorna King stuck her head inside Baxter's office. "Good morning, Joe." She wore a high buttoned black dress with a decorative silver pin in her collar. "Frank, could you drop by my office on your way out?" Lorna's brown hair was slightly streaked and pinned high on her head. Had she worn it shoulder length when she played Fiona? Baxter asked himself.

"How about twenty minutes or so," Alvardi replied.

Lorna beamed a smile at Joe and withdrew from the doorway.

"Probably some administrative matter, kid," Alvardi explained.

Wednesday found Baxter in the Los Angeles office of McKenzie Barber sitting across a conference room table from Ruth Invgold. He had spent ten minutes with Friedman prior to the meeting.

Baxter shared his Grey-gram with Friedman. "Isn't that nice?" Friedman said sarcastically. "All Grey-grams are not as upbeat as this. Sometimes the Grey-grams can be outright nasty. I wonder who writes them."

"One of my project team members is working on a financial management engagement out here. I'd like to share the Grey-gram with her."

"Would you like me to have someone xerox it?" Friedman asked playfully.

"I thought I'd buy her a cup of coffee or its equivalent," Baxter proposed.

"You must be talking about Hillary Stone," Friedman concluded. "I played tennis with her the other morning. She's very competitive. I'd catch her this trip because she goes back to New York on the Thursday before Memorial Day. Hillary's been working on a major branch office profitability study for Golden State Federal. I borrowed a few consultants from New York with prior branch responsibility work. Apparently she came here right from the FSO job. She approached me for a tennis match when I went out to review the engagement team. We played at seven in the morning, which is not my best time for tennis. Hillary has a very powerful serve and she's fearless. Remember that, Joe. I, of course, let her win the first game and then trounced the little minx. I'll have my secretary get you her day telephone number at Golden State. Hillary looked very good in tennis clothes and has an athletic looking body. Hillary's heavy thighed."

"My interest in meeting with her is totally professional," Baxter lied.

"I understand," Friedman said solemnly. "You want to show her your Grey-gram. Now we must discuss and you must meet another lady, Ruth Ingvold. Ruth has been with us for one week and two days and I don't have her applied yet. Today I want you to thoroughly brief Ruth on each of our California engagements. Ruth was Vice President for Compensation Planning at California Interstate Bank. She is very well respected in California banking and personnel management sectors. Ruth is also new to consulting, so I had her fly out to meet Frank Alvardi, and I would like to have her spend a week with you in Chicago."

"How did Frank feel about Ruth?" Baxter asked.

"He thought she was an excellent choice, but would require some orientation into the basic consulting disciplines. That's why I believe you should be a principal resource to Ruth in the months ahead."

"What's her background again?" Baxter asked.

"Ruth's parents are from Iowa and moved out here during the war years. She grew up in Pasadena and graduated from Pepperdine and finished her MBA at USC. Ruth is about 38 and was with California Interstate for about twelve years starting in employee relations and moving up to SVP Compensation Planning. She was very close to the old Chairman, Ned Black. His successor didn't especially care for Ruth, and moved a man she didn't respect over her as Chief Personnel Officer. I've gotten to know Ned through my tennis club. Although Ned's retired from California Interstate, he's still on five or six boards. Ned called me on Ruth and virtually guaranteed me that we would be introduced to the compensation Committee of every board he serves on. Not a thrift in the bunch, and we've never done a dimes worth of consulting with any of them. That's why, Joe, I want Ruth handled with tender, thoughtful care. Properly orchestrated, this can represent a fantastic door opener for us. So you have the next day or so to bring Ruth up to speed, and then I will take her out to meet the clients."

"Will you want me to come out and help bridge things?" Baxter asked.

"No need for that, Joe. I don't want to confuse the clients as to whom they should be contacting. After today, it's good-bye, Baxter, hello, Ruth. Do you get my drift? If this goes well, there may be another Grey-gram in it for you."

Ruth Ingvold turned out to be a heavyset blonde woman of around forty or so with icy blue eyes behind her square designer eyeglasses. She had a firm handshake and the air of a pit-bull about her. The conference table was filled with McKenzie Barber working papers, and there were empty coffee cups and a full ashtray at the end of the table where Ruth had been sitting.

"I've been reviewing these files, Joe," she greeted him. "This looks like the biggest give-away program I've ever seen." She looked across the table at Baxter with her icy eyes and he knew it would be a long morning.

"Well, Ruth," he began, "Suppose you and I begin to define our terms. Let's start there right now."

The first hour of their discussion was contentious. As a banker, Ruth Ingvold, had always looked down at the Thrifts. Ruth was exactly as Alvardi had described her, a brilliant, rigid technician, who had spent her entire career with a single organization.

Baxter went through each engagement, plan by plan, participant by participant, and the rationale for the cost and funding of the plan concepts, excusing himself at 11:30 to call Hillary. He used the phone in an unoccupied office next to the conference room.. Closing the door, he carefully punched in the number Friedman's secretary had provided. It was a long shot. This would be his last night in Los Angeles for quite a while. The phone rang three times before a crisp voice answered;

"Hillary Stone."

"Joe Baxter here. You may not remember me. We worked together on the FSO engagement and had drinks together in the Sherry Netherland. I received a very laudatory note from Ernie Grey on our work. I'm out here today and part of tomorrow. Can I buy you a drink or a cup of coffee while I'm out here?"

There was silence on the other end of the telephone for a period of about ten seconds.

"Well, hello stranger," the voice replied finally. "Do you have any idea of where I'm being kept? I'm in Glendale. It's not like going from Wall Street to mid-town. What did you have in mind?"

"How about dinner?" Baxter proposed.

"Do you have a car?"

"No."

"Where are you staying?"

"The Sheraton Grande."

"That's very civilized. I'll come by there. They serve drinks in the lobby. Suppose I meet you there at 7:30 and we can eat in the hotel."

Hillary didn't arrive at the Sheraton Grande until ten minutes after eight. Baxter nursed his way through two Canadian Clubs while he listened to the piano player during the wait. Baxter decided that if Hillary hadn't arrived by nine, he would simply have a hamburger in the coffee shop and go to bed.

Hillary entered the room through the revolving doors at 8:10 wearing a pink suit with an open neck and carrying a shopping bag. She was a striking, full bodied young woman with tan skin and her sun glasses perched stylishly on the top of her head. Baxter stood up from his chair and called out her name. Hillary walked confidently across the room to Baxter. The men in the lobby followed Hillary with their eyes.

"Joe," she smiled. "I never should have agreed to 7:30. I should have told you 8:30 and then I would be early." She kissed him lightly on the cheek and asked Baxter to order her a white wine.

Hillary seemed full of energy. She had been out in California since the first week in April and would be going back in two more weeks. She finished her wine quickly and Baxter ordered her another.

"The work is tedious and boring, but the social life has been great. I've learned a lot about another industry in another part of the country. I don't ever want to work on another Thrift assignment. It's a dumb industry. They make single family residential loans during stable interest periods and they make a decent return on their money. They make loans to commercial developers and they risk everything they make on the single family residence business."

"The people in the industry are low paid, happy, and suspicious of consultants. Your friend, Friedman, watches costs like a hawk watches stray chickens. We're living two to a room in a Holiday Inn."

"McKenzie Barber has no flexibility on the per diem. The prospect of a free dinner with you was enough to bring me in from Glendale."

"I heard you played tennis with Bob," Baxter said.

"I challenged him. I'm a pretty good tennis player and I thought I'd check him out. He suggested 7 PM at his tennis club, but I knew what that would lead to. SO I got him out at seven in the morning and he drubbed me. The man is a wicked tennis player. He's also a wicked man."

"Have you socialized with Bob beyond tennis?" Baxter asked.

"No. He leaves the help pretty much alone. He's full of a lot of double entendres, but I've concluded that he's controllable. What he does away from the job is probably the stuff of legends."

Baxter showed Hillary the Grey-gram and they reminisced back to FSO.

"That was the best engagement I've worked on at McKenzie Barber and I credit you for that," Hillary said. "I've never worked for anyone at McKenzie Barber who had the skills to pull together a large group of junior people and lay out a structure where they had the latitude to perform. The engagement out here is boring and tedious compared to FSO. I'd like to work with you again while I'm still at McKenzie Barber."

"Where would you like to eat?" Baxter asked.

"Your room," Hillary answered. "I have some accessories in the shopping bag.

They rode in silence in the elevator to Baxter's floor. It was his understanding that he would be bedding down with this attractive, intelligent, full bodied young woman. Friedman had always told him that good things happened in California.

Once inside Baxter's room, Hillary stood in front of the bathroom door. "Thank you for not mussing me in the elevator. I love men that show restraint when you tell them you're prepared to sleep with them. Now call room service and order me a seafood salad and a couple of bottles of California Chardonnay while I get gussied up in my shack-up outfit."

Baxter did as he was instructed, ordering a club house sandwich for himself. He found a soft music station and took his tie off. As he waited, his mind wandered off to Beth Gold in the Duluth Hotel, Jennifer in the Pennsylvania Hotel, and the evening he had spent with Andy in Washington. His experience in hotel rooms with women was limited. The women Baxter had met with Friedman seemed to prefer oral sex in automobiles.

Hillary emerged from the bathroom in a black two piece shorty night gown, high heeled black slippers, and her suit on a hanger. "It's not Frederick's of Hollywood, but it's damned close to it. I was spirited away to Palm Springs two weekends ago and this and a swim suit appeared to be the uniform of the day." Hillary carefully hung her suit in the closet and they met near the foot of Baxter's bed and enjoyed a long wet kiss. "By the way. this is a one night stand. I will be announcing my engagement when I get back to New York after Memorial Day."

The room service knock at the door came before Baxter could fully process Hillary's statement. Hillary slipped back into the bathroom. A short Mexican man in a red jacket unfolded the room service table and fumbled through opening both bottles of wine. Baxter signed the check and tipped the waiter ten dollars to get him out of the room. Hillary emerged from the bathroom at the sound of Baxter closing the chain at the door.

"Hello again," she greeted him.

Baxter poured two glasses of wine. He could see through the thin fabric of the black gown. Her body was athletic with developed muscled arms and legs. Hillary Stone had the body of an athlete.

"Did I hear you tell me that you're about to become engaged?" Baxter asked incredulously.

"I thought I had better explain the rules to you before we went too far. I had the hots for you in Washington and again that time in the Sherry Netherland. I would have gone to bed with you both times if you would have asked me. You called me today out of the blue and asked me to dinner. I came prepared for more than dinner. But tonight is it. After Memorial Day, I will be an engaged woman, diamond ring and all. In September I will be a married woman. Therefore we can have a nice evening together and we won't have to tell each other lies."

"Best wishes for a long and happy marriage," Baxter said raising his glass in toast.

Hillary didn't raise her glass. "Put your glass down, Joe." They kissed and Baxter felt his belt being unbuckled. "And look what I found!" Hillary exclaimed.

There was sex and there were drinks of wine and occasional nibbles of food. "Let yourself go," Hillary said. "I've been on the pill since I was a college freshman."

Later, she sat in his lap in the sofa chair and they watched the television news together. "This is so nice," Hillary said kissing Baxter lightly on the cheek. "I just knew it would be like this." Hillary refilled their wine glasses. "We're getting low. You had better call up Miguel and order in new supplies." Baxter dressed and undressed again for the wine delivery and this time Hillary emerged from the bathroom naked. "It's bed time again, Joe. As you may have suspected, I'm planning to stay all night."

Around midnight, Baxter began to ask Hillary questions about her forthcoming marriage. "Who's the lucky man? Somebody with the firm?"

"His name is Craig and I've been seeing him since I was a senior at Skidmore. He finished at Tuck and then spent four years as a naval officer. Now he's with Chase and they want to send him to London in the fall. I've been talking with your friend Andy Bourke about a transfer to Barber in London. She really hasn't been much help and really got testy when I tried to make an appointment with Clyde Nickerson. I may have to terminate here and apply over there, but that seems dumb. How friendly are you with Andy? Were you two ever like this? She certainly looked daggers at me the night of the party in Washington. It was obvious to me, she wanted you all for herself."

"My relationship with Andy Bourke is quite proper and professional."

"Will you call her and tell her you ran into me in LA and I told you about my marriage and my fiancé transferring to London. See if you can get the straight skinny for me." Hillary began to fondle Baxter. "Think I can get this dog to hunt one more time?"

"I will call Andy by Friday," Baxter pledged.

"Good. Maybe we could be a two night stand. Now tell me about your wife and family. Are you naturally unfaithful or are you just very unhappy?" Hillary asked.

Baxter then told Hillary, a woman whom he hardly knew, what he had only told in edited pieces to Naomi. He began with Willard Green meeting him at graduate school and concluded the picnic one week before. He included a full account of Mr. Tom and Jennifer and his strange empty marriage.

"Oh. Joe," Hillary said when Baxter had finished his story.

"That is the saddest story I've ever heard." She wrapped her arms around Baxter and began to sob.

"Hey, I should be crying, not you," Baxter said stroking her hair.

"I don't want to leave you in the morning. This has to be a two night stand. Maybe I'm drunk, but I'm falling in love with you."

Baxter concluded that Hillary was drunk, because her words had become slurred. "How old are you, Joe?" she asked.

"I'm 39."

"And you're a Manager?"

"I've been promised a promotion to Director in October."

"Fast trackers make Director by the time they're 33 and Partner by the time they're between 36 and 38. You're on the slow track because you joined the firm so late. Craig is off to a late start because of his four years in the Navy. He's a second year man in Capital Markets at Chase. I'm 25 and I'm a second year consultant. My reviews have been good on every job I've been placed on and I will make Associate in October."

"You have two young children and probably some child support obligations coming up or two kids who will be living with you. You live in the Midwest and I like the East Coast. I also love the idea of living abroad for a couple of years. Craig is quite good looking, charming and a good lover. The problem is that I like men. I love their attention and I like to go to bed with a few of them. No." Hillary shook her head. "My future lies with Craig, not you, Joe! What time is your flight in the morning?"

"I'm on a 10:30."

"Take a later flight and love me in the morning. Hold me tonight," Hillary said and she slept in his arms with his hands on her breasts.

Baxter changed his flight and they stayed in the room until 9:30 the next morning. Hillary repacked her shopping bag and put on her pink suit. They summarized together over coffee from room service.

"I will call Andy and probe about your transfer after I get back to the office. Shall I call you in the New York office?"

"That's best. You can call me at my apartment during the week, but not on weekends. Craig is usually there on weekends. I want to sleep with you one more time before I get married, but I don't want to sleep with you after I'm married."

"Agreed," Baxter said.

"Then I must go and work on branch profitability," Hillary said getting up. Baxter opened the door and she left, shopping bag in hand.

He was packing when a loud knock on the door came five minutes later. He opened the door and found Hillary in tears.

"I don't want to leave you. Love me just a little more!" Baxter and Hillary left the room together for the last time close to noon. They stood together waiting for the doorman to get them taxis. "This isn't the end of us, Joe. We're going to have a two night stand. Do you have your Grey-gram?" she asked. Baxter produced it and Hillary began to write on the back side of the grey paper. Then she folded the Grey-gram and returned it to Baxter.

"Read it on your way out to the airport." Hillary took the first cab. He started forward to kiss her, but she shrugged him off with a quick shake of her head.

Hillary entered the taxi wearing her sun glasses and waved back to Baxter as the taxi pulled away.

Baxter unwrapped his Grey-gram on the way to the airport.

It read:

To Joe Baxter:

The presentation of this note will entitle you on demand the second night of your two night stand. This offer expires September 9, 1974 and is unlikely ever to be renewed.

I love you!
H.S.

Baxter refolded the Grey-gram and carefully buried it in the deep pocket of his brief case. He wondered if he would ever redeem the Grey-gram.

Baxter talked with Andy the following afternoon from his office in Chicago. He began the conversation with a discussion of the Grey-gram on the FSO engagement. Andy was aware that a Grey-gram had been sent and suggested that a copy be forwarded to each member of the project team.

"I had coffee with one of our consulting team members when I was out in LA. She told me she was getting married and trying to get a transfer to Barber-London," Baxter said nothing more and waited for Andy to respond.

"That sounds like Hillary Stone to me. Did she put you up to calling me?" Andy asked suspiciously.

"No. But I think you may get a call from Bob Friedman. They play tennis together."

"She's a pushy one," Andy commented. "Hillary is a political and accustomed to getting her own way. Her family is Stone Resources, big oil and gas people from Denver. I talked to London yesterday and it appears that they may be willing to take her. She's been working on these branch office profitability studies for banks and Barber-London apparently has a number of banking clients interested. It just may work. Clyde is handling this personally now, and we may have an exchange of rotational Associates. That little bitch will get her way one or the other. Did she offer to sleep with you?"

"She thinks I'm sweet on you," Baxter replied.

"If only you were, Joe. Are you aware that Naomi is leaving June 30th. She's been hired as Director of Personnel for a large Jewish medical center and she is getting married in August. I'm coming out for the party and I know you will be invited. See you, then. I've got to run," Andy said closing off.

Baxter called Hillary the first of the following week and left a message with her answering machine that things looked good for London.

Hillary called back a day later. "I miss you," she began the conversation. "I've done nothing but think about you since you left. Suppose

I come back through Chicago on my way back East on the day before Memorial Day. You told me you lived near O'Hare."

"There's a Hilton across the street from the airport. It's not as neat as the Sheraton Grande. I've still got my Grey-gram coupon."

"That's for all night. This is going to be six hours between planes," Hillary explained.

Baxter took the day before Memorial Day as a vacation day. He checked into the Hilton at 11 AM, ordered champagne, and proceeded on to the Admiral's Club to wait for Hillary. She had taken a 7 AM flight which was scheduled to land at 1 PM and was going to leave on a 8 PM flight to New York. It was the first time Baxter had entertained an airport liaison.

Hillary's flight was a half-hour late and she was one of the last passengers off the plane. She emerged in a tennis top, white trousers, athletic socks and tennis shoes. Hillary had remained heavily tanned, wore dark glasses and carried a large blue tote bag. She greeted Baxter with a radiant smile. There was no embrace. Rather she shook his hand.

"I would like a long kiss when we're in the hotel room, Joe. You never can tell who you will see at O'Hare."

"We'll slip over to the hotel through the dark back streets," Baxter said taking Hillary's tote bag which turned out to be surprisingly heavy. "You've got more than nighties in here," he observed.

It wasn't the same at the O'Hare Hilton.

They kissed in the room as soon as the door was closed. "Open the champagne, Joe. I need a shower. That was a stinking flight and the air conditioning was screwed up." Hillary emerged from the shower only after an extensive drone of her hair dryer. She wore a towel around her waist and was bare breasted. Baxter handed her a glass of champagne and they shared a light kiss. Hillary seated herself in a chair at the desk across from Baxter, who had seated himself in a stuffed chair.

"Well, Barber-London has agreed in principal to take me. Now all I have to do is marry Craig. Thanks for calling Andy."

"My call wasn't needed," Baxter explained.

"I've never done anything like this before. You know, fly half way across the country to shack up with some guy for a few hours, and then fly the other half of the country back to New York. Give me time to relax, Joe."

"I'm working on it."

"That night two weeks ago was simply too good."

"The morning was better," Baxter observed.

"I've done nothing but think about you since I caught that cab in front of the Sheraton. How about you?"

"I've thought about you too, Hillary," Baxter said. The truth was that he plunged himself back into his work and really hadn't anticipated seeing

Hillary Stone again. She was a 'political' at McKenzie Barber. Hillary was from a wealthy family who was about to announce her engagement. What future was there for her in this relationship with Baxter?"

"Do you think there's a chance for us to be long term, Joe? I felt for you in California. I thought you were neat in Washington and at the Sherry Netherland. But LA at the Sheraton Grande placed you at another level."

"How many times a year do you fall in love, Hillary?" Baxter asked and refilled her champagne glass.

"Touché! I'm always falling in love. English professors, tennis pros, consulting pool guys, associates, ski instructors, managers in my Dad's business, and now my last engagement manager. I fall in love 4.5 times a year. I'm going to be officially engaged next week. My Dad and Mom are flying in from Denver, and Craig's parents are coming down from Boston. Here I am in an airport motel room in Chicago, waiting for a big redheaded man named Joe to take off his goddam clothes and put his arms around me. I want it to be the Sheraton Grande again, because that was the best night of my life." Baxter took off his shirt and trousers and dropped to his knees in front of Hillary's chair. She dropped the towel and Baxter began to kiss her in what Doctor Barry would define as strategic places.

"This is more like it," Baxter heard Hillary sigh.

It was good, but in Baxter's estimation, not equal to the Sheraton Grande. They seemed to be attempting to repeat an experience that they could never really duplicate again. As they embraced, watches were checked, and Baxter called the desk for a wake-up call when Hillary wanted to nap. As in LA, Baxter held Hillary in his arms as she slept.

At 6:30 the telephone wake-up call came and Hillary returned to the shower. This time Baxter joined her. He sat on the toilet seat and watched Hillary blow dry her hair. She clicked off the hair dryer and leaned down to kiss Baxter.

"Joe, what if I were to call Craig and say the engagement is off. I've met this guy named Joe and I'm going to marry him. I know my parents would like you over time. We can leave McKenzie Barber and my Dad will give you a job. We'll move to Denver, or better yet Boulder, and live happily ever after. What do you think of that?"

"I don't think it will work. We barely know each other. We like having sex together. That may not be enough to get us through. You've found someone that you're matched with in Craig. You and I have had this afternoon and had better get on with our lives."

"You still have one night coming," Hillary reminded him. "And you have documentation to prove it."

They had a quick drink in the Admiral's Club and Baxter saw Hillary to her gate, H-3. "Remember, you have until September 9th, to redeem your night with me," Hillary said as she joined the line for boarding. They locked hands for a few seconds and she disappeared down the boarding ramp. Baxter assumed that this was the last time he would see Hillary Stone. There was no future for them.

In mid-June, Baxter was asked to move his department from the tenth floor to the twelfth floor of McKenzie Barber's Chicago office. This placed his practice on the same floor as the Industrial Engineering practice. A number of pool consultants were assigned to practice units in advance of the traditional October 1st promotion date. The largest group of MBA recruits in the history of the firm had been hired for July and August start dates. The Chicago office seemed bursting at its seams. Baxter's department had grown to six consultants in addition to Carl. They generally represented Pool rejects. Executive Compensation was regarded as a second class practice that churned out a lot of data and boilerplate, operating with a lot of backroom consultants. The ambitious fast track consultants competed with each other to work on the Business Strategy or Marketing engagements. Others positioned themselves for work in the Banking and Commercial practices. Still others were assigned to the IE or the Manufacturing practice for grunt work. Executive Compensation was considered the backwater of the McKenzie Barber Chicago office.

Baxter, however, had built an excellent book of business after the conclusion of his California work. His reputation in the firm had been enhanced when the word got around that the work at FSO had greatly pleased the Chairman. Baxter and Carl had initiated a sweeping spring collection of proxy statements and massaged the pay data against a number of performance variables. Baxter had the ideas, but Carl was the superb technician who could find ways to organize, tabulate and present data. Dr. Barry loved the industry reports and used them in initial corporate strategy discussions with CEOs. Dr. Barry loved to entertain CEOs with peer group analysis and Joe would then review senior management compensation against peer group analysis company management compensation. Engagements flowed from these discussions. Executives either wanted to be paid at or above their industry peers or wanted someone to rationalize their pay levels to their boards.

Alvardi wasn't always pleased with Baxter's initiatives.

"Kid, I want to see that stuff you're passing out before it gets in front of clients," Alvardi said after one of his New York people had discovered inaccuracies in some of Carl's data.

"We blew it, Frank. I'll take accountability and I'll make certain that every client gets an update. But if you believe that you have to have prior approval on everything we release, I want a 24 hour turn around," Baxter told his mentor.

"You're dictating to me, kid?" Alvardi asked with a slight edge to his voice.

"I'm not dictating, Frank. I'm asking for your assistance and support to build this Mid-Western practice."

"You're miscast, kid. You ought to be in the goddam State Department. Run everything by me on these special studies from here on in, kid," Alvardi said and he hung up.

Baxter was furious with his mentor and angry with Carl who had exposed him to criticism. An hour later, Baxter's telephone discussion with one of Dr. Barry's clients led to a $150,000 engagement, the largest fee in Baxter's consulting career.

Baxter moved to the 12th floor with a new level of individual confidence, and his practice followed him in similar spirit. Baxter was provided a Director-size office which silently confirmed his October promotion. He was now two doors from Ian Snow, the Partner-in-Charge of the Chicago IE practice. Ian Snow was a white haired, mustached Englishman in his late fifties. He was a short man who wore ill-fitting bland colored suits, but he was also a man with a command presence. He spoke softly, but people jumped into action when Mr. Ian Snow spoke. He greeted Baxter collegially on his first day on the 12th floor.

He entered Baxter's office mid-morning on the first day on the 12th floor. His jacket was off and Snow displayed braces with small golden camels on a field of blue.

"Baxter, isn't it?" he said offering his hand.

"Mr. Snow," Baxter acknowledged. "I appreciate your dropping by."

"I'm hearing good things about you, Baxter. I heard you did a ripping good job on the FSO and that you have succeeded that New York Italian fellow, Alvardi. Is he still with McKenzie Barber?"

"He's in the New York office now, Mr. Snow."

"No need to call me Mr. Snow, Baxter. Most people call me Mr. Ian. We do some pay plan work in our practice. Basic stuff, internal equity structure, point evaluation, job comparison ranking, and bonus plans. Doesn't quite have the sizzle of this stock scheme stuff you do, but I believe our chaps do a very competent job."

"I'm sure they do, Mr. Ian," Baxter responded recognizing for the first time that the IE practice represented a competitor in certain segments of clients.

"Your friend, Mr. Alvardi, wouldn't agree. He used to raise a lot of scope of practice issues. Our chaps were uncomfortable with him."

"There is plenty of work for both of our practices, Mr. Ian," Baxter observed.

"I like your attitude, young man," Mr. Ian said, and he shook Baxter's hand.

"Please use me as a resource, any time I can help," Baxter offered.

Two weeks later, a query came from one of Mr. Ian's Directors, a man named Merrill. "Joe, what do you know about Scanlon Plans?" Merrill asked.

As it turned out, the IE practice had agreed to develop a Scanlon Plan for a manufacturing company in Cleveland and the plan construct was wobbling. Could Baxter take a look at it? The plan was not a complete mess, but required considerable tuning. The plan construct was mechanical and inflexible. Baxter remembered the axiom that Alvardi had taught him on the first week in Executive Compensation.

"These plans have to pay off, kid!"

Baxter tactfully reviewed what the IE practice had produced and tuned it into a plan that would deliver. He was asked to assist in the final presentation, and wound up presenting most of the oral report of recommendations. The report was well accepted by the client and Baxter had not charged an hour of his time into their engagement. His reputation was made with the Chicago IE practice.

As the summer months warmed into July and August, Baxter began to develop a rapport with Ian Snow. Both tended to work long hours during their days at the office. Mr. Ian, after seven o'clock liked to pad around his office in his stocking feet.

Mr. Ian would call Baxter late in the evening and summon him down, presumably to look over something. It was usually a pay system of some kind. Then he would ask Baxter to join him in a cup of tea which he brewed on a hot plate in his office closet. At first, Baxter believed the old man had some kind of hidden agenda and wanted to test or probe him. Later Baxter concluded that Mr. Ian was simply lonely and had taken a liking to his new floor neighbor.

They started having chats in Mr. Ian's office. The chats generally lasted 20 or 30 minutes and then they would return to their offices and work. When one would leave, he would go by the other's office, announce they were leaving and bid the other good night. One night, Mr. Ian paused in front of Baxter's door. "Joe, how about a spot of supper?" They had dinner together that evening for the first time. Mr. Ian lived in a near Northside Hotel called Hampton Court and liked the hotel dining room.

"You live alone in a hotel room?" Baxter asked.

"I used to live in Barrington, but I moved downtown after my wife passed away so that I could be closer to the office. I have a small suite and can prepare things when I choose to. There's daily maid service. All my needs are looked after. I'm really very comfortable here," Mr. Ian affirmed as he scanned the menu in a small mirrored hotel dining room.

"Do you have children, Mr. Ian?" Baxter asked.

"I have a son who teaches Economics at the University of Oregon and a daughter who is Director of Nursing for a hospital in San Antonio, Texas. It's called St. Something or other. They are good children and they have begat grandchildren to whom I am obligated to send presents and cards on their birthdays and holidays. What do you say that we share a bottle of wine, Joe?"

Mr. Ian was a discerning selector of wines and discussed every entry on the wine list before making a selection of a Merlot.

"How long have you been with the firm, Mr. Ian?" Baxter asked.

"36 years tomorrow. That is, with credit for my military service. I'm a Barber man, you know."

"Then you joined Barber before the war?"

"August 5, 1938 I was hired as a Methods Engineer Consultant at the same time as the Anschluss. The war, of course came a year later, and I wound up as a supply officer. I became very good at organizing retreats and later I became skilled at supporting advances. I got out in 1945 and was sent over here on a six month assignment in the Liquor Industry and have been here ever since."

"Then you knew John McKenzie?" Baxter asked.

"Everyone knew Mr. Mac in those days, Joe. He was everywhere at once. he was a marvelous man, Joe. I wish you could have met him. Mr. Mac was gentle, but firm. I met Barber too. He was crisp and bright, but the war ruined him. Mr. Mac handled the war years in his stride and emerged stronger."

Wine was served and they clinked glasses. "We were essentially an Industrial Engineering firm after the war. We knew how to identify efficiency issues and how to solve them. Then this Robson-Allen-Harbridge bunch emerged and they wanted to solve all the problems of the world through linear programming and pay-back analysis. They were simply mechanics at a different level. They bothered Mr. Mac. He considered them the new wave of management consultants."

"Were you in the Chicago office, then?" Baxter asked.

"New York! I was in New York until 1962. Harvey Randolph invited me out to run the Chicago IE practice after he came up from Atlanta. I will finish out my career in Chicago."

"Did you watch Ernie Grey coming up?" Baxter asked.

"Chairman Grey was one of a number of bright young men who came to the firm right out of business school after World War II. They all looked the same to me. They were bright-eyed and ambitious after tying up three or four years of their careers in the service of their country. In some ways, they represented the best generation of Americans. I haven't seen a better one since. Chairman Grey became one of Mr. Mac's Executive Assistants. Generally they stayed a year on that job and then returned to a practice. Chairman Grey stayed and stayed, and it was obvious that Mr. Mac had taken a fancy to him. Then he was promoted to head the Banking practice. Chairman Grey hired a number of good people and called on all the friends of his father. Chairman Grey's father had been President of a large Philadelphia bank which certainly helped his acceptance as a consulting resource. He was really more of a salesman than he was a consultant. After a year or so, Chairman Grey was elected a Partner. Many of us thought at the time, that he was too young and inexperienced but Mr. Mac had his way just as Chairman Grey has had his way now. Shortly after becoming a Partner, Chairman Grey was positioned as Chief Administrative Partner for the firm, and three months later, Mr. Mac managed to install Chairman Grey as the operating partner of the firm. As a testimony to Mr. Mac's cleverness, the old line partners never saw Chairman Grey coming. He wasn't taken that seriously and then suddenly he was the senior partner and our lives and McKenzie Barber were changed forever."

"Then Ernie Grey succeeded Mr. Mac?" Baxter asked to keep the conversation going.

"Joe? Haven't you attended the catechism classes they hold for the Pool Consultants during their first two years?" Mr. Ian questioned Baxter. Baxter went on to explain how he had missed the training and had worked exclusively for Dwyer initially and now in Alvardi's practice since joining the firm seven years earlier.

"Excellent, Joe," Mr. Ian said. "Then you haven't heard all the fibs and myths that Chairman Grey has invented about himself. The roundtable training sessions are the brain child of Mr. Nickerson. I suspect he brought the concept here from Pennsylvania Steel. Of course everyone will look at the same set of events from a different perspective. I have my own personal historical perspective of the rise of our Chairman. Let me ask you first. How much time have you spent with Chairman Grey?"

"I was in a conference room with him for two hours presenting the FSO report and I received a Grey-gram from him this Spring. That's it. Dwyer and Alvardi talk a lot about him."

"Neither one of those two gentlemen have what I would call an informed opinion. They are outsiders and the personal selections of Chairman Grey who brought them in to McKenzie Barber in order to befuddle us. Your Mr. Dwyer is a brilliant unstable eccentric with the morals of the gutter. I regard Mr. Alvardi as a car salesman." Mr. Ian's eyes were bright and deadly and Baxter made a note never again to bring up either Alvardi or Dwyer in the old man's presence.

"Mr. Mac was willing to work until he was 75. He wanted to build a powerful world-wide management consulting firm and the depression and the war slowed him down, so the time from 1945 until 1955 was critical to put into motion the foundation for the McKenzie Barber of the 1970s. The people who had stuck it out with the firm through the 1930s and the 1940s were old, rigid, and worn out. There I was, a young Brit, over here working on a distribution study for Glen Roy Scotch Whiskey. It was supposed to last a month, but I found some fraud and wound up working with their auditors and pretty soon one month became six. I guess Mr. Mac started to wonder what was taking me so long to finish the job, so he invited me out for one of his breakfasts. Mr. Mac had a business breakfast with someone six days a week. He picked Saturday for me. He wanted to know every detail of the Glen Roy job and he was mad as hell that no one had told him about the fraud. I made the mistake of telling him that I regarded myself as a Barber man and that the Glen Roy job was Barber business. The old man hit the ceiling and blistered me. His soft voice thundered that morning.

"'Young man!' says he to me. 'All of our business is McKenzie Barber business and I expect to be fully informed about matters such as this when I have allowed you to work in the United States.'"

"Then he started to check me out on my qualifications and I knew I was in the deepest of troubles. Our breakfast lasted two hours and Mr. Mac finally called for the check and looked me coldly in the eye. 'Ian, why don't you stay over here? We can use you on this side of the pond.'"

"That's the way it was with Mr. Mac. He told me he'd see that I was a partner before he retired. That was back in 1947 and I was a partner by 1950. McKenzie Barber needed experienced consultants at the time. They needed men who could run large engagements. We had old men and bright young men and there I was, in my early 30s with heavy logistics background and I had run engagements for a couple of years. Mr. Mac, had more work than men to run the engagements. He was determined never to have this problem again. That's when the first training classes were developed and people like Chairman Grey entered the firm."

"Mr. Mac went as Senior Partner in those days. A partnership was something a man worked very hard to achieve and he was nominated and elected by his partners, and then expected to contribute his capital and work like hell. The highest honor you could receive in those days was to be elected to the Board of Directors. I was elected to the Board in 1953. I was under forty and running a large practice for the firm. The Board was a rubber stamp for Mr. Mac. He had seen to it that we were elected and he wanted us to stay together and run the firm if something happened to him.

He was 73 then and knew time was running short to pick a successor. He said that his choice was Paul Reynolds, but thought he would need someone who could back him up administratively. 'Young Grey should be able to do that nicely,' Mr. Mac informed us."

"We all sat around the table and looked at each other. Grey was a bright young man, but he really hadn't distinguished himself as a consultant in most of our minds. Outside of the banking practice, the only thing we could remember was that Grey was Mr. Mac's personal secretary for years. Everyone agreed that he was bright, smart, and fair in administrative matters, and Reynolds was a man in his early fifties. He could run the firm and then someone in the room could step forward and run the firm after a term of five years."

"Paul Reynolds was a good professional consultant who hated to be in the office. He traveled a good deal and left the administration of the firm to Grey. Paul liked a good time and smoked a lot. We elected him Senior Partner in 1956 and Mr. Mac retired. He continued to come in the office every day, but he was beginning to look tired. A year or so later, Reynolds was diagnosed with cancer and he went fast. The Board met with Mr. Mac and Mr. Mac asked Grey to excuse himself and talked us into supporting Grey."

"Grey was elected Senior Partner in 1960, and he was seven years younger than me. He took control of the Board from the first day and began to manipulate his own directors to the Board. He wanted me out of New York and sent Harvey Randolph up from Atlanta to Chicago. When I got to Chicago, it was concluded that we had too much Chicago office representation on the Board. Mr. Mac called me from his retirement in San Diego and asked me personally if I would mind stepping down for a term. Mr. Mac assured me that Grey would put me back on when the terms ended in five years. I was never nominated again and I knew that I would finish my career in Chicago. That was twelve years ago, and they have been fine years."

"Chairman Grey, as he became in 1966, began to change the firm. I give him credit for some fine contributions. He turned Europe around. Opened up Germany, got us into computer consulting, forced the operating offices to grow, elevated his people into power. He brought in Nickerson to be his court Rasputin, started hiring the children of client executives, and hired women consultants. Now don't get me wrong about women, Joe. I was a husband and I fathered a daughter that I'm very proud of. I've had some excellent secretaries over the years and have known a number of very competent office administrators, but women do not belong in consulting serving clients. It's bad enough to make use of these shavetail MBAs, but when you're asked to use women in plant consulting, we've gone too far."

"Now I understand that you were very effective using a team that was heavily comprised of women on the FSO review. Now Joe, you had women and men together staying in the same hotels, were there any improprieties during that engagement?"

"Not that I was aware of," Baxter answered.

Mr. Ian shook his head. "Women don't belong in management consulting. There is a place for women like Lorna King. She is very thoughtful and competent. But she is up from secretarial and recognizes her limitations. Shall we have another bottle, Joe?" Mr. Ian offered and Baxter accepted.

"How does the partnership work?" Baxter asked.

"What do you mean by that, Joe?"

"Who owns the firm?" Baxter asked.

"The partners. Each partner is awarded units of interest based on what the Board believes is his level of contribution. There is a capital deposit required from each partner based on the number of units he holds. At the end of the year, the profits are distributed according to the number of units held by each partner. Unit holdings are adjusted up and down each year according to the perceived contribution of each partner. The unit allocation is highly politicized and the Board decides on the units. Then you are really dealing with five firms. McKenzie Barber in the US. Barber UK, Barber France, Barber Canada, and Barber Latin America. Standing out there by itself is FSO which is a corporation owned by the McKenzie Barber partners that Mr. Mac bought in February 1950 as a favor to the government. All of the firms belong to an umbrella partnership which is largely a ceremonial organization which meets once a year and usually makes a good boondoggle for the Board and their wives. Chairman Grey runs all of it along with his entourage. He has run McKenzie Barber for fourteen years. In October 1975 he will run unopposed for Chairman again and will be re-elected for a fourth term. He will then be 59 years of age. Most firms have a mandatory retirement age of 58 and a successor named by age 56. McKenzie Barber does not. Unless there are revisions in the bylaws, Chairman Grey can work as long as Mr. Mac."

"What's your prediction, Mr. Ian?" Baxter asked.

"My prediction is that by 1980, it will be clear to everyone who Chairman Grey's choice will be. There will be a two or three year transition period and there will be an election in 1983 or 1984 before the completion of Chairman Grey's 1980-1985 term. My comment is that twenty to twenty five years is a damned long for a man to run an organization. If I were Chairman Grey, I would pick my successor in the next three years, install him a Deputy Chairman around 1978, and step down in 1980. Twenty years should be enough for any man."

"Who will succeed Ernie Grey?" Baxter asked.

"I have no idea nor do I care. I will have retired. Perhaps I'll live on an island with an airport. I have a theory, Joe. I believe that none of today's front runners will make it unless Chairman Grey should suddenly die. I suspect that Chairman Grey will pick out some young comer and groom him. I guarantee you that the next Chairman will not come from the IE practice. He regards us as dinosaurs. We just stay around, take up space, and make money year after year."

Dinner consumed, they clinked glasses one more time. The second bottle had been finished. "I've enjoyed this, Joe. It's been my kind of dinner. I've talked and you've listened."

"What advice do you have for me and for my future career at McKenzie Barber?" Baxter asked.

"Advice? I'll give you some advice. Stay here in the Chicago office and build a practice and stay away from New York. You will earn a good living and certainly be a partner one day. Serve your clients well and stay aloof from the politics of the firm if you can." Mr. Ian rose from the table and held out his hand. "It's been a good night, Joe, so now it's good-night."

Mr. Ian's office was dark for two days before the news was out. He had died in his sleep sometime during the evening after the night they had dinner. Ernie Grey came in for the funeral service and sat in the front pew with Mr. Ian's son and daughter. Baxter wondered if they knew the way the old man felt about Ernie Grey. He wound up drinking with Lee Heller at the Tip Top Tap at the Allerton.

"Ian Snow certainly was a strange old bird," Lee commented.

"He was a rebel from another time. He had been a Board member once," Baxter explained.

"Board Member? When the hell was that?" Lee asked.

"In the late 1950s. He was one of the Board members who elected Ernie. Ian Snow was once a power in this firm."

"Joe, I don't know how you do it," Lee said. "I didn't think you had a snowball's chance in hell of lasting longer than a year here. Now you're the firm historian and I saw Ernie go out of his way to shake your hand. He still doesn't know who I am. This Fall you're going to be promoted to Director and you will be even with me."

"We're not in a race, Lee," Baxter said.

"We are to win a race, Joe. The clock is running on us. I've got to see a way through to Partnership in the next year or I'm dead."

"You need clients, Lee," Baxter counseled him.

"I need sponsorship. Any idiot can get clients." Baxter asked for the check.

Hillary Stone did not go away after Memorial Day. Rather she became a frequent correspondent. She wrote to Baxter far more frequently than Jennifer. Her correspondence generally came in the form of contemporary greeting cards with short notes. In July she sent a New York Times clipping of her wedding announcement complete with photographs. Craig was a handsome young man with a bright smile. Hillary's hair was shoulder length and she wore a white dress with a V neck. Baxter had from time to time over the years brushed by the society section of the New York Times. This represented the first time he could point to someone he had slept with.

Other times there were little notes on creamy blue paper printed in elegant calligraphic quality letters.

> Dear JB:
>
> I'm taking the summer off to prepare for the wedding and am scheduled to start at Barber London on October 1st. The wedding will be in Denver and I'm going to put Mr. and Mrs. Joseph Baxter, Jr. on the invitation list. Please send a nice gift.
>
> HS

Dear JB:

I'm mad for you! Why don't you find an excuse to fly into Denver and we can accomplish what we did at O'Hare at Stapleton. The Stouffer Inn should be just right. You can write me back C/O P.O. Box 1974 B, Denver, Colorado, 30329.

HS

> Dear JB:
>
> Why in the hell haven't you written me? I need to see you one more time. (Maybe two more times. Maybe for the rest of my life!) I just may show up in Racine for the weekend. Be forewarned!
>
> HS

Baxter was settled into his life without Jennifer. She sent post cards to the children each week and Celeste, the au pair, had proven to be a quiet vegetarian who dressed herself in sweat shirts and jeans and spoke very precisely. She was cheerful around the children and called Baxter, Mr.

Baxter. Her only vice seemed to be the marijuana cigarettes she smoked in the evening in her third floor sewing room bedroom.

Agnes resented Celeste and referred to her as the Hippie. She remained Baxter's evening drinking buddy and they continued to listen to classical music together on Friday night.

Baxter generally arrived from Chicago at the house on Palmer Street Friday nights around eight o'clock. On the first Friday night in August, he worked late and didn't arrive until close to nine o'clock. He noticed a white Pontiac in the driveway that he hadn't seen previously.

Agnes greeted Baxter at the front door. "That girl from your company is here. She brought the package, but wants to go over it with you first," Agnes said knowingly. "She's in with the children watching television now. She's a very nice young lady."

Baxter said nothing and walked directly to Mr. Tom's old study which had been converted into a downstairs family room. Hillary was sitting with Joel and Muffin in a recliner chair watching television.

"Daddy!" they greeted Baxter. "Hillary's brought you a package and she's going to be in Racine all weekend." Hillary was wearing a white Colorado sweatshirt, blue shorts, sweat socks and tennis shoes. She was heavily tanned and held Muffin in her lap.

"So you brought the package," Baxter said.

"Yes, Mr. Baxter," she said rising up from her chair. "And I have been getting to know your wonderful children. I have business here this weekend and would like you all to be my guest at lunch tomorrow including my new friend Agnes."

"Well, we should go upstairs and go over the package right away," Baxter said. "You guys can be up for thirty more minutes and then you must go to bed."

Hillary picked up a large manila envelope and followed Baxter up the stairs to the second floor sitting room. "This is quite a house, Joe. It's the kind of place where they film Dracula movies."

Baxter guided Hillary inside the doorway of the master bedroom. "What in hell are you doing?" he whispered.

"I've come to see you and meet your kids. It's been over two months and I've been going crazy for you. I write, but you don't write back. I've called a couple of times, but didn't leave my name. I packed a bag and checked out one of the staff cars from my Dad's company and drove up to see you. One month from now, I'll be married. I want a weekend with you!"

"You can't stay here!" was all Baxter could think of saying. Hillary was fresh-faced, attractive, and full bodied. She was far too delicious looking to send away, Baxter decided.

"I've checked into a motel two miles down the road. It's called the Deer Lake Inn," Hillary explained. "I expect that you will sleep there with me tonight."

"I expect that I will be there to redeem my Grey-gram."

"This doesn't count toward the Grey-gram. You have one more night after this weekend."

There was a soft kiss and then a longer one. Baxter placed his hand under Hillary's sweatshirt and touched her nipples.

"Jesus I want you, Joe," Hillary said.

"What's in the manila envelope?" Baxter asked.

"The sexiest black night gown you've ever seen, buster."

They got the children off to bed and drank coffee and brandy with Agnes while listening to the classical station.

"Well, I have no idea what you two do at that McCarthy-Barber place, but it must be very important for Hillary to drive here all the way from Colorado," Agnes concluded after her second glass of brandy.

"Agnes, I had other business here in Racine, so this was very convenient," Hillary lied.

Baxter knew from Agnes's face that she was not buying any of Hillary's story. When Hillary excused herself to use the bathroom, Agnes looked at Baxter. "Hillary's a nice young lady and she's in love with you, Joe. She's also good with children. How old is she?"

"25 or 26."

"How old are you?"

"39."

"She comes from a good home. I can tell." They sat in silence listening to Dvorak. "I'll watch the children this weekend, Joe. You're a lonely man. You spend some time with this Hillary this weekend. She's young, but I think she's better for you than the Misses."

They spent the evening at the Deer Lake Motel and Hillary changed into a black sheer shorty nightgown complete with a garter belt, black stockings and spiked heels. "Now Joe, if I don't look like a hooker right this minute, I never will."

"You look great, but you could have come out in a towel and looked just as good," he said.

"I thought I'd pull out all the stops tonight. I want you to ask me to marry you by Sunday afternoon. Time is running out for us, Joe."

It proved to be one of the happier weekends of Baxter's life. Baxter left the Deer Lake Motel at 5 AM and Hillary was back at Palmer Street with sweet rolls and coffee by 9 AM. They spent the day with the children, and had a picnic at the Deer Lake grounds in the afternoon. Large Indian blankets were spread out on the grass and Agnes accompanied them. They drank beer, listened to the classical station on Agnes's radio and watched the sailboats glide across the Deer Lake. Some of the former Caribou Street Plant workers were on the grounds and they came by, one by one, to say hello.

They had different jobs now and hated the British owners from Henry Wiggins who had moved the jobs to Mississippi. They greeted Baxter cheerfully and shook his hand. They had heard Baxter was doing well with some big company in Chicago. Was he still playing basketball? How was Jennifer? No one stayed long and Baxter introduced Hillary as the children's governess.

One maintenance man named Cal lingered on. He was in his early fifties and wore a billied cap. "It worked out for me, Joe. I caught on with Case, but a lot of fellas never picked it up again. The family should have looked out for us. Instead they looked out for themselves. I know you stuck up for us and walked out when you found out what those British bastards were up to." Baxter nodded and waited for Cal to go away.

"And where are you from Miss?" Cal asked Hillary.

"I'm Agnes's niece from Spokane." With that, Cal tipped his hat, shook hands again with Baxter, and walked away slowly across the picnic grounds. Joel and Muffin were twenty yards away at the swing sets and it was a balmy Wisconsin Saturday afternoon."

"You two are a pair," Agnes said after a swig of beer. "That will be all over the shop tomorrow at Case and will work its way back to the Washburns," Agnes scolded them.

"I really don't care what the Washburns think," Hillary said.

Agnes pushed her bulk to her feet. "This one's like a son to me," she said brushing Baxter's head with her hand. "I'm going to see after those children. We should think about going home soon so the whole town doesn't have to meet my niece from Spokane."

"She's a dear," Hillary observed. "Very loyal to you and the children and she hates Jennifer. Those men really seemed to like you, Joe."

"It may have been the best job I ever had, but the company was poorly run. I may have let them down when I left. But they were well paid and taken care of by the family for years and had come to expect it. Mr. Tom liked to make all the rules and in return he was very paternalistic. He had no successor trained to run the business when he had his stroke, and then they made a poor choice when they hired Willard."

"And you went to become a McKenzie Barber man and stole my heart at FSO and now I want you for my man," she whispered.

"Hillary, for the sake of argument, suppose the two of us get together. How in the world can you extricate yourself from all of your commitments?" Baxter asked.

"I've thought about that. I will call Craig first and say that I just can't go through with it right now. Then I will call my Dad and Mom and tell them I can't go through with the wedding. I will then tell McKenzie Barber, I'm not coming back and will move in with you in Chicago. You will start working on your divorce and we will be married in two years time. The children will live with us and we will have two more to go with these two. My parents will take me back into the fold after I start producing children and maybe Dad will find a job for you in the company."

It was all so simple to Hillary, and it seemed so slapdash to Baxter.

After dropping off Agnes and the children, Baxter drove Hillary by the Deer Lake offices and the Caribou Street plant. They settled in at Bud's and danced to the juke box, but the selection had changed.

"Where are we going, Joe?" Hillary asked on the dance floor.

"I've got to know. I can deal with those children. They're nice kids. I want to be your wife. I know we can work things out. But I know I've got to call things off next week or I'm stuck. I want to spend the rest of my life with you."

"Hillary, if I were to settle down with you, we would have a scandal on our hands. You are engaged. I am a married man with children. My career at McKenzie Barber would be tainted. You're a political! Your father's company is a client! Your fiancé will be embarrassed and furious."

"Goddamit, Joe. We're right for each other and you won't step up and claim me!" Hillary began to cry and demanded. "Take me to the motel and get out of my life! Right now!"

There was no embrace or kiss at the end of the evening. Hillary slammed the door of his car shut. Baxter called her three times that evening, but there was no answer. He tried again first thing in the morning, but was informed that Miss Stone had checked out.

In November, Baxter received a wedding announcement, Stephens/Stone nuptials from the Denver Post in a Barber London envelope. Written across the top of the clipping in green felt tip pen was;

You Fool!

Life continued forward for Baxter. His practice grew from the dual synergy with the Strategic Planning practice and the IE practice. He now had ten consultants busy and was promoted to Director effective October 1st. His interest in Lorna King continued to develop. They had a long talk at the promotion party during the first week of October.

The promotion party was an annual ceremony at McKenzie Barber. Promotions were made only once a year with the firm. Partners were usually welcomed into the firm at a country club dinner with their wives. The other promotions were celebrated at the Chicago office promotion party generally held in a party room at the Palmer House. There were always a number of

Associate promotions, several Managers, and a few Directors. This year Baxter had been promoted to Director which was portrayed as a Partner-in-waiting. The party was paid for by the promotees and Lorna King organized the event.

Partners like Paul Brimmer, Mark LoveJoy, and Dr. Barry stayed for one drink and then departed. After that it was an Associates party. They were escaping from the Pool and the room was full of drunken congratulations. Carl, who had been promoted to Manager, was feeling his oats and passing on career advice to the newly minted Associates. Baxter had brought his people together that afternoon and counseled them not to group together, but get out and mix and build their network relationships.

He found Lorna King sitting at a table in the corner nursing a club soda.

"Good party," Baxter greeted her. "Is anyone sitting here?" There was an empty chair across from Lorna with a half-filled glass.

"Mark LoveJoy was sitting there and I believe he left." Lorna looked tired. She wore a brown wool suit and matching brown pumps and her hair was pinned up.

"Mind if I sit down?" Baxter asked.

"Why not? It's your party." Lorna answered coldly.

"Anything wrong?" Baxter asked.

"What do you think of the hors d'oeuvres?"

"They're fine. Not great, but certainly adequate."

"I've had three of those young twirp new Associates come up to me and complain about the hors d'oeuvres. Are they getting noisier every year? It seemed to me that they used to be quieter. God, I get tired of being the housemother at these things."

"It's six to seven-thirty, isn't it?" Baxter asked.

"The piano player quits at seven and I'll be lucky to get them out of here by 8:15. I've got a cold and a headache and I don't feel like being at a party."

Baxter started to get up from the table and Lorna reached out and caught his hand. "Stay and keep me company, Joe. I'm sorry I was so grumpy."

Baxter sat down again. "Congratulations," Lorna said.

"I've heard that before tonight," Baxter replied.

"You seem to be making a name for yourself. I arrange the new Partner parties too, but I sit outside at a desk and make certain everything's served properly. Here I just sit here and listen to them. I would prefer sitting outside at a desk. In about twenty minutes the Directors and the Managers will begin to leave and I'll be stuck with a room full of hard-drinking Associates and Consultants. They will be told 'last call' at 7:15 and they will load up on drinks and hang around 8:15. Then they will go off to dinner together and some of them will go off to bed together. We have a number of

115

shipboard romances this year in the pool. Tomorrow none of them will be good for anything. I told Brimmer we should have the party on Friday night, but he believes they are entitled to a work night and that he couldn't get the Partners to show up for one drink on a Friday night. Now that I've told you all my problems, I feel better, Joe, and my headache is starting to go away. May I ask you to bring me something from the bar. Possibly a white wine spritzer."

The evening progressed exactly as Lorna had predicted.

The piano player left at 7:00, last call was announced at 7:15, and the Associates and the Consultants lingered until 8:00 when Lorna had the waiter flicker the lights.

"Will you let me buy you a promotion dinner?" Baxter asked.

"I just want to go home, Joe. I don't want a late evening tonight. Why don't you come out to Sonny's on Saturday night. You can buy me a drink there. Sonny can use the business."

"What's playing?" Baxter asked.

"Nothing's playing, but Buddy and I are doing songs from Company in a cabaret show."

"What's Company?" Baxter asked.

"Come out and see us and Buddy and I can take you on a musical tour of Stephen Sondheim."

Baxter stood and waited for Lorna as she talked to the hotel people and signed bar checks.

"Are you seeing anyone, now?" he asked when Lorna returned.

"I'm always seeing someone, Joe."

"Do you have room for one more admirer?" Baxter asked.

"Are you still unhappily married?"

"My wife's staying in Europe through the Spring. I have live-in people and I'm quite alone."

"The man with the phantom's wife who lives in Racine and goes off to Europe. You've been here seven years and no one has seen your wife."

"She's not much for socializing. She's a dwarf and sensitive about her size," Baxter said.

"A dwarf wife. I'll put that along side your peanut butter caviar sandwich. I'm not clever enough to make this kind of patter tonight. Come out and see me at Sonny's."

Lorna put her coat on without Baxter's assistance and gave him a sad smile when she said goodnight.

Baxter visited Sonny's Supper Club for the first time on the second Saturday in October of 1974. He told Agnes, Celeste, and the children that he had a meeting in Chicago which would run late, and that he might have to stay over. Agnes saw Baxter out the front door and whispered through her soft brandy breath, "Are you going out to see that young Hillary?"

"No that's over," Baxter said.

He drove his car out of the driveway after taking one last look at the directions Lorna had provided. He was coming in the back way. South from Racine as opposed to west from Chicago. Baxter had stopped Lorna in the hallway the week before and asked, "Where's that place again?"

"What place?" she asked although Baxter sensed from her eyes that she knew precisely which place he meant.

"The place where you sing on the weekends."

"Sonny's! I'll write you the directions," Lorna had said leading Baxter into a darkened Associate's cubicle, flipping the light switch and sketching directions on a legal pad that had been left behind on the desk.

"It's a fairly large complex and you want to go in the dinner theatre entrance. Buddy and I are playing in the Cabaret which opens up to the dinner theatre. We are between shows right now. We open up Bells Are Ringing in December. Buddy and I have been doing a Sondheim show since Labor Day. I sing on the weekends and Buddy plays piano Monday through Thursday in the Cabaret. Buddy and I have sung together since high school."

"High school sweethearts?" Baxter suggested.

"Most definitely," Lorna sketched the highway cut-off from Interstate 94. "You'll be coming in the back way."

Baxter looked over her shoulder as Lorna sketched. Was her hair red-brownish or reddish-brown? It was pinned up as usual, revealing her graceful and regal neck. Her hands were long, elegant and perfectly lacquered. Lorna had been Alvardi's mistress. Could Baxter be next?

"There are a series of billboards, both east and west on 12. They will practically guide you." Lorna passed the yellow sheet to Baxter. "The first show starts at 9. Will you be bringing a guest and will you be coming on Friday or Saturday night?"

"I'm coming alone on Saturday and I'll be there for the first show," Baxter committed.

"I'll tell Sal, the maitre'd to save you a stool at the bar right in front of the piano. They serve food at the bar on weekends. You'll never get a table for one and you should call ahead one week in advance for a table if you're going to bring someone."

"I'll take the stool in front of the piano," Baxter said.

Baxter picked up Highway 12 in Wisconsin and saw his first Sonny's sign on the Wisconsin side.

SONNY'S SUPPER CLUB & MOTEL

LAKESIDE ROOMS, GOURMET FOOD, BROADWAY STYLE ENTERTAINMENT, 24 HOUR COFFEE SHOP, INDOOR POOL
12 Miles

DINE AT SONNY'S SUPPER CLUB. BUDDY MANCINI AT THE KEYBOARD SIX NIGHTS A WEEK
8 Miles

SONNY'S SUPPER CLUB
HEAR BUDDY AND LORNA IN THE CABARET
SING YOUR FAVORITE BROADWAY TUNES
4 Miles

SONNY'S SUPPER CLUB & MOTEL, GOURMET FOOD!
BROADWAY STYLE ENTERTAINMENT!
BELLS ARE RINGING-DEC.
BUDDY & LORNA IN THE CABARET
2 Miles

SONNY'S SUPPER CLUB
1 Mile on Left

It was an enormous complex. Baxter's mental image of Sonny's had been that of a grey stucco roadhouse with a green roof which was situated next to a line of motel cabins. The coffee house jutted out to meet the road and there was a neon sign that flashed "Open 24 Hours". To the left of the coffee shop, set back against the lake was a two story piece of Tyrolean style architecture with a marquee sign that stated;
Ask about Sonny's Honeymoon Special!
The supper club was located to the right of the coffee shop and had a full parking lot. Baxter parked to the far rear and entered the Supper Club entrance as instructed. He was greeted by an attractive, dark haired Italian girl at a maitre'd's stand.
"Cabaret Show. There should be a stool for me at the bar," Baxter said. "My name's Baxter."
The girl scanned a list. "Oh yes, Mr. Baxter. You're Mr. Alvardi's friend. Go to your right, past the coat check, and Sal will seat you."
Sal was a heavy set fortyish man in a tuxedo who stood in front of the cabaret entrance. He shook hands with Baxter.
"Lorna told me to expect you, Mr. Baxter. She said you were a good friend of Mr. Alvardi." His voice was coarse, but polite. "Right this way please."

The Cabaret was separated from the main dining room by a sliding wall which on this evening, was open.

"This is your first time here?" Sal asked when they drew up to the last stool at the bar. The stool directly faced a large piano, some microphones, and a small parquet dance floor. "That's the main stage at the end of the dining room. We put on full dinner shows. Bells Are Ringing is opening in four weeks. We close up this wall when we have a show going. Until then we have Buddy and Lorna doing their cabaret show."

"Will Lorna be in Bells Are Ringing?" Baxter asked.

Sal shrugged his shoulders. "Lorna's trying to make up her mind. We got a new artistic director from San Francisco and rehearsals begin next week."

"I understand they're playing songs from Company."

"Their show changed a little. They play a lot of this guy, Sondheim's music. Sonny doesn't care for all of the lyrics."

"Mr. Alvardi was a regular customer?" Baxter asked.

"Until he moved out to New York, he was out here every Friday and Saturday night. You're going to be sitting on his stool." Sal motioned for the bartender, a short Italian man with slick hair covering a bald spot. "Gino, this is Mr. Baxter. He's a good friend of Mr. Alvardi. Take good care of him. Have a good evening. I'll bring Sonny by later to say hello. He really likes Mr. Alvardi."

Baxter ordered a Canadian Club and a steak sandwich from Gino and watched the main dining room and cabaret fill with customers. His watch said 8:25. Baxter had thirty-five minutes to wait. As he studied the crowd, Baxter concluded there was something unusual about the patrons. The table groupings of four or more were primarily Italians. The couples appeared to be men ten to fifteen years older than Baxter, with young women in their twenties.

Gino served Baxter his drink. "The steak will be served right after the intermission of the first show. Is that okay with you, Mr. Baxter?"

"Gino, where do all of these people come from?" Baxter asked.

"From all over and they've been coming here for years. Sonny opened up after the war. I've been here since 1947. Never worked no place else. The crowd's mostly small business men and working people, some honeymooners, and a few guys with something going on the side. I take it you work with Lorna because Mr. Alvardi did. First time I saw him, I thought it was Joe DiMaggio. We serve good food, full drinks, and put on a nice show. Buddy and Lorna are a show all by themselves. But we put on these big musicals. There's an orchestra and that whole stage up there is filled with singers and dancers. We got Bells Are Ringing coming up. People say that the stuff we put on here is every bit as good as a Broadway show. I ain't never been to Broadway, but I know the entertainment here is damned good and professional." Gino moved away to serve the other customers. The bar was reasonably short with only five other stools, and there was a large service area at the end of the bar with waitresses scurrying back and forth bringing empty glasses and leaving with full ones.

The lights darkened by the piano and Baxter saw a figure carry out something that looked like a bar stool from a side door. Then two figures emerged in the dark from the same door and they stood in silence behind the piano. One was a woman in a cocktail dress with a full skirt while the other was a man of medium height in a white dinner jacket. A spotlight suddenly beamed on the empty high backed bar stool and Sal, the maitre'd, brushed by Baxter, stepped into the light, and picked up a microphone from the piano.

"Ladies and gentlemen! Sonny's Supper Club proudly presents for your entertainment pleasure, our own, Buddy and Lorna! Please welcome them!" Sal led the applause and stepped from the light. The spotlight moved to the man in the dinner jacket who was now seated behind the piano. A piano roll was played and Lorna moved to the stool wearing a beaming smile. She perched on the stool with a microphone in her hand and they began to sing.

"Phone rings, door chimes, in comes company!"

Buddy and Lorna were crisp and good together. Lorna was no longer the proper lady who wore the high necked dresses at McKenzie Barber. She alternatively changed her personality from song to song singing the part of the naive flight attendant in 'Barcelona' to the cynical matron in 'Here's to the Ladies Who Lunch'. They did about thirty minutes of Company. Then Buddy announced that they had some requests. Lorna sang Little Things Mean A Lot, and Buddy sang and played Stardust. Baxter tried to smile at Lorna, but she seemed to look through him. They closed with Lorna singing It Never Entered My Mind. There was long applause and Buddy and Lorna bowed twice. The spot was turned off and Baxter's steak sandwich was served.

Buddy and Lorna were holding hands and talking to customers. Baxter made eye contact with Lorna and could see her breaking off a conversation and leading Buddy to Baxter's stool.

"Aha! A new face in Frank's old stool!" Buddy greeted Baxter in his tenor voice.

"Buddy, this is Joe. He used to work for Frank at McKenzie Barber," Lorna introduced Baxter to a beaming Buddy.

"You're here to take Frank's place. Now look here, I want you to do right by my little Lorna." They exchanged handshakes.

Buddy was short, with thick dark curly hair and a bushy mustache.

"I loved the show," Baxter said.

"Good! Good! The requests were all Sonny's. We're liable to be singing Oklahoma in the 10:30 show. Eat! Eat! I've got to find Dirk." Buddy withdrew smiling and proceeded to bounce his way through the room.

"Gino," Lorna called to the bartender. "A small grapefruit juice." A bus boy brought a bar stool for Lorna to sit on next to Baxter. "You may cut me a small sliver of your steak. I don't eat until after the third show."

"Third show?" Baxter questioned.

"We do three cabaret shows. 9, 10:30 and midnight. The first show is the worst because it's a dinner crowd and they're usually pretty noisy. Midnight's our best show because most everybody's cleared out. Now, Joe, how did you really like us?" Lorna sipped on her grapefruit juice.

"I thought you were both sensational. How long have you been singing together?" Baxter asked.

"Would you believe 8th Grade? Buddy and I were in choir together."

Baxter looked up from his steak and observed a short grey haired man in a tuxedo with his hand on Lorna's bare shoulder. He wore tinted glasses and smiled at Baxter.

"Joe, this is Sonny," Lorna introduced Baxter to the proprietor of Sonny's Supper Club. He got up from his bar stool to shake hands. "Sonny, this is Joe Baxter. He worked for Frank."

"You're bigger than Frank," Sonny observed. "Welcome, Joe. We're pleased to have you with us. Lorna, I have some people who want to meet you," Sonny said guiding Lorna off her stool. "Gino, pour Joe a drink on the house."

Baxter noted that Lorna was four or five inches taller than Sonny in her high heels. Baxter had barely settled down to eat when Buddy returned accompanied by an exceptionally good looking young man in his twenties.

"Where's Lorna? What have you done with my Lorna?" Buddy looked around at the floor. "Dirk! Check under the piano! Joe has stashed her under the piano!"

"Sonny took her away to meet people," Baxter explained. He noted that Buddy's eyes appeared to have grown larger and he seemed more animated.

"Joe, this is Dirk. He's our new artistic Director. Dirk's from San Francisco and will be debuting in the Chicago area with Bells Are Ringing. He's trying to figure out if he wants Lorna to play Ella. Then if he wants her, Dirk will have to talk her into it, because she thinks it will be too much work. Meanwhile Sonny knows exactly who he wants to play Ella. We have a creative conflict here."

Dirk shook Baxter's hand. He was in his late twenties with a baby face, close cropped brown hair, and square even teeth. He wore a blue blazer, grey slacks, red tie, and tasseled loafers. "Joe, nice to see you," Dirk said gripping Baxter's hand. Dirk had a Boy Scout look about him.

121

"Dirk, why don't you take Lorna's place and watch the next show with Joe," Buddy said pulling out the bar stool.

Over time, Baxter and Dirk began to talk. "I understand that this is your first visit to Sonny's," Dirk began. "Tell me, what do you think of it?"

Baxter replied that he had never seen anything like Sonny's before and Dirk then talked continuously through the end of the second show. He had met Buddy in San Francisco at the end of July. Dirk had been Artistic Director for a small dinner theatre in San Jose and Buddy had invited him to meet his Uncle Sonny. The size of the facility and the resources brought Dirk out, but he hadn't realized how active Sonny preferred to be in the productions. Sonny, it turned out, exercised complete editorial authority over all productions. Three songs had been edited out from the Company production because Sonny considered them offensive to his patrons.

"Are you a good friend of Lorna?" Dirk finally asked after he had concluded his assessment and critiques of the creative freedom offered at Sonny's Supper Club.

"We work together," Baxter answered.

"I don't want her in Bells Are Ringing and she knows I don't want her, but Sonny says that Lorna has the lead if she wants it. Her only qualifications to play Ella is that she sings The Party's Over pretty well. This is what Lorna does well. She's getting older, her voice needs a lot of work, and she's really not much of a dancer."

"Will Buddy play in Bells Are Ringing?" Baxter asked.

Dirk made a face. "Buddy's a lounge piano player who sings reasonably well. He sings very well with Lorna. This is what they do," Dirk said as Buddy and Lorna returned for the midnight show. "They keep people in the bar to drink."

The last show ended at 12:30 with Lorna singing The Party's Over. The room was now at twenty percent capacity and Baxter had been on and off his bar stool for nearly four hours and had shared only a momentary exchange with Lorna.

"Joe, you're still here," she greeted him as the lights went on.

"Dirk and I have been sitting here enraptured," Baxter said a little drunkenly.

"I thought you had left after the second show. Come out and have breakfast with us," Lorna invited. "We've got to get some coffee in you. Let me get my coat." Baxter watched Lorna walk away. Her carriage and posture were perfect. She had sung beautifully and had managed to ignore him all evening. Buddy and Dirk were holding a quiet animated conversation three stools down.

Sal, the maitre'd, stood next to Baxter. "How did you like the show?" he asked Baxter.

"I think Buddy and Lorna are wonderful together."

"They've been singing together for a long time. Lorna went out to New York to live for five or six years, but then she came back to us. Sonny treats her as his own daughter."

Lorna returned wearing a silver fox jacket and she linked her arm with Baxter's. "Joe is going to buy me breakfast."

Lorna looked down at Buddy and Dirk. "Hey, you guys, time for breakfast! You all come!"

"Leaping Lizards, Punjab," Buddy shouted. "Annie and Daddy Warbucks are going off to breakfast."

They settled into a large back booth in the coffee shop. Lorna still had her stage make-up on and excused herself leaving Baxter with Buddy and Dirk.

"Well, Joe, did Lorna introduce you to any of our regular customer crime lords tonight?" Buddy asked. The pupils of his eyes seemed enlarged and Buddy had a nervous energy about him. Dirk, in contrast, seemed very tired.

"Dirk, Sal, the maitre'd, and Gino, the bartender, were the only people I met tonight. Sonny did, however, come by to greet me."

"Frank Alvardi used to get out and mix more. This was really his kind of place. A room full of people on the narrow line between criminality and respectability," Buddy said. "Most of them thought he was Joe DiMaggio. They would ask him for his autograph and call him 'Clipper'. Are you Lorna's new suitor. Or would it be suitors? Other bees seem to be visiting our little flower these days. I get to know these things because I'm her accompanist. Lorna has no secrets from me. I know the notes she can't hit anymore."

"And that's a lot of notes," Dirk commented.

"Dirk and I are having a creative disagreement tonight. I thought Lorna and I were really good this evening, didn't you, Dirk. Joe liked us."

"You were fine. Lorna was fine," Dirk said stifling a yawn. Buddy shook his head. "This apple cheeked artistic director needs to get to bed. Come pussycat," Buddy said rising and holding his hand out to help Dirk up. "We'll have our breakfast in the morning."

Lorna returned as they departed and exchanged kisses with Buddy and Dirk and sat down next to Baxter.

"They make a very nice couple," Baxter observed.

"You've caught on. That's very observant," Lorna said and promptly ordered ham and eggs. "I'm starving and very glad that you stayed on. Otherwise I would have no one to have breakfast with. I'm usually too wound up after a performance to go to bed. Buddy and I rehearse on Sunday afternoon and that's all the time we have together when we're not on stage. Dirk is shocked about how little Buddy and I rehearse."

"You're really talented, Lorna," Baxter said draining his third cup of coffee.

"I'm adequately talented to sing with Buddy at Sonny's Supper Club on weekends. I enjoy it and the money comes in handy. I don't want to play Ella in Bells Are Ringing because it will be too much work. Sonny believes I'm some wonderful, late blooming talent. But I know what I've become. A McKenzie Barber administrative person who sings on weekends."

Baxter drank coffee and watched Lorna wolf down her food. Her face was pale without make-up, but her features remained classic.

"I'm interested in you," Baxter said. "Who are you? Where do you come from? What exactly are Buddy and you?"

"I've seen your personnel file, Joe, and you haven't seen mine. I'll do what's fair. I'll recite mine and then we're even. Okay?"

"That's only fair," Baxter agreed.

"Name: Lorna Eleanor King. Real Name: Lorna Eleanor Wisnewski. I changed my name when I moved to New York to become a star of the stage and screen. Date of birth: 5-21-40. Education: St. Albans High School where I received a co-educational Catholic education. Two years theatre arts in three different community colleges, and five years evening school at Roosevelt University. No degree, and probably not a degree candidate. Employment: Carhop jobs, waitress, tour guide, and summer theatres through 1959. 1959 to 1964, actress, waitress, model, hostess, and anything I could make a buck at. 1964 to present McKenzie Barber and Co. Chicago concurrent with employment at Sonny's Supper Club. At McKenzie Barber: receptionist/clerk typist 1964 to 1967, Secretary/Administrative Assistant to Clyde Nickerson 1967 to 1972. Personnel Administrator 1972 to Present. Unmarried, lives with her mother, sings well on most weekend nights."

"You left out Frank Alvardi," Baxter observed.

"Frank Alvardi belongs in the file of my life, not in my McKenzie Barber personnel file. I've seen your file. Now I told you what's in mine. We're even."

"Shall we deal with our life files?" Baxter asked.

"Not this evening," Lorna said. "What I need is a walk. How about taking a walk with me around the yards?"

Baxter paid the check and they began a walk around the far side of Sonny's Motel. The temperature had dropped to the high 40s, and there was a bright quarter moon over the lake. Baxter put his arm around Lorna as they walked.

"Now let me get this straight," Lorna said. "You're married and living in your wife's home while she's in Europe. There's more than meets the eye here," Lorna commented. "I believe you are a married man with a good imagination."

"Believe what you must. My wife and I are estranged and I'm trying to do the right thing," Baxter replied.

"I've known a lot of married men in my life. Most of them are great company overnight, but nothing but misery over the long term. Then there are the men like Frank, who just take and take and never give. Then there are the men like Clyde, who have the inclination to stray, but don't quite have the courage, initiative, or know-how to go about it."

"He may have acquired those skills in recent years," Baxter observed.

"Clyde? Andy, I suppose, took up with him. She looked like the cat who swallowed the canary when she was back for Naomi's going away party. I thought Andy could be a friend when she first came to the Chicago office. Now she's riding high in Executive Office and treats me like the local office char lady. Both of us knew you were sleeping with Naomi. You two looked like you were in heat at Clyde's going away party. Why do people having affairs always believe they are invisible to others?"

"Did anyone else suspect?" Baxter asked.

"Just Andy and me, and we have Clyde in common."

"In common?"

"Clyde's wife is a mess. She's overweight and has diabetes. I used to receive these half-overtures from Clyde and I tried to signal back to him, maybe. Andy probably pounced on him."

"How about Alvardi?" Baxter probed.

"Do you have a thing about Frank? Are you trying to sample your boss's old girlfriends?" They walked around the side of the motel and were now facing the lake. "Frank and I are a closed file, Joe."

"How does one become an open file with you?" Baxter asked.

"Joe, I'm seeing someone now. He's out of the city this weekend. He's a very powerful man and he's single. He's never been married and he's good to me. I have no interest in doing anything to mess up this relationship."

"Do you believe that this man will ask you to marry him?"

"I don't know. But he has far more potential for a long term relationship and less complications than you, Joe."

"You're really a talented singer. Have you ever recorded?" Baxter asked. Lorna was still under his arm and the breeze blew colder from the lakeside.

"Sonny had Buddy and me cut a Christmas album and cassette three years ago. We couldn't give it away. It was a real cutesy family piece, the kind Sonny likes. He finally mailed them gratis to suppliers and customers with a little card that said, 'Merry Christmas from the Gang at Sonny's Motel and Supper Club'."

"What kind of man is Sonny?" Baxter asked. "How would you describe him?"

"That sounds like a therapist question to me. Joe, let's go out on the dock." They walked out on an empty dock under a quarter moon October sky. Lorna remained under Baxter's arm and from time to time, he would squeeze her.

"This dock is lined with power boats in the summer. Sonny relaxes the dress code a little. What kind of a man is Sonny Mancini? First, he's Buddy's uncle. Second Sonny's father, Guido, made his money a little differently. Sonny came back from the war, and Guido staked him to this place. Sonny really built the business and now he's the Sherman Billingsly of Highway 12. A lot of Sonny's father's old associates come here with their families. The place has very tight security and the only drugs around here are what Buddy sneaks in to carry him through the evening. Sonny is a bit of a prude about songs and material and didn't like some of the lyrics in Company, so we cut it out."

"How long have you been singing here?" Baxter kissed Lorna lightly on the ear.

"Joe, anything that's going to happen between you and me is not going to happen tonight," Lorna said brushing Baxter's arm away. "I started as a waitress and was in the chorus of Carrousel, the first dinner theater production back in 1959. The second production was Brigadoon. So you see I have come full circle from chorus to lead. I was a different girl in those days. I was the only child of two very wonderful blue collar people. My Dad was a watchman at a candy factory and my mother cooked at St. Albans School. That's how I met Buddy. We started singing together in eighth grade. Buddy was the brightest, most talented, and best looking boy at St. Albans High School. We used to sing duets in school auditoriums and at PTA Meetings. I became his girlfriend. We used to come out on this pier and neck at night. That was before Buddy concluded that he was gay."

"Buddy started playing dinner music at Sonny's when he was 18. I was a waitress and sometimes I got to sing with Buddy. We used to talk about going off to New York together and getting married. Buddy was a strong Catholic in those days and I thought he wasn't sexually aggressive with me because he was a gentleman. The other boys seemed to be all over me and there was Buddy, gentle and undemanding. To answer your question, I really didn't start to sing with Buddy the way we do now until after I came back from New York."

"When did you go to New York?" Baxter asked.

"I decided on August 21st, 1959, on this very pier. Buddy was with me and he cried. I thought I was hot stuff in those days. I believed I was ready for New York. I told Buddy I would send for him after I was established. I assumed it would be a struggle for a few years and I was anxious to get on with it and get the struggle part over with. I knew it was just a matter of time before I would be discovered and go on to become a great star."

"You weren't discovered, I take it," Baxter observed.

"I was discovered all right," Lorna answered. "I was discovered by some of the most sleazy people in the world. I was used, abused, violated, and trashed. I hated New York City. It was filthy, corrupt, and demeaning. Frank hinted that I should come out there and live with him. All I could see was the same trap at a better location on the East side. I decided to come back in August 1964. I was living in the Village with this piano player who imagined himself a composer. He had just gone off to work and I was lying naked on the bed smoking pot and staring at the ceiling, trying to relax. I asked myself, 'What in hell are you doing out here?' I called Sonny at his office. It was four o'clock Chicago time. I told him I wanted to come back home. Sonny asked me, 'When?'"

"I said, 'That night' but told him I had no money beyond cab fare to the airport. Sonny made a couple of calls and arranged for me to pick up a ticket at the United counter.

I went to the bathroom, took a shower, packed a bag, and left a message in lipstick on the bathroom mirror. I think I wrote, 'I'm gone and not coming back!' Sonny had Sal meet my flight. They had a room for me at the motel and Sonny put his arms around me and said, 'Welcome home, Lorna.' Sonny always treated me as I was one of his family and Buddy as the son he had never had."

"Buddy and I had written regularly over the years. I talked about coming back and he talked about coming out to New York. I told him about the men I was seeing, but Buddy didn't mention any women. I came back home and learned quickly that Buddy was gay."

"The following week I bought a black suit at Carson Pirie Scott, opened up the Chicago Tribune want ads, and interviewed with two employers. The first was some kind of Insurance broker on Wacker Drive. The next was McKenzie Barber. I was overpowered by the pictures of those two magnificent men in the lobby. I knew that this was the place that I wanted to work."

"I had practiced the entire weekend on the IBM electric in Sonny's office and barely got by the typing test. A nice office supervisor type named Eunice let me take the test twice. My only Chicago reference was Sonny, and he told them that I was a very efficient office worker who was always on time. I knew nothing about the business world. The people at McKenzie Barber were so professional and pleasant, and I was determined to be successful and accepted as one of them. There were no women on the professional staff, but there were administrative supervisors who had their own offices. I decided that I would work very hard and advance. Sonny had me sing with Buddy in the lounge one Saturday night, and that was the beginning of the cabaret show."

"I volunteered to work late to type proposals and reports. Soon I became dependable Lorna. The pool consultants tried to date me, but they seemed so young and inexperienced. Then Clyde came in 1966. It was explained to me that he was going to build a new practice in Chicago, and then move back to New York. Frank and Dwyer came about the same time."

"Clyde was very good for me. He explained that I would be his administrative assistant and that he had come to Chicago at the request of the Chairman to launch an Organization and Succession Planning services practice. He gave me a list of books to read, and I read everyone of them in the first two weeks I worked for Clyde. He would receive regular calls from Ernie Grey and close the door and they would talk for twenty and thirty minutes. Clyde would ask me to type certain correspondence in the evening when there was no one else around. It was if he had two jobs. One launching the practice, and the other working for Ernie Grey on special assignments."

"But after six months, we had only one client and six months later, Clyde quit trying to develop new clients and really became the personnel manager for the Chicago and Cleveland practices. I started to handle the routine personnel administration, and suddenly I answered all the personnel questions that came in from Cleveland."

"I told Clyde about how I spent my weekends. He brought Mavis out to see Buddy and me in 'I Do! I Do!' Mavis thought Buddy and I were a cute couple and asked if we were engaged. Somehow Frank heard about Sonny's and became a regular. He brought Bill Dwyer out once and there was almost a brawl. Sonny told Frank not to bring Dwyer again."

"Clyde and I used to have long talks. He took me to dinner once a week and would confide in me about the firm. He asked me for my advice when we brought the first trio of women MBAs in. I suspect that he really hadn't had a lot of experience with women before he married Mavis."

"If Clyde had a pass at you, how successful would he have been?" Baxter asked.

"High profile man, close to the Chairman, and from old family money. What do you think, Joe?"

"It's us poor guys with wives and clients who don't make it in this world," Baxter commented.

"You must be getting cold and getting tired of listening to me," Lorna took Baxter's hand and they walked back to the shore from the end of the dock.

"How's Frank with women?" Baxter asked. "I do so want to emulate him each day and in every way."

"First, you're a smart ass and Frank isn't. Second, Frank is very sure of himself with women. That's all that I'm going to say tonight on the subject of Frank Alvardi."

"How long have you been seeing this other man? You know, the powerful one."

"About a year."

"How did you meet him?"

"Through Brimmer. My life changed after I started to work directly under Brimmer. Brimmer's involved in a lot of civic committees. I had some personal contact with this man and it has developed into a relationship. He's talked about putting me into an apartment."

"Clearly he has all of the old fashioned virtues," Baxter said.

They walked briskly around the side of the Supper Club and found only a few cars scattered across the parking lot.

"Do you want to have one last cup of coffee?" Lorna asked. Baxter's watch said 3AM.

"Why not?" was his response.

They sat at the counter and drank two more cups of coffee.

"I'm always keyed up after a performance. I rarely go to bed until four or five and sometimes I stay up all night." Lorna placed her hand on Baxter's hand. "You have been very patient to walk with me and listen to my life story. Do you think we could just be friends?" she asked Baxter. "I really don't have anyone I'm close to after Frank left."

"Brimmer impressed me as cuddly and fun."

"How do you feel about Brimmer?" Lorna asked.

"In seven years with McKenzie Barber, I have had lunch with him once and received several growls in the hall. That's all I know about Paul Brimmer, other than people have talked about him succeeding Harvey Randolph and eventually succeeding Ernie Grey. Neither of them are on my list of confidants," Baxter observed.

"You're doing very well. I have seen all of the laudatory correspondence about you when you were promoted to Director. All of a sudden people around McKenzie Barber know who Joe Baxter is."

It suddenly became clear to Baxter. Lorna was not to be slept with. Rather she was to be cultivated as a friend. She could be a resource into the inner workings of the firm. Perhaps he would sleep with her eventually, but first he would become her friend and confidante.

"Let's have it your way, Lorna," Baxter said. "We'll be friends."

He saw Lorna to her car and they clasped hands before she turned the ignition. It was a long lonely drive back to the house on Palmer Street for Baxter.

Lorna visited Baxter's office on Monday with a plastic shopping bag in her hand. "Good Morning. I brought you something."

Baxter opened the bag and found four Stephen Sondheim musicals. Included were Gypsy, Anyone Can Whistle, A Little Night Music and Company. "It's a friendship gift. Thank you for keeping me company Saturday night," she smiled. "Let's have a sandwich together soon." She left Baxter's office abruptly without another word.

Over the next few months, Baxter and Lorna became visible friends in the Chicago office of McKenzie Barber. They would meet for afterwork drinks in the Michigan Avenue hotel bars, eat sandwiches in Baxter's office, and occasionally have lunch in the downstairs grill, and he would visit Sonny's on Saturday night. While their relationship was innocent, the office gossips became active. Alvardi, in one of their frequent telephone conversations, closed with a comment about he was proud of Baxter for keeping his old friends from Chicago company.

Dwyer was more direct when Baxter ran into him in the Detroit airport. "I hear you're diddling Lorna now, lad. I'm proud of the way you're filling Frank's shoes in Chicago."

Baxter escorted Lorna to the McKenzie Barber Christmas party on the third Saturday in December and there was more talk. Lorna excused herself before dessert explaining that she was being picked up and Baxter spent the rest of the evening alone and drifting between other couples.

"I really should find someone for you," Lorna said over drinks three weeks later in mid-January. "Some of the new consulting pool ladies look interesting."

"I want nothing to do with McKenzie Barber professional staff," Baxter ruled.

"Have you ever eaten any of the fruit from that tree?" Lorna asked. "Other than Naomi?"

"I'm with McKenzie Barber to serve clients rather than to seek sexual adventures. I just see this administrative lady from time to time."

"Brimmer's out for a week and I'm taking the week off to lay in the sun," Lorna announced.

"Are you meeting Frank?" Baxter asked.

"Frank and I are a closed file, Joe. My friend is flying me off to Naples. I'm very excited. I've never been to Florida."

"Isn't there a McKenzie Barber Board meeting in Florida next week?" Baxter asked.

"It's on the ocean side in Boca Raton. Naples is on the bay side," Lorna explained. "Anyway, Joe. I bring you news. A sweeping change in consulting personnel practices is about to be implemented, and I thought you should know in advance." Lorna had proven to be a valuable source of advance information to Baxter over the past few months and she had been the one to suggest drinks.

"Speak to me lady."

"The consultants' pool concept is going to be changed. MBA hiring is going to be reduced in half. It has been concluded that the consulting specialization practices of McKenzie Barber cannot be exclusively staffed with consultants advanced from the pool. Therefore practices like Information Systems, Manufacturing, and Executive Compensation are going to have the latitude to hire experienced people. You, for example, will have the support to go outside the firm for consultants, rather than take consultants from the pool."

"But this has been going on for a long time. Friedman hired that Ruth Ingvold for the LA Exec Comp practice and Dwyer has been hiring experienced people right along," Baxter reacted.

"That was all ad hoc. Now it's going to be official policy. It's going to change my job, because I will be in charge of experienced hiring for Chicago and Cleveland. It also will change all of the firm's training. Brimmer volunteered you today to serve on a training committee to develop crash consulting orientation courses for all of these newly hired experienced consultants. Also the firm is actively pursuing the acquisition of an Employee Benefits consulting firm."

"Alvardi will love that!" Baxter said remembering how incensed Alvardi had been the previous spring at the thought of the firm entering Benefits consulting.

"Frank may be in some trouble with the Board," Lorna volunteered. "They don't believe Executive Compensation is growing fast enough. The woman out in California isn't doing very well and outside Chicago and New York, the practice isn't functioning. You're going to be asked to establish a resident consultant in the Cleveland office."

"Lorna, where do you get all this information?"

"It's part of being on Brimmer's staff. I get to listen to a lot of telephone conversations and all of the personnel related memos pass my desk. Brimmer trusts me."

"What else is new?" Baxter asked.

"Clyde is on the partnership nomination list and Ernie has enough support to get him elected. Andy's moving up too. I think they are going to make her a Director. If all this happens, it will be effective October 1, 1975."

Baxter ordered another round of drinks. "Any other amazing developments?" he asked.

"Dwyer has been told to clean up his act by October 1. If he does, he will be named co-partner-in-charge of the IE practice."

The drinks were served and Baxter looked across the table at Lorna. The stuff she knew was not recovered from overhearing telephone conversations and reading memorandums upside down. Brimmer or others were openly volunteering information to Lorna. Perhaps a certain amount of it represented pillow talk. Was she sleeping with Brimmer? Baxter said nothing. Communications, after all, were a two way street.

Andy called Baxter unexpectedly on the pretext of discussing Pool Consultant appraisals and then expressed her own concerns. "Joe, it's all over the Chicago office that you're seeing a lot of Lorna King. Is that true?"

"We have been using a lot of Pool Consultants this year and Lorna's my provider. We have an occasional sandwich together in the office," Baxter explained to the voice from Executive Office.

"Are you still married, Joe?" Andy asked.

"My wife has been in Europe for seven months and isn't due back until late spring. I expect that we will begin divorce proceedings then. But I'll be damned if I'm going to put in a firm-wide announcement memo."

Andy's voice seemed to soften. "Oh, Joe. I know how hard you've tried to make your marriage work. I also remember how disciplined you were about personal relationships when we were at FSO. I really wouldn't want you to hurt your career by being openly involved with someone on the administrative support staff."

"Andy," Baxter said firmly, "Any relationship I have with Lorna King is strictly business."

I'm sure it is, Joe. But you must be careful of appearances in a firm like McKenzie Barber," Andy cautioned.

Baxter was shaking when he walked in the front door of the Metropolitan Club in New York in mid-April 1975. He had just left the offices of Leon Harwell for the first time. Alvardi sat in a stuffed chair in a high ceilinged room calmly reading the Wall Street Journal.

"Hi kid. Sorry I got caught in Detroit." Alvardi got up from his chair with a smile.

"I was almost eaten alive by that nice old Mr. Harwell," Baxter said in a low voice.

"He's supposed to be a big buddy of Ernie's, kid."

"Well I sold him some work and it's going to be Chicago office work."

"What kind of project, kid?" Alvardi asked.

"I am to review the senior management compensation in every retail investment his firm owns a position in. He wants me to interview management, collect data, and consult and advice on short and long term incentive norms and limits for management in each one of his investments. He is going to be serving as Chairman of the Compensation Committee on every board he serves on. Mr. Harwell is potentially a gold mine, but he's got to be handled very sensitively," Baxter explained.

"This sounds like a New York engagement that I should be closely involved with," Alvardi said.

"Where in hell were you this morning when I needed you?" Baxter demanded.

"Fogged in at the Detroit airport, kid. I couldn't help it. Did you quote him a fee?"

"I've got the names of all of his investments. I told him I'd be back with a work plan next week and we can work out fee then."

"Make it the week after, kid. I go to Europe next week to work with the Barber people and there's no way I can push it back."

"I'm meeting with Mr. Harwell next week whether you're here or not, Frank."

"I'd be careful not to over step your reach, kid. If you mess up with Harwell, you'll have to answer to Ernie. You will have no one to protect you, if I'm not involved."

The client arrived in the person of two of the senior operating executives of the U.S. branch of a large Italian bank. Alvardi reintroduced the subject when they were in a taxi going back to 311 Park Avenue. "If you have to see Harwell next week with a work plan, then go do it, kid. Just remember to get me involved early in the engagement and don't get greedy about hogging all of the professional time for Chicago."

Baxter knew that the lines had been drawn with his mentor, Frank Alvardi.

Two major events occurred in Baxter's life the following week. Baxter had his second meeting with Leon Harwell on Wednesday and Jennifer returned from Europe on Friday evening. Jennifer had now been gone for over a year.

She wrote the children every ten days and Baxter once every six weeks. Baxter would read the letters in Mr. Tom's old study where there was a globe and a number of maps of Europe. Baxter made the letter reading into a geography lesson, and even Agnes took an interest in where the Misses was staying or had visited.

"I want to go to Europe," Joel proclaimed. "Just as soon as I'm old enough."

"Me too," Muffin joined in.

"Have you ever been to Europe, Dad?" Joel asked. After Baxter replied his 'No', Joel suggested, "I think we all should go to Europe. Mother, you, Muffin, and me. Agnes can watch the house and Celeste can go home. Maybe mother won't be mad at you anymore and we can be a family again."

"We've always been a family," Baxter corrected his son. "It's just that your mother and I have always had to be away a lot."

Jennifer's letter to Baxter had arrived a month earlier.

> Dear Joe:
>
> I'm coming home to Palmer Street at last. As Chuck told you, I've spent the year with a very talented writer who has been away on a sabbatical from the University of Wisconsin. He has been writing a truly fine novel set in the Peace Movement of the late 1960s and early 1970s. His name is Erick Nordquist and I believe he will develop into one of the important writers of the next twenty years. I have served as his editor and occasional typist during the past year.
>
> It is time for the both of us to make decisions about our lives. Would you meet my flight at O'Hare? It's TWA 21 out of Frankfurt. We need to have a long talk. Erick is due back on the Memorial Day weekend. Let's settle this thing between us for once and for all.
>
> Sincerely,
> Jennifer

The meeting with Leon Harwell went reasonably well. They met again in the small conference room around the large oval shaped table. A silver coffee service, sweet rolls, and bone china were on the table when Mrs. Moore escorted Baxter into the room.

"Mr. Leon's on a conference call with one of the investment managers, but will be in shortly. Mr. Baxter, may I pour you a coffee? Mr. Leon specifically said that you could start on the sweet rolls without him."

Mrs. Moore poured Baxter's coffee and closed the door behind her. Baxter took out the workplans from his briefcase, sipped his coffee, and waited. The room was furnished in dark wood and the morning light beamed in from Lexington Avenue. There were some oil paintings of European street scenes on the walls, and a tall grandfather clock ticked away for twenty minutes before Leon Harwell entered the room.

"Sorry to keep you waiting, Joe." Mr. Leon appeared slight and moderately stoop shouldered. "Now, what do you have for me?" Mr. Leon seated himself next to Baxter.

"This is an Alpha listing of the retailers we discussed last week." Baxter had two copies of each passout and looked over his copy as Mr. Harwell scanned his copy of the list. He produced a silver pencil and began to line out one third of the companies on the list.

"I liquidated our position in these companies last Friday based on some information I received. It was time for profit taking. That leaves us———." Mr. Leon counted the companies remaining on the list with his pencil. "Eight, nine, ten. You have ten companies to look into for me, Joe." He returned the Alpha list to Baxter. Three of the retailers he had visited with Lorna over the weekend had been eliminated.

Baxter passed a work plan to Mr. Leon. "Have you ever seen a McKenzie Barber work plan form. I thought it would be useful for us to review the plan so there is no misunderstanding as to scope and extent of the work to be performed for Harwell Management."

Mr. Leon emitted a chuckle as he looked over the work plan form. "I knew John McKenzie. Ernie Grey introduced us and we would have dinner once a year until he retired. I've had McKenzie Barber put this form in front of me before. It usually means quite a bit of money."

"It was my understanding that you wanted McKenzie Barber to study the business strategy, evaluate management's ability and resources to conduct the strategy, critique the executive pay plans to support the strategy, and recommend improvements to more closely relate pay plans to support the best interests of the shareholders," Baxter said.

"That's close," Mr. Leon said with a hint of a smile in his cold blue eyes. "Have you done a lot of this sort of thing before, Joe?"

"I've never done anything like this before. Generally we're engaged by management and we sell the plans to the Board. Sometimes we are pre-approved by the Board. What I understand, Mr. Harwell. is that you are expending Harwell Management funds to engage a consultant to review management compensation as part of your role as Chairman of the Compensation Committee."

"Half-right. You will bill Harwell Management and Harwell Management will pass the billings in due time, on to the corporate entity. As Chairman of the Compensation Committee, I am paid for extra meetings and reimbursed out-of-pocket expenses."

"Has this ever been done before, Mr. Harwell?"

"Call me Leon or Mr. Leon, if you're more comfortable calling people Mister. I think it has been done from time to time, but I doubt as to whether it has ever been an established process. This is not to say that it is not badly needed. Let me give you my thinking on the matter."

"Pay is what it's all about isn't it? Men will work unreasonable hours and accomplish highly risky goals in anticipation of extraordinary financial rewards. There's nothing wrong with paying a President a lot of money in return for achieving high profits or growing the fair market value of the company's stock price. There is plenty wrong with overpaying for poor performance and it is risky to undercompensate management. I am an investor. I can't run these companies. I wouldn't know where to begin. But I do recognize under performance and financial chicanery. Executive Compensation consultants are pretty much in the hip pocket of management. I believe the Board should have their own resources to draw upon."

"Then, Mr. Leon, do I understand that you wish us to proceed down this list of companies?" It looked like $200,000 worth of work to Baxter. Chicago office work!

"Not quite. I want you to do one company first and let me see what kind of product I get from you and then we can consider going onto the others."

"Which company do you have in mind?" Baxter asked.

Mr. Leon's silver pencil moved to the middle of the page. "This one," he said and his pencil came to rest on Hi-Valu Auto Parts in Omaha, Nebraska. "It's close to Chicago and I was appointed to the Compensation Committee in their March meeting."

"Are you on the Compensation Committee of all of these other companies?" Baxter asked.

"No, but I can get myself appointed generally when I choose."

"So we really aren't in a position to proceed on all of these companies at once."

"Oh no. But I certainly got your attention on this matter when I implied it. I'll bet, Joe, you went out and visited some of these stores this last weekend."

"I did and you sold off your holdings in three of the five retailers I visited."

"I called Ernie Grey about you after our meeting. He thinks highly of you, but believes we should have this man Alvardi involved. I told him I liked you and thought you would do nicely. Now shall we talk about fee and then we'll have a sandwich together. Mrs. Moore will order in for us."

Baxter agreed to perform the first study for $15,000 plus out-of-pocket expenses after considerable negotiation with Mr. Leon.

"Do the first one for $15,000. I'll see that you're protected on future assignments. I believe that you and I will have some fun together on these projects. What do you say to some lunch now?"

Mr. Leon and Baxter had lunch in another small conference room. Mrs. Moore prepared sandwiches, and place settings were arranged around a dark wood table. This conference room adjoined a small kitchen. "I really prefer having a sandwich in the office to going out to my luncheon club," Mr. Leon explained.

Baxter sipped his coffee and tried to conjure up the kind of small talk one made with one of the wealthiest men in America.

"What do you know about the Harwells, Joe? Did you talk to Ernie about us?" Mr. Leon asked.

"Ernie Grey is the Chairman of McKenzie Barber, Mr. Leon. We're not exactly intimates," Baxter explained.

"Ernie said that you handled a critical review of one of McKenzie Barber's subsidiaries and did a fine job. He regards you as a comer. Tell me about yourself, Joe. Where do you come from?"

Baxter provided Leon Harwell a highly sanitized version of his life omitting mention of his marriages, but marking his rise from a miner's son to a McKenzie Barber Director level consultant. He included his military service, but made no mysterious claims of dangerous and valorous duty.

"Your kind of advancement is what makes America the country it is, Joe. I was born with a silver spoon in my mouth. I was a Harwell. What do you know about the Harwells?"

"I know that your family made their capital base in coal. Your grandfather founded Harwell Coal and that you sold off the coal interests and became the Harwell Trust. Then you changed your name to the Harwell Management Company in 1946. Your father succeeded your grandfather as President of the Trust, and then your brother became President, and you succeeded your brother upon his death. No one is certain as to Harwell Management's assets under management, but it has been estimated at $5.5 billion. That's what I know. You're smaller than Ford or Kellogg, but right up there among the eleemosynary foundations," Baxter recited.

Mr. Leon sipped his tea and made a clucking noise as if he were processing Baxter's recitation. "You're reasonably accurate, but on the low side" he said finally.

"My grandfather was one of those ruthless coal barons of the late 19th century, and my father was born a gentleman who was accustomed to having money, but had no idea on how to go about making money. Yes, I had a brother named Will, and we took over the Harwell Trust after the war. Will went to war and I didn't. We threw out the investment manager who had served my family and Will, my older brother, became President of the Trust and we became the Harwell Management Company. We were quiet and boring through the war years. My brother, Will, had been a Naval Aviator with Ernie Grey. Will came out of the Navy and he wanted to take over the world. From a careful, cautious, don't-show-your-hand investment strategy under my father's investment manager, Will moved us into an aggressive raiding posture. It was a mistake and it took years for us to correct our image. Will and I were rarely in full agreement on investment strategy, and then Will died in an unfortunate airplane crash, and I was suddenly alone. I pulled Harwell Management back from its aggressive investor position back into the quiet and boring category. We have been very successful over the past fifteen years. I have engaged professional money manager, and we have moved into commercial paper, arbitrage, real estate, and venture capital, but I personally believe that equities are where we will achieve our growth objectives. Now I have my theory on Executive Compensation and its relationship to the fair market value, and I want to see if it will work. That's why you fit so well, Joe. You're with a firm that I highly respect, and you have a fresh open mind about what I'm attempting to do. Who knows? Maybe you and I will be doing business together for a long time."

# CORRESPONDENCE

Dear Captain:

Sorry I missed your call when you came through New York. I was buried in a production scheduling job at a chemical company in New Jersey. I seemed to have drawn all the shit assignments in the New York IE practice and was still at the Associate level. So I took the law into my own hands and finagled myself a transfer to the Atlanta office. Friend Andy, now an important right hand to big Clyde himself, helped arrange my transfer. Story around New York is that Andy is up for Director this fall and I think the closest she ever came to seeing a client was the FSO job. She will probably become a Partner before I move off Associate.

Atlanta is not New York. You don't have a lot of Fortune 500's to work with. A guy named Neil Schmidt has just taken over the office. He told me that Atlanta could use a little New York sophistication when I reported and had my Managing Partner's chat. The first two jobs I was assigned to were for Agricultural co-operatives. I thought back to those good old days when I was working on New Jersey chemical companies. I've been getting out and giving speeches and writing articles like a good McKenzie Barber Associate who wants to be a Manager, but I'm not getting anywhere. The high point of my five year career at McKenzie Barber was working on that FSO job with you. Captain, Andy tells me that they are going to sanitize it and make FSO a case study module in the firm's new training program.

This is kind of a long winded letter, but I don't write you very often, Captain. I'll now come to the point.

It's time for me to leave McKenzie Barber. I know what the rules are. If you want to leave, you tell the Managing Partner that you're considering leaving. Then he'll call up Nickerson, and Nickerson, or one of his people, find you a job. I have heard of a few guys who have been burned by being too open. They have given the people a clock to find a new job and then came up with a couple of second year MBA jobs and told them, 'There's your chance, boy. You better take that one and get out of here because we've got new people moving up behind you.'

It's time for me to go, Captain, but it's got to be on my terms. I have prepared a resume and say that I am currently employed with a major consulting firm that I make sound like Robson Allen. If I get close to something, I want to use you as a reference. Just make the FSO job sound like it lasted a year or so. Also keep your eyes open for me. You're a high flying Director and probably hang around with CEOs, Kings, and Princes. Remember your old pal, Jeff. I am including a copy of my resume for you to share with important clients. McKenzie Barber has become kind of a waste of time for me, and it's time for me to get on with my career. I sure wish you'd look me up when you hit Atlanta again. We could tie our ties to the bar like we did that crazy afternoon with Alvardi and Dwyer, and later that evening with those sweet young things in the Sherry Netherland. That one from Yale went off to do a Doctorate before I could poke her. That little number you were with went off to London/Barber.

Look me up, Captain! I miss your good company.

Jeffrey Lord (ex-USMC)

## MCKENZIE BARBER & CO.
### Internal Memorandum

TO: J. Baxter
Chicago
FROM: H. Randolph
Executive
cc: E. Grey, Executive
C. Nickerson, Executive
A. Bourke, Executive
SUBJECT: Development of consulting training for experienced industry and functionally skilled individuals hired from outside the firm.

Dear Joe (handwritten),

I know that by this time, you have carefully read Ernie Grey's memorandum of May 3 relative to McKenzie Barber's amended consulting hiring practices. I am attaching an additional copy of Ernie's memorandum to this memorandum for your further review.

The firm that John McKenzie founded in 1922 has advanced over its 53 year life from one man's vision to a multinational consulting firm spanning six continents. The clients we serve often require leading edge technical, functional, and industry specific skills which may not be readily located within our present ranks. We have successfully added new executive compensation and manufacturing consulting practices and look to add new skills in order to continue our management consulting leadership through the last half of the 1970s to the year 2000 and beyond. The continued growth and dominance of McKenzie Barber will be predicated on our ability to attract and develop qualified consulting personnel who will advance to form the future leadership of the firm. We remain committed to recruiting graduates from the leading business schools of the country. All of the senior partnership have been developed from the ranks of our MBA hiring.

We now recognize that we cannot exclusively depend on MBA hiring to fill the pipeline of qualified consultants required for McKenzie Barber to compete and grow in the 1970s, 1980s, and 1990s. It has become clear in our forward strategic plans that we must have the flexibility to acquire the services of one or one hundred consultants at a given time. The McKenzie Barber of the 1970s may choose to acquire entire firms of consultants to achieve its goals. With that in mind, we recognized that all of our training roundtables must be revisited and redesigned to provide the critical consulting skills required by our new associates to ensure their success.

The development of these updated training modules will be placed in the hands of the firm's brightest, most able, and successful consulting practitioners. The Operating Committee of the Board has solicited recommendations from the managing partners of the firm and your name was nominated as a course developer and instructor. Ernie has asked me personally to oversee the development process. We are meeting initially at the Hudson Conference Center in Westchester County over the weekend of June 7-8.

You have been selected to participate in this critical kick-off meeting. It is assumed that you will schedule your client responsibilities around this meeting date.

Reservations have been made in your name on Friday, June 6th, and a cocktail reception followed by a group dinner will be held on Friday evening.

We will begin promptly at 8:30 AM on Saturday morning and you should anticipate a full day of group work. We will reconvene on Sunday morning and expect to complete our work by 4 PM on Sunday. An agenda for the two meeting days is attached. Should you have a conflict which you believe will preclude your attendance at this meeting, I request that you telephone Mrs. Applegate, Ernie Grey's secretary at 212-490-1001. I will be in attendance with you throughout the weekend and look forward to a productive collaborative effort.

(Written by hand) Joe, you are representative of the audience we are trying to reach. Ernie speaks highly of you and I look forward to getting to know you better.

HARVEY

Baxter called Andy after he read Jeff's letter and the memorandum from Harvey Randolph. She called back two days later on a Friday morning.

"What's this memorandum from Harvey Randolph all about?" he asked.

"You've read Ernie's memorandum about our change in staffing policy?" Andy answered Baxter's question with her own.

"It's my favorite valentine. I carry it in my brief case nestled next to my Grey-gram."

"You are one of the anointed ones, sixteen in all, who have been invited to help formulate consulting training programs that will set the course of the firm for the next twenty years. It is quite a feather in your cap to have been invited, Joe. I suggested to Paul that he nominate you. I looked at your personnel file and found that you've never attended a roundtable or a training course and you're a Director with eight years with the firm."

"I am a graduate of the Dwyer Technical School and the Alvardi School of Charm and Stealth," Baxter argued.

"You were mentored. Maybe that's a better way. The firm is committed to hiring experienced consultants to contrast with our traditional pool of MBAs and you represent the model of a consultant who joins the firm after a fast track career in industry. Harvey thought it was a great idea. The meeting will provide you visibility with the other fast track partners, directors, and managers of the firm and you can provide personal input from the perspective of the consultant coming into the firm at mid-career."

"I'm at mid-career now. I was early career then," Baxter corrected her.

"You were fast track, Joe," Andy pointed out.

It was the first time anyone had ever referred to his rise with Washburn Manufacturing as fast track.

"And," she continued, "We are considering some case training. One case that has everyone excited is FSO. They have really turned around since our study and it represents a classic case demonstrating engagement management techniques. You and I could write the case together."

"It might not be the best case to show new mid-career consultants, Andy. There was no selling involved. It was a mandated engagement. I'd pick one where there is selling involved. These guys coming in mid-career are going to have to learn how to sell work, and they better learn that in a hurry."

"That's going to be a separate case, Joe."

"Andy, do I sense an implication that I could have some continued connection with firm training beyond this meeting?"

"You could be selected as one of the key trainers, Joe."

"Andy, I want to be out acquiring and serving clients, not training mid-career consulting hires," Baxter explained.

"Joe, no one has selected you yet. If you are selected, you should jump at the opportunity. Joe, only a few people at McKenzie Barber know who you are! This is your chance for visibility!" Andy argued.

"Serving clients is what this game's about, Andy."

"Joe, serving clients is necessary, but the firm leadership opens up the doors to those clients. If you don't serve those clients, they will find someone else to serve those clients and that's what McKenzie Barber is all about. It's important for you to be known within the firm if you want to advance and become a Partner, Joe. The next two or three years are critical for you. I can help! Being part of this training effort will help! I know that Harvey Randolph wants to have a private dinner with you the Saturday night of the meeting."

"Why wasn't Jeff Lord considered for this kind of meeting? He certainly could use some visibility and he's one hell of a good man," Baxter asked.

"Jeff's career is on the beach with McKenzie Barber. He is regarded as competent, but a chronic complainer. Also he was indiscreet in some of his relationships with the support staff, and that got around the office. I worked out a transfer to Atlanta for him, but the firm expects that he will be gone in a year. We know he has a resume out."

"Well, I guess I'll see you at the Hudson Conference Center."

"I will be looking forward to seeing you, Joe. It's been too long," Andy said and then there was a click at the end of the line. Baxter looked at his watch. It was 2:30. Time to head out to O'Hare to meet Jennifer and conclude a phase of his life.

Jennifer was an hour clearing customs. Baxter brought a brief case full of work and waited patiently. He hadn't missed her, and certainly over the years had learned to live without Jennifer's company. Other than the flirtation with Hillary, and his California escapades with Friedman, Baxter had no relationships with women other than his friendship with Lorna. He worked twelve hour days during the week, spent his weekends on Palmer Street, and one or two Saturdays a month in Sonny's Supper Club. Jennifer's letters to the children were warm and full of the details of her life, while her letters to Baxter were brief and contained terse directives. Baxter thought back to the night he put on his tuxedo for the first time He had been on his way to pick up Jennifer. It was the night of the announcement of their engagement at the Deer Lake Country Club. Why had he married her in the first place? The answer always came back the same. The Washburns wanted him to, and in return, Baxter would have eventually been made President of Washburn Manufacturing. Mr. Tom had picked him out for Jennifer. He had wanted Jennifer to marry someone competent enough to run the business. Tonight was going to mark the end of his life with Jennifer Washburn.

Jennifer finally emerged from customs, accompanied by two black skycaps. Her hair was shoulder length, and she wore dark glasses over her saucer eyes. Jennifer was dressed in a white blouse, blue blazer, and jeans tucked into long high heeled black boots. She looked thinner, and reminded Baxter of a princess leading two nubian slaves. Jennifer continued to be a beautiful and striking woman.

Baxter closed his brief case and stood to meet her. She raised her hand to the skycaps signaling them to stop.

Jennifer greeted Baxter with a cold smile.

"Hello Joe. Don't you look like a little piece of corporate America." There was neither a handshake nor a hint of a wave.

"I brought the Pontiac. I'm not certain that I can get all that stuff in the car," Baxter said.

"What did you think I'd have? An overnight bag? Never mind. I'm arranging for the baggage to be shipped to Palmer Street. The trunks should be here next week. Joe, give these men some money and take their names if there are any slip-ups. I don't have any American money. Give me some change so that I can call my parents."

Baxter gave Jennifer all the change in his pocket and she responded with a curt "thank you". Male eyes followed Jennifer as she energetically walked through the airport to the public telephones.

Baxter gave each skycap a twenty and reviewed their instructions on delivering the bags to Palmer Street. Chuck had apparently arranged for a cartage firm to deliver the luggage.

Jennifer made several calls while Baxter waited. He was now becoming impatient to get on with their discussion. Finally Jennifer hung up the telephone and Baxter met her half-way to the street door.

"Well. I'm announced. Let's get the hell out of here," Jennifer said. "I want to be free from airports. Why don't we go to that seafood place on the lake. It's on the way home."

Jennifer chattered about the flight and reminded Baxter that she was six hours ahead of him. They talked about the children and her year in Europe filling the time before Baxter drove into the parking lot of the restaurant. It was a busy Friday night dinner crowd and Baxter insisted on a corner table.

Baxter ordered a Gellhorn while Jennifer had a white wine as they sat in the front bar waiting for a table.

"I don't ever remember being here with you," Jennifer took out a long European cigarette. Baxter made no effort to light it.

"Well," Jennifer said after a long pull on her cigarette. "Let's quit sparring and talk! I want a divorce and I want you out of Palmer Street tonight. You can pick up the rest of your things over the weekend, but I don't want this to drag out. You and I are quits and I don't want you in my house anymore."

Baxter nodded. He had prepared for her demands. "What about the children?"

"They will stay with me at Palmer Street and you will see them on weekends. You can get a motel room, if you think you should stay over. I will require alimony and child support. I have a tax lien against my trust and have spent a little more money than I had anticipated in Europe. You look like you're doing well, so I assume you can afford it."

"I will pay child support, but you will not get a dime from me in alimony. If you pissed away your inheritance, I would suggest that you consider a job."

"Why should I have to get a job? You've been living off me rent free for seven years. It's time for you to start paying me back. I probably will work though, and Erick will be moving in when he's back from Europe in two weeks. That's why I want you out tonight. I'm also going to get that old drunk, Agnes out of the house for once and for all. She has the right to live in the carriage house according to Tom's will, but I don't want her in the house again."

"She loves those children," Baxter reminded Jennifer.

"They don't especially like her. You should see what they say about her in their letters. I'll keep Celeste."

"Celeste smokes controlled substances," Baxter said.

145

"Joe, where the hell have you been? Everyone smokes grass. Erick does and I do it! It's been less harmful than the alcohol Agnes and you use to abuse your bodies. I want a divorce and I want alimony and child support."

"Doesn't Erick want to support you?" Baxter said.

"He's being paid modestly by the University, but should do well after his novel has been published. We have no plans to marry presently. He's five years younger than me. We're very good together sexually, and he's an enormous talent. We're just going to take our relationship a day at a time."

"Settled in at Palmer Street with your reefers and our children," Baxter commented.

"Reefers! You sound like a character in a 1940s movie, Joe. And what makes you think that both of the children are yours?"

Baxter sat motionless in his chair and repeated her words in his head over and over again.

"I'm kidding, Joe. Of course they're ours."

Baxter thought back to a morning in the summer of 1969. He had awakened in the early morning to find Jennifer sitting nude on a bedroom chair. She had been smoking a cigarette while silently watching him. Muffin had been conceived that night. It was the last time, some six years distant, they had made love. Had she been with someone earlier? Was making love to Baxter Jennifer's way of covering herself?

"Jennifer, tell me the truth. Muffin isn't my child is she?"

"Of course, she's your child, Joe. Who's child could she be?"

"Jennifer, you've been running around on your own for six or seven years. I suspect that you have had a lot of relationships outside this marriage. Muffin could well be a product of one of those relationships. You and I made love only once in five years and conveniently Muffin was conceived on the basis on one coupling between us."

Jennifer lit a fresh cigarette and Baxter said nothing. The hostess announced that their table was ready.

They were seated against the wall, one table down from the window looking out at Lake Michigan. Baxter ordered glasses of white wine for both of them. Jennifer started another cigarette and stared at Baxter. She was a striking woman with her saucer eyes, aristocratic features, and athletic body. Men around the restaurant looked at her. Jennifer was 36, and Baxter estimated that she looked five years younger than her age. He had once loved her, and now disliked her. They both had taken lovers, but Baxter's only semi serious relationship had been with Hillary.

"Muffin probably—," Jennifer began. "Muffin is not your child, Joe. Her father is a tall blonde boy they called Starward that I met in the peace movement. He was an organizer for a militant group and stayed in Madison for about two months before he moved on to Canada. I got stoned with him one night, and he called me his 'uptown classy lady'. He had long blonde hair that he wore in a pony tail and wore a headband with stars on it. Starward had a wonderful silky body and I couldn't keep my hands off him. He was from Fallbrook, California where his parents raised avocados. Starward's real name was Edgar something and he had gone off to USC, dropped out, bummed around Europe, and joined the peace movement when they tried to draft him. He was a wonderful, idealistic lover."

"What happened to him?"

"He had to leave in a hurry. They tried to blow up the ROTC building and there was a leak. He went on to Canada and there I was pregnant."

"It's a shame he didn't meet your folks. He could have gone golfing with Chuck."

Jennifer splashed her wine in Baxter's face. "You really stink as a person. Get me out of here and take me to Palmer Street. Then, get the hell out of my life!"

He drove Jennifer home in silence. The children were waiting for her. "Mommy! Daddy!" They ran to the front door in their pajamas. Baxter kissed them, walked upstairs, packed two large bags and announced to the children that he had to go off on a long trip and would be gone better than a month. Muffin squeezed his legs until Baxter lifted her up. Her round face was filled with tears.

"Daddy, why do you have to go right away? You just got back and now Mommy's back. We can be a family again."

"I'll talk to them," Jennifer whispered.

"I'll bet you will," Baxter whispered back.

"I hate that McKenzie Barber, Dad. They make you go places all the time. Even on weekends!" Joel protested.

Agnes walked out to the car with Baxter. "Are you going for good?" she asked him. Jennifer and the children stood framed on the front porch holding hands.

"I believe so."

Tears formed in Agnes's eyes. "And you're leaving me here with the Misses? Is that it?"

"That's the way she wants it. She now has a writer-in-residence program."

"I don't know what you're talking about, Joe. I don't always understand you."

Baxter hugged the bulky woman and smelled her brandy breath.

"Promise me, Joe that you will never abandon those children."

"I won't."

"Say it out loud to me. Swear by your mother."

"I swear by my mother that I will never abandon those children," Baxter agreed.

"Then I'll stay behind and do my best, Joe."

Baxter placed his bags in the trunk and drove slowly out of the driveway of the house on Palmer Street. Jennifer, Joel and Muffin waved from the porch. Baxter wondered how Starward was making out in Canada. He would never abandon Joel and Muffin!

Baxter worked at the office that Saturday until seven. He was going to catch a plane to Omaha and meet with the Hi-Valu Auto Parts people on Monday.

They insisted in starting their meeting with him at 7AM so Baxter made arrangements to catch a late Sunday afternoon flight to Omaha. He considered going back to the apartment in Rosemont and watching the Cubs game, but once on the expressway Baxter continued on to Sonny's Supper Club.

Baxter had been to Sonny's a half dozen times since that first evening in May. He would be seated at the bar stool in front of the piano and would order a steak sandwich and drink Canadian Club. From the bar stool, Baxter would either have a front row seat for the cabaret show or an oblique angle seat for the stage production. He saw *Bells Are Ringing* from the barstool. Lorna did not play Ella, and had sat next to Baxter for half of the performance. Months later they put on *Pajama Game* and Baxter sat through two separate performances. Lorna did not try out for or volunteer to play Babe. Rather Lorna was content to sing on weekends with Buddy in the cabaret show, and began to be picked up by a driver in a black limousine. The limo usually arrived about 10:30 and Lorna would carefully monitor the time on her watch.

"You really should ask Daddy Warbucks to come in and meet the boys," Baxter suggested.

"It's not his kind of place," Lorna would answer.

Tonight was a cabaret night with Buddy and Lorna at the piano. *A Little Night Music* was to open in two weeks and Lorna had agreed to play Desiree.

"Will Daddy Warbucks come in to see you play Madame Armfeldt?" Baxter had asked.

"He might. He's never seem me perform. I do sing to him sometimes though," Lorna had confessed.

Baxter pulled into the Theatre parking lot which was only two thirds filled, and was provided his customary stool at the bar. He was seated at the bar next to Dirk who wore a white shirt with a cravat instead of a necktie and had taken to wearing tinted glasses.

"Well, Dirk," Baxter greeted him. "How's *A Little Night Music* going?"

"Reasonably well. I have been getting pressure from Sonny about a part for Lorna and she's perfect for Madame Armfeldt. She certainly can sing anything Glynis Johns can sing. I've brought in some new voices I worked with back in San Francisco to perform in the strolling quintet and I'm very happy with it. We may have a long run of three or four months. I have a stand-in for Lorna during the week and I think it's going to work. How's it going for you?"

Baxter considered explaining that his wife had thrown him out, was demanding alimony in addition to child support, and he had learned that one of his children wasn't really his, but belonged instead to a hippie named Starward, who was last seen heading for Canada. Baxter elected to say, "Fine. Things are progressing swimmingly. Have you seen Buddy and Lorna this evening?"

"Buddy is getting himself pharmaceutically prepared for this evening's performance. Lorna is in a dither because her Daddy Warbucks mystery friend called her this afternoon and told he would pick her up at 10:15 instead of 12:30. That means she won't be here for the 10:30 show. Buddy doesn't like to go on alone on weekends. Why just weekends I'll never understand. Buddy plays by himself four nights a week. Lorna is trying to get someone of the *A Little Night Music* cast to sing with Buddy in the 10:30 show. I suggested that we just convince Buddy it's Wednesday night and he'll be just fine. Meanwhile Sonny is angry with Lorna for letting her social life interfere with her professional obligations. It's sitcom night at Sonny's Supper Club, Joe," Dirk said. Then he broke into a smile. "Here comes Lorna and it looks like she's got a volunteer replacement. She has Teri undertow."

Baxter looked up to see Lorna clad in a white dress with long white gloves. She was followed by a smaller woman in a dark dress with a low neckline. Baxter noted that her hair was cut short and she had dark expressive eyes.

"Teri has joined our group. She worked with me out in San Francisco and will be in the group of strolling singers in Night Music," Dirk explained. "I wonder where in the hell Lorna found her."

Lorna kissed Baxter lightly on the cheek. "How did it go Friday, Joe?" He had told her about Jennifer's return from Europe.

"I guess I'm a free man at last," Baxter replied. Lorna touched his hand. "We'll have to talk about this next week. I have to make a flying escape tonight."

"Mr. Big is coming early tonight," Dirk commented.

"Teri will do the 10:30 and 12 show with Buddy," Lorna announced. "I've got to catch up with Buddy. Teri, you sit up here with Dirk and Joe. You'll do just fine." Lorna scurried off into the darkness behind the piano.

Baxter fetched a bar stool and the girl sat between Dirk and Baxter. She radiated a broad smile to Baxter and extended a hand. "I'm Teri, T-E-R-I. And you're Joe." Teri's dress was dark blue and she wore matching long blue gloves.

She was large breasted, small waisted, and short, but artificially taller in four inch spiked black high heels. Teri took Baxter's hand and returned his squeeze.

"Joe Baxter. I work with Lorna during the week."

"And do you know this mysterious heavy date of hers?" Teri asked directly.

"No one has ever seen his face, dear," Dirk commented. "He wears an iron mask."

"Dirk and I worked together on the coast. He also directed my older sister who has now gone legit with the San Francisco Opera."

Teri's voice was full and modulated as she spoke. Every word she spoke seemed to have a special character to it.

"Teri may be more talented than her older sister," Dirk reported.

Sal walked briskly by them, patting Baxter on the shoulder in friendly recognition as he made his way to the spotlight. Then he began his introduction which was followed by applause, a piano roll, and the overture to *Company*. Teri ordered a grapefruit juice and beamed a smile at the couple entertaining from the piano.

"I understand that you are going to take the 10:30 and midnight show?" Baxter asked in a low voice placing his mouth close to her ear. He could smell her perfume and Teri's short black hair had a fresh clean smell.

"That's right," she acknowledged.

"Have you sung in the cabaret before?" Baxter asked.

"No."

"Have you sung with Buddy before?"

"A little bit the other night when we were fooling around after rehearsal?"

"Are you nervous?"

"No."

"When did Lorna ask you?"

"About an hour ago in the parking lot. I had come by to pick up my check. You see I just moved out here from San Francisco. I'm working my way East. This dress comes out of wardrobe. I came out here dressed a little differently. I was just planning on going out for a pizza with this friend of my sister's, but now I'm dressed to the nines and I get to sing to a near full house and make a little extra money. Maybe someone in the audience will discover me and whisk me off to stardom. Listen to them! I swear Buddy has a range of just four notes. Poor Lorna has seen better days too. But she's pretty."

Baxter concluded that Teri had more self-assurance than the McKenzie Barber female MBAs. The first set concluded, and Lorna made a rapid exit after the applause. She kissed Baxter hurriedly on the cheek on her way out.

"Can we have coffee on Monday? I thought about you when I was up there."

"Tuesday. I will be in Omaha on Monday," Baxter replied, but didn't believe she had heard him.

Buddy joined them. "Well my dear, I appear to have been abandoned. Didn't we sing together the other afternoon?" Buddy asked Teri.

"Buddy," Dirk interjected. "Teri sang for me out in San Francisco. She has a voice of steel. Why don't the three of us sit down together for a moment?"

Teri looked to Baxter and shrugged her shoulders. She placed her gloved hand on Baxter's shoulder. "I hope you stick around to hear me. I'm really very good."

They moved to a table in the far corner of the room. Baxter drank Canadian Club and watched them talk. Why was he here at Sonny's in the first place? Lorna was off with her lover whom he suspected, but had not confirmed, as Brimmer. His marriage was over and he might have an expensive divorce on his hands. Muffin, the little daughter he loved, was not his. All he really had going in life was his career with McKenzie Barber. What was next for him in life? The answer, of course, was to have another Canadian Club, eat his steak sandwich, and sit through the 10:30 Cabaret show.

The spot came on Buddy at the beginning of the 10:30 show. He was alone seated behind the piano.

"Good evening again, ladies and gentlemen. I'm Buddy Mancini, and Lorna has left me for another man. At least temporarily! We have located a wonderful replacement. Her name is Teri Michaels and she has come to Sonny's from the San Francisco Bay area where she performed under Dirk Baer, our Artistic Director at the Vista Dinner Theatre in San Jose. Teri will be joining us in the *A Little Night Music* production which will be opening in ten days. Tonight we'll give you a little advance treat. Please welcome, Miss Teri Michaels!"

Buddy led the applause and Teri moved to the microphone beaming a broad little girl's smile. Buddy broke into *People Will Say We're In Love*. The audience wasn't prepared for the range, volume, and quality of Teri's voice. She appeared to recognize the limitations of Buddy's voice and carefully carried him through the song. Dirk was at Baxter's side.

151

"Isn't she great? Her sister was fantastic, and Teri's even better. She called me a month ago and said things had gotten slow and that she was trying to work her way East. She's young, Joe, but star quality."

They went on to sing *Stranger in Paradise*, and *The Impossible Dream* before Teri sang *Send In The Clowns* as a solo. "She can sing rings around Lorna," Dirk commented. "She's going to start in the quintet in *A Little Night Music* and I'll move her into the "Anne" role."

Someone requested *Frankie & Johnny* and Teri blew out the room. It had been a long time since Sonny's Supper Club had heard a voice with that kind of range and emotion. Buddy and Teri entertained through 11:30 and left to enthusiastic applause. Teri smiled her way through the crowd to the bar stool next to Baxter.

"How was I?" she whispered.

"You were everything you said you were," Baxter replied.

"The house was a little thin," Teri judged. "There were more people here on Friday night. We had a rehearsal Friday afternoon and I stayed for the cabaret show. They had more people in last night." Teri looked Baxter up and down. "You work with Lorna? What do you do?"

"I run a practice. It's a consulting firm. I get involved in pay plans for senior management."

"Is Lorna a consultant?"

"No. She works in the office on personnel matters. We're just friends."

"Are you important?" Teri asked.

"To some people," Baxter answered.

"I don't know anything about business. My parents were teachers, and my mother taught voice. I'm talented and trying to see how far my talent will take me."

"I guess I'm in the same boat," Baxter said.

"I haven't had much to do with business people," Teri confessed. "Where do you live?"

"In a Chicago suburb out by the airport called Rosemont. I keep an apartment out there because it's close to the airport."

"That's where I live. That is, that's where I'm living. I'm staying with my oldest sister who's a flight attendant with Western Airlines. She lives with two other flight attendants in Rosemont. I've been sleeping on the sofa couch for the last two weeks. I've only been in town two weeks. I'll get my own place after I get settled in. I also need to buy a car. Are you married?"

"I'm separated," Baxter replied.

"You're a rather attractive man. Are you going to stay through the last show? Because if you do, you could drive me home. You live in Rosemont and I live in Rosemont. You could save me some cab fare."

"I'll stay through the last show," Baxter committed. Teri placed her hand on Baxter's. "It's been very nice talking to you. I should mix a little. I'll see you after the show."

The midnight show was better than the 11:00 PM show. Teri and Buddy sang more fluidly. Each seemed to know what could be expected from the other. They sang a medley from *The Fantastiks* that produced heavy applause from the late evening crowd. Dirk put his hand on Baxter's shoulder at the end of the performance. "Teri can sing rings around Lorna. She has an exciting wonderfully pure voice. She won't be at Sonny's longer than a year. She'll be a star."

Teri came to Baxter after the applause concluded for the midnight show. "Are you sober enough to drive me home?" she asked.

Baxter got up from his bar stool and stretched. "I believe so," he responded.

"You're really big," Teri said.

"But gentle," Baxter offered. "How about coffee?"

"I would prefer to get out of here. Right this minute." She took Baxter's hand on her gloved hand and began to lead him out of the room. "We're going to wardrobe where my old clothes are, but I'll be damned if I'm going to change now," Teri stated.

Teri led Baxter into the basement of Sonny's Supper Club where she opened a door marked "Wardrobe".

She produced a shopping bag and then they walked briskly toward a side door. "This dress and these shoes belong to Wardrobe and I'll be damned if I'm going to get changed this time of night." Teri led Baxter out to the parking lot in long quick steps.

"You were really great," Baxter said as he started the car.

"Thank you. I knew I would be a big improvement over Lorna but I wasn't sure whether I could carry Buddy. Boy, is he a mess!"

Teri asked where Baxter lived and it seemed that they were two blocks apart. "Do you have anything to drink at your place?" Teri asked. "I'm wide awake and it's 1:10. My sister is flying and her roommates have dates and sometimes they bring the dates back to the apartment on weekends."

Baxter brought Teri up to his apartment, turned on music and poured her a brandy.

"This apartment is a lot like my sister's except it's smaller. It's white and sterile with a couple of posters on the wall. How long have you lived like this?" Teri asked.

"I used to live in Racine, Wisconsin, and kept an apartment in Chicago. I'm in the process of getting a divorce. That was just settled last night. So I'm a born again bachelor," Baxter announced.

Teri took a long drink of brandy and held out her glass for a refill. "I should be careful about brandy, but pour me another. Tonight was a good night and I want to celebrate."

Teri sat on a lounge chair with her legs extended. She had kicked off her shoes.

"You have me in your apartment, sir. Why haven't you made a pass at me?"

"Because I'm a middle-aged man and you're trying to kill time to allow your sister's roommates to settle in for the night," Baxter responded.

"You're hardly middle-aged. You look around thirty to me. I'm starting to get relaxed. I could stay the night here with a little encouragement."

Baxter leaned over Teri's lounge chair and moved his mouth against hers. There was no resistance and open mouths quickly locked together. He moved his hand to Teri's breast and she pushed it away.

"This is a borrowed dress from the Wardrobe department. Why don't I take it off and hang it up? You should get comfortable too," Teri suggested.

Teri was full breasted with a narrow waist and thick thighs. Baxter pulled out the sofa bed and they reclined together with each additional article of clothing a point of debate and negotiation. They were together after one more brandy.

"I'd like to stay the night," Teri said when Baxter decided to sleep.

"I sure as hell don't feel like putting my pants on to walk you home at this hour of the morning," Baxter responded.

It was better in the morning. Teri had made coffee while he slept and was wearing one of Baxter's tee shirts when she returned to bed. They loved vigorously until noon. It was at breakfast that Baxter found out that Teri was only nineteen years old.

Baxter left for the airport in the late afternoon to make his visit to Hi-Valu Auto Parts. He read the Sunday Tribune, reviewed his notes, shaved and dressed. Teri made no effort to get dressed. She borrowed Baxter's tooth brush, put on make-up, but remained clad in a tee shirt she had located in his dresser.

Baxter had fixed a breakfast of scrambled eggs and toast and Teri had chattered about herself through the meal.

"I want you to know, Joe, that I'm not in the habit of picking up men in bars and going to bed with them. Last night was the first time I've sung east of the Rockies. I was dreadfully hyped, and there you were talking to me and part of things. You really are a very good looking man. Older, smooth, obviously a man of the world, and a very good lover. You really swept me off my feet. I've been singing professionally since I was fifteen and I know I seem older to a lot of people but I'm only nineteen."

"Nineteen!" Baxter had protested.

"I'll be twenty in September. I was really good last night. I expect to be very successful here in Chicago, and then I'm on to New York. I'm a very talented vocalist and believe that I will develop into a star. I grew up around music. My father taught band and tried to compose on weekends and my mother was a voice coach. I'm one of four sisters and we all sing. My oldest sister, Gloria, now sings with the Opera in San Francisco. My second sister, Lou, is the flight attendant, who lives down the street. Then there's me and I have a sister named Jane, who is a Junior in High School. It's generally agreed that I'm the talent of the family."

Teri calmly sipped her coffee, clad in Baxter's tee shirt, with large bosoms, heavy thighs, and attractive calves. An hour earlier they had been coupled. Now she was matter-of-factly discussing herself.

"I'll have to leave for the airport around five o'clock. I have to be in Omaha for a breakfast meeting. Can I drop you at your sister's?"

"Would you mind if I stayed here overnight? I would really appreciate it if you could take a cab to the airport and leave your car keys behind. I need to get back out to Sonny's to bring the dress back and pick up my check for last night. I need the money, you see."

"Let me get this straight," Baxter said. "You want me to take a cab to the airport and you want to use my car and my apartment for tonight?"

"I'll be gone in the morning, Joe. I'm very new in town and I need some help. Were you ever new some place? I'm just starting out in Chicago. Trust me with your car and your apartment for one night. I trusted you last night. Do the same for me!"

Baxter rocked back and forth in his chair. "What kind of driver are you?"

"I'm good, Joe. I've been driving since I was fifteen. Did I ask you last night what kind of lover you were?"

"You did say something about being gentle," Baxter responded.

"And you were gentle. You were very good for me last night and this morning. I'll be just as gentle with your car and your apartment. I'm young in life, but I've learned already that a lot of getting along in life is based on trust. How about it, Joe?"

"Let me see your driver's license," Baxter said.

Baxter took a cab to the airport. Teri saw him to his own doorway and gave Baxter a very wet kiss. He placed his hands on her derriere and felt her body full against him.

"I'll spend the night with you whenever you want. We're really good together, Joe," she said in a husky voice.

My God, Baxter thought on his way in the cab to O'Hare, I'm one night officially separated from Jennifer, and I've left my car and my apartment in the hands of a nineteen year old girl! But then again, she would be twenty in two months according to her driver's license.

The Gauer Brothers in Omaha were glad to see Baxter. They were both full faced, short, and stout and reminded Baxter of pigs. Hi-Valu Auto Parts was a 100 store operation with documented plans to go to 500. They had no idea of who Baxter or McKenzie Barber were. They were in awe of Leon Harwell, and considered Baxter as his emissary. They appeared to be competent merchants with decent controls, but needed to invest in information systems. Neither was paid very well. They had started the business with a single store and both were paid $75,000 with bonuses paid on a discretionary basis. They had substantial non-qualified stock option grants that were in excess of 100,000 shares. Baxter viewed Hi-Valu as a threshold company with upside of about three years. It was obviously a test by Leon Harwell. He already had reached his conclusions about this company. Harwell wanted a professional's view of the relationship of the company's short term business future and the senior executive compensation structure supporting Hi-Valu's relatively primitive business plan. There was a need for two major consulting engagements. One in strategic planning and the other in information systems. At the same time, Baxter recognized that to propose the work directly to the client without reviewing it with Leon Harwell, would bring an end to their budding relationship. Baxter visited the headquarters offices, their distribution center and four stores before he caught the five o'clock United flight back to Chicago.

He could hear Sondheim from under the door as Baxter returned to his Rosemont apartment at 6:45. There was a light under the door and he turned the lock to see Teri in the doorway wearing one of Baxter's red V necked sweaters and a pair of black stretch pants.

"Welcome home, stranger," she greeted him. He set down his brief case and Teri greeted him with fresh lipstick and a wet kiss. "I'm cooking tonight. We're having pasta, French bread, salad, and wine. I'll bet you didn't expect to see me here tonight."

Baxter had seen his car, intact, parked in the carport when he left the taxicab. He had assumed that Teri had used the car for her errands and left his life. Now, here she was, greeting him domestically with dinner.

"I thought you would be getting on with your life," Baxter said seating himself on the hide-a-bed.

"I am getting on with my life," Teri said pouring Baxter a glass of wine from a wicker covered Chianti bottle. "I've decided to move in with you. I moved out of the airline attendant apartment and moved in here."

"I don't recall asking you," Baxter responded.

"If you don't like me after dinner, I'll move out in the morning. Isn't that terrific Chianti? It's pricey, but I wanted tonight to be perfect."

Sondheim's Company played on Baxter's sound system. The Chianti was very good. He took off his jacket and loosened his tie. There certainly was no throwing her out that night. Baxter settled in to make the most of things.

Teri had moved in for the long term. The studio apartment had met Baxter's need in his previous life as a part-time resident, but now he had acquired a full time resident in Teri. She had moved in her wardrobe, cassette tapes, and appliances and was staked out to stay. Teri was easily passionate and a willing lover. There was really only one flaw. Baxter didn't trust her. Teri had obviously been looking for an alternative living arrangement and had discovered Baxter. She was bright, attractive, and possessed a highly desirable body, but Baxter distrusted her.

They came to agreement over morning coffee that Teri would move out as soon as she was able. She needed a car, however, to get around in Chicago. One of the bartender's at Sonny's was selling his car, a 1970 Chevrolet. Could Joe help her buy it? Teri needed to work with a voice coach in Chicago. Could Baxter help out? She would keep track of his advances and settle up when she moved on. Occasionally money would be missing from Baxter's billfold and he assumed that Teri was getting up in the middle of the night to secure still an additional advance. She held her advances to something between ten to fifteen dollars. They met on weekends at Sonny's Supper Club. Teri sang initially in the quintet of *A Little Night Music*, but Dirk placed Teri in role of Anne after two weeks. Lorna was furious when she learned that Teri had moved in with Baxter.

"Joe," she said one evening after a performance. "Why did you let that little bitch move in with you? You're going to be a partner candidate soon. Do you realize how leaving your wife and moving in with a 19 year old girl is going to look?"

"She's nearly twenty," Baxter corrected her.

"Joe. She's a vicious dishonest little bitch. She's getting her hooks into you."

"I'll give you a deal," Baxter said to Lorna. "I'll throw her out, but you have to move in as her replacement."

"Joe," Lorna replied. "You are not only impossible, but also awfully foolish."

Baxter had acquired a mistress. He was not madly in love with her, but Teri had qualities of accessibility.

A Little Night Music raised the curtain at 8:00 PM and ran through 11 PM. Teri usually arrived at Baxter's apartment between midnight and one in the morning. Baxter tried to wait up for her working on McKenzie Barber projects. He would sit at the kitchen table and work spread sheets into the night. Teri would arrive bright and vigorous.

"Com'on, Joe. Take me out and buy me a drink someplace."

He would beg off pleading either an early morning flight or a breakfast meeting. Teri then took to calling him from Sonny's. "Joe, I'm going to go out with the kids tonight. So I'll be out a little late."

After a week or so of staying out with the kids, Teri quit calling. "I was going to call you, Joe, but it got so late and I knew you had to be someplace very early."

Some nights Teri didn't come home at all or came in the door at the time Baxter was sipping his breakfast coffee.

"Have a nice evening, dear?" he would greet her.

"You really don't care what I do, do you Joe?"

"You and I are temporary," Baxter would explain. "You can move out anytime without hard feelings. I do expect you to pay me back for the car and the other money you have borrowed from me."

"I'll pay you back every penny," Teri would promise.

Baxter customarily spent weekends with the children and Teri disappeared on her own personal social agenda. He caught Teri's attention when he packed his large bag on the morning of Friday, June 6th.

She had returned to the apartment at ten minutes before six and Baxter was closing the zipper on his bag.

"You're going away for the weekend?"

"Yes," Baxter replied. He started to say that he was attending a compulsory McKenzie Barber training conference, but caught himself.

"When will you be back?" she asked.

"Sunday night late."

"Are you spending the weekend with someone?" Teri probed.

"Yes. It's a hideaway on the East Coast. Fresh air, horses, swimming, and dancing in the evening under the stars."

"And you're going to be there with a woman?"

"An older woman. She's quite wealthy," Baxter added.

Teri opened the closet and hunted for a hanger for her dress. "We need a bigger apartment," she grumbled. "We need more closet space."

"This apartment is just fine for my purposes," Baxter explained. "You were invited in for a nightcap four weeks ago. It has been an extended nightcap. I have a life to lead."

Teri stood in front of Baxter in a black foundation garment and pantyhose. Her brown hair was slightly mussed and there were faint circles around Teri's eyes.

"You don't want me here anymore?" Slight tears formed in the corners of her eyes.

"You might find some other place to live. How about where you stayed most of last night?" Baxter asked.

"You're angry with me, Joe. But you and I have never really had an understanding. I've liked the freedom you've given me. There have never been any strings and I've always been here for you when you wanted me."

"I'm not angry with you, Teri. But I suggest you think hard about other living arrangements while I'm gone."

Baxter took it as his cue to leave when Teri broke into full tears.

Baxter spent the afternoon of June 6th in one of Leon Harwell's conference rooms. In the dark paneled wood conference room, the white walled efficiency apartment back in Rosemont seemed to be on another planet. What would Mr. Leon think if he knew Baxter had a young tramp with a good voice living with him? Baxter was in the conference room because he was a McKenzie Barber consultant. That made him something special in Mr. Leon's eyes. He was about to begin a meeting with the head of one of America's great family fortunes. Baxter recognized he had advanced up the social mountain from Iron Creek, Minnesota to this room and he vowed to himself to continue his move up the mountain until the air became too thin.

Mrs. Moore brought in the coffee service and announced that Mr. Harwell had been supervising the trading this afternoon, but would be in shortly.

Baxter sipped his coffee for another five minutes and reviewed the Hi-Value Auto Parts report for what he estimated as at least the fifteenth time. The report was comprehensive and included a number of recommendations that would promote retention of key employees without dramatic increases in base salaries. He had discussed the report line by line over the telephone with Mr. Leon. He questioned every finding in detail and asked for back-up data. The $15,000 study now contained $28,000 worth of time at McKenzie Barber standard rates.

"I'm sorry to keep you waiting, Joe," Mr. Leon apologized as he entered the room. He seemed happy and energized on this afternoon. "I liquidated our position in several stocks. I'm a great Friday afternoon trader."

"Do you personally manage all of the money for Harwell Management?" Baxter asked.

"No." Mr. Leon made a face as if Baxter had asked a very naive question. "I engage a number of outside money managers and I run a pool of money personally. Most outside money managers believe that they are required to measure their performance against the S & P. If they want to manage our money, they are measured against my personal performance. The fund I manage personally generally exceeds the performance of the outside managers, and always exceeds the S & P. Harwell is the performance standard around here," Mr. Leon proclaimed proudly.

"Have I ever shown you how we're organized?" Mr. Leon continued. He seemed in a friendly and expansive mood and began to draw boxes on a legal pad that had been left out for him.

"I'm at the top." He drew a rectangle.

L. Harwell
President

| N. Harwell | D. Gasten | S. Greenstein | A. Barlow | M. Dunn |
|---|---|---|---|---|
| SVP | VP | CFO | VP | VP |
| | | | Trading | Investments |

"Now, let me take you through Harwell Management from left to right. We were once the Harwell Trust Company. There was my Dad, his investment manager, a bookkeeper, two secretaries, a receptionist, and a messenger. I started to come in the office in 1941. The Investment Manager grudgingly gave me a desk in the corner that later was closed off into a small cubicle. He vigorously complained to my father that my presence in the office was needlessly raising the overhead."

"Then my brother, Will, came back from the Navy. My Dad became the Chairman. Will became the President and I became Executive Vice President. I retired the Investment Manager whose investment style was low yield fixed income. Will and I became Harwell Management, the feared corporate raider," Mr. Leon sighed. "What a joke we must have been to others! Will had come out of the Navy ready to take on industrial America. He regarded the family money as his birthright. It took me about six years to get Will under control. Ernie Grey was a big help in reasoning with Will."

"I was pretty much running Harwell Management alone when Will disappeared in his plane crash. There is a long winded explanation for the box on the left. N. Harwell is Ned Harwell, Will's oldest son. I promised his mother that Ned would always have a place at Harwell Management. He represents the Management Company in our charitable giving activities."

"The next box, D. Gaston, is Dan Gaston, also family. He married our daughter, Claudia. Dan is our house counsel."

"Then we have Sid Greenstein. Sid's our chief finance person. When I call Sid, our Chief Financial Officer, he corrects me. 'You're the Chief Financial Officer around here, Mr. Leon. I'm really the controller.' Sid's really very good, Joe. We hired him from our public accounting firm ten years ago. He was the manager on our audit."

"Next we have Abe Barlow, our trader. We hired Abe from Broadbaker Brothers about a dozen years ago. He maintains the relationships with all of the clearing houses. Last we have Marcus Dunn, a very bright able young man, whom we sponsored through Columbia Business School. Marcus is the son of my chauffeur, and assists me in running my personal investment fund and supervising the outside portfolio managers. We employ about twenty people here, make money for the family to live on, provide charitable contributions, create jobs for family members, and generally make the world a better place by outperforming the S & P by a country mile."

"It's a very interesting collection of people," Baxter commented.

"It's a very fragile organization. If something happens to me, it will be outright chaos. I, by the way, have a wonderful wife named Adele, and three children. My oldest boy, Wilson, lives in California, and presumably earns a living as a film maker. My daughter, Claudia, is married to Dan Gaston, our house attorney. My youngest son, Bennett, is in his first year of Collegiate School."

"There are a great many more mouths to feed than you see around the office. At last count there were a total of ninety-seven uncles, aunts, nieces, nephews, and cousins feeding from the family trough. It could be worse, I suppose. There could be more of them and they could be militant. Some day, Joe, when we have more time, I'll delight you with a short history of the Harwell family. My Grandfather was reputed to be the most ruthless man of his time."

"I'd like that, sir," Baxter replied.

"Now we should discuss Hi-Valu Auto Parts, Joe."

They had discussed the Hi-Valu Auto Parts report twice in telephone conversations. Their first conversation had been close to one hour long. Their second discussion, two days later, had run nearly thirty minutes. Mr. Leon closed off with, 'I suppose we can really get into your report the next time you visit New York."

The Saturday meeting in Westchester provided Baxter the opportunity to meet Harwell Management on the preceding Friday afternoon.

Mr. Leon began the new discussion of the report with a fresh energy. He repeated his old questions and posed new ones. Mr. Leon's questions had little to do with compensation levels, but were focused on the quality and potential of the people who reported to the Gauer Brothers.

"Mr. Leon," Baxter reminded Harwell. "I was engaged to review the compensation plans affecting top management, not to perform an assessment of their management capabilities."

"But, then again, you did, didn't you?" Mr. Leon reminded Baxter. "You discussed senior management pay plans, you reviewed business strategy, organizational depth, and the other realities of doing business. You have developed an important bi-product for me as an investor. Now, Joe, put yourself in my chair. How long would you stay with Hi-Valu Auto Parts?"

"I'm not in the business of investment advice, Mr. Leon."

"Joe, if your aged aunt, Noreen, back in Minnesota, held this stock, what would you tell her? It closed at 21 5/8s today. Harwell Investment came in at 12 1/2, the IPO price. When do we get out?"

"But you're on the Board. You chair the compensation committee," Baxter protested. "It would send a chilling message to the investment company when you sell your stock."

"Joe, I just went on the board and told them I would serve only a year or so. The Harwell name clearly embellished that group of local luminaries they assembled as directors. Recognizing that I can leave the board at anytime it is appropriate and I don't possess a gorilla's sense of market timing. When should we exit, Joe?"

"I didn't come to this meeting with that kind of analysis, Mr. Leon," Baxter responded.

"I would hope that you brought some judgment with you, Joe. If you and I are going to work together over a long time horizon, Joe, I would like to hear some conclusions from you. Now you've looked at the numbers, the market, and the people. You and I both know that Hi-Valu is not a stock that a shareholder holds forever. Now tell me! When do we get out?"

"Between 35 and 38 which the stock should hit next spring," Baxter answered.

"How did you reach the 35 and 38?" Mr. Leon asked.

"Probably PE ratios based on plan. They will hit their earnings growth over the next two years and they will have price competition and will have grown to a size that will be difficult to manage. The Gauers are looking to do other things. You should, as you already have, provide them a significant incentive to stay and perform. That is a clear recommendation from our report. My estimate, Mr. Leon, is that the stock will peak around 35 and 38 in two year's time. That's based on intuitive judgment and rather primitive ratio analysis," Baxter stated.

"You're probably close to reality, Joe. As I explained before, we engage outside money managers. They are full of quantitative theories and modern portfolio management processes. These managers are all quantitative and portfolio management theory oriented. They see numbers, judge on numbers, hang onto 70% of their stocks in the 90% performance level, sell off the stocks in the next three decibels and they move on. There is no personalized investment oversight, just computer models. No sensitivity to the enterprise, just number junk! I have always been a different kind of stock-picker, and I outperform the portfolio managers. The difference is that I take risks. I bet on people, not numbers. I have some theories about compensation and performance that I want to put in practice. I believe you and I are off to a good start on Hi-Valu Auto Parts. I would like to try you

162

on some others. I suspect that you spent a little more time on Hi-Valu than you had anticipated."

"Yes I did, sir," Baxter answered.

"Then bill me for the excess, but not one penny more. Now, Joe, what is this weekend meeting you're attending?"

Baxter provided a vague explanation about the meeting.

"I'm about ready to leave for the day. The Hudson Conference Center is on my way. I'll drop you."

They were picked up in front of the brownstone by a black chauffeur dressed in a black suit, white shirt, black tie, and highly shined shoes.

"Good evening, Mr. Leon." The black man greeted them, opening the door to a dark blue Cadillac limousine.

"Joe, this is Lamar Dunn, my chauffeur and confidante. Lamar's son is a very able young man who assists me in investment matters."

The black man shook hands with Baxter, and then opened the trunk for his bags. "Lamar, we're going to drop Mr. Baxter off at the Hudson Conference Center. You know, the old Meyerman estate. Go up 87. It's not far out of our way."

"Who was Meyerman?" Baxter asked conversationally when they were settled in the back seat.

"Lamar? Do we have beer in the refrigerator?" Mr. Leon called ahead.

"Yes sir. We have Chinese and German beer back there, Mr. Leon," Lamar called back.

Leon Harwell opened the small refrigerator. "What will it be, Joe. I love to have a beer on the ride home Friday evening. Ever had a Tsing-Tso beer? Maybe it's time you tried one. We even have plastic glasses."

"Then it's Tsing-Tso beer, Mr. Leon."

"A good choice, Joe."

They settled back with their beers and Mr. Leon re-addressed the subject of Meyerman. "Meyerman was a peer of both Broadbaker and Goldman and his investment firm was bigger than Goldman through the late twenties. He built an enormous estate for his family at a time when they didn't want Jews in Westchester. He was nearly wiped out in the depression, and merged his firm with Broadbaker. Meyerman wound up in personal bankruptcy, the house was sold a couple of times, and wound up as a conference center. You'll be meeting, Joe, in a place that was one man's vision of the good life. Poor Meyerman. I went to Yale with one of his sons. He wound up as a dentist I believe. Having a wealthy father is no certain ticket to success or financial stability. I have grown the family fortune and helped others create wealth."

They sipped their Tsing-Tso beer in silence as the limousine maneuvered its way on to the FDR Drive.

"Now, Joe, are you a family man?"

"Yes sir I am. I have a son age 9 and a daughter age 6."

"And what does Mrs. Baxter think about all of your traveling?"

"Well sir, she's recognized that it's part of being a McKenzie Barber consultant," Baxter carefully responded.

"Has anyone suggested that you transfer east?" Harwell asked.

"No sir. Not formally."

"I would think your career would blossom a little faster in New York. You impress me as a young man with considerable ability. You also have a nice way about you. You would do well in New York. Would you like me to talk to Ernie Grey about you?"

"I would consider moving to New York, Mr. Leon. But it is important that my replacement, Carl Miller, is ready to take over for me in the Midwest."

"I understand all of those things, Joe. I would prefer that you were out here to participate in my little investment management experiment."

"I will remind you that Frank Alvardi, McKenzie Barber's National Practice Director for Executive Compensation, is resident here in the New York office," Baxter said.

"I have met your Frank Alvardi. Ernie asked me if I would meet him. Bruce Dinsmore, your managing partner for New York, brought Mr. Alvardi over for lunch. Dinsmore impressed me as a very good man. I've met him over the years. Your Mr. Alvardi impressed me as a smooth talking, shoe salesman. I could see him very well received by consumer packaged goods and apparel companies. I told them I was most happy going forward with you and that I wish you were officed a little closer to me. Then I called Ernie and told him that I may have a series of projects for you to take on. I believe, Joe, after you and I have had to do a number of these studies, you will develop a grasp of what I want and the work will come easier."

"What did you really want or expect from the Hi-Valu Auto Parts review?" Baxter asked.

"I wanted a management audit presented as a review of compensation. When I engage you to do one of these projects, I will expect a quick review of the business, the management, and the pay systems. I talked to Ernie about my idea and he assured me that it's done all the time. He mentioned that you had managed a similar assignment for a McKenzie Barber subsidiary involved in government work. I will simply tell Ernie, that based on your first project with me, I want you to continue forward."

Baxter sipped his Tsing-Tso beer and looked out the window at the East River and the skyline of Manhattan. The signs were pointing to New York City with McKenzie Barber. Baxter was at heart a small town guy who had not really caught on to Chicago. How could he possibly be ready to relocate to and thrive in New York City?

"Joe, have you ever done any international work?" Mr. Leon asked breaking the silence.

"No sir, I haven't," Baxter answered honestly. "I have worked for multinational corporations, but it's pertained to corporate officer positions, which has included the Senior International Officer's compensation. I have yet to work with the pay of overseas country managers."

"You might brush up or do some research on that area. I'm on the Board of U.S. Pharmaceutical and moved over to the Compensation Committee. I've been on Audit Committee for three years and it's a board that I enjoy. There was some talk this Spring about bringing in a consultant to study country manager's pay. They call their general managers, managing directors over there. They couldn't come to agreement in the Far East, but I know they want Europe reviewed. I expect that they will want to consider consultants around April of next year. I will see that you have the opportunity to compete for the work, provided you do some advance preparation."

"I'll talk to Frank Alvardi about it," Baxter said.

"You may talk to and consult with Mr. Alvardi to your heart's content, Joe. But the McKenzie Barber consultant I want to introduce to U.S. Pharmaceutical is Joe Baxter. I don't think McKenzie Barber has done a lick of work at U.S. Pharmaceutical in the last ten years. You will be competing against Robson Allen, and at least one of those actuarial firms. I'll arrange for my office to send you out an annual report, 10K, and a proxy. Think about U.S. Pharmaceutical, Joe. There's no hurry right now, but when it's time, I'll see that you get the chance. I may have another project similar to Hi-Valu for you. I'll be back to you on that."

The limousine pulled in front of a massive iron gate with Hudson Conference Center in large letters over the gate. They drove up the driveway about a half mile to a large mansard roofed stone building. "Think of it, Joe. Someone used to live here. The Meyermans once represented one of the premier family fortunes of America. Now their home serves as a retreat house for corporate groups. There are some lessons here, Joe." Baxter stepped out of the limousine at the main entrance. Mr. Leon waved and Lamar, his driver retrieved Baxter's bags and shook hands.

There was a thick packet with Baxter's name on it waiting at reception for him. It was 6:15 PM. "You're the last one," a uniformed lady behind the reception desk explained to Baxter. "They have been checking in all afternoon and some people from your firm have gotten some tennis in. I'm supposed to tell you that cocktails are at 6:30 in the Monroe Room, and dinner will be served at 7:30 in the Jefferson Room. Your meetings over the weekend will be held in the main auditorium. Your room, Mr. Baxter, is in the annex at the far rear of the estate." She rang a bell and a black attendant clad in white shirt, necktie, and blazer appeared.

"Henry, this is Mr. Baxter. He's with the McKenzie Barber group. He is in the far annex in room 520. Henry will take you out in the golf cart."

"Will I need to take a bus to get back in?" Baxter asked as Henry packed his bags in the back of the gold cart.

"It's about a ten minute walk, sir," Henry explained. "They got the McKenzie Barber folks spread out all over the place. You and a Mr. Grunwaldyt are the only ones out in the annex."

The golf cart proceeded around the side of the building and moved along a cement sidewalk past the tennis courts and over the grounds to a white frame building that looked like a dormitory. "It's nice and quiet back here," Henry observed. "It's just a little walk to the main building and I'll come out and pick you up if it's raining, or you think it's too far to walk."

Baxter was taken to a back room that looked out on a flower garden. His room contained a double bed, a wet bar, a refrigerator, a writing desk and two wicker chairs with foam cushions. The walls were white and the furniture was brown. Baxter left his hallway door open to air out the room and sent Henry off with a five dollar bill after he located the beer.

Baxter decided he would wear a suit to the cocktail party, shave, and put on a fresh shirt. He had just finished shaving when he heard a rap at his door. "Com'on in," he called out. The door opened and a handsome young man entered. His hair was cut short, his features well chiseled, and he had a tall athletic build. It was his grin that made him appear boyish. It was friendly, yet impish. His face seemed to say, 'I know something you don't know. Let's see you get it out of me.'

"Hi, you must be Baxter. I'm Jon. That's J-O-N, Grunwaldyt."

Baxter gripped the hand extended. Grunwaldyt wore a blue blazer, blue and red club tie, grey slacks, and tassel loafers. He held a beer can in his left hand.

"You and I are the only ones out in the annex. I'm a first year associate. Where are you from?"

"I'm from the Chicago office," Baxter answered.

"You look too old to be an Associate."

"I'm a Director. I run the Executive Compensation practice in Chicago."

"I didn't know we had an Executive Compensation practice in Chicago. I thought Alvardi was the whole thing."

"I used to work for Alvardi in Chicago. He moved to New York and I succeeded him," Baxter explained. "How long have you been with the firm, Jon?"

"I was in the hiring class of 1973 and made Associate in October 1974. I'm in the IE practice and they had me in college recruiting this Spring. I'm a last minute substitution for Norb Benson, who's at the Director level like you. He got called off to Barber Germany to manage a major engagement that apparently got into trouble. When he tried to cancel, Executive Office had a fit. I was called Thursday night and told to show up here for the weekend. Apparently Executive insisted that the New York IE practice be represented. So here I am, a first year Associate hanging around on a weekend with the Deputy Chairman, Partners, Directors, and Managers. If nothing else comes from this, I certainly will get a lot of exposure. Now I know why I'm out of the annex. I'm a junior man. Why did they put you out here? Don't they like you?" Grunwaldyt asked bluntly.

"I'm expected to mentor you and keep you out of trouble," Baxter replied unwrapping a fresh shirt. "Sit down, Jon, and tell me a little more about yourself," Baxter invited.

"What's all this about?" Grunwaldyt asked sitting on the edge of Baxter's bed.

"Have you read the memo from Harvey?"

"Um hum."

"Then you know what I know, Jon. When McKenzie Barber asks me to go somewhere, I show up. Here I am."

"Are you one of those people that the firm hired from outside the firm?" Grunwaldyt asked.

"It's not like we're from broken homes, Jon. But for the record, I did join the firm after serving as a senior officer for a consumer durables company," Baxter explained.

"Are you the one that Wild Bill Dwyer likes to talk about?" Grunwaldyt queried.

"That depends on what he has to say," Baxter responded.

"He describes a young plant manager without any real manufacturing skills who used common sense and the ability to manage people to be successful."

"That's not me," Baxter observed. "How's Bill doing?"

"He's five levels up from me. They're trying to combine the IE and the Manufacturing practice with co-directors. I don't know how it's going to work. I'm an IE, so if you're a friend of Dwyer, you shouldn't ask me."

Baxter knotted his tie. "I understand that there's a cocktail party at 6:30. What do you say that we walk in together?"

"I'd love it. Do you have a business card, Joe?"

Baxter produced a card. "Do you want one of mine?" Grunwaldyt asked.

"No," Baxter said. "I think I know how to find you if I need you."

*Dwight E. Foster*

They walked down the pathway to the mansion in the fading seven o'clock light. Grunwaldyt was clearly disturbed that Baxter did not ask for his business card and his confidence seemed momentarily shaken.

"This is quite a place," Grunwaldyt remarked. "Do you suppose someone used to live here?"

"The Meyermans lived here," Baxter announced. "They were as big as Goldman before the crash. They sold to Broadbaker eventually."

"I didn't know that," Grunwaldyt acknowledged.

The cocktail party in the Monroe Room was in full attendance when Grunwaldyt and Baxter entered the room. Andy was standing near a chafing dish and waved to Baxter as he entered the room. Most of the other faces were strangers. They wore blue blazers and grey pants as if they were uniforms. Andy at first appeared to be the only woman in the room. She wore a high necked dress with short sleeves. Later as Baxter looked around the room, he observed a second woman. She was stocky and wore her hair short. Baxter went over to greet her after he ordered a Canadian Club from the bar. "Hi, I'm Joe Baxter," he greeted her.

"Alice Dungler," she greeted him and extended a moist hand.

"What office are you from?" Baxter asked.

"You don't have a name tag on, do you?" She moved her shoulder to display her name tag over a large breast. Her nametag read "Alice Dungler, Los Angeles."

"I'm from Chicago."

"You should get a nametag. They're out front," she said dismissing Baxter and resuming conversation with a lantern jawed man on her left. Andy caught Baxter at the door. She had his nametag and pinned it over his left hand breast pocket below his handkerchief. Andy waved across the room to a greying man with a crewcut. "That's Harvey Randolph, the Deputy Chairman. He really wants to meet you, Joe."

"Who is Alice Dungler?" Baxter asked.

"An absolutely dreadful woman from Los Angeles. She was an Operations Research Analyst and now she's a Manager in the Systems Practice. We were desperate to have women participate and had to settle for her."

Harvey Randolph, the Deputy Chairman of McKenzie Barber, now stood in front of Baxter. He was about five foot nine and heavy set. His close cropped hair was salt and pepper and his smile was radiant. "Joe, I've heard so much about you. I'm Harvey Randolph." His handshake and smile were warm. Harvey impressed Baxter as a man who presented a self-effacing image, but was accustomed to being in charge.

"I'm going to have to leave early this evening," Harvey explained. "Mrs. Randolph had something planned well ahead of this meeting. I want

168

to spend some time with you, Joe. What do you say we have dinner Saturday night after the session?"

"I'd like that," Baxter agreed.

"I've heard so much about you from Ernie, Clyde and Frank, that I thought it would be good to spend some time with you when you were out and get to know you better." Harvey emptied the glass in his hand. "I've got to get going," he announced handing the glass to Andy. "Joe, I'll see you in the morning." Harvey kissed Andy on the cheek and then walked briskly out of the room. Grunwaldyt had drawn up beside them. Baxter introduced him to Andy and looked over the room.

He scanned the name tags. All of the up and comers he had heard about were in the room. The only ones who knew Baxter's reputation were Andy, Clyde and Harvey Randolph.

"Am I the only one here from Chicago?" Baxter asked Andy.

"We tried to get three from Chicago, but you were the only one Brimmer agreed to send," Andy inspected Grunwaldyt's nametag. "I don't remember your name on the invitation list, Jon."

"I'm a last minute substitution for Norb Benson," Grunwaldyt explained. "Norb was called off to handle a crisis for Barber Germany. I guess they picked me because I helped out in campus recruiting last year. I've also worked a lot in client training."

"You're a Manager, then?" Andy said.

"No, I'm just an Associate," Grunwaldyt replied.

"But he made it in one year," Baxter commented. "We didn't."

Baxter placed his hand on Grunwaldy't shoulder. "It's young men like this that will sustain the growth of this firm into the year 2000 and beyond," Baxter said.

Andy made a face and excused herself.

"So that was Andy Bourke," Grunwaldyt observed. "Do you know her well?"

"We started at McKenzie Barber on the same day. We filled out health insurance forms together. We once worked on a major internal review together and we talk by phone every two weeks. She's what I would classify as a friend. Do you have any dirt on her, Jon?" Baxter ordered a second Canadian Club. Grunwaldyt blushed a little and joined him in a white wine.

"Do you want to sit together at dinner?" he asked timidly.

"I wouldn't consider sitting with anyone else. Not even that nice Alice Dungler."

Baxter could see Clyde Nickerson in the room. He was grinning and shaking hands as he made his way through the room. Andy was now at his elbow apparently playing the hostess.

"She's bloomed into a fine looking woman," Baxter observed.

"And they make a nice couple," Grunwaldyt said with a rigid cherubic face.

"Is that the talk around the New York office, Jon?"

"That's what's talked about. I'm sure it's not true," Grunwaldyt confirmed.

Clyde and Andy had traversed the room and were drawing up to the place near the bar that Grunwaldyt and Baxter occupied. It was the first time Baxter had seen Clyde as a Partner. He seemed more cheerful and confident than Baxter remembered him in Chicago.

"Joe," he greeted Baxter with a handshake. "I'm glad you're here. We're looking forward to some real contributions from you tomorrow. By the way, did Harvey get to you? He couldn't stay tonight, but I believe he wants to have dinner with you tomorrow. Why, I don't know. The Deputy Chairman doesn't always confide his inner most thoughts to first year partners."

"Jon!" Clyde greeted Grunwaldyt. "I heard the news about Norb Benson and I think you're a sensational replacement. We need an Associate's input into the process."

"I'm glad and very flattered to be here, Clyde," Grunwaldyt replied.

Clyde got a glass and a spoon from the bartender and rattled the spoon against the glass for the room's attention.

"Ladies and Gentlemen! Dinner is served in the Jefferson Room. There are placecards at the table which will provide you the opportunity at dinner to continue to get acquainted. Bon Appetit!"

Baxter and Grunwaldyt were seated on each side of Alice Dungler. "Hello again, Alice," Baxter greeted her. "I have a name tag. This is Jon Grunwaldyt from the New York IE practice."

Alice shook Jon's hand and began talking loudly to the Manager from the San Francisco office named Fred Tabor. "You have no goddamned business doing work for that Bakersfield cooperative! You have no resident competence in the food processing industry and I'm going to get to Harvey Randolph tomorrow about this," she threatened Fred, a balding scholarly man in his late thirties, who stared at the ceiling as Alice shouted.

"Jon," Baxter said across Alice Dungler, "Shall we say grace?"

"You say it, Joe," Jon responded.

Baxter bowed his head and Grunwaldyt followed suit. "Lord, give Alice Dungler the power to smite her enemies! Amen!"

Alice grinned at Baxter. "Are you supposed to be funny?"

"No," Baxter replied. "I'm deeply religious and highly supportive to you. Put in a good word to Harvey for me tomorrow if you can!"

"You're outrageous!" Alice concluded and she clinked glasses with Baxter. Then the table of six shook hands. Alice was the only woman at the table. They were all Managers with the exception of Baxter and Grunwaldyt. Fred Tabor was a Manager in the San Francisco Systems practice. Harley Dimon, a dark haired young man with high cheekbones and long eyelashes, was a Manager in the Atlanta IE practice. Lastly at the table was Tom Ruffle from Dallas who wore a crew cut and turned out to be a Naval Academy graduate.

They were given a choice of fish or steak and two bottles of red and white wine were placed on each table. Everyone consumed and the table became convivial. Alice and Baxter became buddies after two glasses of wine.

"Now, tell us Joe. How did a hotshot Director like you get stuck in a table with a bunch of Managers and an Associate? You should be up at the head table with Nickerson and the other Partners, and that world famous consultant, Andy Bourke!" Alice pulled on Baxter's arm. "Look at her up there. Looks like she's the damned queen of the manor! I don't think she's ever seen a client!"

Grunwaldyt told Alice in a low voice that Baxter and Andy were good friends.

"Ha!" Alice said pulling on Baxter's arm again. "Your good friend, Andy, gives women in business a bad name." Alice was heavyset, but firm. Her glasses were now resting on her forehead. "Fred, I apologize for yelling at you earlier. You're a good professional, but you're in way over your head in food processing. Let me spend a day with your people up in Bakersfield. I won't charge you a dime!"

"Alice, I wanted you on the engagement from the beginning, but Floyd wanted San Francisco consultants on the engagement," Fred answered.

"You put a bunch of people with banking experience on a system with a lot of logistical variables. That lead consultant, Alan what's-his-name, called me and asked thirty minutes of the dumbest questions I ever heard."

"He's a smart young Stanford MBA a year out of the pool. What he needs is some nurturing, Alice. He knows he's on the line on this engagement."

"He's working with a Co-op, Fred. They are well meaning, not very bright, fee sensitive, and vindictive when they don't believe they got what they paid for. We're probably going to get sued by that Co-op up in Sacramento. That was another engagement that nobody talked to me about until it was out of control. Our systems practice is in deep doo-doo, guys. That's one of the reasons why we're out here. Today's systems problems of America's business cannot be solved by smart, apple cheeked MBAs. Either we hire experienced people or we train them up." Baxter looked at Grunwalydt's cherubic face. His wine glass was barely touched. His eyes and ears were carefully recording and processing the talk around him. Alice turned to Baxter.

"This firm used to pretend that computers didn't exist until the early sixties. The IEs were into linear programming and modeling, but there was no hardcore systems data processing consulting. They should have gone outside to hire someone like Dwyer, the manufacturing practice leader."

"What's your background, Alice?" Baxter asked.

She squeezed his arm again. "I thought you'd never ask, big boy."

Everyone around the table grinned with the exception of Grunwaldyt who remained stone faced.

"I'm Cal Poly double mathematics and MS in OR from Carnegie, and mercy me, I hold a doctorate in applied mathematics. I worked for Rand Corp, Hughes, and DOD before I got my doctorate scholarship at Carnegie."

"How did you come to work for McKenzie Barber?" Grunwaldyt asked.

"I went to work for FSO, the business no one likes to talk about, in 1972. I was out there a year and the LA office borrowed me for a big job for the Tomato Processing business of Hortense Foods. I came in when it was a near disaster and turned it around. LA asked me to come out permanently and I've been there two years. I'm what they call a non-traditional McKenzie Barber Manager. I guess that's why I'm here at this shindig. How about the rest of you? If Andy Bourke planned tomorrow's program, we will all be asked to stand up and say a few highly edited words about ourselves. She learned that little trick from her college sorority. But here we are. Let's get down and dirty and tell the truth about ourselves! Let's start with you, big boy!" Alice again squeezed Baxter's arm. "My name is Joe Baxter. I'm from a small town in Minnesota where my father was in the Mining business. I served in the Army and hold a couple of degrees from the University of Minnesota with my graduate degree in Industrial Relations. I was recruited in a campus interviewing process to join a medium sized manufacturer of housewares in Racine, Wisconsin. I joined Washburn Manufacturing as Executive Assistant to the President and later became a Plant Manager. My final job was that of Vice President and Secretary of the Company. I was hired into Bill Dwyer's Manufacturing Practice in 1967 and transferred after two years to Frank Alvardi's Executive Compensation practice. I was made Director in September 1974 and I run the compensation practices in both the Chicago and Cleveland offices."

"Seven years to Director. That's good," Tom Ruffle observed. Alice looked down at Grunwaldyt. "You're on, cutie pie."

"I'm Jon Grunwaldyt. I hold a BSIE degree from Michigan and a MS Industrial Administration from Purdue. Both degrees were conferred with honors. I served six months after duty with the Army Corps of Engineers between my undergraduate and graduate degrees and I hold the rank of

Captain in the US Army Reserves. I was heavily recruited by both Robson Allen and McKenzie Barber in graduate school, and was a summer intern at Robson Allen. I chose McKenzie Barber because I consider it a much stronger firm. I joined McKenzie Barber in 1973 and was promoted from the pool to Associate in October 1974. My industry experience to date has been in consumer packaged goods and cost analysis, and cost reduction has been my strength. I expect to become a Partner with McKenzie Barber and I find your comments and insights very interesting. I am learning from all of you and very pleased to be here and sharing this table with all of you."

"Ha! How's that for Mom and apple pie!" Alice exclaimed.

"Let's hear it from you, Harley."

"My name's Harley Dimon and I'm from the Atlanta office. I graduated from Georgia Tech with a BSIE, and I hold a MBA from Emory University. I served two years in the Army with a year in Vietnam as a Supply Officer. I joined the Atlanta office in the IE pool in 1970, made Associate in 1972 and Manager in 1974. I work extensively on inventory and production control systems in the textile and fabric conversion industries. I think my name was picked out of a hat to show up here this weekend. Harvey Randolph opened up and built the Atlanta office, and Neil Schmidt runs the practice now. I have never visited or worked with another practice of McKenzie Barber and outside those forums, this is the first time I've really had the opportunity to talk with managers from other offices. I'm really enjoying it."

"Bully! Harley!" Alice said. "Now you're up Fred. tell'em about your Doctorate!"

"I am Dr. Fred Tabor," Fred began. "I started to work for McKenzie Barber as a para-professional in office accounts as an undergraduate. I finished an undergraduate degree at Cal and attended Stanford as a John McKenzie scholar. I completed a MSIE in Operations Research, joined the San Francisco office full time in 1969, took eighteen months off to finish my doctorate and came back to the firm in 1972. I was appointed a Manager in 1973. I'm responsible for the Information Systems practice in the Pacific Northwest and Northern California and I will never go to Bakersfield again unless I'm accompanied by Alice."

"Well, I guess that leaves me," said Tom Ruffle from Dallas. His hair was cut short in a sandy grey crew cut. He had the look of a trim military officer. His white shirt had a crisp starched collar and he wore a plain dark blue linen tie with a military knot. "I'm Tom Ruffle. I graduated from the Naval Academy and went regular Navy where I was a submariner. Later I worked on Admiral Rickover's staff. My wife hated the Navy. I resigned my commission after eight years. My last CO had flown with Ernie Grey in World War II and he set me up to meet with Ernie and Clyde. I wound up with my choice of going to work for FSO as a program manager or going into the pool in the Dallas office. I took the pool in Dallas. I spent about a year in the pool and a Manager named Lon McMasters kind of picked me out to work with him in Cost Management. He told me that he intended to become a partner, and if I was any damned good, I would help get him there. McMasters was elected a Partner last October and I made Manager. He told me two weeks ago that I would be coming up here, and Lon instructed me to keep an eye on those assholes up at executive office. I'm like Joe. I come from a place outside McKenzie Barber and management consulting wasn't the career I had in mind when I graduated from the Academy. But I'm here now, and I'm good at what I do, and I'm making more now than I was in the Navy. I intend to stay at McKenzie Barber and become a Partner."

"How long have you been with the firm?" Grunwaldyt asked.

"Three years," Ruffle answered.

"Three years to Manager," Alice commented. "That's good!"

"How do you compare the Navy and McKenzie Barber?" Grunwaldyt asked.

"They're about the same, except working for McMasters is easier than working for Rickover."

"What in the hell did you learn about business in the Navy?" Alice demanded.

"A little. Not as much as you learn in business school, for example. But you learn a lot about leadership, organization, information flows, budgeting, politics, policy, and motivation. I was ready for McKenzie Barber," Ruffle looked to Baxter.

"Joe, did you learn much in the service?"

Baxter took a sip from his wine glass. "I learned organization and administration at the feet of a master, a black Sergeant Major named Wilson."

"Well, here's to him, godamit!" Ruffle said raising his glass followed by the others at the table.

"Sergeant Wilson!" Baxter toasted.

"Where is he now?" Alice demanded.

"Dead!" Baxter replied.

"Then let's raise our glasses once more," Tom Ruffle toasted.

"To Baxter's Sergeant Wilson and to the very able chiefs I served with!"

"Hear! Hear!" Grunwaldyt said, a little too loudly.

They were now a group. Jokes were told and gossip exchanged. Table mates left to attend to their needs and returned to the group. The surrounding tables broke up, and finally they were the last occupants in the Jefferson Room.

Andy stopped by the table, standing behind Baxter's chair and placing her hand on his shoulder. "You certainly are night owls!" Andy said. "We're going to start promptly at 8AM tomorrow morning and we have a very long day."

"8AM, dearie," Alice said with a refilled wine glass. "is like sleeping in! As line consultants, we're usually out at our clients at 7AM."

Andy rolled her eyes toward the ceiling. "I'm pleased that you all have another hour's sleep. I'll see you all at eight! Good Night!"

Baxter looked around the room for Clyde, but there was no sign of him. The table mates watched Andy walk through the Monroe Room and out of earshot. "I believe we are ready for after dinner drinks, my dear."

"Many after dinner drinks," Tom Ruffle seconded.

The waitress, a college age, fresh scrubbed, plain featured young woman, said something about them moving into the bar but Alice caught her short. "We'll lose the continuity of our discussion." She waved a ten dollar bill in front of the waitress. "This is cash over the house gratuity. Keep the booze coming, lady, and there will be another ten when we leave."

They all ordered double brandies and Alice asked for a cigar.

"I'll be discussion leader, guys," Alice declared. "Let's talk offices. The only communication I ever get in LA, outside the McKenzie Barber Global Report, which I might add, is absolute bullshit. The other source is from visiting consultants which is first class hearsay. In LA, we recognize that San Francisco is the enemy. They slip down to Bakersfield in the cover of night to sell jobs that they can't deliver to unsuspecting co-ops. We fear McKenzie Barber-San Francisco more than Robson Allen-LA. So let's talk about our offices, guys. This whole bullshit program may bomb by noon tomorrow and they'll send us all home. Let's seize the moment and communicate!"

"I believe we must define the parameters of communication," Tom Ruffle suggested.

"It should be relevant to our individual information needs," Grunwaldyt added.

"I believe we should succinctly describe the operating culture of our respective offices," Harley recommended.

"That sounds very behavioral," Baxter concluded. "I volunteer to go first. Otherwise we will never agree on what should be said and left unsaid." Alice gripped Baxter's arm. Her full breast brushed against Baxter's upper arm. "I think Joe's got it! Go to it, Joe! Then we can go around the table and hear what we all have to say. The house rules have to be, tell it like it is or don't say it. Is that agreeable to all?"

"Hell, yes!" was registered around the table.

"Go to it, big boy!" Alice urged. "Tell us about the operating culture of the Chicago office."

"I operate at a disadvantage" Baxter began. "I'm not intimately involved in the Chicago practice. I lead the Executive Compensation practice and I report up to Dr. Barry Keller, the Partner-in-Charge of the Business Strategy practice. I rarely see him personally and generally communicate with him through short notes. I don't think Dr. Barry really understands the CARS reports. Dr. Barry operates through an Administrative Director named Lee Heller. Lee is strictly a numbers man."

"I'm glad he's at least a numbers man," Alice interjected.

"That turkey was once on a systems engagement with me that we were supposed to co-manage. I had to carry him. I think he's flopped in every practice he's been in. I'm surprised he's not an outcounsel nominee."

"Thank you for sharing that with us, Alice," Baxter continued.

"There has been a significant interaction with the Business Strategy Practice because Executive Compensation represents the reinforcement agent for strategic planning. I've worked with the IE practice and have come to realize that they occasionally carry out assignments for their clients in the areas of incentive plans and basic pay plans. The Commercial Practice goes their own way, and I really don't pay much attention to the rest of the office. The only time I did was when I was asked to manage a review of FSO down in Washington. I had a temporary problem obtaining people to staff the engagement, but that worked out over time. The Chicago office seems to run itself. It also runs the Cleveland practice which is about fifty consultants. I supervise a compensation practice there and spend one day in ten in Cleveland. I have been with the firm for eight years and met once with Paul Brimmer, the Managing Partner, when I was hired, and once for lunch just before I was promoted to Manager. There's a Christmas Party in December. It is understood that everyone will attend. There is an off-site day long meeting mid-year, called a roundtable, that everyone attends or finds a good excuse to avoid the formal meeting and show up for cocktails. There are no other management meetings or any other feedback on how well the office is doing. The only other feedback is from the CARS reports. I rather like it that way," Baxter concluded.

"Any questions for Joe?" Alice asked in her assumed role as chairperson.

"I got one," Harley Dimon said. "Is it true you have an administrative lady up in Chicago who sings in nightclubs?"

"Harley, her name is Lorna King and she handled personnel administration. She does not sing in night clubs, but does sing on weekends at a suburban dinner theatre called Sonny's Supper Club," Baxter explained.

"Is she somebody's girl friend?" Harley asked further.

"She's not my girlfriend," Baxter responded. "I'm not into the Chicago office social scene."

"A very good vague report, Joe. You've managed to tell us very little in a smooth evasive presentation," Alice commented.

"You're up Ruffle," Alice instructed while lighting up her cigar.

"The Dallas Office opened up in 1963. It had about seventy people when I showed up three years ago. The office is very IE oriented. Everything is coded in the CARS reports as an IE engagement regardless of the function. I think they keep a lookout at the airport to make sure Wild Bill Dwyer doesn't come to town and walk off with some business. Rex Binger, the Managing Partner, is a tough, straight talking Texas A & M graduate who thinks the New York office is bullshit. We are now up to about 100 consultants and we operate in a high control, low trust work culture. We do, however, do damned good work and make a lot of money for McKenzie Barber."

"Remind me never to show up in Dallas?" Alice said between puffs on cigar. "How many women do you have on consulting staff?"

"Oh," Ruffle answered. "We get a lot of letters from Executive Office, I guess. Every year we interview a mess of women from the B School and then bring 'em in for interviews and scare the hell out of them. We make two offers a year and they're always declined. The only women we employ in Dallas are on administrative support staff."

Alice blew a large smoke ring. "Let's hear from Harley and possibly we will hear about an enlightened office."

"Atlanta's about 150 consultants, and I would estimate that 20% are women. Most of the women are in the Systems practice. Neil Schmidt, our Managing Partner, is a highly respected old school, Industrial Engineer, who is very active in the community. We do a lot of work in state and local government, banking, food processors, cooperatives, textiles, and furniture. It's all either systems or quantitative work measurement or cost reduction studies. We tend to do large projects and we are asked back. We borrow New York consultants, but Neil insists that Atlanta consultants participate on the engagement."

"He's been having Joe's friend, Frank Alvardi, down from New York lately, and has been talking about starting an Executive Compensation practice in Atlanta. Neil loves Bill Dwyer as a professional. His night owl hours bother Neil a little because Neil is a strict Baptist. But Neil told me that Bill Dwyer is the smartest manufacturing consultant he has ever seen. From an office culture point-of-view, we're collegial and a little parochial. People love to come to work in the Atlanta office and there is a sense of family."

"How is Jeff Long doing?" Baxter asked.

"He's leaving, Joe. Jeff's a fish out of water in the Atlanta office. He's got a little too much New York office in him to succeed in Atlanta. He's smart enough, but there's an edge about him that clients don't like. Neil counseled him out about a month ago. He thinks he got sold a bill of goods by Clyde and Andy. Transfers are tough because there's always so much distressed Associate level consulting merchandise around. Anybody else have a question?"

"Harley, you've made the Atlanta office sound like the Consulting Garden of Eden. You just be careful a snake doesn't get in there," Alice commented. "Let's get on to Fred so that he can lie about San Francisco."

"San Francisco is the best place to live in the United States. We love to bring in outside resources from other offices and they like to visit us. We have about 150 consultants and every discipline that the firm offers is represented in the San Francisco office. It has sophisticated clients that range from financial services to Silicon Valley. We have the youngest Managing Partner at McKenzie Barber in Floyd Piper. Floyd was elected a partner at age 30 and was named Managing Partner at age 35. Floyd's Stanford B School, and he's wired into the Bohemian Club. His family is prominent and our biggest fear is that a client will hire Floyd as CEO. Come by and see us! We'll show you some Northern California hospitality."

"Oh Jesus, Fred. What a goddam bullshit commercial for an office of pirates and territory invaders! This discussion has degenerated into PollyAnna time. How about you, young Seigfried?" Alice pointed toward Grunwaldyt with her cigar and flicked an ash into her coffee cup.

"You must recognize that I'm junior to all of you. I'm an Associate and you're all Managers and Joe's a Director. I'll give you my view of all the New York office through a first year Associate's eyes. I believe it is the best group of consulting talent ever assembled. Because it's so large, there are a number of bureaucratic practices that are required to maintain the equilibrium of the office. Bruce Dinsmore, the New York office Managing Partner, has been in place for a dozen years and will retire in about three years. A lot of the coffee and cocktail hour talk is concerned about who will succeed Mr. Dinsmore. I just listen because I'm not qualified to contribute. I did ride up in the elevator once with Mr. Dinsmore. He's a very distinguished man with a nice smile and tends to wear blue pinstripe suits with red ties. Most of my engagements have been financial analysis oriented, and I've yet to be out on a shop floor. I expect to be with McKenzie Barber long term, and New York is the office I want to be in."

"I believe we've touched bottom," Alice commented.

"No, Alice," Ruffle said. "Bottom has to be LA. Let's hear the real guff about LA!"

Alice turned to Baxter. Her cigar had gone out. "Got a light, handsome?" Baxter re-lit her cigar with a book of table matches. "The LA practice is a lot like the Oakland Raiders from a reputation point-of-view. We're bad guys, disliked by the other offices, and we make a lot of money. It's a Loony-Toons office headed by Ben Sydes, who spends most of his time hanging around the Jonathan Club either in the restaurant or the men's room. I don't think Ben has set foot in the office for at least three years. He spends his free time in Beverly Hills. The Partners are all free spirits, movie star handsome, and fancy themselves cocksmen. Everything is kind of free flowing. The Directors and Mangers seem to run the office. Consultants work godawful hours and everybody seems to be sleeping with everyone else. We love to borrow other office consultants. We bring them in and corrupt them. The ones we completely corrupt, we transfer in so that they can help us corrupt others. We especially like when Ernie Grey comes to visit because then Ben Sydes is required to come in the office and greet Ernie."

"We have very smart, independent consultants who spend their free time doing drugs and bitching about how dumb and pompous McKenzie Barber is. Bob Friedman is our up and comer, and will take over the office as soon as the dummies out in Executive Office catch on to what a flake Ben Sydes is. Friedman is slick, smooth, smart, a free spirit, and an incredible tennis player. He sells one hell of a lot of work at his tennis club, and his father-in-law is one of the biggest real estate developers in Southern California. Friedman owns the S & L industry in California. After working in LA for three years you will never fit into a conventional office of McKenzie Barber. That, boys, is the plain unvarnished truth. Any questions?"

"How is Ruth Ingvold doing?" Baxter asked about the woman Friedman had hired to run the Executive Compensation practice.

"She'll never make October," Alice answered. "She has no business. I asked Friedman what he was going to do about her. He told me that he had a transfer in mind. Transfer from where I asked him. No answer from handsome Bob."

"Well that's everybody," Ruffle said getting up from his chair. "Like the lady from EO said. Morning comes early around here." Ruffle was followed by Harley and Fred leaving Baxter and Grunwaldyt with Alice.

"Cinderella time!" Baxter said rising to his feet with Grunwaldyt quickly following his lead. Alice put out her cigar and pushed herself up next to Baxter.

"Want to see me to my room, big boy?" she asked.

"Jon and I wouldn't have it any other way," Baxter said and they saw Alice to the elevator in the main building. Grunwaldyt and Baxter walked out of the main building and started their walk across the lawn to the Annex.

"My god, that was an education!" Grunwaldyt exclaimed in a low voice. "Could you believe the way they described Dallas and LA?"

"Jon," Baxter explained to his newly found friend. "I had more trouble with the way they described Atlanta and San Francisco."

"I've got to think about that," Grunwaldyt said.

Baxter found a note under his door. It read:

Dear Joe:

You certainly have turned into a night owl. If you get back to your room before 12, give me a call at room 1064. If you come in after midnight, meet me for breakfast at 7AM in the Garden Room off the lobby. We would like you to take Norb Benson's spot as a discussion leader. Clyde thinks that Jon Grunwaldyt is too young and inexperienced. I'm sorry that you didn't find time to come over to our table at dinner. Communication is a two way street. Let's you and I start communicating with breakfast.

Andy

Baxter's watch read 12:30 AM. He undressed and stared at the white ceiling of his room through the half-light from the yard lights. What in hell was he doing here? he asked himself.

Andy greeted Baxter in a white pants suit and flat shoes. "That was a boisterous group last night," she greeted Baxter.

"You shouldn't ask consultants to give up their weekends, Andy," Baxter replied. "They tend to get surly and turn to drink. They're used to working Saturdays, but do it on their own terms."

"It was picked up at our table and Bill McIvor, the Managing Partner from Toronto, commented to Clyde, 'Is that the way your people behave in the U.S.? I hope they conduct themselves a little more professionally in front of clients," Andy scolded Baxter.

"I didn't meet him last night. Point him out to me, Andy and I will make a personal point to introduce him to Alice Dungler this morning."

Andy winced. "Let's talk about today's program. The objectives are to begin a training process for newly hired experienced consultants. I need you to take over a group after the ten-fifteen coffee break, stay with that group through the morning and afternoon and deliver your group feedback at 4:30. Your group will convene at 8AM on Sunday morning for more discussions and then you will participate in a general feedback session at 10:30 Sunday morning. Following lunch, everyone will be assigned action steps, and the date of the next meeting will be decided."

"Andy, are you telling me that I have been drafted into this project for the duration and that I will be expected to continue attending these meetings?" Baxter asked.

"Joe, you are earmarked as one of our trainers. You're ideal. A successful outside hire with well developed engagement management skills."

"Andy, I have clients to acquire and look after," Baxter protested.

"Joe, this is very important to the future of the firm. This is your opportunity to be highly visible within the firm. My goodness, you're having dinner with Harvey Randolph, the Deputy Chairman tonight. You should take this meeting very seriously."

"Who's going to be in my group?" Baxter asked.

"I have the name tags set out with the receptionist in front of the auditorium. Your tag will have a blue ribbon on it that will say, group leader. The tags under it will make up your group. I had lists printed, but we had to do some juggling when there were some last minute cancellations. I arranged the tags this morning, and Patti, my assistant, will have the lists and break-out rooms prepared by the time we're done with opening remarks and orientation."

Baxter nodded, they ordered breakfast, and made small talk before Andy began to probe again. "Why is Harvey Randolph having dinner with you tonight?"

"I have no idea, Andy."

"I hear you're separated now. Are you going to get a divorce?" she asked.

"It's in the works."

"Your wife will have the children?"

"I would assume so and I will have visitation rights."

"I think Harvey's going to sound you out about coming to New York. I know Friedman has asked for you in Los Angeles. Which would you prefer?"

"I would prefer to stay in Chicago and do my job there," Baxter answered.

"You might have a lot of weekends as a trainer."

"How long am I expected to be part of this program?"

"Two years minimum, three years max. You'll be a partner by the time you go off."

Baxter sipped his coffee and digested Andy's words. It was another FSO assignment, but Andy was right. It was an opportunity to become visible in the firm. Baxter excused himself to check on his group. He found Alice

Dungler standing in front of the reception table drinking from a coffee mug. She was wearing a blue UCLA sweatshirt, running shorts, sweat socks, and tennis shoes. Her body, while heavy set, appeared muscular and athletic. "Good morning handsome," she greeted Baxter.

"Have you located your group?" Baxter said looking over the table. He saw his name and blue ribbon name tag at the top of a line of name tags. The tags were the same people at the dinner table the night before.

"It's our dinner group from last night," Baxter observed.

"What a coincidence."

"Coincidence hell! I got out here early and rearranged them and then I volunteered to help Patti type up the group lists. Our Group is cast in stone for the weekend, handsome. You will make a wonderful Group Leader and we can move through all this bullshit efficiently so that we can get in some social time. Poor little Queen Andy will have a conniption when she sees the lists, and it will be too late to change them."

The Saturday meeting in the auditorium began with Clyde Nickerson at the platform lectern. The uniform of the day was short sleeved sports shirts and wash trousers with loafers or athletic shoes. Alice Dungler was the only one in shorts. Baxter seated himself in the back row with Grunwaldyt on one side and Alice on the other.

Nickerson greeted the assembled group of consultants and said that they had a great deal of very important work to accomplish on this weekend, and that the firm extended its thanks in advance for giving up their weekend. He then introduced Harvey Randolph.

Baxter read over the agenda. It was to begin with a historical overview and a keynote of the meeting's objectives by Harvey Randolph. Harvey would be followed by Andy who would introduce the meeting process. After that, it was all group work with presentations at the end of the day followed by Sunday assignments. Finally there were cocktails and another group dinner.

Harvey Randolph was greeted by polite reserved applause as he stepped to the platform.

"Good morning! We all have a very important and busy day ahead of us. The task of developing our consulting professional is critical to the growth of this wonderful firm of ours. Saturday morning meetings, I might add, are a long time tradition of McKenzie Barber. John McKenzie believed that we should serve our clients during the week days, meet for training on Saturday, and spend Sunday with our families. Ernie Grey and I date back to the days of John McKenzie and the time after World War II when the firm enjoyed its first period of robust growth. I joined the firm in 1948, and Ernie came in 1949. So, as you can see, I had seniority over Ernie for a while. He ultimately passed me up, as you are all well aware."

"Back in those days, the consulting trainees were different. We averaged between 26 and 30 in age and most of us had forfeited four years of our career in service for our country. We were damned proud of what we had accomplished for our country and we were very anxious to get on with our careers."

"McKenzie Barber consultant training in those days usually meant a week in a downtown hotel room. During my week of consultant training, I can remember the staff service taking the beds out of the hotel room and putting folding chairs into the space where the beds had been. We spent a week in that room in July New York heat. Classes would begin on Saturday morning at 8 AM and we would have Sunday off. Then we went Monday through Friday lunch. The course was concluded about eleven-thirty on Friday morning and we all changed into fresh white shirts because John McKenzie was coming to lunch."

"Lunch was always served in a private room, and we knew it was acceptable to have a drink at that luncheon as long as it was a single drink. We had survived the week, and we were now ready to be McKenzie Barber consultants. Mr. Mac was well prepared and knew us all by name and knew where we had gone to college. He would shake each man's hand and greet him with 'How do you do.'"

"Mr. Mac would always order a sherry, and his glass was barely touched at the end of the luncheon. After lunch, Mr. Mac would excuse himself. We sat around the table for ten or fifteen minutes listening to our training leader summarize and sermonize until we were excused. Then we packed up our bags, went over to Greenwich Village and drank until the bars closed. It was graduation day! We were McKenzie Barber consultants! Bring on the clients!"

"Needless to say, consultant training has become more refined over the years. In the 1950s we began to recruit two kinds of consultants to McKenzie Barber. We recruited from the foremost Industrial Engineering Programs of universities and from top Business Schools in the U.S. These graduates were distributed into two separate consultant pools, which in turn, fed talent into traditional services and new services. We had an IE pool to co-exist, and in many offices like Chicago, Atlanta, and Dallas, the pools were simply merged together. Other offices such as New York, San Francisco, and Los Angeles maintained separate pools. Some of our IE hires have wound up working very effectively on traditional MBA functions such as strategic planning. MBAs, in turn, have migrated into the manufacturing, cost engineering, methods, plant rationalization, and the traditional industrial engineering services offered by the firm."

"In the early 1960s, we identified other areas of consulting opportunity to serve our clients. These areas included computer services, advanced manufacturing services, and executive compensation. To launch each practice area successfully, we concluded that leadership was required from outside the firm. To that end we recruited Dr. Bolyard, Bill Dwyer, and Frank Alvardi as functional practice leaders and began to fill in behind them. We weren't always successful with our transfers from the pool into these practices, and began to look for other solutions. We hired experienced consultants and individuals with outstanding functional skills and we paid them market rates to join us. Some were quite successful, and others we quietly told that they were not cut out for consulting at McKenzie Barber. During the period 1970 to 1974, 15% of our hires were experienced people with advanced functional skills. These consultants generally joined us at the six to eight year experience level and a few of the more successful ones are here today in this room."

"The question before us this morning is how to train these new consultants. We have developed a series of seminars for our incoming consultants such as Consultants Forum I for incoming hires, and Consultants Forum II for newly promoted Associates. The experienced consultants were hired at odd times of the year and always applied on engagements. We never seemed to be able to group them together long enough to get them trained. We had to count on a mentoring system. To the rescue, Clyde Nickerson's department managed to design a three phase correspondence course that all of the new consultants were expected to complete. This splendid course, regrettably, was completed only by a small number of the eligible, experienced consultant population. While its content was first rate, the course was not delivered effectively, and we have concluded that it was time to drop the correspondence course."

"Now, in June 1975, we are on the edge of a new era at McKenzie Barber. We are at a time when we are looking beyond hiring selected experienced consultants. We are actively considering the acquisition of entire firms of consultants and providing them the advantage of our culture, values, approaches, accountability systems, and access to our cherished client base. We are going to require training and development exercises to bring these acquired consultants up to the overall McKenzie Barber standards of excellence. The group in this room was carefully selected to provide input to the design of the professional training standards of the 1980s. The group in this room will become the first standard bearers of the McKenzie Barber professional development programs that are expected to carry the firm into the twenty-first century. The firm has come a long way from those week long sessions in economy priced hotel rooms in lower Manhattan. We are a world class firm serving clients throughout the free world. This group has been asked to assume an enormous responsibility. I know that you will be up to the task! I'm certain that you will have questions and I would be pleased to answer them at the coffee and luncheon breaks. I will now turn this morning's program over to Clyde Nickerson, Partner-in-Charge of Organizational Services. I thank you for your attention."

There was light applause for Harvey. Alice leaned over and whispered into Baxter's ears. "Have you ever heard so much bullshit from a grown man? He talks like the firm's going to buy Robson-Allen. Jesus Christ, what have we gotten into?"

Baxter nodded and watched Clyde Nickerson move behind the lectern. Clyde talked for a few minutes about the rich traditions of competence at McKenzie Barber and then was followed by Andy. Andy had a long carousel slide presentation, a lot of training jargon, and mission talk.

"Fucking A!" Alice whispered to Baxter. "I wish that cunt would shut up!"

They broke for coffee at 9:58 and a group immediately surrounded Harvey Randolph. Baxter poured a cup of coffee from the urn and headed off to his assigned breakout room. Grunwaldyt was in hot pursuit.

"Don't you want to hear what Harvey has got to say?" Grunwaldyt asked as he drew abreast of Baxter.

"Anything he has to say in front of a group of people will be very vague and general. I'm scheduled to have dinner with him tonight. I can then ask my questions directly. What quality of answers will I get in a room full of consultants?" Baxter asekd.

Grunwaldyt followed Baxter into the Iris Room. "I see your point," he agreed.

"We have a great deal to do, Jon, to get ready for our group. I would like you to serve as recording secretary during our sessions," Baxter instructed his newly acquired protégé.

Harvey Randolph approached Baxter during the afternoon coffee break. "Joe, I've got us set up for the dinner at my golf club. Suppose we meet at the cocktail party and take off around 6:45. We'll go to Arrowfoot Country Club. It's about fifteen minutes away and be sure to wear a tie."

"Is a blazer okay?" Baxter asked.

Harvey nodded and moved off to another group.

Baxter delivered the first group report of the day. His group had recommended trashing all of the firm's current training programs and installing a series of minimum competency development modules. Baxter, in his role as Group Leader and presenter, had simply let his group speak their minds, accepted their recommendations initially, and then ruthlessly tested each final recommendation. Their report generated a lot of discussion and opened the door for criticism of the existing programs. Clyde Nickerson hadn't anticipated that the consultant's correspondence course would be so universally criticized and appeared very uncomfortable in the group discussions. He sat in his chair with a flushed face, while Andy tried to moderate the discussion. Harvey Randolph sat in a far corner of the room and smoked his pipe in silence.

Clyde stopped Baxter after the conclusion of the group discussions. Baxter had lingered behind to chat with some of the other group members while Nickerson shuffled, sorted, and collected papers on the speaker's platform. At 5:45 Baxter and Nickerson were in the room alone and each had completed the assembly of their papers.

"For a man who has never attended a training course, you have turned out to be quite a critic," Nickerson's voice cut through the room like a knife.

"I was just the group spokesman, Clyde. Most of the group had been through Consultants Forum I and II and the rest had taken that Introduction to Consulting course with the audio tapes and booklets. I was the only untrained consultant in the group. The recommendations came from the group, not from me, and I thought the feedback was pretty constructive. The forums and the consulting audio tapes have served their purposes and provide building blocks for the training programs of the future," Baxter answered.

"I'll bet you're one hell of a bullshitter in front of a client," Clyde said closing his brief case and walking out of the room past Baxter without another word.

Baxter's group was comprised of the dinner table assembly of the previous evening. There was Harley Dimon from Atlanta, who spoke slowly and chose his words carefully to avoid offense. In the daylight of the breakout room, the group appeared differently to Baxter from the evening before. Harley was quite handsome with dark eyes and long eyelashes. His words were Southern soft, and his manner seemed gentle and courteous, but Baxter suspected that Harley's face was a mask. There had to be more of an edge to him to advance to Manager. He was very party-line in his convictions and would only shift an opinion when the rest of the group had reached a consensus.

Tom Ruffle from Dallas had been tough, blunt, and tended to be a nit-picker. He was also very negative about executive office, Clyde and Andy. "Those Consulting Forums would be okay if we were in the Girl Scout or Bible School business. It's Chairman worship. First we make all these young virgin MBAs be introduced to John McKenzie worship and then they behold Ernie Grey, his spiritual successor, and he pumps them up with the celestial mission of McKenzie Barber, and they come back full of platitudes. What they need to hear is that this is a damned tough business and they're going to have to work like hell if they want to stick around here."

Grunwaldyt surprised Baxter. He was tall, blonde, appeared like a young god in the mid-morning light. Grunwaldyt's baby blue eyes locked into the grey naval officer's eyes of Tom Ruffle and said, "You're exactly right, Tom. We need to put the new hires through boot camp, not charm school."

Alice Dungler had shed her running shoes and sat with one sweat sock covered foot on the table as she listened. From time to time she alternated feet. She was a large breasted woman, but her body was firm and her cut-off sweatshirt revealed muscular arms. Hair short, face square, complexion fair, intelligence keen, she was capable of igniting the room with a raucous laugh. Alice Dungler was a woman with a man's presence. She was capable of intimidating the men around her, and she commanded respect. Baxter had been careful to sit on the opposite end of the table from Alice. From time to time Baxter looked at her and found Alice's intense brown eyes trained on him.

"Throw it all out and start over again. That training tape is the dumbest thing I've ever heard. I think our little Andy wrote it and everyone knows what a crack consultant she is. That voice over on the tape sounded like one of Andy's unemployable sorority sisters. That course is an embarrassment," Alice proclaimed.

Fred Tabor was thoughtfully concise. "I believe that in the group presentation, Joe should touch on the positive aspects of the existing programs, and say in a nice way that they have outgrown their usefulness to fully achieve the firm's training objectives. I further believe that the rest of this discussion should be spent identifying the critical bodies of knowledge required to be a successful McKenzie Barber consultant, Associate, Manager/Director, and Partner. There are principals of competence at each level, and we could develop the course into continuing education modules. All of Nickerson's development courses are amateurish and he really doesn't know the difference. They tell me he lifted everything from the Pennsylvania Steel training guide. I know we all consider the man a horror, but this is the chance to put something right."

Fred seemed intelligent, thoughtful, and a little effete to Baxter. His semi-bald head seemed to shine in the mid-morning sun.

"Oh Fred, what a statesman you make!" Alice commented.

"I agree with Fred," Grunwaldyt piped. "There's a lot wrong here and Joe has let us all say our piece. Now we have the opportunity to put things right."

They each looked around the room at each other waiting for one more comment. "Then let's go on with it,' Baxter said and they began to make constructive progress.

Andy served as the discussion leader for the late afternoon group presentations. She had visited the Iris Room during late morning and listened to their deliberations for ten minutes and then exited without a word.

"Nice to have you by my dear," Alice said when the door had been closed after Andy's departure. "Do stay longer next visit."

Now Andy was at the lectern, with Clyde seated at the far chair on the platform table. Baxter's presentation had been first and he used an easel to present the critical bodies of competence concept. Clyde was not pleased when Baxter presented his group's conclusions to scrap I and II forums. Baxter's boldness set a tone for the other groups to be outspoken and aggressive in their comments and recommendations. Andy was besieged by comments from the floor and was becoming flustered. Clyde jumped to her defense and informed the group that Ernie Grey would be very disappointed to hear of their disapproval of the Forums and cited the many complimentary letters he received from the consultants and associates who attended the Forums.

"Hell, Clyde," Tom Ruffle called out from a seat in the back of the room. "Those guys just want to get promoted."

Baxter looked over to Harvey who sat motionless in his corner chair sucking on his pipe with his legs crossed.

Nickerson moved to the lectern next to Andy to help her take control of the meeting. "They make a nice couple, don't they," Alice whispered to Baxter. Grunwaldyt giggled.

Around 5:20 it was concluded that they would take the evening off and begin thirty minutes earlier on Sunday at 7:30 AM. Andy thanked the group for their candor and stated that their input today was very productive.

Baxter showered, changed into a jacket and tie and found Grunwaldyt waiting downstairs prepared to accompany him back to the main building.

"My compliments on a superb presentation, Joe," Grunwaldyt greeted Baxter. "I believe our group showed rather well, don't you?"

"There's no prize awarded for best group, Jon," Baxter warned.

"I was a little overwhelmed last night at dinner about being the junior man, but I really believe that I held my own today and contributed," Grunwaldyt observed in his best self-serving manner.

"You did just fine, Jon," Baxter said walking faster.

"Why do you think Harvey Randolph is having dinner with you?" Grunwaldyt asked.

"He wants my opinion on a number of firm governance issues," Baxter replied.

"Do you suppose he's looking you over as a partner candidate?" Baxter shrugged his shoulders and walked even faster.

Andy was standing near the bar with Bill McIvor, the Toronto Partner, who had been concerned about Baxter's table's conduct the evening before, and today had defended Forums I and II and the correspondence course.

McIvor was a man of medium height with a craggy Scottish face and sandy hair. He greeted Baxter by name.

"That was an excellent presentation, Joe. I didn't agree with your group's conclusions. You were a little hard on the traditional training because I believe it's worked very well in Canada. Your group did, however, show a lot of insight into the challenges of indoctrinating experienced people into the consulting practice. We haven't chose to go that route in Canada."

"I just spoke for the group, Bill," Baxter replied. "Jon Grunwaldyt here, developed most of the criticism of the existing training programs. Many times young Associates bring fresh insights into old problems." Baxter pulled Grunwaldyt forward in front of McIvor and stepped away with Andy following him. She was wearing a print cocktail dress, white pumps, and showing a lot of tan.

"Is Clyde pissed at me?" he asked in a low voice.

"He was embarrassed in front of Harvey, Joe. The new training programs are our mandate from Ernie. We know the old programs were dated, and we had no real funding for the local office delivered training programs. Of course, they were crude, Joe. But they were better than no training at all. Harvey was one of the partners who really challenged Clyde's nomination. You made Clyde's programs sound foolish and you're right. He's pissed!"

"Andy, I just presented the group's consensus."

"Joe, I don't know how that group was formed. I checked my notes at lunch and the six of you weren't even supposed to be together. You could have at least soft-pedaled the criticism in front of the group, and told us privately how the group felt. Joe, I know how powerful and entertaining you are in front of an audience. You can sell anything you want to. You're going to be one of our trainers and you had better keep on Clyde's good side if you want to be a partner," Andy scolded him.

Baxter decided to say nothing. His eyes met Andy's. Her dark hair was swept to one side and she stared back at him. "Why don't you call me in my room when you get back from dinner? I have a bottle of Chardonnay on ice," she invited. "2064."

"I should just knock on the door?" Baxter offered. There was a pull on Baxter's arm and it was Harvey Randolph.

"You ready to go to dinner, young man?" he asked.

They drove in Harvey's black BMW to the Arrowfoot in Westchester. Harvey sucked on his pipe as he drove and talked between sucks.

"This is a damned good club!" Harvey explained as they drove up a winding drive through the late June twilight. "It took me damned near four years to get in. When I moved to Chicago from Atlanta, I was in the club I wanted inside of a month. Out here it's an eternity. I'm not used to sucking up to people to get into a golf club, but I was willing to in order to get into Arrowfoot. Mrs. Randolph and our girls have used the club extensively. On most Saturdays, I'm out on the course. This Saturday, however, was my Hudson Conference Center day. Do you play golf, Joe?"

"No sir," Baxter answered. "I never really have had time to take up the game."

"You ought to start playing," Harvey counseled as he parked the car. "You're a big athletic looking fellow. You must have played some sports in your time."

"I played football through my junior year in high school and I captained the basketball team my senior year."

"Did you play in college?" Harvey asked.

"I went into military service after high school," Baxter said slightly editing his history. "Then I enrolled in a Big 10 school and playing basketball as a walk-on was an impossibility."

"I played at Furman. I was starting guard in '40 and '41 and then went into service. That was a godawful long time ago."

Harvey led Baxter through the parking lot to the front door of a building that resembled an ante-bellum mansion.

"We're going to have a half-hour wait that usually runs forty-five minutes. What do you say we have a toot?"

They had three toots in the long angular front bar of Arrowfoot and looked out at the 18th hole. Harvey Randolph appeared to be in no hurry to be seated.

"What did you think of today's proceedings, Joe? Was it a waste of time and money?"

Baxter sipped his Canadian Club and let it slosh through his mouth before he answered. "Not at all, Harvey. It was almost Hegelian, thesis, antithesis, and synthesis. I believe we were on the edge of a real forum of ideas when we broke up. I look for us to have a very productive day on Sunday."

"Hegel!" Harvey snorted. "That's a name you don't hear much about at McKenzie Barber! What are you, Joe? Some kind of intellectual?" Harvey signaled for the waitress and held up two fingers. Baxter knew that introducing Hegelian concepts in a conversation with Harvey Randolph had been a mistake.

"How long have you been with the firm, Joe?" Harvey asked after the waitress had acknowledged the new drink order.

"I hired into the Manufacturing practice under Bill Dwyer in 1968, advanced to Associate in 1970, Manager in 1972, and Director in 1974," Baxter recited.

"How old are you now?" Harvey asked.

"I just turned 40."

"When do you expect to be a Partner?" Harvey asked.

"1977 or 1978 at the latest," Baxter answered optimistically.

"That may be rushing it. Do you have a good man behind you?"

"Carl Miller is quite competent. He lacks some flexibility in dealing with clients and he tends to be very quantitative. Carl probably doesn't sell as well as I do, but he's improving," Baxter explained.

"Does he run around quoting Hegel?" Harvey asked playfully.

"Carl is not a Hegel man, Harvey. He's into heuristic modeling."

"That's unfortunate, Joe. Maybe you should take him aside and explain to him about Hegel. In fact, you can take me aside and explain about Hegel when it fits your schedule. Joe, "Harvey began again. "I hear you have done some business out in California and then it dried up after Friedman hired some lady from a bank. Is that true?"

"I did some business in California. I was not aware that it had dried up. I never see any of the national numbers. I know that Ruth has less volume than anticipated," Baxter said politically.

"Ruth has been a disaster. Friedman wants you out in California. Do you want to transfer? Bob has talked to me conceptually about you transferring out to LA. He's brought it up to Ernie and our Chairman likes Friedman. Now for once and for all, are you interested in transferring or not?"

"Would I be a Partner when I moved?" Baxter asked.

"No. But you could be a Partner over time, and you would have the whole West Coast from San Diego to Seattle for a consulting practice. What do you think of that? Bob Friedman really wants you."

"I'd be willing to go to LA as a Partner, not as a Director!" Baxter responded.

"Joe, you would have to go out to LA as a Director and prove yourself as a Partner candidate," Harvey explained.

"I've already proved myself at the Director level in Chicago, Harvey. I'm billing out in excess of $1 million in Chicago which I understand is a Partner's requirement for billing. I believe I can grow Chicago into a $2 million practice by 1980, and on that basis I will become a Partner with McKenzie Barber. Why would I want to move to California and place all that at risk?"

"People get at risk, Joe, when they put their own careers ahead of firm needs. I've moved four times with the firm, and Ernie talked to me about a year ago about going overseas. I was and I am ready to go, if Ernie believes that is the place where I can best serve this firm. If you want to be a part of the firm, you don't go around demanding this or that. You just do it! You'll be well taken care of over time, and any transfer is pretty well thought out before it's presented to someone. Now do I understand that you're going through a divorce?" Harvey asked.

"I'm separated, but will be divorced sometime this year," Baxter explained.

"Do you have children?"

"Two. A boy nine, and a daughter five," Baxter recited. Harvey shook his head and sloshed his whiskey as if he were preparing to say something. "We've got a lot of divorced men in the firm. Women are still so new that we don't have a fix on it. But all over the firm, we've got men with broken homes and they're good men, too. We ask our consultants to work very hard and make personal time sacrifices to serve our clients, and small wonder their marriages don't work out. John McKenzie didn't marry until he was in his sixties. Mrs. Randolph is a real trooper. She lived outside a couple of Army camps before I went overseas, and we started out pretty humble when I first went to work for the firm. Our generation was a little different, I guess. I'm not being critical of you, Joe. I'm saying that it's not unusual for a man at your level or higher to go through some kind of martial discontinuity. We may have to set up some kind of divorce counseling resource in Nickerson's department. It's getting bad. Would you say that your marital difficulties were caused by your work with the firm?"

Baxter wondered if the question was some kind of trap. "No sir. My wife had a nervous breakdown following a family tragedy, and that occurred four years before I joined the firm."

"Where were you before the firm?" Harvey asked signaling the waitress for a refill.

"A company in Deer Lake, Wisconsin, a town just outside Racine, called Washburn Manufacturing."

"Housewares and small electrics!" Harvey responded.

"That's it!" Baxter acknowledged.

"That was the company that Burke sold!"

"Bill Dwyer did some work for us. Then the President died suddenly, and Hamilton Burke was assigned to work with us. It was Ham who concluded that we should sell the company."

Harvey broke into low convulsive laughter. "So that's how you came to us! Burke's famous M & A engagement!"

"I wasn't aware that McKenzie Barber's work with Washburn Manufacturing had reached the Deputy Chairman's office," Baxter commented.

"It shouldn't have. How well did you get to know Mr. Burke, Joe?"

"Quite well. The first McKenzie Barber people I met were Mark Lovejoy and Lee Heller from the Chicago office. Then Bill Dwyer came in with Lee Heller and I was the client liaison manager. When Hamilton Burke came to work with us, I was appointed to be the principal interface. We put together the offering booklet on the company and went around the country making presentations to potential buyers. Finally the company was sold to a British company called Henry Wiggins Plc. I elected not to stay with them after the merger, and Ham arranged for me to interview the manufacturing practice."

Harvey again sloshed the ice cubes around in his glass.

"Hamilton Burke was and continues to be a free spirit within McKenzie Barber. Ernie Grey loves him. Burke used to be a military man, and most military men are supposed to be accustomed to taking orders. I was in the Quartermasters, and all I did was what the people over me told me to do. Ernie was a fighter pilot. He was used to free-lancing in order to stay alive. Burke was in some Special Forces outfit where they had to do a lot of improvising, and he was used to making up his own rules. He came to McKenzie Barber and thought he was still in the Special Forces when he went to the Emerging Companies practice. We had a heck of a time getting people to transfer into that practice because nobody wanted to work with medium-sized companies. It was probably the only practice that would have taken Burke, and as you know, we're out of that sector now."

"Burke wasn't supposed to go around and sell companies. I'm not saying that it wasn't the right solution for Washburn, but we should have referred the sale opportunity to at least three investment banking firms and helped the client pick out one they could work with. Burke decided that McKenzie Barber should sell the company and earn some more fees. Had Burke ever sold a company before? No! Was McKenzie Barber in the business of selling companies? No! Did we occasionally try to match one client with another? Yes! Did we send them a bill when it was successful? Sometimes! Most of the time we sold them more work from our traditional practices and we got it as a sole source because the client recognized that we had helped them. Now we had Mr. Burke out in some small town in Wisconsin, blatantly selling a company for a fee. Some of the firm's friends in the investment banking business who had been referring clients to us for years, called us up and told us that if we were going to compete with them, they were going to quit referring clients to us. The Chairman of Broadbaker personally called Ernie Grey. Well, Burke got lucky and sold the company. We collected our fee, folded up our M & A business, and discontinued the Emerging Companies Practice a year later. Ernie arranged to send Burke off to Barber-Paris. A lot of us figured Burke would spend a year or so in Paris and then quit and go back to his family business. We figured him for one of

Ernie's "political" hires. Damned if he didn't fool us and make Partner in Paris. Then he went off to London where he was very successful, and now he's coming back to Executive Office this fall."

"This fall? Executive Office?" Baxter asked.

Harvey stood up from the table. "Looks like we got our dinner spot in the dining room. What do you say we get something to eat, Joe?"

They were seated in a corner table at the far end of the dining room. The room was crowded and seemed filled with attractive middle-aged people who waved at Harvey. They stopped at several tables to exchange handshakes and Baxter was introduced as an associate from McKenzie Barber. The men wore blazers, neckties, casual shoes. The women were dressed in smart casual outfits and wore a great deal of jewelry. There was talk of tennis and golf dates, and a general lament for Harvey after they learned that he was spending the weekend at a conference.

"Ernie Grey is a slavedriver, Harvey," one stylish woman with blonde hair sporting diamond bracelets on both wrists commented. "I'm playing doubles with Millie next week. I'm going to tell her that Ernie shouldn't wreck your weekend."

Harvey patted on her bare tanned shoulder. "I don't know if Millie can help much with Ernie, Grace. She doesn't see much of him herself."

Harvey ordered two more toots when they were finally seated and asked the waitress for the wine list.

"Ernie Grey belongs to Arrowfoot?" Baxter asked.

"Yeah, he belongs all right, but I don't think he's been here twice in ten years. Millie Grey comes here and plays some tennis, and their daughter, Kathleen, swims here. Ernie only plays golf when he absolutely has to. He could be one hell of a golfer if he wanted to. I play every Saturday. We have a regular foursome of presidents and we all do some business together. This club has paid off for the firm. It's one of my favorite places in the world."

The waitress brought menus, and Harvey mandated that Baxter try the trout and the house salad, and they would start with the seafood chowder. He ordered a bottle of Sauvignon Blanc and Baxter found himself looking into the owl eyes of the Deputy Chairman.

"You said that Ham Burke is coming back from London. What will he do in Executive Office?" Baxter asked to pick up the conversation.

"He's going to work in Executive Office for Ernie. He will be Partner-in-Charge of firm-wide Strategic Planning. Executive Office is in a dynamic growth mode. I just hope that the firm can keep up with Executive Office so we can pay for all of these people and still make some money for the partners."

"What will the Partner-in-Charge of Strategic Planning do?" Baxter asked.

"Whatever Ernie wants done," Harvey answered. There was a silence and Baxter didn't speak while those owl eyes trained on him. "Joe, the firm is entering into a time of dramatic change. This meeting today is part of that change. Ernie Grey believes that the firm has become complacent. Our growth has flattened. Ernie likes 15% a year minimum. This year we will probably come in around 8% growth in the US and 12% worldwide. Ernie's not happy with these kind of numbers. Some of us old-timers tell Ernie, 'Hey, it isn't that bad.' It had to slow down sometime. Ernie always tells me that a slow growth practice is a dying practice. Ernie wants to expand the firm in new growth directions. He's getting impatient with the performance of start-up practices. Ernie Grey has very high expectations, and when he brings in people to make a difference, they had damned well better make a difference. McKenzie Barber is going to start to acquire other consulting firms. These consultants are going to have to be trained in our values and way of doing things. That's what this meeting is really about."

"Mr. Burke is being brought back from Barber London to work with Mr. Grey on the new directions of McKenzie Barber. Mr. Burke will be in charge of acquisitions. What the hell! He sold your old company. He should be able to handle the buy side." Baxter now could clearly sense that Harvey Randolph resented and disliked Hamilton Burke.

"I haven't seen Ham in seven years," Baxter stated innocently. "Has he changed much?"

"He's quite the European bon vivant. He's still single, but has a lot of ladies around him. He took up polo and is quite a horseman. Both the French and the British liked him. That's unusual. Now if only we can get the Americans to like him."

"He arranged for me to meet with Clyde Nickerson in 1968 and I never heard from him again," Baxter said establishing his independence from Burke.

"Well, I would renew your acquaintanceship with Mr. Burke. His star may be rising in the world of McKenzie Barber." Chowder was served and Harvey ordered an additional toot. Baxter passed, having nursed his last Canadian Club.

"Now at this point, Joe, you're probably wondering why I invited you out to dinner," Harvey continued. "It's time to talk about your career. You're a bit of a phantom in our personnel system. There are very few appraisal forms completed about you, and you have had no documented career planning interviews. Why is that?"

"I've always been busy. Bill Dwyer was always simply on the run. Frank Alvardi once gave me an appraisal in which he told me to dress better. I started buying my suits at Brooks Brothers. Dr. Barry is awful on any kind of paperwork, and I refused to have Lee Heller conduct an appraisal of my performance. He's a peer and really only runs administration for Dr. Barry's practice. I know my numbers by heart and I know I make some money for the firm."

"That you do," Harvey agreed. "I'm familiar with your numbers. They're decent. Ernie is not happy with the growth of the Executive Compensation practice. He is not happy with the growth of several practices. He is tired of being number two to Robson Allen. Frank Alvardi was recruited to make us number one and he hasn't accomplished that yet. I'm not being critical of Frank, mind you. He's put us on the map as a number two, but the actuarial firms may push right by us this year and we may be number 4 or 5 by year end. That's intolerable to Ernie. I'm not telling you any secrets, Joe. Ernie has had this conversation with Frank, and he's had Roger Dirks in the room. Do you know Roger?"

"Just by reputation," Baxter acknowledged.

"We need to do something to juice up Executive Compensation. Ernie believes we must buy one of the actuarial firms and overlay the Executive Compensation practice with an Employee Benefits firm. How do you feel about that?"

"That would depend on the firm. I have no objection as long as we grow and make money," Baxter studied the owl eyes and suspected that he had made a point.

"New York is doing well in Executive Compensation now that we have Frank in New York. He stayed too long and seemed to be getting comfortable in Chicago. You can't lead a national practice out of Chicago. It needs to be in New York. You're doing fine in Chicago, and I agree that you will have a two million dollar practice by 1980 in Chicago. I anticipate that it will be closer to $2.5 million. Atlanta is going through the motions. Dallas has a little business. The West Coast is a major market opportunity. You have already demonstrated that you can be successful out there. Bob Friedman wants you to come out. We've had a failure because you declined to go out two years ago."

"Wrong, Harvey," Baxter interjected. "The failure was a result of Bob Friedman's choice of practice leaders, not my reluctance to relocate to Los Angeles."

Harvey nodded his head as if in agreement, but said nothing.

"Joe, will you go out to Los Angeles?"

"Only with the assurance I will be elected a Partner in September 1976."

"1978 is probably your year, Joe. Get used to it, if you plan to stay with us," Harvey decreed.

"Am I being told to transfer to Los Angeles if I know what's good for me?" Baxter queried.

"You have some other options, Joe." The wine was served and Harvey made a major ceremony out of tasting the California wine he had ordered. "One other option for you is a new job in Executive Office. As I said before, Ernie is going to expand Executive Office. That's why Clyde was elected a Partner last year. We need someone to work along side of Andy Bourke to be in charge of training. We're going to come up with some training principles at this meeting. We need someone who can build the programs and then rotate off after a couple of years and return to an operating practice. You were recommended and are acceptable to Clyde. Are you interested?"

"I want to serve clients, Harvey. I'm willing to serve as a trainer to serve the best interests of the firm. I'm unwilling to serve in a staff role. I do, however, have a suggestion for you."

"Who's that?" Harvey asked. His owl eyes seemed cold.

"Lee Heller in the Chicago office. He's at the Director level working for Dr. Barry as his administrator. Lee's worked in a several practices and he really knows the CARS system inside out. If we're going to acquire a number of consulting firms, I assume they will have to go on CARS. Lee knows CARS inside and out."

Harvey nodded his head. "That sounds like a good suggestion."

Harvey produced a pad from his jacket pocket and wrote down; Lee Heller, Chicago, works for Barry Keller.

"There's a third option for you, Joe. Come out to New York and be Alvardi's number two. If this Carl Miller can continue on and make 75% of your numbers, and if you came out to New York, we can have a strong national resource."

"Has this been discussed with Frank?" Baxter asked.

"It will be. We wanted to hear what you thought about it, first. Leon Harwell has been talking to Ernie about you. There are some strong ties between Harwell and Ernie Grey. They talk back and forth a lot and socialize. You have made quite an impression on Leon Harwell. He didn't take to Frank Alvardi, but he is taken with you for the moment. He's suggested to Ernie that you be transferred out to New York. Leon's a strange duck. There are very few people he takes to. He likes you though. Ernie remembers you from that FSO study of a couple of years ago. I reviewed that report Friday afternoon and I didn't think it was anything special. Andy Bourke wants to use it as a case study in the training program, but I think that's because it was the closest she's ever been to being a consultant. But you made an impression on Ernie that time and he remembers you. Would you come to New York, Joe?"

"Only if I'm a Partner coming out," Baxter replied.

"You're missing the point, Joe," Harvey said. "No matter where you go, you'll transfer at the Director level. The local office will have to nominate you to be a Partner. You're going to have to run around the track a couple of times before they will be willing to sponsor you."

"Then, how would you guarantee me a partner nomination coming off the training job?" Baxter asked.

"We couldn't. You would have to spend a year or two in the practice so the local partners would know you well enough to sponsor you for partnership," Harvey explained.

"Then my real options are Los Angeles, New York, or to stay in Chicago! Taking the training job would simply set me back."

Harvey returned to smoking his pipe and sucked in silence. "Your options, Joe, are where you will best serve the firm. There are lots of men and women in the firm who could do the training job. I talked to Brimmer about you. His attitude was 'What the hell does Baxter know about training? Leave him here in Chicago where he can make some money for the firm.' That's the way it is with Brimmer. You make enough money for the Chicago office, and he'll see that you're made a partner so that he can keep you. Brimmer is a lot like Ernie. He's all numbers and charging ahead. The only difference is that Brimmer was a real consultant and Ernie kind of dabbled in it." The waitress refilled their wine glasses and the fish arrived. Harvey ordered another bottle.

"Ernie Grey dabbled in consulting?" Baxter asked.

"Ernie Grey came in with the consulting class of '49. I was in '48. He was a bright, hard working, young fellow who took his work seriously, but hell, we all did. He had flown with Leon Harwell's older brother in the war. The older brother, Will, was buying companies and doing all kinds of wild things. They bought a company with a lot of problems and Will asked Ernie what McKenzie Barber could do for them. We got a decent sized job out of it, fixed up the company and they were able to sell it a couple of years later and get their money back. Getting the work got Ernie a breakfast with Mr. Mac and he took a liking to Ernie. He made him an Executive Assistant. Mr. Mac used to have two or three bright young men, in those days running around doing odd jobs. Most of them would stay a year and go back to a practice. Ernie stayed on and on. Mr. Mac had adopted him. Then he sent out Ernie to organize a banking practice. He used all of his Dad's contacts to get him into banks, hired a lot of people, picked out a fellow named Perkins to run the practice. Mr. Mac announced Ernie a great success, got him elected a partner, and moved him up to the equivalent of my job. The partners elected Paul Reynolds to succeed Mr. Mac when he retired. All any of us can remember about him is that he was a four pack a day smoker and pretty good in front of an audience. He died of cancer after a year or so, and there was Ernie holding all the cards, and I was a second year manager. So, Joe, that's a long story about how we got a Chairman who had only dabbled in consulting. Don't get me wrong. Ernie Grey has been wonderful for this firm. Mr. Mac made a very wise selection when he picked Ernie out and groomed him. He has grown the firm, picked the right people worldwide to run McKenzie Barber, and he's made a lot of money for the partners. He has no loyalties to any practice or any partner except maybe to that fellow who's running this weekend's conference."

"You produce year after year, or there's no place for you at McKenzie Barber. He has a lot of ideas and he'll take on risks, but he'll never stay with his losers too long. Ernie hates Robson Allen Harbridge. They have damned near drawn even with us. We're stronger than they are overseas, but we suspect they may have passed us in the U.S. Ernie wants to be biggest and he's ready to make acquisitions to get there. The last one we made was FSO in 1950 and Mr. Mac made that one as a favor to his old pals in the DOD. It's making money again, by the way."

"Now let's get back to what you call your options, Joe," Harvey paused between bites of trout. "Your options are what's good for the firm. This is especially true if you become a Partner. If you share in the profits, you must do what's good for all of the partners, not just for yourself. Now let's face 1975 reality for a moment. We've been talking about the past and your future, but we've been skirting the reality of 1975. The Executive Compensation practice has under-delivered in Ernie's eyes. We hired Frank Alvardi, RAH's number two, to make us number one. It hasn't happened. Now we're looking at acquiring an actuarial firm, and Frank is running around crying about how he won't report to an actuary and that the practice must be placed under the Strategic Planning practice. We have two real practices and a lot of hobbies. You have been asked to go out to Los Angeles where you have already demonstrated that you can be successful. Bob Friedman is someone that Ernie has singled out for more responsibility. I never thought I'd see the day when we would have an LA Jew as a Managing Partner, but it's going to happen this fall. Now keep that in confidence. I think you should go out and see Friedman again. Spend a week out there. You will not go out there as a Partner, but we'll give you a big raise. What are we paying you now?"

"My base is $75,000 and I received a $20,000 bonus last fall," Baxter replied.

"We'll make it worth your while to go to Los Angeles," Harvey said. "You will have to earn your place as a partner out there." Baxter rolled the transfer around in his mind. Friedman was going to be named Managing Partner, which would automatically place him on the Board of Directors. It would be starting over again, but his life had to change anyway.

"Now, how much work have you really done for Leon Harwell?"

"I've finished one engagement, and we have talked about additional work. He gave me a ride Friday afternoon to the Hudson Conference Center."

"Leon Harwell tends to make a lot of fuss, but really doesn't send us that much work. he usually goes right to Ernie when something goes wrong, and has thrown a lot of people's careers off track. He will fall in love with a consultant for a while, and then turn on him. I wouldn't count a lot of Leon Harwell as a business builder, Joe. You impress me as a bit of a free spirit. You should go out and work for Friedman. He's probably read a lot of Hegel."

The waitress brought coffee and a dessert menu. Harvey ordered a cognac and Baxter followed suit. "This has been a good dinner, Joe," Harvey ruled. "I like to get out with our high potential people and talk about the firm and their careers. You're a little older than the seven year MBA or MSIE, and I recognize your impatience to be a partner, Joe. The partnership will come in due time. All you have to do is to accomplish what's expected of you. In a firm like McKenzie Barber, you'd be amazed to learn how many people get ahead just by coming to work every day. Just don't go around delivering ultimatums about having to go someplace as a Partner. It could rub some people around here the wrong way. Now, Joe, I recognize you may have some questions for me. Tomorrow will be a busy day for both of us. You and I have been having a fairly private conversation. I'm the Deputy Chairman of the firm. At least I was Friday afternoon when I came up here. Ask me some questions. If I can't answer you, I'll just say PASS. Like if you were to ask me how much money I made or something like that, I would say PASS. Okay?"

Baxter looked into those owl eyes and sipped his coffee. The evening now appeared to be moving into a new phase.

"Why did you ask me out to dinner tonight?"

"Three reasons. 1.) Ernie's been hearing about you from both Leon Harwell and Bob Friedman. He wanted me to size you up. It was probably the first and last time Ernie will ever hear about the same person from those two. 2.) I was supposed to feel you out on the new training job. That was Clyde's idea, but I suspect that it came from Andy Bourke. 3.) I wanted to know what you thought of today's meeting." Harvey sat in silence sipping his brandy awaiting Baxter's next question.

"What is the new organization for Executive Office?"

"Ernie and I will continue as #1 and #2. The senior staff will report to Ernie and FSO, Barber Canada, Barber Paris, Barber London, Barber Asia, and McKenzie Barber Latin-America will report to Ernie. I think that's too much and we should appoint a Deputy Chairman, International."

"Ernie won't accept a layer between the Chairman, and the International leadership right now. I think he'll come around in a year or so."

"Who's on senior staff?"

"Clyde's Partner-in-Charge of Organization Services. That gives him Staffing, Manpower Planning and Training, Compensation, Benefits, and Pension Plans. He's got Andy, Betty Ryland, and the Manpower Planning and Training job. Ernie now has a Chief Financial Officer, a fellow named Lickens, that Clyde recruited from one of the accounting firms. Lastly, Ernie has Public Relations, and our newly hired General Counsel. I've got the US Managing Partners reporting to me and I sit on about fifteen standing committees that Ernie has operating. If we saw our organization at a client, we'd tell them that they had a real span of control problem. Ernie likes flat organizations and has no problem working six days a week. I do, and I like my job better. The last job in the world I ever want to hold is Chairman of McKenzie Barber. I'll leave that temptation for others to contemplate."

"What is the relationship between Ernie Grey and Clyde Nickerson?" Baxter asked.

"Now there's one where I should say PASS, but I've had a few toots tonight, so I'll offer you an insight there. Keep your eye on Clyde Nickerson! A lot of people get down on him and he has a very thankless job. Ernie uses Clyde for dirty jobs and all the miserable little tasks that have to be done to keep the firm going. One of the reasons Clyde did so poorly on the line in Chicago is that Ernie kept on using him on little special projects."

"The Grey and the Nickerson families go back a long time. Clyde has always idolized Ernie. He works even longer hours than Ernie. The ironic thing is that Clyde doesn't have to work like that. He's got trust income that exceeds what he makes from McKenzie Barber. Clyde is going to have a strategic role in this firm as long as Ernie's here. After Ernie's retired, Clyde's anybody's game."

"When will Ernie Grey step down as Chairman?"

"Ernie's only 54. I figure he'll go to 60. There are others who figure that he may work five years longer than Mr. Mac. There's nothing in the McKenzie Barber partnership by-laws that require the Chairman to step down. Joe, you may retire before Ernie Grey does. There are several fellows that are angling about to succeed me when I retire, and to succeed Bruce Dinsmore, the New York Managing Partner, who will go out about the same time I go. If you ask me to discuss the contenders, I will PASS."

"Why is McKenzie Barber a partnership as opposed to a corporation?"

"To avoid double taxation of earnings. We're operated like a corporation, but you're not going to find much democracy around here. If you go across the street to Robson Allen, you're going to find the same thing. Just a different letterhead."

"What is the partner making process?"

"It starts in January. Every Director level management employee is reviewed by the local office partners and agreement is reached on the list of partnership nominees. The list is reviewed during the first week in March by the Operating Committee which is comprised of the firm's US Managing Partners. Certain names are withdrawn on the basis of discussion in that meeting. There are a bunch of deals made in that meeting. It's you-support-my-boy and I'll support-your-boy stuff. Ernie and I are there to keep things on a level playing field. Following that meeting, a confidential list of nominees is circulated to all partners world-wide for review and comment. That list always elicits a few negative comments and we lose about 10 to 15% of our nominees. The local nominating office has the privilege to withdraw their nominees without prejudice. They can also fight for their nominees, but that's generally discouraged. The final list is rubber-stamped by the board and then a ballot is distributed to the partnership at large for ratification in August. We announce Partners right after Labor Day and Bingo! October 1st, we have a new batch of Partners and the process begins for another year."

"What happens to the new Partner?" Baxter asked. No one had ever taken time to explain the details of the partnership brotherhood. All Baxter knew was that the Partners appeared to have the power, prestige and the money. He wanted badly to be one of them."

"There's a formula applied to the compensation of the Director, we used to call them Managers, and that represents his or her units of interest at admission. The unit value is the same for all, and represents our profitability divided by the number of units in the pool. How many units of interest a partner holds is predicated on where he stands in the partnership. Partners are required to put up capital in proportion to their unit holdings, and are paid annual interest on their capital accounts. Unit holdings increase in proportion to the Partner's influence on overall profitability. That's all I'm going to say on the matter. Unit allocation can sometimes be a very ugly matter and a point of continued dissonance in the firm. You will find out soon enough when you are elected a Partner. McKenzie Barber will shower money on high performers, but will not tolerate marginal performers." Harvey seemed to bristle when he discussed Partner's compensation. He had felt obligated to answer Baxter's question, but was obviously uncomfortable about going into a detailed discussion.

"Well, Joe. I don't know about you, but I feel I've talked enough for one night. My comments to you were quite open and I assume that they will be held between us."

"Of course," Baxter agreed.

They weaved a little as Harvey returned Baxter in the BMW to the Hudson Conference Center. Baxter was dropped at the front door of the building by a quiet pipe smoking Harvey Randolph. He appeared to have had his fill of talking back at Arrowfoot. On the drive back, Harvey was content to suck on his pipe and humming along with the car radio.

"Well, you get a good night's sleep now, Joe, and we'll have at it in the morning. Keep tonight's gab under your hat." Baxter paused outside the front door and watched the BMW lurch forward into the night. He had survived dinner with the Deputy Chairman and vowed that he would never bring up Hegel in front of another McKenzie Barber partner.

Baxter stopped by the downstairs bar for a nightcap, and discovered his group seated together around an oval shaped table. They were all assembled with the exception of Grunwaldyt. Alice, Harley, Tom, and Fred were seated at a table littered with half-filled glasses, and Baxter heard their boisterous laughter from the front lobby. Alice was the first to see Baxter. "There he is! The Deputy Chairman's pet!" She pulled out an empty chair next to her. Come over here and sit down, big boy. Tell us about your evening with the firm leadership. Then we'll reward you with an account of the high spirited events that took place right here in this very room."

A round of guffaws followed Alice's greeting. Alice brought the waitress around and more drinks were ordered including a brandy for Baxter.

"Well, Joe. While you were off cavorting with our beloved and rarely seen Deputy Chairman, we've had a little excitement back here at the ranch," Alice continued.

"We've had music, dancing, unwelcomed advances, rejection, and finally rightful rescue by a knight in shining armor. And it all happened right here in the Elbow Room of the Hudson Valley Conference Center," Fred added.

"My evening was fairly boring. We just talked about training," Baxter said sliding in next to Alice where he was greeted by a brush of her thigh.

"The excitement was here, Joe," Alice said placing her hand affectionately on Baxter's shoulder. "It all came after dinner. A trio played and we were all dancing. Guess who took a shine to our little Miss Andy?" Alice was not waiting for a guess continued, "It was our Mr. McIvor from Toronto. They danced the evening away with McIvor displaying his best Canadian ballroom moves. Clyde, our leader, sat and watched ecumenically. Then McIvor got romantic. It was obvious top all of us that Andy was driving him wild and uncontrollable."

"McIvor then made an advance or two on our Andy. She pushed him off at first and finally slapped him. Clyde was off his stool like a tiger tempered with Diet Pepsi."

"He proceeded to deck McIvor," Tom Ruffle interjected. "I believe I heard old Clyde say, 'Take that you, cur!' under his breath. We were present at an international incident."

"A border dispute between Partners," Harley ruled.

"Where's McIvor now?" Baxter asked.

"He's rounding up a second to call on Clyde," Tom Ruffle predicted.

"And where's Clyde?" Baxter asked.

"He's calming Andy, I'm sure," Alice said. "Either that or he's working her up to new passions."

"I was supposed to call her when I got back," Baxter said.

"Call her in her room, Joe. If a man answers, simply say McIvor please!" Alice advised.

"So you're telling me that McIvor made a pass at Andy and Clyde took him to task," Baxter asked for final clarification.

"You're making it sound boring, Joe. The whole drama was played out in front of us. It was breathtaking!" Alice exclaimed. "Andy, with men fighting over her! It was something to behold! I'm sure that she's dreamed about something like this all of her life. Now she's experienced it! And her triumph was shared with us! If only we had pictures! Poor, dumb old pompous McIvor, who was bitching about our decorum last night, getting in his cups and patting Andy on the ass. How could he know that he had reached an area reserved for Uncle Clyde?"

"Now this is serious stuff, Joe," Harley observed. "McIvor is the Managing Partner of the Toronto Office and reports directly to the Senior Partner in charge of Canada. Why he was here for this conference, I'll never understand."

"He wanted a crack at Andy, Harley. They heard up in Canada that she was hot stuff."

"You can bet Ernie Grey will get a call on Sunday from the Senior Partner in charge of Canada. I think his name is Arnold McIcecube. He will denounce this scurrilous attack on one of his key Managing Partners," Harley predicted.

"And Ernie will tell him, 'Don't send guys down here who can't fight'," Ruffle countered.

"And where is Grunwaldyt?" Baxter asked.

"He was led away," Alice answered. "There are some things as Associates shouldn't see. One is lust and violence between Partners. He will consider it acceptable behavior and turn lusty and violent."

Baxter drained his brandy. "I have a telephone call to make to my mother who worries about me when I'm away and out late." He left the table and located the house phone, dialing Andy's room number. Nickerson's voice answered.

"Clyde, Joe Baxter here. I heard what happened and it sounded to me like you did the right thing. Is Andy there?"

"Joe, I'm afraid I lost my temper with that fellow, but he was really out of line. Here's Andy."

Baxter now had Andy on the line. "Joe, I presume you've heard about our little drama tonight. How was your dinner with Harvey?" Her voice sounded very calm and controlled.

"Fine, I'll tell you about it in the morning. He wants me to go to LA. I'll leave you in Clyde's good hands," Baxter said.

"You're welcome to join us. I have a chilled bottle of Chardonnay here," she invited Baxter.

"I'll pass, Andy. I have a big day tomorrow," Baxter said and then hung up the receiver. He went to bed that night and dreamed of John McKenzie and Ernie Grey.

In later years, when Baxter looked back to contemplate the flow of his life and career, he designated the period between 1975 and 1977 as his transition period. It was the beginning of the excursion that would take him to New York, but the journey began pointed toward LA. Baxter marked the Hudson Conference meeting and the dinner with Harvey Randolph as the beginning of the transition period. Baxter knew that he would be compelled to leave the Chicago office sooner or later, and he had gotten a glimpse of a larger, more complex and Byzantine world of McKenzie Barber.

Sunday had been surprisingly productive and calm at the Hudson Conference Center. McIvor showed up early and was contrite. Nickerson shook hands with him, followed by Andy, and the group work moved forward on a serious basis. Alice insisted on referring to Nickerson as KO, but the name didn't stick after the conference. Harvey asked Baxter if anything had happened the evening before, and Baxter replied that he hadn't personally seen anything. He left the conference around four o'clock for LaGuardia, after having informed Andy that he would decline the Executive Office training job if it were offered. It was agreed that he would serve as a conference trainer and Baxter would return to his work in Chicago.

Brimmer's secretary contracted Baxter on the Monday afternoon after his return to Chicago and a breakfast meeting was set for Wednesday morning at Brimmer's club.

"What in the hell do you thing you're doing?" The bald-headed mustached Chicago Managing Partner greeted Baxter. "Aren't you happy in Chicago?"

"I don't understand your question, Paul," Baxter said seating himself across the table from his glowering leader.

"You've been whoring around soliciting transfers to other offices. I had three calls on you Monday morning. I took a big risk when I put you into

Alvardi's job and we've moved you along compensation-wise. What in the hell is this transfer campaign of yours?" Brimmer was obviously angry with Baxter. Baxter had tried to call Lorna twice to see if she knew the reason behind the meeting, and she hadn't returned either call.

"Paul, I love working in the Chicago office. I want to stay here the rest of my McKenzie Barber career. It's everyone else that wants me to go other places in the interest of the firm. The way I see it, I'm in the middle of the country and can get to either coast within two or three hours. I want to stay here in Chicago and build this practice into a multiple partner practice. Let me tell you how all this got started." Baxter then recited the story of his relationship with Friedman, Leon Harwell's discussions with Ernie Grey, and the Director of Training overture that he had declined. Brimmer cooled by the time Baxter was finished with his narration, and they ordered breakfast.

"That goddamned Friedman!" Brimmer observed. "A classic young Turk! Ernie finally got around to pushing Ben Sydes out, which was the right thing to do and about five years overdue. Sydes was being protected by Harvey, but Friedman has finally been selected as his successor?" Brimmer shook his head. "Our Jewish swashbuckler! He'll wear better long term in a place like Cleveland or New York rather than Los Angeles. I wasn't aware that he had initiated these discussions. This kind of behavior is unacceptable to me! The Executive Office job would have been a poor choice for you, but it could be right for Lee Heller. Now look, Joe, when you suggest a name like Lee Heller to someone like Harvey, you just don't blurt it out over dinner. What you do is say—-I may know of someone who would be perfect for that job, but I must check it out first. Then you call me and ask. If I agree, then you call Harvey and say, 'I've checked it out and believe you should call Brimmer.' That's how it's done. Joe, you've a very good consulting practitioner, but you're going to have to sharpen up on the inter-office relationships and life with the mother office, if you're going to advance here. Keep going as you are. Build your practice! I guarantee that you will be a Partner with McKenzie Barber. When it's time for you to transfer to another office, I will tell you. Until that time, do your job, serve clients, and defer the politics to me."

Breakfast was consumed quickly and they were out the door by 7:45. Baxter received Brimmer's message clearly. He was in the Chicago office until Brimmer gave him permission to discuss other career options.

Teri stayed through October when she received an offer to tour with a road company of *A Little Night Music*. She campaigned for them to move to a larger apartment, but Baxter countered that he had only invited her up for a nightcap, and she had now stayed nearly a year. Teri departed and promised to write. She had taken up with an orchestra percussionist named Bud, and explained Baxter away as a friend of her sister, with whom she maintained a platonic relationship.

Chuck Washburn made an active attempt to reunite Jennifer and Baxter. It seemed that her writer friend had moved back to the Madison campus to write his great American novel. Chuck and Didi hosted a dinner in their Whitefish Bay home in Milwaukee and invited Baxter and Jennifer.

Jennifer was waiting for him in the family room when Baxter arrived. She had her hair cut short in a pageboy and wore a black dress with a V neckline, black pumps, and a silver necklace that Baxter had not given her.

"This is just like old times," Didi said after drinks were poured. Jennifer talked about the children, Agnes's banishment to the carriage house, and how empty the house was without Baxter. The children missed their father. Nelson was enjoying his retirement and the Henry Wiggins people appeared to have made a go with Washburn Manufacturing, although they had closed the plants in Racine and Deer Lake.

"I think it's time for you two to get back together rather than divorce," Chuck began his plea.

Baxter was noncommittal and polite through the main course. He deferred confronting the real issues until after dessert.

"This is all very pleasant and I'm enjoying this evening very much, but I believe it's time to review the issues at hand."

"Spoken like a true McKenzie Barber consultant," Chuck acknowledged.

"There's really no going back," Baxter started with three sets of eyes on him. "This is a matter between Jennifer and me and shouldn't be discussed around a dinner table as an after dinner subject."

"It's a bit of a family matter, Joe," Chuck said tactfully. "Didi and I simply wanted to get you two together and begin some kind of dialogue. We don't want to be privy to private discussions between Jennifer and you. We just want you to have them. We could take a drive and leave you here with the kids."

Baxter stood up from the table. "It's a nice August night out. We can go for a walk." Jennifer took a sip of coffee and stood up from the table. "Then a walk it is."

They walked down the sidewalk of a treelined street in the fading nine o'clock half light. It was a neighborhood of large homes and rolling lawns. Jennifer lit a cigarette and they walked in silence for the first block. Baxter decided she was a beautiful woman in the half-light. If he had just met her for the first time at the dinner table, he would probably be falling for her at this time. Too much had happened since that wedding day and Mr. Tom's death. He disliked Jennifer now, and perhaps that dislike would evolve into outright hatred over time. Jennifer held her cigarette in her right hand and extended her left hand for Baxter to grasp. He allowed it to remain empty.

"I think you should come back," she said finally. "I want you back. The children want you back. I'll let Agnes back into the house if you'll come back. Chuck tells me that you have done very well at McKenzie Barber. I was a little surprised at first when Chuck told me that you were close to becoming a partner, but then I remembered how hard you work. You always were full of initiative. The family was very impressed with you. Tom was really the matchmaker, though. He picked you out for me. We have two lovely children and we should be a family again. I'm prepared to be a good wife to you, and I'll sleep with you again. I'll sleep with you tonight if you want me to."

"No dice, Jennifer," Baxter said.

"Do you still have that young girl living with you? Chuck arranged for some pre-hearing investigation. You picked her up right after you moved out of Palmer Street. She's only 19 or 20. Are you appealing to young girls?"

"She's moving out. I'm just a brief stop on her path to international stardom," Baxter explained.

"That's another thing. You've been hanging out at some supper club that's owned by Mafia connected people. What does McKenzie Barber think about that?"

"It's not Mafia connected. Sonny, the owner, has a broad acquaintanceship with a number of Italians engaged in a great many activities. He knows contractors, public accountants, and grocery store owners. He knows about as many gangsters as he knows bullfighters. Were you and Chuck hopeful of damaging my character? All I do is work and I've never missed a payment on our child support agreement although I admit I've been remiss to visitations. I'll try to do better there."

Jennifer started a fresh cigarette, stamping out the butt against the sidewalk. They walked another block in silence. Baxter wanted to turn around. "There was another girl, wasn't there?" Jennifer said staring ahead of her. "She was seen at the park with Agnes and the children. Agnes tried to palm her of as her niece. The children remember her. They said she was with McKenzie Barber. It all happened when I was in Europe."

"I'm sorry, Jennifer. But it was all quite innocent. The young lady was a consultant who had dropped off an important package. She had some time between flights, and we asked her to come for a picnic with us. Her name was Hillary and she was engaged to be married at the time. She is someone's wife now, and living in London. For a first rate libertine, you seem to be really scratching for evidence of any of my transgressions. Jennifer, just get the hell out of my life and stay out!" Baxter said.

He was angry over the introduction of Hillary into their discussion. She would come into his head when he was sitting alone in lonely airport motel bars. The memory of the last meeting with her in front of the Deer Lake Motel stayed with him.

"Godamnit! We're right for each other and you won't step up and claim me!" The words stayed with Baxter. "What if——?"

"If that's what you want, let's do it. I'll want alimony!" Jennifer said drawing to a stop and turning back.

"You're not getting alimony. You'll get child support."

"I don't have as much money as I expected to have. You'll have to make up the difference somehow."

Baxter stepped up the pace of his walk. He wanted to get to Chuck and Didi's house and into the safety of his car.

"If we go to court, we go to court," he said.

"The children should come first," Jennifer said nobly. "Would you consider taking them?"

"What would I do with the children?" Baxter demanded.

"You could get a bigger place, move that little piece of baggage you have now out, and I can start a new life unencumbered with motherhood. I'd like to study to be a museum curator. That's my new job with the Gellhorn Institute and it's paid."

"Jennifer! I will not pay you alimony and child support too."

"Just $12,000 a year and child support will keep me even. Chuck believes we could be final by November."

"Jennifer, what happened to the great American novelist?" Baxter asked.

"It didn't work between the two of us," Jennifer lit a third cigarette.

"Do you have someone new?"

"There is someone that I have been seeing, but I'm willing to end the relationship if you want to reconciliate."

"I'll have to think about this," Baxter said as they reached his car. "Give my best to Chuck and Didi. I have to go. I'll call you next week," Baxter said unlocking his car door.

"No kiss?" Jennifer asked standing on the curb.

"Sorry. It's not something I want to do," Baxter said and started the car. He could see her standing on the curb through his rear view mirror. They both knew it was all over and had known it for years. Tonight had been a meaningless ceremony. Poor Joel! Poor Muffin! They had been unfortunate enough to have been born. Where was Hillary tonight? He decided he would call Barber London on Monday morning.

Baxter called Barber London on Monday and was bounced to personnel. Hillary Stone had left six months earlier on maternity leave. He took down a forwarding address but crumpled up the paper after he hung up. Another

chapter in the book of his life was closed forever. After Teri moved out in
October, Baxter was truly alone, except for the weekends with the children.
He moved to a larger apartment down the hall, and began to pick up the
children on Friday nights and keep them with him until Sunday morning.
Sometimes he would drop in on Agnes in the carriage house on Sunday
morning when Baxter returned the children. She had aged dramatically,
complained of varicose veins, was drinking heavily, and still listened to
classical music. They found her dead in November. Baxter arranged for the
funeral service and explained about death to the children.

Baxter remained busy with his practice, and everyone at McKenzie
Barber waited for the acquisitions to begin, but none happened. Hamilton
Burke was announced as the new Partner-in-Charge of Strategic Planning
reporting directly to Ernie Grey. Bob Friedman was named the new
Managing Partner for Los Angeles, and Alice Dungler began to call Baxter
on a weekly basis. The rest of the group at Hudson Conference Center also
stayed in contact with Baxter. Mostly they wanted compensation
information for their clients. They always shared the gossip in their own
offices, and inquired about other offices.

"Burke was down in Dallas last week," Tom Ruffle shared. "I think he
was looking at a software firm. Lon McMasters introduced me to him. He
looked like the kind of man who will make things happen."

Hamilton Burke seemed to be everywhere and he appeared in Baxter's
office during the first week in December. Baxter hadn't seen him in eight
years. He stood framed in the doorway of Baxter's office. Burke looked the
same. Sandy, close cropped hair, erect stature, sparkling eyes, and he
addressed Baxter in his melodic voice. "Joe, how are you!" came his
greeting. They clasped hands. "You've gotten bigger! I've been hearing
good things about you. I brought you into the Manufacturing practice and
now I understand you have become an expert in Executive Compensation.
How did all this happen? Tell me about it." Burke seated himself across
from Baxter. Their conversation started focused on Baxter's move into the
Executive Compensation practice, but early on he concluded that Burke
really wanted to discuss the practice as a business unit

"Why is Alvardi so hung up on us getting into the Employee
Benefits/Actuarial Consulting business?" Burke asked point blank.

"I don't believe Frank is against the firm entering Employee Benefits
consulting. He just doesn't want Executive Compensation to be part of
Employee Benefits. Executive Compensation is strategic and concerned
with providing tailored incentives to achieve defined operational goals.
Employee Benefits represent cost incentive work force programs that have
little to do with Executive Compensation. It's a different business. That's
Frank's case."

"Then, Joe, explain to me why the large Actuarial Consulting firms are in Executive Compensation?"

"They're in it for the money, but their work is very mechanical and is dominated by actuaries who have real problems with issues more strategic than pension funding assumptions."

"Do you and Alvardi rehearse your stories together?" Burke asked.

"My views are my own, but I respect Frank's thinking on this. It's okay if the firm goes out and acquires an Actuarial Consulting firm, but maintains Executive Compensation as a separate business. Exec Comp belongs under Strategic Planning," Baxter stated.

"Joe, why isn't the practice growing faster?" Burke asked.

"I don't see the numbers, Ham Exec Comp here in the Midwest has grown 20% a year. I believe that exceeds the Chairman's hurdle rate."

"Alvardi doesn't share the national numbers with you? You're a Director, Joe, and I understand close to being a Partner. Don't you and Frank communicate?"

"We're on the phone two or three times a week. We co-published twice last year. I know that we're about a $5 million practice nationally."

The practice was $4.65 million in FY '76. Frank has a plan of $5.3 million for FY '77 and he's counting on $1.4 million from Chicago. Can you hit those numbers?" It was the first time Baxter had ever had a McKenzie Barber conversation with Burke. His wolf grey eyes were merry enough, but they seemed merciless. This was a man who had once killed people, Baxter reminded himself.

"That's a soft budget, Ham. We'll blow in about $1.6 million this year."

"Good boy," Burke said and glanced at his watch. "I have to be with Brimmer now. I thought I'd just drop in. Ernie and I had dinner the other night with an old fellow named Leon Harwell. He seems to think the world of you, Joe. I believe he wants you out in New York pretty soon. When you're out, please look me up. Maybe we can have a dinner, or at least a drink. It's been a long time, Joe." Burke rose from his chair.

"Ham," Baxter called after him. Burke stopped and looked back at Baxter.

"There was a consultant who transferred to the London Barber office that I worked with. Her name was Hillary Stone. Did you meet her?"

"Hillary Stone, Stone Resources in Colorado. Yes I did, Joe. I played tennis with her a couple of times. She had a very powerful serve. Was married to a nice young fellow who worked in the London office of one of the money center banks. She got pregnant and he went to work for her father's company back in Denver. Moved into an officer level position. How well did you know her, Joe?"

"Just through a couple of consulting engagements," Baxter answered.

"I'm sorry to hear that you didn't get to know her better. She was a damned fine looking woman. Look me up when you're in New York again," Burke said taking his leave.

An image of Hillary popped into his mind for a moment. He remembered two words. 'Claim me!'.

It had become obvious to Baxter that Alvardi was in trouble at McKenzie Barber, but it was recoverable. He called him the next day and recounted his conversation with Burke.

"Burke's dangerous, kid. Be damned careful what you tell him. He's a lot like Ernie. He wants everything to happen right now. They had been fiddling around on a lot of things at EO, but with Burke up there with Ernie, things are going to happen. Not everything is going to be good."

"Frank, can you keep me better informed?" Baxter asked. "Burke asked me a lot of questions about the practice nationally and I didn't have the answers. I felt dumb."

"I'll do better, kid. I got a call coming in from a client. Adios." There was a click and a dead line. A classic Alvardi exit!"

Mrs. Moore, Mr. Harwell's confidential secretary called on January 2, 1977. Mr. Harwell had several projects for Mr. Baxter. When could he come out?

"What sort of projects?" Baxter had asked.

"The International Division of U.S. Pharmaceuticals, a company called Brookline Fashions, and a restaurant company named El Tortilla," Mrs. Moore recited.

A week later, Baxter was waiting in one of Harwell Management's conference rooms with U.S. Pharmaceutical's 10K, 10Qs, proxy, and annual report. He wanted the U.S. Pharmaceutical engagement badly. Neither McKenzie Barber nor Baxter had any real experience in the pharmaceutical industry, and this was an opportunity to break in. Brookline Fashions was a $50 million revenue specialty retailer headquartered in Queens. It was thinly traded and managed by the Greenstein family. It looked to Baxter like a nothing company. Brookline had been taken public at 81/2 and now was trading at 3 5/8. Harwell was obviously looking for a fast upside return. El Tortilla was headquartered in San Antonio and franchised Mexican restaurants. Baxter had read the financial material three times on the plane and concluded that their accounting was aggressive. El Tortilla appeared to be a high risk investment. The stock was trading at 7 1/8.

U.S. Pharmaceutical was the reason why Baxter was in the Harwell Management conference room.

"Good morning, Joe," Mr. Leon greeted Baxter ebulliently. "I believe I've got some very interesting work for you. Let's start out with El Tortilla."

They spent nearly an hour on El Tortilla. Harwell wanted Baxter to visit San Antonio and do another Hi-Valu Auto Parts. "What I want you to do, Joe, is to make a qualitative assessment of top management's integrity."

"Do you believe I'm qualified to do that, Mr. Leon?" Baxter asked.

"As qualified as anyone I'm acquainted with. I wouldn't ask you to do it, Joe, if I didn't think you could handle it," Mr. Leon snapped back.

Next came Brookline Fashions. "This company may have substantial upside, or they may be going nowhere. It's a family company and I want you to look their ability to really grow the company. I called Seymour Greenstein, the Chairman, personally and told him that one of our family trusts is examining the possibility of making a substantial investment in the company. A couple of days in Queens ought to do it."

"Mr. Harwell. I'm not a retailing expert. I am not qualified to evaluate their merchandising strategy."

"No one asked you to do that, Joe. You just go in and look at the people and tell me whether they can get where they say they're going. It's as simple as that. I want your people's judgment on Brookline. Now you write me letters confirming what we've discussed and you get started, Joe. $15,000 per engagement and expenses as we agreed on Hi-Valu Auto Parts. I have to be going, Joe." Mr. Leon rose up from the conference table.

"Mr. Leon, we haven't discussed the International Division of U.S. Pharmaceuticals," Baxter reminded him.

"Oh that. I have a name you can call. They have agreed to talk to you on the basis of my recommendation." Harwell picked up the telephone and dialed Mrs. Moore, his confidential secretary. "Mrs. Moore, what is the name of the international personnel person at U.S. Pharmaceutical whom Mr. Baxter is to call. Spell again, please." Harwell scrawled a name and a telephone number across a piece of paper. "Here it is, Joe. The man's name is James Hopper-Jones. I believe he's British and he's International Personnel Manager or something like that. He knows I'm on the Compensation Committee and his superior, Reg Naisbett, should have alerted him for your call. This work should be competitive and Robson Allen is proposing. I can guarantee nothing, but I have put in a good word for you. Good luck and good-bye," Harwell said and left Baxter alone in the conference room. He had come all the way to New York and received two assignments which he would have declined in Chicago and he had the telephone number of a middle manager in U.S. Pharmaceutical."

Baxter got the work at U.S. Pharmaceutical's International Division. They wanted a private survey of European Managing Director and senior staff positions for eleven European subsidiaries and a number of firms had been invited to propose for the work. Hopper-Jones was a conservative personnel bureaucrat with slicked black hair who wore vented suits and

Italian shoes. Baxter wrote one of the most creative proposals of his life and McKenzie Barber was awarded the work. Baxter was to visit Europe in June 1977 where he would be assisted by one Barber-Paris multi-lingual consultant. Ham critiqued Baxter's proposal and promised that he would make some calls to assist Baxter should he get the work. Ernie Grey sent Baxter a Grey-gram when McKenzie Barber was awarded the assignment.

The El Tortilla management group impressed Baxter as unethical hustlers. Everyone in senior management appeared to be a cousin of someone else, their financial statements were replete with pockets of costs that had not been expensed, there was no financial planning process, the accounting systems were primitive, slow, and inaccurate, and the food was lousy. Baxter wrote the first draft of his report in a Best Western motel with a bottle of Canadian Club and a bucket of ice as companions. He produced a report that Leon Harwell believed should be placed in the New Yorker. He called Baxter the day he received it in the mail. "Joe, I've read this report twice and it is one of the freshest, wittiest pieces I've read in a long time. I am intrigued by the Mexican segment of the restaurant market, but obviously El Tortilla is not a Harwell quality investment. I must confess that I called Mrs. Harwell to read the part about your kitchen visits. She loved your humor. I made a xerox and sent a copy over to Ernie Grey. I know he will enjoy it."

Oh! Oh! thought Baxter. The Grey-gram arrived three days later.

TO: J. Baxter
Chicago
FROM: E. Grey
Executive
cc: F. Alvardi
New York
Subject: El Tortilla Restaurant Report-Harwell Management Co.

Mr. Harwell forwarded a copy of your El Tortilla Restaurant report. He was very pleased with your work and the report. I was personally not happy with the findings presented to clients laced with editorial comments. Please, in the future, see that my office receives one copy of all future reports issued to this client.

Baxter called Alvardi after reading his Grey-gram the second time. "Don't worry, kid. Your numbers are great. Just always remember this. Chairmen rarely have a sense of humor, this one especially. Numbers engineer his emotions and he only exhibits two emotions, joy and rage."

Brookline Fashions was a new and different experience for Baxter. It was his first Jewish, family owned retailer. Brookline was headquartered in a section of Queens just beyond the Midtown Tunnel. It was $8.35 by taxi from the Waldorf, plus tolls, and located in a tangletown of warehouses.

Brookline was formed in a curved rainbow colored sign over the front doorway. There were some cement steps, iron railings and glass block windows on each side of the door. Two signs were posted with tape on the glass blocks.

Employment Office-Side door

Salesmen-Thursday-Friday only or by Special Appointment

The front door was locked and Baxter pressed a buzzer. "Yes?", a Queens accent greeted him through the speaker over the buzzer. "Mr. Baxter to see Mr. Greenstein," Baxters said clearly into the speaker.

"We have a number of Mr. Greensteins. Sy, Herb, Fred, Sy Jr., and Zave. Which Mr. Greenstein?" the voice demanded.

"Mr. Seymour Greenstein," Baxter requested.

"Seymour, Sr. or Seymour, Jr.?"

"I have a meeting with the Mr. Seymour Greenstein who is the Chief Executive of Brookline Fashions."

"Are you a salesmen with a confirmed appointment?"

"I am not a salesman. I am expected. My name is Baxter. Mr. Harwell arranged for me to see him to discuss some business matters."

"Are you seeking a position? Then you should see Mr. Feldman at the side door."

"Mr. Greenstein expects me at 10 AM. My name is Joe Baxter. I am neither a salesman nor a job seeker." Baxter had his face close to the speaker and said his words loudly and slowly. A voice from behind him shouted, "For Christ sake, Florence! Let him in. He's well dressed, white, and peaceful, and he has an appointment with Sy, Sr!" Baxter turned and saw a young woman in her twenties standing next to a large corrugated box. A battered white convertible was parked next to a fire hydrant at the curb and the door was swinging open. She had short brown hair and was only wearing a white blouse, black skirt, and black flat shoes in the cold winter morning air.

The voice from the speaker shouted. "Is that you Bridgette?"

"At your service, Florence. Now open the godamned door. That's not Fort Knox you're guarding!" the girl commanded. There was a buzz. "Grab the door, Mister, before Florence loses her conviction!" she instructed Baxter. He opened the door and looked back at the girl. She was trying to move the box up the steps. Baxter placed his brief case in the door as a stop and hopped down the steps to help her with the box.

"Let me help, that looks heavy," he said and the two eased the box up the steps. Baxter took the front and backed up the steps with the girl pushing the box upwards. "I didn't hear you drive up," Baxter said as they reached the landing at the front door.

"I didn't drive up. I coasted. I ran out of gas three blocks ago. Lucky I was pointed down hill," she explained.

Florence turned out to be a white haired lady with shell rimmed glasses who operated from behind a switchboard panel. The reception area was comprised of two red naughahyde chairs, a formica table and a six foot high plant.

"Thanks, Mister," the girl said when the box was in the reception area. She held out her hand for Baxter to shake.

"Bridgette Morgan! Thanks a million!"

"Joe Baxter. It was my pleasure."

Bridgette turned to Florence. "Get LeRoy up here from the warehouse. We're sending this shit back to the supplier."

"Mr. Greenstein don't like boxes in the reception area, Bridgette."

"Florence, call LeRoy right now and get him up here and then call Leon, the guard. I'm out of gas in front of a fire hydrant. Tell Leon to hotfoot down to the Standard station and get me a can full of gas."

"Aren't we Miss Pushy this morning?" Florence commented and proceeded to make those calls.

Bridgette turned to Baxter smoothing out her hair. "So, Joe, what brings you to Queens on a Wednesday morning in February?"

"You've been running around in a convertible with the top down in February. Aren't you cold?" Baxter asked.

Bridgette rubbed her arms. "There, I'm getting my circulation back. I have a jacket in the car. Thanks for reminding me."

She turned to the door. "I'll knock and you let me in. Florence can't be expected to do two things at once. Right now she has her calling to do. Get on with it, Florence, time is slipping by," Bridgette said as she bolted out the door.

"LeRoy! Come up to reception right away, Bridgette has a big box of goods she wants to charge back to a supplier and tell Leon he should go to the Standard station and get a can of gas for Bridgette. I don't know how many gallons! Get enough gas in the can so Bridgette can start her car. This is an emergency, LeRoy! Step on it!"

There was a pounding on the front door behind Baxter. He opened the door and Bridgette reappeared with a Yankees warm-up jacket around her shoulders.

"Mister!" Florence called out. "Only I open that door! Don't ever do that again!" she scolded Baxter.

"Florence! Be polite to this man! He's a guest!" Bridgette took a cigarette pack from jacket pocket and extended the pack to Baxter. "Want a cigarette?" she offered.

"Don't smoke," he replied.

"Rats! That means you won't have a light."

"Bridgette, Mr. Greenstein don't like people smoking in the reception area. He thinks it makes the lobby look cheap," Florence scolded.

"Florence, he's already done that with the furniture," Bridgette countered.

"And you, sir," Florence returned to Baxter. "Who did you want to see again?" Baxter again asked for Mr. Greenstein, Sr.

"Why didn't say so before. You're Mr.———?"

"Baxter."

"Spell it please!" Florence demanded.

"Jesus, Florence! Call up Sy, Sr. and tell him Joe Baxter is here for his appointment!" Bridgette urged.

Florence was soon on the phone with someone named Ethel.

"You're expected in the executive conference room upstairs. Mrs. Miller, Mr. Greenstein's Sr.'s executive assistant will be right down to escort you to the conference room," Florence announced.

"Look like you're getting the red carpet treatment, Joe. It was just a matter of persuading Florence to tell them that you were here. What do you do for a living?" Bridgette asked.

"I'm with a firm called McKenzie Barber, and one of my clients has asked me to come by and meet with management here. What do you do here?" Baxter asked.

"A little bit of this, and a little bit of that. This morning I was a District Manager. This afternoon I will be a Buyer. Tonight I will be a student."

A small wiry black man entered through a side door. He was clad in a green janitor's uniform and wore a pencil behind one ear.

"LeRoy," Bridgette greeted him in a command voice. "I have gathered up all of this Hush-a-Bye crap from six of our stores. We are shipping it back to Hush-a-Bye express collect. I have all of the stock numbers. See Sonya and get a charge back form typed up. I will stamp it with my FUCK YOU! TAKE IT BACK! stamp when it's typed up. Now get this box out of here before Ethel comes down and has a fit!"

"Yes, Miss Bridgette!" LeRoy acknowledged, and began to push on the box.

A fiftyish woman with white hair, wearing a dark suit and dangling earrings entered the room. She smiled and extended her hand. "Mr. Baxter? I'm Ethel Miller, Mr. Greenstein Sr.'s Executive Assistant. We're very pleased that you could come today to meet with us. Welcome to Brookline Fashions." She clasped hands with Baxter. Her hand was talon like and ring laden.

"You wouldn't have a light, would you Ethel?" Bridgette asked brandishing an unlighted cigarette.

"Bridgette, you know Mr. Greenstein's rules about smoking in our reception area," Mrs. Miller said in a patronizing voice. "I'm sorry, Ethel. I have allowed a nicotine craving to over ride the grandeur and dignity of this beautifully appointed room,"

Bridgette said rolling her eyes and starting off in the same direction of the door into which LeRoy had exited. As she reached the door, Bridgette stopped and beamed back a smile. "Nice to meet you, Joe!"

"I see that you've met our Bridgette," Mrs. Miller said as they started up a staircase.

"I met her in the front of the building. She certainly has a lot of personality and energy," Baxter commented.

"Bridgette's grown up with Brookline Fashions. She started out as a stock girl when she was a senior at St. Agnes High School. The late Mrs. Greenstein took to her and taught Bridgette about buying. Now she seems to do a little bit of everything around here. Mr. Greenstein Sr. is very interested in her development. He had been sending her evenings, at company expense, to the Fashion Institute."

"That's very magnanimous," Baxter commented. "How long ago did Mrs. Greenstein pass away?" he asked climbing the stairs a step behind Mrs. Miller.

"Three years now. She trained her son Zave to replace her. She used to do the buying, and Mr. Greenstein, Sr. ran the stores. Now we're much larger and we have a number of senior executives."

Mrs. Miller led Baxter into a large walnut paneled conference room across from some windowed offices. Five Greensteins awaited him. Sy Senior greeted Baxter. He was a man with a mane of white hair and of medium height. He greeted Baxter with a firm handshake while brandishing a cigar in his left hand.

"Mr. Baxter, I'm Seymour Greenstein, Sr. I'm the CEO of Brookline Fashions. This is my older son, Sy, Junior." Sy was in his late forties and he sported a Groucho Marx mustache. "Sy is our Executive Vice President and Chief Operating Officer." Then he turned to a tall dark haired man, who was wearing a blue glen plaid suit.

"This is Herb Greenstein, my nephew. He is our General Counsel and Chief Administrative Officer." Sy, Sr. moved on to a short fat man who wore an olive colored three piece suit.

"This is Fred Greenstein, our Executive Vice President of Stores. Lastly, this is Zave Greenstein, my younger son, who is our fashion merchandising genius." Zave wore a white shirt open at the neck with a black cravat and dark trousers. There was a round of handshakes and hellos, and Baxter was shown to a place at the end of the table where he could face all five

Greensteins. There was a coffee urn, a pitcher of orange juice, and a large platter of sweet rolls and bagels at the center of the table.

"Brookline Fashions is honored this morning to have a representative from the Harwell Trust meet with us to talk about our fast growing company," Sy, Sr. began. Ethel poured coffee and started the platter with Baxter. He passed it to Fred, who took one bagel and one sweet roll, before passing it on to Herb.

"I must tell you, Mr. Baxter, that I was floored about two months ago when I heard personally from Mr. Leon Harwell of the Harwell Family Management Trust, and he said that his trust had been studying our company as a possible investment. He said that he would have his advisor, Mr. Baxter, meet with us when you were in New York again. So we are very pleased to meet with you to tell you about our very well established and promising company. Each of these busy executives has cleared his schedule to attend this meeting on this morning, Mr. Baxter. Mr. Harwell is regarded world-wide as an astute and important investor. Yet, at the same time, there was some dread on our part. The stock market has not properly valued us as a company."

"Herb," Sy looked down to his General Counsel and Chief Administrative Officer, "said to me just yesterday, 'Suppose Mr. Harwell wants to take over our company in a proxy fight. Then what do we do?' I told Herb that Mr. Harwell wasn't the kind of man who took over companies on an unfriendly basis. I told Herb that Mr. Harwell usually bought a large block of shares, and sometimes took a seat on the Board of Directors. If that is the case, Mr. Baxter, we would welcome Mr. Harwell on our Board as a very senior advisor. It's only a matter of time before this company is on the Big Board taking our place beside The Limited and the GAP. We've got the team and the merchandise concept that will put this company on top and make a lot of money for our investors." Sy, Sr. ashed his cigar and smiled down at Baxter. "What would you like to know from us this morning?"

Baxter asked questions that would compel the Greensteins to talk. He had been through this twice before for Harwell. The companies, personalities and markets changed, but the agenda was the same. People knew who Leon Harwell was, and they respected his financial clout. Baxter was his emissary.

"Suppose that you describe in your own words, the history of the company, its strategy in the current operating climate, and your collective forward plans." Baxter opened his brief case and produced a legal pad and appeared poised to take notes.

They all contributed over the next thirty minutes. Sy, Sr. started and one by one they interrupted and contradicted one another to tell the story of

Brookline Fashions. Baxter had leafed through their eleven page annual report on the plane. Their accountants opinion letter was from a firm called Goldman & Waxman located in Garden City, New York. Sorting and sifting through their commentary, Baxter formed an initial image of the strange company that called itself Brookline Fashions.

Brookline Fashions had been formed after World War II by Seymour Greenstein, Sr. and his wife, Maxine. Sy, Sr. had returned from the service, gotten a GI loan and Maxine's family had provided the rest of the capital. Maxine's maiden name was Brookstine which was anglicized into Brookline. Sy ran the stores and Maxine was the merchant. They started with a ladies and young women's ready-to-wear store in Brooklyn. Later they extended to infant's and children's wear. Stores were opened up in Queens, Staten Island, and extended throughout Long Island. Now Brookline operated stores in New Jersey, Connecticut, Westchester, Upstate and Western New York and Eastern Pennsylvania. Their fashion image was contemporary styles at high value prices. They now operated 100 stores with total aggregate revenues of $50 million. They expected to be $100 million by 1980 and $300 million by 1985. They would be a Big Board company approaching one billion dollars by 1990.

Sy, Sr. talked on confidently about the bright future of Brookline Fashions, and then he instructed Herb to pass Baxter the earnings per share estimates for 1976, 1977, and 1978. The earnings per share estimated for 1978 were one and one/half times the value of the stock at the conclusion of yesterday's market close. "That's not adjusted for splits, either," Herb added enthusiastically.

"That's very impressive, gentlemen. Mr. Harwell likes to assess the ability of management to meet their earnings goals. May I ask a few questions?" Baxter began. "Let's start with your individual senior management roles. Mr. Greenstein, Sr., as Chief Executive, I assume you have overall responsibility for the company. What do you believe are your principal accountabilities?"

"I'm the Chairman of the Executive Committee, which is this group of executives, and I'm responsible for stockholder relations." Sy, Sr. ashed his cigar and looked around the room. "Is that it boys?"

"Don't forget your outside work, Dad," Sy, Jr. added. "Dad is active in a number of community associations and attends all of the NRMA meetings in the city."

"How often does the Executive Committee meet?" Baxter asked.

"Whenever it's necessary. Brookline Fashions operates like a well oiled machine. We all like to get out, visit stores, shop competition, and look for new store sites," Sy, Sr. answered.

"One by one, Baxter asked them about their jobs in the company and inquired about their subordinates. Zave, the merchant, had three buyers. "Well three buyers including Bridgette," Zave corrected himself. "My mother held my job until she passed away three years ago. She started Bridgette buying accessories about five years ago. She's buying teens and missy sportswear now, too," Zave added vaguely.

"Bridgette works for me, too, in Stores," Fred Greenstein added. "She's kind of a Junior District Manager for the Queens District. We had a guy quit last summer and Bridgette stepped in for him, and we haven't been able to find a replacement yet. So she's kind of kept the job. She also has Ernestine, our Display Coordinator, reporting to her."

"Bridgette," Sy, Sr. interjected, "is just one of many of the devoted and motivated young people who made up the dynamic middle management of Brookline. She's been with us since high school, and we have paid for her continuing education at the Fashion Institute. Bridgette is one of our young managers of tomorrow. You can't give her too many jobs to do. That's the way it is with our enthusiastic young people."

Baxter moved the subject to their merchandise control and inventory management systems.

"We have a very advanced computer system, Mr. Baxter," Herb answered. David Gerstein, our Director of Information Systems, is a brilliant mathematician, and he's worked with World Computer to develop a leading edge merchandise control system. "We're considering licensing it to other companies," Herb Greenstein said proudly.

Baxter went through the motions of taking notes. He wanted to get out of the conference room and see what Brookline Fashions really looked like. He thought about Bridgette in her Yankee warm-up jacket. Was she really that motivated?

"Now, Mr. Baxter, may we ask you a few questions?" Sy, Sr. asked. "How long have you been doing this for Mr. Harwell?"

"Several years," Baxter lied.

"Your card says Chicago," Sy, Jr. observed. "Why would Mr. Harwell use someone from McKenzie Barber in Chicago to visit a New York company?"

"Because he prefers it that way," Baxter answered.

"How big an investment do you think he'll want to make? We've got some preferred in Treasury with a guaranteed ticket," Herb offered.

"Mr. Harwell does not discuss his investment strategy with me. My total mission is to meet management and make a quick review of operations."

"Are you looking at a number of companies like ours?" Sy, Sr. asked.

"I can't answer that. I do, however, appreciated your candor and forthrightness. Now I'd like to walk through the warehouse, have a few words with your controller, meet your Director of Information Systems, spend some time with Zave and his buying staff, and visit a few stores."

Sy, Jr. and Herb exchanged suspicious side glances. "Mr. Baxter," Sy, Sr. said, "we weren't prepared for you to walk around the building and see stores. We just thought you wanted to meet with us as a group and get to know us."

Where did Harwell find these companies? Baxter asked himself.

"Why would you want to visit the warehouse, accounting, and the computer room?" Herb asked. "I can see visiting stores, but I don't understand the other departments. You're not an auditor, are you?"

"Mr. Harwell likes assurance that the management and the systems are in place to support the company's growth plans."

"Do you mean to tell us that you can spend a few hours and determine that?" Herb challenged Baxter.

"I'm quite fast. I'd like to see stores tomorrow. Today I'd like to visit internal operations," Baxter said.

"Mr. Baxter," Sy, Sr. protested. "This is like inviting someone into your home and having them want to inspect the bedrooms, the bathrooms and look under the sink."

"Mr. Greenstein, haven't you ever been visited by a Securities Analyst in your positioning as a public company?" Baxter asked.

"We've had them call-up, but nobody has ever come out to see us before," Sy, Jr. admitted.

"Boys," Sy, Sr. announced, "Let's show Mr. Baxter what he wants to see. Herb, you take him to the warehouse first, and I'll go down to Accounting and the computer room and explain about Mr. Baxter's visit. Then tomorrow, we can show Mr. Baxter some stores."

"Bridgette can take him around," Zave volunteered. "I'll talk to her about it."

Good! thought Baxter. The Bridgette he had met this morning, properly primed, could provide a wealth of information.

The Controller was a young man, three years with Brookline, following employment with their outside Auditor, Goldman & Waxman. His name was Stan Feldman, and he appeared gentle and easily intimidated. There was no evidence of a budgeting or profit planning system, and he was not involved in inventory control. It appeared to Baxter that Zave's buyers did what they believed was right, and the Controller kept score. The inventories were financed at 2% over prime. The payables systems was convoluted and there were a few murky supplier relationships. Baxter toured two warehouses in adjacent buildings. One was a neat firetrap and the other was a modern building bulging with merchandise. Baxter made tests of the inventory system and could only match two of the five SKUs he tried to locate. He decided that he wanted to talk to Zave's buyers last, after meeting with David Gerstein, Brookline's reigning computer genius.

Gerstein was a heavyset man in his early thirties with a beard. He wore a white shirt open at the neck with black trousers and a gold necklace. A MS Computer Science diploma was framed on the wall of his cubicle, and there was a picture on his credenza that showed him with Zave Greenstein. They were both clad in colored Brookline tee shirts and bermuda shorts.

"Mr. Baxter, I'm pleased to see you," David Gerstein said, remaining seated while staring intently at a computer screen. "Excuse me for a moment," he gestured for Baxter to take a chair and began to punch instructions into the keyboard. Baxter opened his *Wall Street Journal* and read three pages before Gerstein brought himself to speak. "I understand that you're from McKenzie Barber, Mr. Baxter. Do you know Aaron Goldstein? I understand that he's one of your top computer people."

"I'm not familiar with the name. Is he in the New York office?" Baxter asked folding up his *Wall Street Journal.*

"Yes. He's moved very fast and he's pretty high up. Aaron is an Associate. We both serve as Adjunct Professors in Computer Science at the New School. I assume you're at the consultant level," David commented.

"No," Baxter corrected him. "I'm at the Director level. I was once classified as an Associate, but that was many years ago. Can we talk a bit about Brookline's systems?"

"Are you familiar with the world of computers?" Gerstein asked.

"Passably," Baxter replied. "Suppose you lead me through the merchandise information system starting with the vendor purchase order to receiving to the sales floor and then show me how you reflect vendor returns. Go slow when you describe the stock-keeping unit systems. It didn't make a lot of sense to me when I was over in the warehouse just now." They stared at each other for at least thirty seconds before David said, "Let me show you the vendor information file to start."

The systems were brilliant in concept, but Baxter concluded that Brookline had major documentation flaws. Nearly all of the computer systems were directed toward merchandise control or selling services. Accounting seemed to be neglected. "Do you report to Herb?" Baxter asked.

"I report to Zave on most things, and to Herb on some things," Gerstein responded with a shoulder shrug. "That's the way it is in a family company."

The meeting with Zave Greenstein was the last of the day for Baxter. Zave occupied a large office on the second floor which was decorated with modern art and cluttered with swatches and merchandise on rolling racks. Zave had a large oval shaped blonde desk and a matching round table. The credenza behind his desk contained a picture of his father and a picture of an attractive blonde haired woman who reminded Baxter of Betty Grable.

"That's my mother," Zave said when he detected Baxter staring at the photograph. "That's the way she looked in the 1950s. She was the merchant here and my mentor."

Zave seemed gentle and relaxed. He had been the most quiet in the morning meeting. "I would think you would have started with me and talked about the merchandise planning and selection first. But instead you started at the warehouse level and worked your way back to me. Why did you do that?" Zave sucked on a mechanical pencil as they talked. He took it in and out of his mouth from time to time as if he were smoking a cigarette.

"Mr. Harwell expects me to report on the company's ability to support growth. He assumes growth when he identifies an investment opportunity," Baxter said making up an answer.

"That's very interesting," Zave said nodding his head and taking a long drag from the eraser head of his pencil.

"Tell me about your buying organization," Baxter requested.

Zave took a piece of graph paper and began to draw boxes.

"We tend to run thin. I'm the head merchant, and have had the job for about three years. I've really have had it longer because my mother was diagnosed with cancer about five years ago and she began to get me ready and cut back her time in the office."

Baxter looked up at the Betty Grable-like picture. She certainly could have done better than Sy, Sr.

"Under me I have three buyers, Denise, Lucille, and Bridgette. All three were trained by my mother. Bridgette also handles Display and has been an acting District Manager since last Fall. She was my mother's favorite. It was mother's idea to send Bridgette off to night school. Denise and Lucille are good mature buyers, and I work well with them. Bridgette is a rebel and can be very argumentative. She does have more ability than Denise and Lucille, but she lacks their maturity. She is always having wars with vendors, store managers, and even David Gerstein, our Information Systems Director. We're going to have Bridgette take you around to visit stores tomorrow. If nothing else, she will be extremely entertaining."

Zave went on to talk about Fashion and lost Baxter. He knew he was out of his element when he could talk about people and numerical relationships. He listened politely and attentively, but Zave could be talking about Solid State Physics as far as Baxter was concerned.

"So that will give you a picture of where we're going from a fashion forward perspective," Zave concluded.

"Now we should call Bridgette and arrange for you to meet her in the morning." Zave dialed four digits on his telephone and then spoke into the phone. "Bridgette, dear, did Fred talk to you about showing our visitor, Mr. Baxter, around to some stores in the morning? That's right, you should rent a car. I'll have him come by and you can work it out. I'll send him right down. Dad had to leave early, but sends you his best," Zave peered at his watch. "David and I have a squash date. Nice to see you." They shook hands, and Baxter left with instructions that took him back down to the first floor to a small office without windows. The sign next to her cubicle said, B. Morgan-Buyer. Bridgette was on the telephone when Baxter looked into her office. Her desk was a series of neatly stacked piles of papers, and there was a large ash tray littered with cigarettes.

Bridgette faced the wall as she spoke on the telephone. Her Yankee jacket was hung over the back of her swivel chair.

"Look, Jack. I don't give a fuck what Zave said. I don't want anymore back order bullshit. If you can't ship us this week, you're gone and I'm shipping all those tacky belts back to you. It's your decision, Jack and if you try to go slinking around me, I'll break both of your fucking legs. What do you mean that's not very ladylike? If you'd ship us like you're shipping our competitors, I'd be a perfect lady. I'd even have tea with you."

Bridgette hung up the phone and turned her chair to see Baxter in the doorway. "Hello, Joe," she smiled. "I was informed that I will be taking you to see some stores tomorrow morning. How many do you want to see? You can't see the whole hundred because it will take too long. You and I would have to spend weeks together, and it would be sure to cause talk. How many would suit you?"

"Four will do!" Baxter said standing across from the desk.

"How about two in Queens, one in Great Neck, and one in Massapequa. It will make a full morning and I've got business in everyone of those stores. Meet me out in front here at 8:30 tomorrow morning. I will have a car with a top."

"That sounds outstanding. I assume I will meet you where we met this morning," Baxter responded.

"Expect I won't have a box with me, and there will be no need for Florence to buzz you in." Bridgette picked up her telephone indicating that the conversation was over as far as she was concerned.

"Can someone get me a cab?"

"Where are you going?" she asked.

"Back to the city."

"Where in the City?"

"The Waldorf," Baxter acknowledged.

"I'll get you a car." She pulled a voucher from her desk and dialed a telephone number. Three minutes later she had a car number and instructed Baxter to wait out front.

Baxter waited out in the early February darkness at the front steps of Brookline Fashions until 6:05. As the car pulled up, he saw Bridgette's battered, top down convertible leave the parking lot. She wore a white scarf and her Yankee jacket was zipped up to her neck. She waved as she drove by. Baxter settled into the back seat of the sedan, and once again asked himself, how did Leon Harwell learn about this company?"

He had dinner with Ham that evening. He had tried before and called him by chance from the airport the evening before.

"I've just had a trip canceled, Joe. I would be delighted to have dinner with you," the melodic voice agreed.

Ham was staying on a street called Beekman Place, and he told Baxter that he could walk it from the Waldorf.

He entered a building called the Belgrade, and was greeted by a uniformed doorman who inquired as to Baxter's business in the building.

"Mr. Burke's in the penthouse," he called ahead. "It's Penthouse C." Baxter rode the elevator up 16 floors to the penthouse level. It was the first time he had ever been in a building like this. Penthouse A was on the right hand side of the elevator while B was on the left. C was at the end of the hall. The door was slightly ajar. Baxter knocked twice and heard Ham's voice. "Come in Joe. I'm on the telephone." Baxter entered into a room of thick carpets and dark wood. There was a fire burning in the fireplace, and Ham was seated in a chair talking on the telephone. "Yvonne, my dinner guest is here. I must say good-bye." Then he said something in French and hung up. "A lady I know in Paris. It's one-thirty in the morning there, Joe. Good to see you. I've got a bottle of port open. I can pour you a glass of port or something else. Let me help you with your coat." It was gracious host, Ham, who greeted Baxter. The man who came into his life, launched his consulting career, and disappeared.

Hamilton Burke had his jacket off and greeted Baxter in a dark vest and trousers. His jacket was laid across a table. Burke's sandy hair remained close cropped, and he moved about the room with a stiff drill field carriage.

"Joe, what brings you out to New York?" Baxter requested port. He had never had a glass of port in his life. It reminded him of the time he had gone to Harry's Cafe in Minneapolis with Willard and had his first martini.

"Harwell work. He pays me to review absurd companies."

Ham raised his glass. "Here's to absurd companies that we can get paid to review! Tell me about it, Joe."

Baxter described his visits to El Tortilla and Brookline Fashions.

"My God! They're not exactly McKenzie Barber profile clients are they? Whatever you do, don't write another funny report on the one you reviewed today. Ernie doesn't have a funny bone for a lot of things. I thought your report on the Mexican restaurant chain was a scream. Harwell apparently liked it. You may have just caught Ernie on a bad day."

Baxter told Ham about the engagement with U.S. Pharmaceuticals and again asked his advice about overseas staffing.

"That's wonderful, Joe. That's the kind of work we should be getting through Harwell, not those strange retail companies. I'll call Paris for you and make sure that you get a competent multi-lingual consultant with a reasonable billing rate. This is the firm's first engagement with U.S. Pharmaceutical. Ernie will be excited!" Ham observed Baxter's glass. "What do you say we have one more glass of port and take off. I've got reservations at this Italian place on 1st Avenue and 57th Street. It's called Supremo and it's quite hot right now."

"Tell me about what you're doing! I know what Barry Keller does in his strategic planning engagements for clients. But what does the Partner-in-Charge of Strategic Planning do for McKenzie Barber?" Baxter asked.

Ham sipped slightly on his port and his eyes closed for a minute. "I've been thinking about that, Joe. I've concluded that I'm a portfolio manager. Let me explain—-McKenzie Barber was in its beginning an Industrial Engineering Consulting firm. It evolved into a Specialized Industry stage where the firm selected industries where they believed they could profitably differentiate themselves. They coasted on with that for years. Next they added new disciplines and new industry specializations. In addition, they opened up new offices. Suddenly it has been recognized that in order to be competitive, McKenzie Barber may have to make acquisitions of other consulting firms. The last acquisition the firm made was in the Spring of 1950 when they acquired FSO. The job I have taken on reports directly to Ernie with the objective of looking hard at the existing portfolio and determining which should be grown, which should be abandoned or divested, and what should be acquired. I have complete access to the Chairman, wide access to information, but no staff. Ernie and I are completing our honeymoon period, and it's time for results. It's one of the toughest jobs I've ever taken on. But if I'm successful, McKenzie Barber will be a different firm. If I'm not successful, McKenzie Barber will slip seriously in the 1980s."

"I've heard that Ernie Grey is tough to work for," Baxter commented.

"Ernie's a pussycat," Ham corrected him. "He pushes, but he pushes patiently. Ernie's demanding, but he's not unreasonable and he's open minded about looking at the business in new ways. Ernie knows that the firm cannot continue to operate as it did in the 1960s. FY '71 and '75 were damned scary to Ernie and he knew the firm has got to be better prepared for the next down cycle."

*Dwight E. Foster*

"Down cycles?" Baxter questioned. "I haven't seen any down cycles over my nine years with the firm."

"That's because you have always been able to keep yourself busy, Joe. Others haven't, and have failed to keep others busy. That's where Nickerson comes in so handy. Clyde has been very successful in moving Associates, Managers, Directors and even Partners out of the firm and convincing them that it's their idea. I used to wonder what Clyde was good for and now I know. He's got a network of headhunters and clients who believe McKenzie Barber people are the greatest pool of resources in the world. Ask me where we really have the lead on Robson Allen and I'll tell you it's Clyde Nickerson. Whether you like the bugger or not, he is a national treasure to this firm."

Baxter had never heard Nickerson referred to as a national treasure before.

"Ernie needs to build up a decent critical mass of Executive Office resources. Some of them are going to have to be Partners of the firm. All Ernie really has had over the years has been Clyde, Marv, the Controller and the four or five Associate level rotationals who come in for 12 and 18 month cycles. By the time they're any real help, they're back out in operating offices again trying to get back on Partner track." Ham looked at Baxter's glass. "What do you say we have one more touch of port and then take off for Supremo. I love to hear the sound of my own voice," Burke said pouring a little more port into Baxter's glass and then emptying the bottle in his own glass.

"This is a lovely apartment," Baxter said.

"Well come on. I'll give you a tour." They had been talking in a small sitting room located inside the front hallway. They now moved through a large L shaped living room with an adjacent full dining room. "Let me show you the kitchen. I could run a restaurant in this place." They walked into a huge kitchen with a large ten foot by five foot butcher block working area in the center of the room. "This used to be the New York townhouse of an Austrian Baron. Baron Putzi von Hofnagel."

"And you bought it from him?" Baxter asked in awe.

"No. Don't own it. Just use it as interim digs. It belongs to a French lady who lives in Paris and visits from time to time." Ham led Baxter out of the kitchen into a short hallway with two closed doors. "Those are servant's quarters. There's another door out of the kitchen that leads to the outside hallway. This door was about as far as they were allowed to go in the house other than to pick up during the daytime." Ham opened the door into a study lined with books with a large rolltop desk. "That's where Putzi used to do business. He left Austria after the Anchsluss to either seek freedom as an independent business man, or serve as a Nazi agent. No one's ever been able

228

to prove either." They walked through a succession of large bedrooms including a master bedroom with a giant canopy over the bed. "I just can't bring myself to jump into that thing alone," Ham commented. "So I usually sleep in one of the other two."

"How often does the French lady visit?" Baxter asked.

"She was here over Christmas and is expected back in May. Yvonne has a husband and feels socially obligated to be with her husband and her son. I've known the woman on and off for about two years. She insisted that I move in here when she visited in December."

"How's her husband feel about it?" Baxter asked.

"I don't think he knows. They're both enormously wealthy and Yvonne has her own money. He could send seconds to call upon me and challenge me to a duel, I suppose. But then I would have the opportunity to kill the son-of-a-bitch. I'm very good with pistols, sabres, and foils. Shall we go on to dinner, Joe?"

They knew Hamilton Burke well at Supremo. A distinguished grey haired man in a white dinner jacket greeted Burke with a warm handshake, and snapped his fingers for the check room girl to take their coats. The maitre'd's name was Antonio and he shook Baxter's hand. "Pleased to meet a new friend of Mr. Burke. I can put you on the main floor, Mr. Burke, but you're a half hour late and I seated someone at your table on the second floor."

"No, Antonio. Mr. Baxter and I want to talk a little business and first floor is too noisy." Burke looked into the bar beyond the piano player. "How long Antonio?"

Antonio shrugged his shoulders. "Maybe twenty minutes. Thirty minutes on the outside."

"Seat us at the bar next to those two ladies," Burke said nodding his head toward two well dressed thirtyish women seated in the far two bar stools.

"They are waiting for their escorts, Mr. Burke. They have been delayed. Something about delays in the Boston shuttle."

"Then Antonio, you must seat us next to them at the bar. Ask that one gentleman to move down."

"Mr. Burke?" Antonio gestured with open hands that what he was asking him to do was very difficult.

"See to it, Antonio," Ham commanded. His melodic voice had steel in it.

"Yes, Mr. Burke," Antonio agreed with some resignation. They followed some ten feet behind him as he requested a man in a dark suit to move down and Burke slid into the stool next to the ladies. They ordered martinis, and Baxter studied the women through the mirror behind the bar.

They were well dressed, immaculately groomed, and five years older than they appeared from the maitre'd's stand.

"Good evening, ladies," Burke greeted them after their martinis had been served. To his right was a brunette in a blue suit with diamond earrings and beside her was a woman with reddish brown hair in a brown knit suit and matching pumps.

The brunette looked at Burke for a second and returned a flat and uninterested 'good evening' and continued to talk to her companion. They took out cigarettes, but the bartender beat Burke to the light.

"Are you ladies waiting for a table, husbands, or both?" Burke persisted.

"We're waiting for husbands and then a table," the brunette replied coldly.

"I'll bet they got caught on a delayed shuttle," Burke continued.

"You've been talking with Antonio," the brunette replied coldly.

"I've seen you in here before," Burke continued. "You live over on Sutton Place. I see you in that little grocery from time to time." The brunette raised an eyebrow. "I live on Beekman Place. I'm just back from Europe. I was posted there eight years and don't know a soul in New York."

"I was in Paris for five years and London for the past four." The brunette's companion was now leaning forward. Baxter listened to the piano player with one ear and to Burke with the other.

"Where did you live in Paris?" the companion asked.

"It wasn't very fashionable. I had a flat in Montmartre overlooking the city. The view was spectacular and the neighbors were on the eclectic side. I was just there on weekends because I traveled a lot. I lived in Marble Arch and later in Mayfair in London. Now I'm on Beekman Place," Burke said qualifying himself to his audience. Baxter wondered if he should volunteer that he had lived in Iron Creek, Minnesota, Racine, and now Chicago.

"You must lead an interesting life," the brunette answered.

"How about you ladies? My name's Hamilton Burke, III which means there were two more before me. This is my friend, Joe Baxter from Chicago." Burke slid back from his stool revealing Baxter.

"I'm an Astro-Physicist/Neuro Surgeon and I'm visiting New York to learn from this man," Baxter greeted them.

"You're a what?" the woman with reddish brown hair asked.

"I'm not going to repeat it again in a public room," Baxter said rising up from his bar stool. "I'll whisper it in your ear." Suddenly the four were in a cluster. The brunette's name was Rhonda, and her companion's name was Sybil. Rhonda was married to a partner of Wellington Barr which Baxter identified as a premier New York law firm. Sybil turned out to be a literary agent who was seeing a Partner of Rhonda's husband. Tonight was to be their first dinner together.

"And they're stuck in Boston!" Rhonda lamented.

"Ladies, should your escorts for some reason, not be able to appear, you may join us on the second floor," Burke offered. Antonio was now beside them. "Mrs. Windom, your husband has just called from LaGuardia. They will be here in a half-hour and I have a table for you on main floor. Mr. Burke, your upstairs table is ready." Baxter shook hands with Sybil while Burke kissed Rhonda's hand.

"Well, Joe," Burke observed when they were seated at a rear table upstairs, "It looked like we had a shot at getting laid back there. I will bet you that Rhonda Windom looks us up before the evening is over."

"What makes you say that?" Baxter asked.

"She has the eyes of a player. So has her friend. A little more bad weather and we could have bedded them tonight," Burke speculated. "What's your martini status these days?" Burke asked while scanning the wine list.

It was a long dinner. They started with the house tortellini and enjoyed a Sauvignon Blanc. Baxter told Ham about his marriage. He shook his head. "Never met your wife. Heard from some people that she was a looker, but difficult. You seem to have a high tolerance for abuse, Joe. You should finalize that divorce, Joe, and come out here to New York."

"I had dinner with Harvey Randolph in June. He brought up Los Angeles. Brimmer had breakfast with me when I got back from the training conference and gave me hell about talking transfers with people. So I'm keeping my head down and doing my job. I want to be a Partner and believe I have the qualifications."

"Joe. You will be a Partner with McKenzie Barber. Keep your powder dry. If Ernie buys the recommendations I will make to him next week, and we can sell it to the operating committee, I will have the influence level to push you into the Partnership. New York is where I want you and I can use this Harwell relationship of yours to get you out here."

"What about Brimmer? What about Friedman?" Baxter questioned.

"Brimmer will give you up if Ernie asks him. I'll handle that young Turk Friedman. Just do your job and give me time, Joe. Executive Compensation is a small, but strategic practice. Leadership must be centralized. Alvardi will be number one in charge of New York and you will be number two and will orchestrate the other U.S. practices. You'll have to travel a lot, but that won't kill you."

"Ham, I'm getting mixed signals from people," Baxter observed as the veal was served.

"Joe, the only signals you need to listen for are my signals. I work for Ernie Grey and he asked me to help him restructure McKenzie Barber. I will need key lieutenants and resources in the years ahead, Joe. I want you to be one of them. Don't pay any serious attention to that old drunk, Harvey Randolph, and recognize Friedman for what he is, an up and comer, but not a finisher. It's you and the others I select who will run the firm in the mid 1980s."

Baxter looked into those cool grey eyes and he recognized Burke's goal for the first time. He wanted to be Ernie Grey's successor. Burke wanted to be Chairman!

"Speak of the devil!" Burke announced. "Our old friend, Rhonda, from the front bar, is coming this way. She's a sure bet for a nooner."

Baxter crashed into his room at the Waldorf at 1:30 in the morning. Burke had virtually confirmed an assignation with Rhonda in front of him. Then Burke talked about the international practice. He took him through each of the practices, and the personalities of the Managing Partners. "In London, Joe, they perceive the U.S. as the farm team. They were flat on their ass after the second world war and Mr. Mac and later, Ernie bailed them out. They have conveniently blotted that period out of their minds. London was a tough office to break in. London has U.K. clients. The other offices primarily serve non-resident multi-nationals. The Paris office is just beginning to serve French clients. They did a major job with the de Hartog interests this year. But the Paris office's clients are generally French subsidiaries of American and British companies. Frankfurt, Milan, and Zurich are in the same boat. The clients are primarily multi-national subsidiaries of American, British, and now Japanese companies. The same is true in Latin America and in Southeast Asia. McKenzie Barber lives and dies with its multinational clients. That's why the U.S. Pharmaceutical engagement is so meaningful, and why the junk you're doing with Harwell is so meaningless. McKenzie Barber must carefully farm it's multi-national clients! The Emerging Companies practice that hired me was a joke. It was a whim of the chairman that didn't work. Realistically, Joe, McKenzie Barber never should have been performing consulting work for Washburn Manufacturing. It simply was not the firm's kind of client."

"Harwell is not our kind of client, unless the stuff you're doing for him will lead us into more U.S. Pharmaceuticals. McKenzie Barber has been run like an amalgamation of Indian tribes. Each tribe has its chief and their tribal lands. They sit on councils together, smoke peacepipes, and swap skins at the conclusion of hunting season. But McKenzie Barber is not one nation of warriors. That's what the new chief must accomplish! The new chief must bring in new tribes and train them and the old tribes in the new ways! And that, Joe, is the task ahead. I hope you're with me!"

Baxter's wake-up call came at seven, and he woke with a stunning headache. The last thing he wanted to do was to visit Brookline Fashion Stores. The Harwell work was irrelevant unless it led to U.S. Pharmaceutical class engagements. Perhaps he would ease out of the arrangement with Leon Harwell. He was not going to become a Partner at McKenzie Barber grinding out $15,000 engagements for Harwell Management.

Baxter shaved, showered, had a quick cup of coffee, and bought newspapers. He passed the flower shop with his newspapers and turned back. On impulse, Baxter purchased six red roses for Bridgette. She was giving up her morning to show Baxter stores when she had better things to do, and he was obligated to pan Brookline Fashions to Leon Harwell. It was more poorly managed than El Tortilla. Flowers made Baxter feel better when he hailed a cab in front of the hotel.

A black Chrysler was parked in front of Brookline Fashions when Baxter arrived in his taxicab. He started up the steps to begin the entry negotiations with Florence, but was called back by a honk from the Chrysler.

"Joe, I'm here." Bridgette emerged from the driver's seat. She seemed a different person from the day before. She was wearing a black suit with white pearls and held a paper cup in her hand. Baxter climbed in the passenger seat and held out the flowers to Bridgette. "I know taking me around to stores will be a burden on your schedule and I'd like you to have these as an advance thank you."

Bridgette inspected the top of the flower cone and took several short smells. "Jesus! Roses! I'm just driving you around to some stores. You'd think I spent the night with you!" Bridgette opened her car door. "I'm going to put these in water." When she was outside the car, Bridgette peered back in at Baxter and her bright pretty face smiled back at him. "And thank you. I'll be right back."

Baxter watched her run up the steps to the front door. Black pumps and pretty legs, there was a marked difference from the girl in the satin Yankees warm-up jacket of the day before. "Open up, Florence! This is a raid!" Baxter heard Bridgette shout into the speaker. Then he watched her disappear in the front door of Brookline Fashions.

Baxter was at page nine of the *Wall Street Journal* when Bridgette returned, prancing down the steps with a coffee in each hand. Baxter got out to meet her and was proffered a coffee in a paper cup. "Hope you drink it black!" Bridgette said. "Those flowers are lovely. You didn't have to. I'm just doing my job by taking you around. But thank you! Flowers always make my heart happy. What's the newspaper?" Bridgette asked, sliding back into the driver's seat.

"The *Wall Street Journal*," Baxter said.

"I've seen it on Zave's desk. All the Greenstein's look at the *Wall Street Journal*. They all check the stock quote page and shake their heads because the stock hasn't moved. Zave, and possibly Herb are the only ones I've ever caught reading the *Wall Street Journal*. Zave passes his copy to David. They share a lot of things together. I read *Women's Wear* every day."

"As a manager in business, you should read the *Wall Street Journal* in addition to the *New York Times* business section, every day," Baxter lectured her.

"Right!" Bridgette answered and started the car. "I figured we'd start out in Massapequa and work our way back. I picked the stores we're going to visit because I have business there."

"This isn't the car you were driving yesterday," Baxter thought back to the battered white convertible.

"I was told that you were a hot ticket guy, Joe. My instructions were to get gussied up, rent a nice car to drive you around in, and maintain a positive and cheery attitude. No one mentioned anything about you bringing me flowers," Bridgette said.

"Please, no more about the flowers," Baxter requested.

"So, dear," Bridgette maneuvered the car through the congested morning Queens traffic in the general direction of the Long Island Expressway. "What is it that you do that's so important to the Greensteins? I'm supposed to drop you at Sy, Sr.'s favorite restaurant in Queens after we're done."

"At our first stop, call Mr. Greenstein and tell him I appreciate the invitation, but I can't make lunch. I have another commitment," Baxter concluded that there could be nothing more depressing than one more meeting with the Greensteins.

"So, Joe," Bridgette continued. "I know you're with McKenzie something or other, but what are you doing with Brookline Fashions?"

"McKenzie Barber is a well known management consulting firm. I am a consultant and do work for a very wealthy investor named Mr. Harwell. Mr. Harwell makes a certain number of investments in businesses that are best described as high potential companies on the threshold of significant growth. He has engaged McKenzie Barber from time to time to visit these companies, meet management, perform a quick review of the business, and make a recommendation relative to management's ability to meet their goals. I have visited a number of companies on Mr. Harwell's behalf. This time he has asked me to visit with Brookline Fashions."

"Joe, you sound just like a night school business professor at The New School," Bridgette commented.

Baxter sipped his coffee and they drove in silence for a few minutes. Bridgette appeared to be processing what Baxter had told her.

"What happens if this Mr. Harwell buys a lot of stock?" she asked.

"The price of the stock will go up for a while and other investors may be attracted to invest in Brookline Fashion," Baxter speculated.

"What if the company doesn't do well?" Bridgette asked.

"The stock price will go down and Mr. Harwell will be unhappy. He will be unhappy with Brookline Fashions and he will be unhappy with me if I recommended the management was prepared to meet their plans and they didn't," Baxter responded.

Bridgette punched in the car lighter and placed a cigarette in her mouth. Baxter made no effort to light it. She took a long drag at a red light.

"I understand that you have been with Brookline since high school," Baxter said, wanting Bridgette to continue talking.

"I have worked for two businesses in my young life, dear." Bridgette accelerated the car for the entrance to the Long Island Expressway. "I worked in Goldberg's Bakery from age 13 until my junior year at St. Agnes. I used to wait on Mrs. Greenstein when she came in. Sometimes I'd carry things for her out to the car and we'd talk. I thought she was the most beautiful, elegant lady I'd ever met. The Goldbergs used to bitch about losing sales when I was out of the store. One day I was carrying out some bags of baked goods for a party Mrs. Greenstein was giving. It must have been a $100 sale, and Mrs. Goldberg shouted after me, 'Don't take the long way back, Bridgette!' Mrs. Greenstein, Maxine, turned around and glared at Mrs. Goldberg. 'She'll be back when I send her back, Hedda.' Then when we were outside at her white Cadillac, Maxine put her hand on my shoulder and said, 'You go back in there and quit, Bridgette. I want you to come to work for me at Brookline.'"

"Well, I didn't ask when or what will I do, or how much are you going to pay me. All I knew was that this beautiful, elegant lady had asked me to come to work for her and I was good and damned tired of working for those damned Goldbergs who were always accusing me of stealing chocolate chip cookies. I remember I announced my big move at the dinner table that night. My Dad, who's an Irish cop, just shook his head an said he didn't know why I had to work for Jews all the time. I came to Brookline right after Easter in 1966. I just showed up in my St. Agnes jumper and Maxine put me to work doing stock records."

"I saw her pictures on Zave's desk. She was a very beautiful woman. She reminded me of Betty Grable," Baxter commented.

"Maxine was a lot classier than the Betty Grable I see in all those old movies. She didn't have a daughter. She had Sy, Jr. and Zave. Maxine kind of took me under her wing. I was very close to her and I'm still not comfortable about talking about her with people I hardly know. She was the brains behind the business. Maxine had the final say on store locations in addition to merchandise. She worked 12 hour days and after a few years, I was with her most of the day. We merchandised during the day and looked at stores from late afternoons until evening. Then we would have dinner together. I would get in at about eight in the morning and we'd have a bagel together and go over the figures from the day before. Maxine didn't come in on Saturdays, but she was there on Sundays and I would come over after mass. We'd usually have Sunday lunch together. Sometimes we'd go off to their country club and she would introduce me as her assistant. I just felt proud as hell being with this beautiful sophisticated woman."

Bridgette stamped out her cigarette and started a fresh one as she weaved through the Long Island Expressway traffic.

"Now I'm not saying that Maxine was perfect. She had a hell of a temper and she screamed a lot. She made me cry a couple of times, but Maxine would always apologize. She's the one who got me started going nights to Fashion Institute and The New School. 'Bridgette' she'd tell me. 'It's not important that you have a college degree, but it is important that you get an education from people outside Brookline Fashion.' We would go through the bulletins together and pick out courses. A couple of times we took courses together, but Maxine would never complete the class. She didn't have a degree. I guess she went a couple of years to Hunter College. But Maxine was a damned smart woman."

Bridgette gave the finger and a long honk to a pick-up truck that pulled in front of the car. "Up yours, buddy!"

"Maxine was always on my case to be more of a lady. She would have had a fit yesterday if she saw me at work in my brother's jacket, but I had to get into a bunch of dusty stockrooms."

"I met you on the steps at ten o'clock. How many stores had you visited?" Baxter asked.

"Not stores, dear! Stockrooms!" Bridgette corrected him. "I started gathering up all that Hush-a-Bye crap at a quarter to seven. That was," Bridgette closed her eyes for a second and counted as they nearly rear-ended an oil truck. "Nine stores. I wanted a hundred pieces even to send back to those bastards, and it took me nine stores to do it. I'm at war with one of our suppliers!" she explained.

"Now, this store in Massapequa, is in a strip mall. We prefer enclosed malls, but we'll take good leases where we can get them. It grosses about $800,000, which makes it one of our larger stores. My sister works there. I'll introduce you. There's Ellie, the Store Manager, Estralta, who takes the train in from Brooklyn, my sister, and Ruby, the stock girl. Ellie's okay. Pushy, but good with customers, and she lives a mile away from the store. Estralta is a P.R. She's awfully good at selling kid's clothes, but dangerous near the cash register. Ruby, the stock girl, weights 225 and spends her free time eating Twinkies in the stockroom. Last year, my sister, was known as Sister Clare in the Little Sisters of Something or other. This year she's in the Brookline organization. Clare quit the order last February after trying to get out for two years. My brother thinks that the Catholic church is worse than the Marine Corps to get discharged from. Clare's pretty good with the cash register and filling out sales slips, but she can't sell worth shit. As you can see, the meld of superb merchandise and key manpower has made this store one of the outstanding performers in the Brookline Fashion family of stores."

They reached the strip mall shortly after 9:45 and there were customers in the store. The store was nestled between a drug store and a hardware store. Bridgette started with the window display and explained a great deal about merchandising themes which Baxter didn't fully comprehend. He had no further interest in Brookline Fashions, but listening to Bridgette Morgan was outright fun. She was quick and outrageous.

"That's Clare waiting on the lady in the blue coat with the little girl. She wants me to get her some dates and she refuses to wear make-up. I told her the other day, 'Clare, you put on some goddam make-up and I'll get you some dates.'"

Clare was a tall, large-boned woman with long hair tied with a blue ribbon. Her shoulders were slightly stooped and Clare displayed healthy square teeth when she beamed a smile.

"She used to teach first grade. I figured with that background she could cope with the Greensteins. I don't see a wedding ring on you, Joe. Think you'd like to go out with her?"

"I don't have personal relationships related to my work," Baxter answered.

Bridgette stood in front of him. Her brown hair had been curled and there was a touch of eye shadow today. "You've dashed my personal hopes, dear. Shall we go in and look around?"

Baxter concluded, after visiting four Brookline stores, that they all looked the same. It was Bridgette who explained the subtle differences. "Look, Joe," she explained over mid morning coffee in a Queens enclosed mall. "You have to have three things to be successful in retailing. Merchandise, people, and location. If you've got all three, you're going to be successful. If you have two of the three, you'll make some money, and if you have only one of the three, you've got a loser on your hands. If you have none of the three, you have a disaster. Our merchandising is generally good. The Brookline customer recognizes that our goods are high value/low price. Our location selection isn't as good as it used to be. We're trying to grow too fast, and Sy, Jr. simply isn't as intuitively good as his mother. He gets snowed with a lot of fast talk and funny numbers by real estate guys. Our people are so-so. Ellie, for example, is a good store manager. Zoe, at that last store, is terrible. David and Zave love to develop these computer models about how big Brookline is going to be, and they feed that stuff to

Herb who massages the figures around for Sy, Sr. and Sy, Jr. These guys have no idea what goes on at the stores—-." Bridgette stopped herself in mid-sentence. She knew that she had said too much to Baxter. Bridgette calmly lit another cigarette and looked Baxter directly in the eye. "And what other questions can I answer for you, Mr. Baxter? We have one more store to visit and this morning is just bolting by." She fluttered her eyelashes.

Bridgette was subdued after coffee and said little to Baxter as they completed their store visits. They left the last store shortly after noon. "Now where is your luncheon?" Bridgette asked as they stood outside at the Chrysler.

"I had hoped you would join me, Bridgette."

"So, you could pump me a little more? You have a face of a bartender, Joe. I'll bet people tell you a lot of secrets."

"I'm through gathering information for Mr. Harwell. I've learned a lot about retailing that I didn't know before, and I've enjoyed this morning," Baxter said trying to turn on his charm. "And you're the first person who has ever told me I have the face of a bartender."

"God! You're tall!" Bridgette said looking up at Baxter. She was five feet three to Baxter's six feet three. "Do you have any place in mind?"

"You pick," Baxter said.

They drove to Brooklyn Heights to an Italian restaurant called Naples which had a long awning that reached out to the curb and valet service. "I've been here with suppliers. It's a sneaky place where suppliers bring customers, and men bring women who aren't their wives," Bridgette announced as they left the car with a teenage boy in a white jacket.

Naples had waiters in tuxedos, a long bar, dark wood and red velvet booths. They were promised a table in fifteen minutes and shown to a small table in the front bar. Bridgette ordered a mineral water and excused herself to call the office. Baxter watched her way away from him in quick short steps. She was an attractive little imp. Why had he brought her flowers? Why hadn't he just grabbed a cab back to the Waldorf to pick up his bag? What in hell was he doing in an Italian restaurant in Brooklyn Heights? He had a five o'clock flight back to Chicago. He was unlikely ever to see this girl ever again. Still she had other qualities he hadn't seen in other women. She was smart, combative, and quick. Bridgette Morgan could probably eventually run Brookline Fashions if the Greensteins would give her the chance.

Bridgette returned with a broad smile and a full wine glass. Her mineral water was waiting in front of her empty chair. Baxter stood up and held Bridgette's chair for her.

"School's out! You've corrupted me, dear. I was going to use the Lincoln to visit stores this afternoon, but now it looks like I'm going to have a long lunch. Salute!" she said raising her glass.

"Bridgette, my work for Mr. Harwell has been completed. This is an off-the-record personal lunch," Baxter said.

"Sure. Now, Joe dear, you look married to me."

"Used to be!"

"Are you Catholic?" Bridgette asked.

"I was brought up Lutheran in Minnesota," Baxter explained.

"Where in the hell's Minnesota?" Bridgette demanded.

Baxter drew an outline of the United States on a cocktail napkin and drew dots showing New York, Chicago, Minnesota, and Iron Creek on the napkin.

"You're from the middle of nowhere," Bridgette observed. "You come across as very corporate in your Brooks Brothers suit, button-down shirts, red ties, and wingtips. You look, at first to be very predictable and trustworthy, Joe. But I also see you as very manipulative. Maybe you better stay away from my sister. All she's seen until last year were priests and they were always after the altar boys."

The head waiter showed them to a table near the back of the dining room. "I want a booth," Bridgette protested. She pointed to a booth in the corner. "The signora wants to sit there, dear," she commanded the waiter.

They were seated in a velvet upholstered booth. "This reminds me a little of Ernie's in San Francisco," Baxter commented.

"I've never been to San Francisco," Bridgette said. "I've been as far north as Buffalo, as far west as Philadelphia, and south to Baltimore. Maxine always talked about taking me to Paris. She loved to go to Paris and used to bring me little gifts. You know——things like scarves and gloves. Maxine took Zave a couple of times. Now I hear Zave and David are going together this summer and Sy, Sr. is footing the bill. I would have loved to have gone to Paris with Maxine. Tell me this, dear. Did you grow up rich, middle class, or poor? Poor doesn't mean poverty. We grew up lower middle class. I learned that term in a Sociology course at The New School. I don't know how much people learn in college. But they do teach you the codes so that you can talk to other people who have gone to college. Anyway, we had five of us living off my Dad's pay as a policeman. We were very Catholic," Bridgette signaled the waiter. "The large redheaded man wants to order a bottle of Chianti, please." Facing Baxter, Bridgette continued. "It's all your fault. You threw me off when you brought me flowers and then you got me talking about Maxine. Joe Baxter-with-the-face-of-a-bartender! We grew up in a flat in Queens. There were five of us. Three sons and two daughters. Clare was the oldest, and my Mother had her as a nun candidate when she was barely out of the cradle. I was second youngest and the tomboy. We all had to work as soon as we could bring in money. We had to save up for Clare's dowery to the big church. I had the bakery job with the Goldberg's, and figured I'd finish St. Agnes and go to work as a secretary or something. Then this beautiful Jewish woman comes into my life and changes it. I'm like her daughter, but not her daughter. Then comes the cancer. It got messy. She was in chemotherapy and was losing her hair and wearing these funny turbans all the time. Then Maxine was gone, and I found myself in a company managed by incompetent schmucks. You saw right through them. You looked at them and picked them apart. You're going back to your Mr. Harwell and you're going to tell them that Brookline Fashions is a company held together with spit and library paste. These assholes are going to grill me and ask, 'What did you tell the Baxter guy, Bridgette?'"

"Nothing that he hadn't figured out the day before," Baxter interjected.

"So what about you, Joe? If you're going to start seeing my sister when you're out here, I should know a little about you."

The bottle of Chianti arrived along with the menus.

"What would you like to know?" Baxter asked.

"You look successful. Are you?"

"Reasonably so."

"You live in Chicago. How often could you get back to see my sister? She loves to roller skate by the way. She couldn't do much of that as a nun."

"I may be asked to transfer to New York," Baxter offered.

"Then you could move to Queens. You could take Clare to movies and bowling."

Baxter ordered the snapper, while Bridgette ordered a veal steak. "I think I would like to have my sister write you," Bridgette announced. "Do you have a business card?" Baxter produced a business card.

"Director?" she read his title. "Are you on the board of directors?"

"It's a title," Baxter explained. "It's one step down from a Partner. The firm is very large and powerful and Brookline Fashions would not be the kind of company we would have in our portfolio. We deal with the Fortune 500 industrials, the top 100 banks and insurance companies, the top fifty transportation companies, and we work with individuals with great personal wealth like Mr. Harwell."

"I've never met anybody before who does what you do," Bridgette stated. "I'm good at reading people. Maxine was the first one to tell me that. You look straight, but you're tricky."

"I don't know how you reached that conclusion," Baxter responded.

"I don't believe you're divorced."

"It will be final this summer."

"Do you have children? Clare is very good with children."

"I have a son ten and a daughter six," Baxter confessed.

"Do they live with you?"

"They will live with their mother in Racine, Wisconsin."

"Another new place. Show me where that is on the cocktail napkin."

Baxter drew another outline of the United States on a cocktail napkin.

"Jesus! It looks like Queens and New York," Bridgette commented.

"How about you, Bridgette? Do you have a man in your life?"

"Don't you want to ask me about my sister, Clare?" Bridgette asked.

"I'm more interested in you," Baxter said.

"Is that why you brought me flowers?"

"I brought you flowers for another reason," Baxter replied. "Now my question is, Bridgette, do you have a man in your life?"

"I have a married man in my life," she confessed. "He's Jewish, has a family, and he sees me on the side. That's why my sister is so right for you. I'm more or less taken on a part-time basis. It's my first affair with a married man and—-Jesus, I hope it's my last."

Baxter held his hand out across the table and Bridgette accepted it. "How long has this relationship existed?"

"Jesus, you sound clinical," Bridgette reacted.

"Look, Bridgette. I once had an affair. I had a very unusual and unhappy marriage," Baxter said in his most consultative tone.

"The guy is a very successful merchant with a very large department store. He was brought in as a guest lecturer at Fashion Institute. He was attractive, funny, and he made sense. I stayed behind to talk to him. I started sleeping with him that night, and it's been going on for three years now. I felt so damned alone after Maxine died. I shouldn't tell you this, but I will. I've told you too much already. I'm resigning from Brookline on Monday. I'm going to work for a specialty store chain called Incognito as a buyer. My friend had a lot to do with getting me in. Last night I finished at Fashion Institute. It's time for me to move on and get the Greensteins behind me forever. I don't know where I'm going with this guy, but he's very wise and very hip, and I'm in love with him."

"I understand," Baxter said.

Bridgette drove Baxter to the Waldorf to pick up his bag and on to LaGuardia. "Do you think we will ever see each other again?" Bridgette asked as she parked the car in front of American Airlines.

"Probably not," Baxter concluded.

"Thanks again for the flowers. Do you want to kiss me good-bye or something?"

"Why not?" Baxter said and he slid across the seat. Their lips met closed mouth and then tongues reached. Baxter's hand was on her back and he could feel the outline of a brassiere strap.

"You're a good kisser," Bridgette observed as she pushed Baxter gently away. "We should do this again."

"We probably won't," Baxter said climbing out of the car and retrieving his bag from the back seat.

"Don't count on it, dear," Bridgette said and she drove off leaving Baxter at the curb.

Europe was on Baxter's mind after he had returned to Chicago. The U.S. Pharmaceutical engagement was his to begin, and Baxter expected to be gone for two weeks. Alvardi appeared to resent Baxter handling an international assignment.

"I want to review that report in draft form before you take it to the client, kid," Alvardi demanded. "I should have been in that proposal meeting. You're working the wrong side of the country thanks to your buddy, Harwell."

"Frank, the job is no big deal. They have ten subsidiaries in Europe and they want Managing Director and senior staff compensation levels studied. If it were a US company with ten divisions spread out in California, Washington, Illinois, Michigan, Missouri, Texas, Georgia, Florida, New York, and Pennsylvania, and they wanted General Managers and direct reports, we wouldn't be having this conversation."

"Kid, you will be dealing with overseas resources and you have no experience with multi-cultural subtleties. The firm wants to do business with U.S. Pharmaceutical, and this is the first time we've had a chance to propose on any consulting in two years."

"And I was introduced by a Board Member," Baxter reminded his mentor.

"You're getting too big for your boots, kid. Don't blow this one!" Alvardi hung up without saying good-bye. Baxter thought back to his discussion with Burke. It had been suggested that Baxter transfer to New York and work directly for Alvardi. Baxter now preferred to keep 750 miles between them.

Burke called a day later. "I made some calls overseas for you, Joe. I've got some people positioned for you in Europe to assist on U.S. Pharmaceutical. In the U.K., I have lined up a young man at Barber London named Byron Locke. He works in what they call the remuneration practice, and is very keen to work with Knoll Labs, the U.S. Pharmaceutical English sub. They're located in Bristol, which is an easy train ride from London. Now in Paris, I have a young woman for you. Her name is Dominique Beaufort, and get this, she is a Harvard MBA and speaks English, German,

Italian, and Spanish fluently. She is considered to be a shoe-in for Associate this fall and regarded as bright and hard-working. I asked Michael Stokes, the Managing Partner, what she looked like, and he said that you wouldn't be disappointed. If I were you, I'd simply cable them and tell them when you will be coming, approximately how long you will need the consultants, and send them a pouch of your supporting materials a day or two after your cable. You negotiate their rates with their department heads. Stokes in Paris is a peach and will be very fair about Dominque. Be on your toes with Julius Green, the head of the London remuneration practice. He loves to screw American consultants and he's gotten good at it. Call any time if you need help."

"Ham," Baxter held on the telephone. "Were you serious the other night about me coming out to New York and working directly for Frank?"

"Quite. But it's our little secret for now! I believe it's the only way we'll ever get your practice off the ground to the height Ernie likes to see things. We can have Frank handle New York and coordinate with International and you can oversight the rest of the U.S. The Comp practice needs a critical mass practice to provide the resources for a national network of local office resources."

"Has this been discussed with Frank?" Baxter asked.

"I want to try it out on Ernie, first," Burke replied.

Baxter looked out his window at Michigan Avenue. While he was in Europe, people were going to decide what was best for his career, and inform Baxter what was best for him after he returned.

Baxter received two memorable pieces of mail in the afternoon office delivery. The first was a note on personal monarch sized stationary from Lee Heller.

> Dear Joe,
>
> We both have been traveling and I really wanted to tell you my news personally. You and I go back a long time to those days at Washburn Manufacturing when I was the consultant and you were the client representative. I remember we used to drink beer together in a place called Bud's. Joe, I'll come to the point quickly. I have been offered and have accepted the position of Director of Manpower Development & Training in Executive Office working for Clyde Nickerson and working side by side with Andy Bourke. I have been assured that I will be a Partner nominee within a year. I know that this position was discussed with you, and it was decided to look further. The appointment is a real high visibility plum and has ample exposure to Ernie and Harvey. I feel very honored to have

been chosen over so many others. Joe, no hard feelings please. I will do my best to put in good words for you, and it is my fondest hope that one day, we will both become partners of McKenzie Barber. Margo sends you her love.

Lee

And on orchid colored stationary and marked "extremely personal" was a letter unopened by the mailroom from someone named B. Morgan. Who in hell was B. Morgan? Baxter asked himself. He opened the flap and Baxter guessed the identity of the writer before the letter frcc from the envelope. It was from that little imp, Bridgette.

Dear Joe:

I'll bet you never thought I'd write you. First the news! I resigned from Brookline two days after your visit. I thought I'd give it a day of grace after your departure. I'm going to Incognito Stores as a buyer. As you can see by my card, Incognito is located in the Empire State Building. I have always wondered who offices in the Empire State Building and now I know. Me!

The Greensteins took it badly. Sy, Sr. tried to talk me out of it. He pulled out all the stops. He offered to pay for more night school! A truly generous man, that Sy!

The next day when it became clear that I was really going to leave, a security guard and Herb came around. They told me I had one hour to clear out my desk and leave the premises. Herb said the family appreciated my efforts over the years but couldn't understand my disloyalty in going to a competitor. I tried to explain to Herb that Incognito served a young business woman customer as opposed to all those frumpy, bargain seeking housewives of blue collar workers who poked their heads in our stores looking for mark-downs.

"That's not our customer at all," says Herb. He wouldn't know a goddam customer from a parking meter. So there I was, cleaning out my desk and there were your beautiful roses on my desk which had opened and were just beginning to droop.

'Okay, Herb,' I said. 'Have it your way!' I grabbed my picture of Maxine, took your flowers, my brief case, and walked with the security guy past Florence like a convicted criminal. I asked to see Sy, Sr. to say good-bye, but Herb said he was not available. Personally, I got a better send-off when I left the bakery. They gave me some day old doughnuts at least. Florence was the warmest. 'I guess we won't be seeing you around here anymore,' she said as I walked by her with the security guy.

'Up yours! Florence!' I told her, instead of good-bye.

So there you have it, Joe. I have taken leave of my home and career with Brookline Fashions. I fondly remember a lovely lunch in Brookline with a silver tongued,, red-headed man who had the face of a bartender. He was very nice and I let him kiss me. I wouldn't mind kissing him again. My new office number is 212-701-2635. That rings in my office. I know you're going off to Europe, but maybe you'll look me up when you come through New York again. I hope you don't think this letter is too forward, but you were the guy who brought me roses and kissed me. After all, I'm just a slip of an innocent girl!

Yours,

Bridgette

P.S. There's a $2 million inventory bust in the computer system. Tell your nice old Mr. Harwell about that one. It will be a year or so before the auditors catch it.

P.S.S. Those bastards fired my sister at the end of the day. Keep your eye out for an opportunity for an ex-nun with a good personality who roller skates and bowls.

Baxter folded the letter, returned it to the envelope, and placed in the recesses of his brief case next to his first Grey-gram. He couldn't explain to himself why he was keeping it. Baxter crumpled Lee Heller's note and flipped it in his waste basket. It was a good place for Lee and Baxter had helped engineer it. He dialed Lee's extension to acknowledge the note and a voice answered, "Lorna King."

"Lorna? Baxter here! Where is Lee?"

"Executive Office. He thinks he went to heaven. I've been given his job."

Jesus! Baxter thought. New information! "Stay where you are. I'm coming over!"

"I'm in the small Manager's office next to Lee's old office," Lorna explained. "But I rather have you buy me a drink tonight because I have to be in with Dr. Barry in fifteen minutes."

"The front bar of the Regimental Grill, sixish," Baxter suggested.

"We have much to talk about. Also I need your help on how to manage Dr. Barry."

Lorna was fifteen minutes late. Strawberry blonde hair swept to one side, blue high necked dress, gold necklace, blue pumps, smooth face and immaculately groomed. Baxter was one Canadian Club down when she joined him. There was a handshake and Lorna ordered a martini straight up. She took a deep breath and then the information flowed.

"Lee Heller was practically shot out of a cannon to Executive Office. they had him out there four times. Brimmer called Ernie and said, 'Either he goes in that job or he goes out. He's the highest priced clerk we have in the firm.' It was okay for Clyde, but I think Andy fought it in her typical internecine way. Brimmer told me that you were her first choice and you had turned it down personally to Harvey."

Baxter looked across the booth at Lorna as she paused to take a first sip from her martini. It seemed to be in the open now. Brimmer that! Brimmer this! Many exchanges were probably made with their heads on pillows.

"You're going to take Heller's job permanently?" Baxter asked.

"I'll have it as long as Brimmer and Dr. Barry believe I can do it. And —," Lorna raised her glass again. "I love it! I'm in the center of a business for the first time in my life. I know the CARS pretty well, and Dr. Barry is brilliant, but bitchy! HE may have the biggest ego in the firm! I know the firm pretty well administratively, and Dr. Barry admitted to me in our first meeting that he didn't know where all the land mines were. He really likes you, by the way and he had grown to despise Lee. Lee was very arrogant with the university people Dr. Barry brought in. The strategy people went to Barry as a group in January and told him, 'Let's get rid of this guy!' I got a nice adjustment and I'll get a big raise in October," Lorna beamed.

The discussion moved to other subjects, which included for the first time, the name of Hamilton Burke. "Do you realize that Burke has formed a firm wide long range planning committee?"

""Who's on it?" Baxter asked.

"Dr. Barry, Bob Friedman, Neil Schmidt from Atlanta, and Roger Dirks from New York. Burke apparently insisted on keeping the committee small and he's chairing it. Getting Dirks and Dr. Barry in the same room is a real challenge. Friedman is apparently on his way up. He leap frogged a lot of partners to get LA."

"A sound man!" Baxter commented.

"Neil Schmidt is Harvey Randolph's protégé and Harvey campaigned for him. Dr. Barry refers to him as Mr. Dull-Normal and believes Schmidt's been placed on the committee to be Harvey's spy. Nobody knows what to make of Burke. He's someone who has been out of sight a long time and suddenly he has Ernie's ear. Dr. Barry and Dirks absolutely hate each other. Dirks won't let Chicago work east of Cleveland. They just had a minor war over a client in Pittsburgh. It was the Allegheny National Bank and it was kind of a strategy and how-do-we-support-the-strategy-with-our-executive compensation-engagement." Baxter listened to Lorna rattle off on the work of the firm. She knew the terms and had probably been carefully tutored over the last year.

"Dirks made the point that the compensation piece was critical, and Alvardi was needed for us to compete for the work. He told Dr. Barry that this guy Baxter back in Chicago was a lightweight. Then Brimmer took Dirks on with Bruce Dinsmore, the New York Managing Partner. Dirks prevailed. We lost the engagement to Robson Allen and Barry rubbed Dirk's nose in it. I heard we lost it on price because Alvardi over bid the compensation piece."

"We should never lose a job on price, Lorna," Baxter pontificated. Baxter was tempted to say, 'But you've traded up.'

"Frank knows how to take care of himself," Baxter observed. "What do you hear about Wild Bill?"

"He's turned over a new leaf. He's stopped drinking and is now living with a lady who is an Associate Professor in the NYU Business School. He brought her to Harvey's open house and she made a great impression on everyone."

Baxter thought back to the afternoon at O'Grady's Bar after the FSO job when Dwyer had been all over the young, ugly Irish nurse. It was a shame he hadn't brought his camera.

"Is there a lot of socializing like that in New York?" Baxter asked.

"Chicago is unusual, but because the Managing Partner is a bachelor, Joe. We have two parties. The promotion party and the Christmas party. Attendance at both is mandatory in Chicago. I hear in New York there are a number of parties and it's important to be invited and to show up. Especially to the ones given by the senior people! When you're not invited, you know you're slipping. Lee Heller will go crazy in that kind of a political environment. Even Nickerson gives an annual house party."

"Does Andy come in and help?" Baxter asked.

"I hear that she comes with an escort, brings flowers for Mavis, works the room, and leaves early. She never brings the same escort twice and there are some catty people who thinks she gets them from a service."

"What do you hear about me going to New York?" Baxter asked bluntly.

"It's been rumored. Dr. Barry wants you to remain in Chicago, Carl's considered okay, but he thinks you're far better in front of a client. I doubt that you will be nominated in 1977, but 1978 may be pretty good for you. How's your divorce coming?"

"It will be final by the time I get back from Europe. She has the kids and I pay $1,500 a month child support and alimony. How do raises and bonuses look this year?" Baxter asked. Lorna had all kinds of information. Why not pay?

"You're having a good year. Brimmer has a matrix of revenues and Director profitability. You come out very high. I hear Teri moved out."

"She's gone on the road and left no forwarding address," Baxter explained.

Lorna shook her head. "You simply have terrible luck with women. I believe you have some basic flaws in judgment. She ran around Sonny's telling people you were too old for her and that she didn't know how to get out of the relationship without breaking your heart."

"I'm very careful who I bring up for a nightcap these days. I'll give you a ride home anytime, though."

"No need for that. I've moved over on Hampshire to a one bedroom. I can walk to work now," Lorna announced.

Their eyes met and without exchanging another word Baxter knew what the move implied. Brimmer had set her up in an apartment.

"Will you still be singing at Sonny's on weekends?" Baxter asked.

"No, Joe. With the new job that part of my life is over," Lorna replied coolly.

# May 1977-Paris

"Joe, this is Dominique," Michael Stokes said introducing Baxter to a tall dark haired young woman. She wore a white blouse with a blue Hermes scarf, dark suit, black stockings, and shoes with low heels. She had a very serious smile and held out her hand.

"I'm very pleased, Mr. Baxter, to have the opportunity to be your assistant on this very important engagement." Her words were spoken slowly, as if she were trying to form every word perfectly. Baxter accepted her hand and squeezed it gently. Dominique squeezed back firmly.

"Dominique, as we discussed, lived in the United States, and is a graduate of the Harvard Business School. She joined us a year ago," Michael Stokes said repeating what he had told Baxter earlier in private.

Stokes was a round bodied Englishman who had been sent by Barber in 1953 as a young manager to open up the Paris office. "They told me at the time," Stokes had explained to Baxter, "that I would be here a year or two. I have now been here for twenty-four years."

"Please call me Joe," Baxter instructed Dominique. She had beautiful dark eyes. Dominique was tall, 5'7 or 5'8 and she had a narrow body with small breasts.

"I would be pleased to call you, Joe," Dominique forced another one of her serious smiles.

"Well, I'll leave you two to start your work. Giselle, my secretary, has set up an office for you. She'll handle any needs you may have, Joe. I hope that you and I can find time for lunch before you head back to the States," Michael said taking leave. He shook hands with Baxter and added something in French for Dominique.

They were shown to a small office with two desks facing each other. Dominique said something to Giselle in French when they were shown into the office, and Giselle answered by shaking her head.

"This is a very small office for someone so important from the United States. Giselle said that this is the best she can do. But I think she can do better. Do you want me to try?"

"No, Dominique. This will do nicely," Baxter said raising his hand.

"Giselle will have someone bring coffee and Evian. Now I must tell you one thing right off. My English is a little rusty, but will come back quickly as we talk more. I must also confess that I have no previous experience in compensation work. I learn very quickly and I am most anxious to learn from you."

"I really need you as a translator, Dominique. I understand that you are fluent in French, German, Italian, and Spanish."

"That is right. I am a little nervous around you this morning, but my English will improve as we talk. You will see."

"I'll show you what was accomplished during the London phase of the work." Baxter spoke slowly and methodically took Dominique through each step of the work plan. She took notes on a yellow lined pad and began to interrupt with questions after ten minutes. Dominique's English improved quickly as she became more confident in her words.

The UK phase of the work had gone reasonably well. Byron Locke had been very helpful. They had taken the early train to Bristol and enjoyed a breakfast together of bangers and eggs in the first class car. Locke was a lanky young man with soft eyes and an easy laugh. He was good company during their interview visit with Knoll Lab management. Locke also helped bridge the McKenzie Barber/Barber cultural differences. Julius Green, Byron's department head, had tried to negotiate additional time for the London office to perform analysis and technically review the London portion of the work. He also volunteered French speaking Barber consultants for the European work. "There's no need for you to burden yourself with Barber Paris consultants. They really aren't very good," Green counseled Baxter.

Baxter brushed Green off, and then went out with Locke for dinner and a tour of London jazz clubs. They had been out until three in the morning. Baxter had gotten up at 5:30 AM in order to catch an 8 AM flight to Paris. Now he was seated across from his French consultant with a dreadful hangover, taking her sequentially through a complex engagement work plan.

They were to fly first to Madrid, then Milan, Zurich, Frankfurt, Brussels, Amsterdam, and finally Paris. "You have visited all of these cities?" Baxter asked.

"Oh yes. I have been to Madrid and Milan many times. Zurich I know well. Brussels, yes. I have been to Frankfurt twice. I will be a very good guide and support consultant for you, Joe."

On a Saturday morning two weeks and three days later, Baxter awakened in Dominique's apartment. The windows were open and Paris sunlight streamed into the tiny bedroom that opened out to a side street.

Jesus! Where the hell am I? Baxter asked himself as he looked across the room. He was lying in a bed with a saggy mattress that faced a small dressing table with a mirror. Beside the dress table was a wardrobe and a small chest. The walls were filled with prints and posters, and he spotted his trousers folded over a chair facing the dressing table.

Baxter pulled up the memory of the luncheon at Jardin Elysees Lenotre. He had enjoyed a superb luncheon with Dominique. They had walked back to the Barber Paris office to pick up the final drafts of the U.S. Pharmaceutical reports and assure that two copies were included in the

Chicago Office mail pouch. Baxter had placed an additional copy in his brief case. Then he had taken Dominique to the Crillon for drinks. Their relationship had been very correct for twelve working days. Dominique had grown more attractive with each day. She had left Baxter in Frankfurt in order to return to Paris on one weekend, but rejoined him in Brussels on the following Monday. Baxter found himself missing Dominique's company.

Baxter could remember strolling down St. Germain with Dominique after the Crillon. She was going home to change and they would go out to dinner at her favorite brasserie. Her hand clasped Baxter's hand as they crossed a street, and he knew that he would be sleeping with her that evening.

The single elevator in Dominique's building was being repaired and they walked up four flights to her small apartment.

"Paris is very expensive. I have a small apartment which is similar to a studio apartment with a tiny bedroom," Dominique warned as she turned her key on the door. "And I share the apartment with a good friend."

Dominique opened the door and was greeted by a large black cat. She picked up the cat from the floor and stroked it lovingly. It was a large, furry black cat with probing green eyes. "This is my room mate, Joe. This is Cybelle," Dominique spoke in French to the cat and Baxter concluded correctly that there was a promise of milk.

"That's a big cat," Baxter observed.

"She belonged to a lady next door who moved away and I took the cat. We have only been together for six months, but we get along very well."

Cybelle became busy with a milk saucer in the doorway of the tiny kitchen area. Dominique turned her attention to Baxter. There was a wonderful first kiss by the couch with Dominique's hand tightly gripping the back of Baxter's neck.

"Our reservations are not until ten," Dominique said. "We have time to love."

Baxter remembered showering with Dominique, putting his suit back on, and going off to a wonderful brasserie where they ate in a downstairs room. There was a little old man who played the piano. He played a lot of Satie, and later played some Sondheim.

"You know music and you are a very good lover," Dominique said as she picked at her salad. Baxter looked across the table into Dominique's dark eyes. He would be back in bed with her in two to three hours. What a delicious evening!

Now it was Saturday morning in Paris and Baxter lay naked in a narrow bed, barely capable of holding two occupants. The bedroom door opened and Dominique appeared in an apron carrying a small tray with coffee and croissants.

251

"Good morning, Joe." She was wearing nothing under the apron. "I have dressed and undressed again. I have some breakfast for you." Dominique set the tray on the edge of the bed. Cybelle took a position next to the tray as an observer prepared to help with table scraps. Dominique poured a coffee for Baxter and then slipped off her apron.

"I hope I don't embarrass you. Cybelle is accustomed to seeing me like this."

Dominique stood in front of Baxter. She displayed her long thin body with narrow hips and breasts the size of champagne glasses. This morning her nipples appeared to be very hard. Baxter sipped his bitter French coffee and contemplated lunging for her.

"I have a day planned for us," Dominique announced. "It is now 10:45. You must eat your breakfast, take a shower, and then we can check out of your hotel and bring your bag here. You checked in here very late last night and I believe you will be a wonderful guest. Then we will go to the Cafe Lipp on the Left Bank for a late lunch. After lunch we will take a boat cruise. After the boat cruise, we will return here and love. Then we will catch the eleven o'clock show at Crazy Horse. Men love the Crazy Horse. After Crazy Horse we will have a midnight supper. Then we will return here and determine how consistent you are as a lover. Does all the interest you?"

"It sounds like an interesting, well planned, full day," Baxter said nibbling on his croissant. Dominique sat on the edge of the bed and Baxter leaned forward to kiss Dominique's right nipple. Their mouths met.

"Our work plan allows for some flexibility," Dominique pointed out. Cybelle remained perched on the far end of the bed and was noncommittal.

A perfect Saturday was followed by a perfect Sunday. They walked the streets of Paris with arms around each other waists and they kissed periodically. In Montmartre, a street artist drew a picture of them as they sipped brandy at the outside table of a small cafe. They walked around the neighborhood, and Baxter wondered just where Hamilton Burke had lived.

Each day, Baxter related the edited episodes of his life. He included Iron Creek, Washburn Manufacturing, his marriage to Jennifer, and his career at McKenzie Barber. Baxter excluded the episodes of his earlier marriage to Maggie. His life sounded fairly interesting as he completed his recitation at the entrance of the Louvre.

Dominique exchanged the episodes of her life. She started with her little girl images of America. Then she went on to describe her childhood in a small village outside Lyon where her father and mother taught science and mathematics in the high school. Dominique was an only child.

"Much was always expected of me," Dominique said as they held hands only glancing from time to time to the paintings. "My parents were very intelligent and were disappointed that they had not risen further. They were rigorous in my discipline. There was much study and little time for friends and play. I grew up very bookish and wore glasses early. I was unattractive to boys. Then I won the Roosevelt Scholarship for study in the United States. I am still not certain as to which Roosevelt family provided the scholarship. Suddenly I was at Mills College in California. My parents gave me contact lenses for my graduation, and I started a new life."

"I became a different person in California. My parents were surprised at the change in me when I returned the summer after my freshman year. My father was quite shocked, but I believe my mother was pleased. I learned to play tennis and golf and had known men. The work at Mills was not that hard. It may have been hard for others, but it was not difficult for me. That is when I wrote to Mrs. Grey."

"Mrs. Grey?" Baxter questioned.

"Mrs. Ernest Grey. Her name is Millie. She attended Mills College, but it was war time and she married before she could graduate. Mrs. Grey was very active in alumni affairs and has helped Mills students in advancing to graduate school. She visited the school and interviewed me. We hit it off rather well. Mrs. Grey is an attractive, vivacious woman, who does not take herself very seriously. She calls herself an old Gimbel's handbag buyer. I told Mrs. Grey that I wanted a business career, and would like to attend the Harvard Business School. Mrs. Grey told me that Harvard had been her husband's school, and that she would like to have me meet her husband. That was how I learned about McKenzie Barber."

"I met Mr. Grey that spring, and he arranged for me to spend a summer internship in the San Francisco office. I worked with the CARS system and saw how much the work was reported. I became more and more interested in McKenzie Barber. I wrote a research paper on McKenzie Barber for an advanced Industrial Sociology course that was included in my application to Harvard. Mr. Grey wrote a letter of recommendation, and I was accepted. I worked at the New York office of McKenzie Barber one summer. That's when I first heard about you from one of the consultants. They talked about the time you took a number of first year women consultants to review the Washington government business and gave them real responsibility. Also, I spent two days in Mr. Alvardi's department inputting proxy pay information into that antiquated computer model he uses. I took some interviews my last year at Harvard, but I knew that McKenzie Barber was the only company for me. I wanted to start in New York, but I was told by Mr. Nickerson that I would be more useful at Barber-Paris."

"Barber-Paris was not McKenzie Barber-San Francisco or McKenzie Barber- New York. It is very old fashioned by comparison. I was the first woman ever hired on the consulting staff. I was also a special consultant because I had contact with Chairman Grey. The Greys took me to lunch when they visited in October last year and I was highly respected when I returned to the office. They tried to treat me like a clerk and I protested. Finally I was given a very responsible assignment with a large and well respected family business, the de Hartog family. I was given the responsibility to study administrative costs at their headquarters offices and I did well. The Baron de Hartog wrote a very nice letter to Michael about my performance. I was delighted when Michael informed me of this work with you. I was planning on a vacation, but postponed the vacation to work with you. So here we are together not looking at pictures when it is a nice day outside. Why don't we come back on a rainy day? Let's go back and love again. We have so little time until Tuesday morning."

That night as they walked along the Seine Baxter told Dominique that he loved her.

"I love you also, Joe," Dominique said as she started to cry.

"What's wrong?" Baxter whispered.

"I wanted to sleep with you, but I did not want to fall in love with you," Dominique protested.

"I want you to come to the United States to be with me." They stopped to stare out at the Seine and Baxter's hands were clasped on Dominique's shoulders. "I love you and I want you to be my wife. I have two children, a boy and a girl, and their mother has custody, but little interest in them. You have so much love in you, Dominique. I need your love. My children need your love. Come with me to America and be my love."

Dominique continued to sob. "Oh Joe. If only I could! I would love to be your wife in America! But it is very difficult for me. I wanted to be with you since that first day. But this is so new. I must have time. Please give me time!"

Baxter kissed Dominique on the eyes, her ears, and her neck before settling on a long kiss on her mouth. "Oh Joe, take me back to bed! We have one more golden day left before you have to leave. I want you to hold me and love me as soon as possible." They walked up the steps to the street. Baxter found a taxi and Dominique was in his arms again.

Monday was better than Saturday or Sunday. They had a long lunch at a brasserie on the Champs Elysees and watched Paris parade by them. They sipped brandy and held hands and enjoyed their closeness.

"How soon do you want me to come to America?" Dominique asked.

"As soon as possible," Baxter responded.

"I would have to quit my job here. I doubt whether there could be a transfer. I could, however, call Mrs. Grey."

They sat in the sunlight only partially protected by a green Perrier umbrella. Dominique's eyes were obscured by sun glasses. "Where would we live?"

"In Chicago at first. I expect to be asked to move to New York later this year."

"And you will be a Partner in New York? I could find work more easily in New York than Chicago. I believe we should live together for a while," Dominique shook her head. "This is just too fast. We have only known each other for three weeks. I need more time! You need more time! We are infatuated. I don't go around falling in love with new men coming into my life. We should have had sandwiches sent in on Friday instead of going to Jardin Elysees Lenotre with all of the tourists. You should go back to Chicago and I could be on the vacation I had planned. Now I have to go into the office tomorrow and I'm starting to get very sad over you leaving me. My life was far less complicated before I met you. Also I expect that I will be sore for a week after you leave. I'm not used to all this sex. I could get quite used to it, mind you. Cybelle seems to accept it. She sits on the bed and watches us. Perhaps she is writing a book."

Dominique patted Baxter's hand. "What is to become of us? Why can't we just live for the present? I think Americans see too many movies with happy endings and that's why they rush into marriages. I think you were very calculating when you married this Jennifer. Now you think you should marry me. Is marriage always the answer? Why can't we just see each other from time to time as lovers, and stay with our careers?"

"On that basis, we will be fated to fade away from each other, Dominique."

"I will remember this weekend forever, Joe."

"As will I," Baxter agreed.

"Let's go back and put on another show for Cybelle. I think she's become quite bored without us," Dominique ran her hand over Baxter's thigh. He signaled for the check.

Baxter sipped champagne for the first hour of his flight from Paris to Chicago. He wanted to savor the moment. Joseph Baxter, Jr., son of Joseph Baxter, Sr., a miner from Iron Creek, Minnesota, was riding back to the U.S. in the first class section of Air France. He was close to becoming a Partner with the world famous management consulting firm of McKenzie Barber & Co. and he had just made love to the most beautiful woman in France in the back seat of a taxi-cab. Did it ever get better than this?

Baxter was in love. Hopelessly in love! He would have given $5,000 to have had Dominique in the seat next to him instead of the heavyset snoring Italian.

Baxter would have his arm around Dominique, and her thick, black, sweet smelling hair would be in his face. Baxter would have asked the flight attendant for a blanket for his wife. Once covering Dominique with a blanket, he would begin to touch her. Dominique loved to be touched and stroked. She was a hot French woman, the first he had ever known.

He remembered kissing Dominique in the rain by the cab stand. She had been wearing only high black boots and a grey raincoat. Baxter's bag was in the front seat with the driver and there had been a long lingering wet kiss. Baxter could feel Dominique's body under the rain coat. He had taken Dominique's arm. "Come with me to Charles DeGaulle. You'll be good company."

"Joe, I must not and you know why!" Dominique protested. Baxter pushed her ahead of him into the back seat of the taxi. He thrust a 100 franc note to the white-haired, black cab driver. "Charles De Gaulle Airport, if you please. Look straight ahead and watch the road."

The taxi driver grinned, displaying his gold fillings and responded with a "Oui, Monsieur."

"Joe," Dominique continued her protest. "You are being very naughty." Baxter kissed her and untied the belt to Dominique's raincoat. "I love you, Dominique!"

"And I love you, Joe. But you are a crazy American."

Baxter from time to time looked ahead at the driver's face. Dominique was atop Baxter with her raincoat open. The driver could only see the rise and fall of the raincoat, and Baxter could make out a subtle grin on the driver's face as the taxi moved through the wet, early morning Paris streets.

The report was good! U.S. Pharmaceutical would be pleased. There were a number of finds. Baxter had, at last, visited Europe, the site of his ex-wife's frequent disappearances.

Baxter continued to drink champagne while he waited for lunch to be served. There was only one direction for his life to go from here. Up! He had met the woman with whom he would spend the rest of his life.

Two weeks later, Baxter was at the low point of his life when he arrived in New York to present the final report to U.S. Pharmaceutical. He had talked to Michael Stokes to days before and learned about the de Hartog connection. Michael's words were locked in his memory. "She may come back a baroness." What the hell was a baroness anyway?

He sat in Alvardi's office drinking coffee while his leader scanned the report. "Don't you dare change one fucking word, Frank," Baxter warned Alvardi.

"You don't seem happy, kid. Is there something wrong?"

"I just want to present the findings and get this job over with. The work was damned good!"

"Dirks is coming with us this morning," Alvardi alerted Baxter.

"Frank, this is not a major engagement. We're presenting to a couple of human resources guys, and maybe we'll be invited back to present to the VP International. Roger Dirks is kind of overkill for this kind of audience."

"He wants to come! The firm has never done any work for U.S. Pharmaceutical. It's a major target client for his practice. Kid, Dirks is like the two thousand pound gorilla in the New York office. He goes wherever he wants to. He should be the next Managing Partner of the New York office, and may be Ernie Grey's eventual successor. Dirks wants to get into U.S. Pharmaceutical in the worst way."

"We're on at 10 AM and I don't expect we'll be there through lunch," Baxter predicted. All he could think of was what the report was the product of his work with Dominique. It was the off-spring of their relationship. Would he ever see her again? He had been so confident on the Air France flight back to Chicago. Now there was silence. Baxter had even written Dominique a note from O'Hare the evening before.

Dearest Dominique:

I'll start this letter by repeating what I've told you before. I love you! I had never loved anyone before as much as I love you! I talked with Michael and learned about your cruise with the de Hartog's. I understand why you're on the cruise, but I want you to know that I love you more than any other man in the world. I think of you constantly and I want you beside me. I need to hear from you! Tomorrow I will present our report to U.S. Pharmaceutical. I will be brilliant at the presentation because it is our work. Please let me hear from you. Soon!

Totally smitten,
Joe

Roger Dirks wasn't what Baxter had expected. He turned out to be a short, muscular man who came dressed in a light-weight, grey three piece suit. It was the first time Baxter had ever seen a summerweight three piece suit. Roger had salt and pepper close cropped hair, large shoulders, narrow waist, and the bearing of a military officer. He also reminded Baxter of an alert killer bulldog when Alvardi and Baxter met him in the lobby at 9:45.

"Report look all right to you, Frank?" Dirks asked as they started to walk. U.S. Pharmaceutical was on Madison Avenue between 55th and 56th streets which was a short walk from McKenzie Barber.

"Report's fine, skipper," Alvardi replied.

"We've done what the client expected us to do and we have several finds," Baxter said as he tried to adjust to Dirks brisk walking style.

"Well, don't fuck up this morning. That's all I ask," Dirks snapped.

"I resent that kind of talk," Baxter said.

"We've done a damned fine job for this client. Neither you nor Frank was involved in bringing in this client, and your presence certainly isn't needed in this meeting. I would advise you to sit back and shut up this morning. I'll handle the client," Baxter shot back. Alvardi winced.

"I hope you are as good as you think you are, Baxter," Dirks said.

Baxter gave one of his better performances that morning. He had good slides, crisp analytical work, and what Frank Alvardi would call a good story line. Baxter told himself when he snapped on the projector that this presentation belonged to Dominique.

James Hopper-Jones, the International Human Resources Manager, and Neville Christopher, the Corporate Director of Compensation, were delighted with Baxter's presentation. Alvardi made a few comments to support Baxter's findings and Dirks gave a brief general commentary on the complexities of compensating overseas managers that was insightful.

"Joe," Hopper-Jones said at the conclusion of the presentation, "We would like to have you back to make your presentation to Reg Naisbett, our International MD. No changes! What you have told us is spot-on! Nice job! We recognize that an additional presentation represents extra costs and ask you to bill us accordingly." Then turning to Dirks, Hopper-Jones said, "Thank you so much for joining us this morning, Mr. Dirks, and you too, Mr. Alvardi."

They were out on the street again at ten after twelve.

"Excellent! Excellent!" Dirks exclaimed. "What do you say we go over to the Plaza for lunch. I'm buying." Dirks slapped Baxter on the shoulder. "Wonderful presentation. There will be some more work from U.S. Pharmaceutical. See that I attend the meeting with Naisbett. I'll juggle my schedule. And Frank, if you're busy, I'll just go along with Joe."

They lunched in the Edwardian Room with Dirks doing most of the talking and Alvardi periodically looking at his watch.

"Skipper, I've got a two o'clock meeting down at Chase. I've got to run," Alvardi said, finally rising from the table.

"Joe, do you have a meeting too?" Dirks looked to Baxter.

"No. I was going to catch the four o'clock flight back to Chicago," Baxter answered.

"Good. Then you can stay with me and finish this bottle of wine. You're excused Frank. Godspeed to Chase, and for Christ's sake, sell something!"

Alvardi exited the room rapidly, but every waiter in the room waved as he left. "They think he's Joe DiMaggio or at least his son or nephew. Our man Frank is a real piece of work," Dirks commented between sips of chardonnay.

"Why does he call you skipper?"

"I commanded a ship in Korea, and I sail competitively on the weekends. A few people around the office call me skipper. Frank is one of them."

"How long have you been with the firm, Roger?" Baxter asked.

"Oh Christ, Joe. Let me think!" Dirks held up his wine glass and stared through it. "I was an ME with an IE option out of Cornell in 1950. Four years in the Navy. A year of graduate school at NYU. The firm hired me as a summer intern and I never went back. I had a wife and young kids in those days and had to make some money. I started in the old IE practice in 1955. That makes twenty-two years. I made Partner in 1960, the same year Ernie Grey crowned himself Chairman. I run two/thirds of the New York office and may pick up the other third when Dinsmore officially retires."

"Officially?" Baxter questioned.

"He's been retired from active work for about five years now. Bruce is primarily ceremonial. There is a network of these old IE dinosaurs around and they have kind of a protective league that's headed by Harvey Randolph. They are paid a lot of money and they pontificate at the drop of a hat, but they really don't contribute. Do you know Friedman out in LA?"

Baxter nodded his head. Boy, did he ever know Friedman!

"Ernie's just sent a message to the old boys when he retired Ben Sydes and replaced him with that young Turk/Jew. Friedman won't retire out in LA either. Give him three to four years in that job. He'll have someone else groomed and he'll be out in New York." Dirks stared at his wine again. "Did Burke talk to you about coming to New York?"

"It was mentioned."

"Do you want to come?"

"What would I do?" Baxter asked.

"You'd be number two to Frankie. Frank would do New York and International and you would help out in New York and manage the other practices in North America."

"Would I come out as a Partner?"

"That's a given. You show up here next Spring and you will be a Partner October 1, 1978."

"Has this been discussed with Frank?"

"It's been talked about. He'd just as soon that you stayed in Chicago. He doesn't want this to happen, but he refuses to say why it won't work. Frank is very good at what he does. He has put us into the high end of the Executive Compensation business, but he hasn't built a dominant practice. Robson Allen has stretched out its lead, boutique single discipline comp

259

firms are being formed and rapidly becoming serious competitors. The actuaries are licking their lips at the compensation consulting marketplace."

"What about the acquisition of an actuarial firm and all of those other proposed consulting firm acquisitions?" Baxter queried.

"That's why Burke is back from Barber/London. Burke will make it happen! Right now, Burke is Ernie's fair-haired boy. I had dinner the other night with Burke. He spoke very highly of you, Joe. That's one of the reasons I showed up today. Burke told me to catch you in action. I'm glad I did. Burke's mission with Ernie is to rethink and re-invent McKenzie Barber. What you see today is not what you're going to be seeing ten years from now. In two years, Dinsmore retires, Harvey Randolph retires, and six years Ernie Grey will retire. We're going to have a new McKenzie Barber, larger, more profitable, and we'll run away from Robson Allen."

Dirks placed his napkin on the table. "Let's take a walk, Joe."

They walked slowly down Fifth Avenue on a warm summer afternoon. Dirks didn't seem to be in any kind of a hurry. They stopped in front of shop windows and Dirks would explain about each store. They finally entered a store called Escadrille where every sales clerk on the floor acknowledged Dirks.

A matronly woman in a black high necked dress greeted Dirks in French and he replied in kind. Baxter thought once again of Dominique. Would he ever see her again?

Diamond earrings were produced from behind the counter and Dirks held them up to the light. "Gorgeous," Dirks said. "Absolutely gorgeous!"

"For your wife?" Baxter asked.

"She gets alimony. This is for another lady." Burke turned to the saleswoman. "Wrap it, Annette! Deliver it to my office between 4:30 and 5 today. Include a small card."

"That's a lovely gift," Baxter commented as they resumed their stroll down Fifth Avenue.

"Some of the most beautiful women in the world are here in New York, Joe. They are also highly skilled gold-diggers. Let's go have a coffee. I know a place on Madison Avenue."

This time they entered an office building and made their way to an empty coffee shop in the rear of the building that looked out on 47th street.

A bald man with steel rimmed glasses, pencil thin grey sideburns, and wearing an apron greeted Dirks warmly. "Hey Roger, com'on in. Haven't seen you for a while. You must be eating lunch uptown again."

"George, shake hands with Joe Baxter from Chicago." It was a narrow L shaped room with a horseshoe counter and three small tables. They sat at the counter and George shook Baxter's hand.

"George and I have been doing business for twenty-two years," Dirks explained.

"This is Mr. Dirks office away from the office," George said proudly and he affectionately patted Dirks lightly on his back.

"Joe and I need to talk a bit. We'd like to sit over at the table by the wall phone. Bring us coffee until we tell you to stop," Dirks said and they moved to a small table that looked out on 47th street.

"I found this place by accident when I was an intern. I came in here about 1:30, ordered an egg salad sandwich at the counter and found that I left my wallet on my desk. I explained to George what happened and he wasn't having any of it until I found my Navy ID in my jacket pocket. What the hell it was doing there, I'll never know. I showed him my old Navy ID. I was still a reservist at the time and found out George had been in the Navy and served as a cook in an officer's mess. Apparently he had been treated pretty well and he respected officers. He wrote down my name and said 'Pay me tomorrow.' I have been coming here ever since. I come over sometimes in the afternoon when I don't want any calls or interruptions or general McKenzie Barber bullshit. I consider George to be one of my best friends. You can't be friends with people that you have to constantly push, threaten to fire. It's important to have a life outside of McKenzie Barber that stands on its own. Now let's see. I looked at your personnel file this morning——You're 42, divorced, and have a base salary of $85,000 and your bonus for this year has been accrued at $20,000. If you agree to come to New York no later than April 1, your base will move to $100,000 on October 1st and your bonus will be guaranteed at $25,000 for FY 1978. Brimmer will nominate you in January for Partnership and you will be elected in the summer ballot. October 1, 1978! You're a New York partner!"

"Will someone put this in writing for me?" Baxter asked.

"Sure! I will!" Dirks pulled a napkin from the holder on the table. He started to write everything out on a paper napkin including the relocation benefits. The total agreement took up two napkins and Dirks signed his name at the bottom of each napkin.

"Read it over, Joe. See if I've left anything out."

Baxter read through the napkins twice. It was a good complete offer and included an upfront bonus for moving and a six month apartment allowance.

"Now we need a witness," Dirks said. "George, come over here and witness something," Dirks commanded.

"Are you going to have this typed and reviewed with Brimmer and Nickerson?" Baxter asked.

"We'll call Brimmer now. That's why we're sitting by the pay phone. Nickerson will get confused. He'll want to research this deal and make certain that you didn't get anything that somebody else didn't get when they moved from Chicago to New York. We could both be retired by the time Nickerson got this kind of arrangement approved. Take the napkin with you! For Christ sake don't lose it! Xerox a copy and sign "accepted" and the date. Now let's call Brimmer."

Baxter was prepared to bet that they would never reach Brimmer. It usually took a minimum of two days to reach Brimmer. The call went right through.

"Paul! Dirks here! I'm with Joe Baxter in a quiet corner of an exclusive New York eatery. We have reached a tentative agreement on terms and he wants to come. Let me read the terms to you." Dirks proceeded to recite from the napkin. "No, Paul! I want Joe to come out to New York happy, and to be productive and I will not be part of nickel and diming him!" Dirks said emphatically.

"Sure, I'll put him on the phone." Dirks handed the phone to Baxter.

Baxter got a "Hi Paul" out and Brimmer cut him short. "Joe, are you sure you want to do this?"

Baxter looked to Dirks. He had cold blue eyes. Roger Dirks was clearly not a man to cross. He had signed the napkin and there was no going back. "Yes, Paul. I believe the move is best for the firm, the practice, and my career."

"I want an orderly transition to Carl and your personal commitment to make plan in Chicago, this year and next year. If the Chicago Executive Compensation practice goes to hell in a handbasket after you transfer, I'll catch up with you. Do you understand that, Joe!" Brimmer threatened.

"I'll do it."

"You goddam well better do it, Joe. Now, good luck! You and I will work together again. Let me talk to Dirks!" Brimmer demanded.

George witnessed the napkin and poured more coffee. Baxter stared out the window at 47th street and Dirks seemed to be talking to Brimmer about new subjects. Where in hell was Dominique at this moment? Baxter asked himself.

Dirks finally hung up and replaced the receiver on the wall. "Well, Joe, welcome to the New York office. I'll arrange for you to meet Dinsmore sometime. Ernie called Brimmer this morning and explained we were moving you. Ernie is the only one Brimmer ever pays any attention to. Burke engineered this! I guess Ernie asked him who you were, and Ernie remembered you as the big red-headed fellow that Harwell likes who did the work at FSO. Nickerson tried to scotch the Partnership nomination as part of the deal, but Burke overrode him. You might as well know this now, Joe. We're close to acquiring a Benefits firm. The firm will report to me and Executive Compensation will be folded under Benefits. I've got to make a meeting. Have some more coffee! George will take care of you."

Baxter had a third cup of coffee and watched the passersby on 47th street. He re-read the napkin three times. They had positioned him into making a career decision that afternoon that he had not anticipated making when he left the Waldorf that morning. Baxter's life was about to change dramatically. Where was Dominique? Baxter pictured Dominique somewhere in the Mediterranean Sea, sunning herself in a one piece bathing suit and sunglasses, reading a book. Would he ever see her again?

It was never quite the same again after Baxter returned to Chicago. His move to New York was not announced until the September promotions, but everybody down to the mail boy in the Chicago office seemed to know that Baxter was transferring to New York.

Baxter returned two weeks later to repeat his presentation to Reg Naisbett, the Managing Director, International for U.S. Pharmaceutical. Dirks accompanied Baxter and he didn't believe that Alvardi's attendance would be required.

"Three's too many, Joe," Dirks explained.

Baxter had received a memorandum signed by Bruce Dinsmore, Managing Partner of the New York office, which confirmed the contents of the napkin agreement, and Nickerson was copied. Baxter signed one copy and returned it to Dinsmore's office.

Hopper-Jones and Naisbett sat at one side of a conference table with Baxter and Dirks on the other. Naisbett was a tall, thin, greying aristocratic man who wore a stylish blue, double breasted suit of European design, in contrast to the blue, light-weight pinstripes worn by Baxter and Dirks. Naisbett asked a great many detailed questions, which Baxter had not anticipated, but he responded well.

Dirks carefully positioned comments and questions about the overseas business units that led to a lengthy discussion about G&A allocations and transfer pricing. They adjourned to a private dining room after Baxter completed the presentation and Dirks continued his transfer pricing schedule.

"Reg, I'll make you a proposition. Let me have a couple of our bright young associates come in for a couple of days and review your methodologies. Maybe we'll even agree with you. We won't bill you for walking around and talking to people. Then if we should be doing some real work, we'll write you a proposal."

"Roger, I'd have to think about that one," Naisbett smiled. Hopper-Jones looked at his shoes.

"I'll drop you a note on how we've done it in the past for other multi-nationals and messenger it over to you in the morning," Dirks said.

Naisbett looked at his watch. "Very well then," he said rising from the table. "I have to make a meeting. Jimmy will show you out," Naisbett said. "Good show, Joe. A very interesting report indeed."

Hopper-Jones alias "Jimmy", showed Dirks and Baxter to the front lobby where Dirks paused to use the lobby telephone to call his office.

"Your Mr. Dirks certainly isn't bashful, Joe," Hopper-Jones commented in a soft voice. "Came along presumably to observe you perform, and tried to plug new work. I really don't know how that set with Reg, Joe. Let's you and I stay in contact. I hear you're moving out here in a few months."

Baxter stayed over to have dinner with Alvardi that evening after dropping by Harwell Management for coffee in the late afternoon.

Mr. Leon greeted Baxter warmly in a front conference room facing the street. "I really liked the depth you displayed in the Brookline report, Joe. I've never seen anyone ferret out information you did in two days time. Your report sounded as thought you were pulling your punches a little. I showed it to Mrs. Harwell. She asked if Mr. Baxter had lost his sense of humor."

Baxter shook his head. The change in writing style demonstrated the power of a Grey-gram. "What's next on the retail industry list, Mr. Leon?" Baxter asked.

"I'm finished with retail, Joe. I liquidated all of our retail holdings last Friday," Harwell explained. "I will have some fresh investment directions that I want you to look into this Fall. You've done some very good work to date and I believe it's time for me to use your services in a different set of industries. I must tell you, Joe, that I was delighted to learn from Ernie Grey that you will be transferring to New York. It will make it a lot easier for us to work together. Why don't you and I pick out a date in October to get together? I'll have some new work for you then. I understand that you won't be out here permanently until spring. When you're settled in, I'd like you to come out for dinner one evening and meet Mrs. Harwell."

"Ernie Grey told you personally that I was transferring to New York?" Baxter asked incredulously.

"No. It was Ernie's senior assistant. That man named Burke. Mrs. Harwell and I attended a Historical Society dinner and sat at the same table with this man, Burke. He was the one who let your cat out of the bag. Needless to say, I was delighted with the news."

Alvardi was less ebullient over dinner. "I'm not happy about this, kid," he announced after martinis were served. "I wasn't consulted and it was served up to me by Dirks as a fait accompli. You're needed in Chicago and further west, not New York. Then I found out that they are on the verge of acquiring Frederick Partners and folding the comp practice under them."

"What or who is Frederick Partners?" Baxter asked.

"They are a goddam boutique Benefits/Pension consulting firm. We are a bigger practice than they are. The way they talked around Executive Office, they were going to land a large multi-national Actuarial firm. What we're going to wind up with is some rug merchant who's convinced Hamilton Burke and his Strategic Planning Committee that they have a going concern that has been only constrained by capital. To top it off, Dirks showed me a copy of your memorandum of understanding. Kid, you have guaranteed making plan in two different offices for FY 1978! That is about the dumbest thing I've ever seen anyone do. Kid, you're not superman! You're only a fair technician. You're a good salesman and you work hard! That may be enough for you to get by in the Midwest and running out to California, but it won't be enough to get you by in the New York market. This is the toughest consulting marketplace in the world! Who told you that you were good enough to come out here and make a difference? I like you, Joe. But, Jesus, why couldn't you have stayed in Chicago where you belong?"

"Decisions were made about our practice because you're falling short of the goals that were expected of you," Baxter said throwing down the gauntlet. "I'm being asked to leave my children to come to New York! I don't like coming out here any more than you want me out here. As far as meeting plan in both offices, you watch, Frank. I'll goddam do it! As for technical skills, I'm ready to let the marketplace decide. I'd just as soon work with you and be your Partner. I sure as hell don't believe I'm ready to challenge you for your job! I believe that the two of us can really build this practice for the firm."

Alvardi sipped his martini in silence and waved the waitress for a refill. "Kid, were you a goddam cheerleader in high school?"

"Negative! I was an ass-bumping, elbow throwing, shorts pulling basketball center," Baxter corrected him.

"That's good, Kid, because you will have to draw upon those skills to stay afloat in the New York market." Alvardi raised his glass. "Well you're coming and we're stuck with each other. We might as well make the most of it."

They enjoyed a leisurely northern Italian dinner, washed down by two bottles of Chianti on top of two martinis. Over time, Alvardi mellowed from his early evening Italian tough guy pose.

"Frank you've been in both offices," Baxter began to probe. "What are the principal differences between the Chicago Office and the New York Office?"

Alvardi smiled a tired Joe DiMaggio smile. "Sometimes, kid, you're transparent as hell. Right now you want your Uncle Frank to tell you all about what you've managed to get yourself into, when you didn't ask me in the first place. Okay, let me tell you about McKenzie Barber and Frank Alvardi from the beginning.——I was a little like you at one time, kid. I had been at Robson Allen about 7 or 8 years and was working for Art Perrin, the father of Executive Compensation consulting. Art was in his late forties, and I figured I would spend the rest of my career at Robson Allen. We looked at McKenzie Barber as a firm dominated by old IEs with a young Chairman, and assumed that it was just a matter of time before we passed them up as a firm. One day I got a call from one of those search firms that Clyde Nickerson uses. He tried to be mysterious and I narrowed his client down to McKenzie Barber about five minutes into the conversation. The recruiter emphasized that it was a number one job building a practice from scratch with all kinds of resources to support the business. I met the recruiter about two weeks later, and about a month later, I was sitting across the table from Clyde Nickerson. He started with what-makes-you-think-you're-good-enough-to-work-for-McKenzie Barber routine and I almost walked out. The talks stretched on over a year. They must have talked to everyone in the country. It got back to Art over time and he took me aside, and over lunch asked me point blank if I was talking with McKenzie Barber. I told him yes. Art's a great guy, kid. I'll introduce you to Art when you're out here for good. I have dinner with him every six weeks. He's the finest gentleman I've ever worked with. That day at lunch, he just looked at me over his clubhouse sandwich and said, 'Don't go over there, Frank. You won't be happy. McKenzie Barber is too structured for a free spirit like you. You will have my job at Robson Allen when I step down. If you get an offer, talk it through with me before you take it.' Well, kid. McKenzie Barber finally got serious, and I met a whole bunch of the senior people. Two partners swung me over. One, of course, was our magnetic Chairman, who said Number One a lot. The other was Brimmer. Brimmer made sense. He could see the integration of consulting skills to solve a client's problems under a single client service partner. I walked away from Brimmer feeling that I had talked with a giant."

"What about Ernie Grey?" Baxter asked.

"Just another CEO pushing people to be number one. I gave him a B- in vision and an A on getting people to behave the way he wanted them to. They gave me everything I wanted. Ernie proposed that I join in the Chicago office to beat the non-compete clause in my Robson Allen Partner's agreement. All Robson Allen clients were two years off-limits. More money! Number one! I went back to Art and told him, 'Frank,' he said to me. 'Don't say a word about quitting. I'll go to Charley and work out some money for you.' "Art," I told him. "I'm going to do it! It's not the money. It's the opportunity.' We talked for a while longer and then Art excused himself and I knew he was going up to see Charley Robson. The three founders had always split up the functions of the company and Charley handled administration. The three of us, Charley, Art, and me, met for breakfast the next morning at the University Club. It was a long breakfast. We started at seven and we were the last ones in the dining room at 9:30. Charley, who was usually a lot of fun, was very serious that morning. That was my first clue about how much Robson, Allen, and Harbridge all hated McKenzie Barber. There were a lot of jokes around the firm about second prize as a weekend in Cleveland with your favorite McKenzie Barber Partner. But I didn't fully realize how much they hated McKenzie Barber until that breakfast at the University Club. Charley went over ever aspect of my offer. Art seemed a little embarrassed over Charley's behavior."

"Then about 9:30, Charley looked me straight in the eye and asked, 'Do you still want to go to McKenzie Barber, Frank?' 'Yes I do,' I said. Charley looked at me with a cold hard stare and said, 'Then Frank, don't bother to go back to the office. We'll ship your personal things wherever you want them sent.' 'What about my clients?' I asked. 'They are Robson Allen Harbridge clients, not your clients, Frank.' Charley got up and walked away without shaking hands. Art stayed behind. He was obviously hurt by the way Charley had behaved, but there was nothing he could do about it. Art said, 'It's not too late now, Frank, to turn this thing around. The only thing to do is to handle this matter professionally and not embarrass ourselves to the clients. You and I will always be friends.' Art put his arm around me in the elevator and squeezed. He was very gentle and clinical, but hardly affectionate, and I've never forgotten the shoulder squeeze in the elevator that morning."

"So there I was, kid. Bridges burned and McKenzie Barber in my future. I was supposed to stay two years, maybe three years on the outside, in Chicago. I stayed five. I tried to run the national practice out of Chicago. It wasn't a bad strategy. I was in the middle of the country. I worked for a rational man, Paul Brimmer. Brimmer was concerned with serving clients and making money. He didn't fall asleep at night wondering how he was going to be number one! Brimmer regards his business plan as a sacrosanct covenant with Executive Office. He is cautious and thoughtful in the development of the plan and he carefully negotiates acceptance from each one of his Partners. Then Brimmer delivers his numbers and that's why Ernie loves him. That's also why Ernie pulled Harvey Randolph out of Chicago to make room for Brimmer. Harvey didn't always deliver his plan, and sometimes got a little cute to protect some of the old IEs. So Ernie brought him up to Executive Office as Deputy Chairman where he couldn't hurt anyone."

"You asked what the difference between Chicago and New York offices are? New York is where it is! Chicago is where it isn't! I got comfortable in

Chicago. I had Brimmer to work for! A man who liked quality work and Partners who hit their plans. There was no talk of number one or beat Robson Allen. Rather, it was what are you going to do this year in revenues and operating income? What investments will you require? It was simple. Develop your plan! Commit to your plan! Make your plan and you're fine. Miss your plan and you're in trouble! I got comfortable, kid. I was making my plan, doing good work, got chummy with Lorna, started buddying around with Dwyer, and hung out at Sonny's Supper Club on weekends where they treated me like a visiting prince. I was living the good life in Chicago, and all of a sudden, and I should have been watching over my shoulder, I'm in front of the Operating Committee and they're demanding to know why we're not number one yet! That's when you and I had our breakfast, kid. Then I got out here and there was all this talk about Human Resources consulting and acquiring an Employee Benefits Consulting firm that I will report through. Then, Dirks, who incidentally is a super guy in my book, tells me that he has arranged for Joe Baxter to come out and work with me and help us be Number One. How the hell am I supposed to feel? Number one is hard, kid! It's easier done on paper than accomplished in the marketplace."

"What about Brimmer and Lorna? Is there really something going on there?" Baxter asked.

"I never saw that coming, kid. I thought you'd take up with Lorna. I knew your marriage was on the rocks, and here was this fine intelligent, attractive woman that I didn't need anymore who was going to be lonely."

"She told me that you had invited her to New York," Baxter commented.

"That's her side of it. The best I ever offered Lorna was a front of the plane roundtrip weekend ticket to New York. Instead she stayed behind to enrapture Brimmer."

"It's hard for me to imagine Brimmer in a state of rapture," Baxter observed.

"Whatever it is, kid, those two have found each other, and you have missed the window I tried to leave open for you," Alvardi ruled.

"How much talk is there about Brimmer and Lorna?" Baxter asked.

"It's beginning to build. He keeps on promoting her and there's been talk of Lorna having other qualifications."

"How much talk is there about Nickerson and Andy?" Baxter asked.

"That's been all over the place for years, kid. It's getting boring because it's been accepted. Now back to Chicago and New York," Alvardi began his thesis again. "Chicago's easy, kid because Brimmer's setting the rules. There's not a lot of politics. There's no Mrs. Brimmer to cow-tow to! He sets the rules and they're enforced. New York is a mega-practice. Bruce

Dinsmore pretends to run it, but it's really pockets of power. The New York office is fundamentally unmanageable! Dirks has the biggest piece of it. What do you think of Dirks?"

"I couldn't believe him in the meeting with the International Vice President at U.S. Pharmaceutical. He came on like a shoe salesman!"

"That's Dirks! We have done zippo business with U.S. Pharmaceutical and suddenly that little bastard had a foot in the door. Dirks is successful because he's one of those guys who puts one arm around a client's leg and never lets go. That's Dirks! He brings in clients and keeps them in the fold. That's why he has two thirds of the New York consulting practice. Dirks is what New York is about! He's foxy, greedy, and never lets go! Dirks could be the successor for Harvey. He's not classy enough to succeed Ernie!"

Baxter asked a number of other questions that evening about where he should live. Should he keep a car in the city? Was the firm sensitive if you had someone living with you? Who were the bad guys in the office? What should he do about Nickerson? They left the restaurant with their arms drunkenly entwined under the awning as they tried to hail a cab at midnight on a rainy night in New York. Baxter let Alvardi take the first taxi. He was going north to West 85th Street. Baxter was going south to the Waldorf.

"Welcome to New York, kid!" Alvardi said running out to the taxi.

Baxter waited ten minutes under the awning for a second cab.

The rubicon had been crossed. He was going to become, for better or for worse, a New Yorker!

Baxter did not give up easily in his quest to find Dominique. She was officially on a leave of absence from Barber-Paris, and had vacated her Paris apartment at the end of August. A post office box number had been left for mail forwarding. He finally asked for Ham's help at the end of September. Baxter, first had to explain to Ham why it was necessary to locate Dominique Beaufort.

"Joe, how long did you know this woman?" The melodic voice on the other end of the telephone in New York asked.

"A little over two weeks, Ham," Baxter answered.

"How old are you now, Joe?"

"I'm 42, Ham."

"Joe, you're acting like one of my young Second Lieutenant platoon officers after a long weekend in Saigon. They always met their own true love among the local maidens. You're a little long in the tooth to go off the track like this. And a staff consultant too! You should know by now that it's managers and up around here, and you throw the associates back when you catch one and wait until she grows to manager," Burke lectured Baxter.

Chicago based oil companies. Carl had taken an undergraduate degree in Mathematics at Ripon, and a MBA at the University of Michigan Business School. He had met his wife, Eileen, in graduate school when she was pursuing a Masters in Nursing. Eileen was a plain looking, intelligent young woman who bore Carl children every other year until they stopped at five. Eileen dutifully attended the few McKenzie Barber-Chicago functions that were required of her. She always asked about Joe's wife, but had quit asking on cue from her husband, two years earlier.

Carl lived in Wilmette, and his working hours were subject to train schedules. Baxter had always handled the heavy travel while Carl worked with the Chicago area consultants. He took the early train in and was on the job at ten after seven in the morning and left at 6:15 each evening in order to catch the 6:37 home. Once home, he ate with his family, and then worked in the study until eleven or so. Carl Miller had the work ethic of a true McKenzie Barber man. He worked until he dropped each day and came back for more the next day. Carl, however, had to be kept busy. Someone other than Carl had to sell the work. If the other Partners sponsored and introduced him to their clients, Carl would be successful. He tended to wait for the opportunity to come to him, as opposed to scratching clients up in the manner Alvardi had taught Baxter. Baxter's major concern in leaving the Chicago practice behind to Carl was his successor's ability to develop business. Carl tended to over intellectualize in client presentations and leave them confused.

Baxter had communicated this in their annual reviews but Carl tended to discount the assessment.

It was at the promotion party that Baxter and Carl decided to go out for a private drink and discuss their relationship. Brimmer had announced the promotions, and indicated that Baxter would be transferring to New York in the Spring. He declared that Carl would be responsible for the Chicago Executive Compensation practice, but still would report to Baxter. It stuck in Carl's craw, but they agreed to meet after the party for drinks and a hamburger.

They regrouped in a tavern next to the train station to presumably clarify their roles. Carl wanted to operate with autonomy while Baxter doubted whether he could operate without Baxter's active participation in the business development process. After a couple of drinks, Carl displayed his insecurity.

"What does Alvardi say about me?" Carl asked after a second Scotch and water.

"Frank believes, as I do, that you are very good technically, but that you need some help in communicating with the client," Baxter responded tactfully.

"Alvardi has been in only in one of my client presentations. He has picked that up from either Dr. Barry or you," Carl protested.

"There have been other Chicago Partners who have seen you in front of clients," Baxter explained. "You're viewed as very bright, but rigid, and sometimes doctrinaire."

"Doctrinaire!" Carl protested loudly. "I don't give the store away as Alvardi and you do! One day, you two will be called to task about favoring the clients. I'm hardly doctrinaire! If anything, I'm breaking fresh ground by bringing sound mathematical and analytical criteria to executive performance measurement. You and Frank are like a song and dance team. You carefully assess what your audience wants and then lead a loud chorus line across the stage to sing the songs that they want to hear."

"Carl," Baxter replied patiently, "The business is reviewing client's short and long term strategy and determining what compensation schemes are required to support these goals, but we don't recommend plans that are not responsive to shareholder objectives."

"That's all very nice, Joe, but I have seen Frank and you bend very low for clients. You are biased to serving the management of the clients who engage McKenzie Barber. Presumably we are engaged to serve the shareholders and we respond to management."

"Carl," Baxter began his lecture, "The clients are ultimately the shareholders, but you must recognize that senior management and the board represent our ultimate contact point with the shareholders."

"You're a whore, Joe," Carl said.

"You're full of manure, Carl," Baxter defending the practice. Carl seemed to Baxter to be a closet liberal who perceived himself as the ultimate arbitrator of pay. He was going to represent a sensitive control problem for New York office direction.

Baxter worked very hard in the Fall of 1977. He had two offices in which he had committed to making plan and was dedicated to achieving his dual objectives. Baxter worked six days a week most weeks and neglected his weekend visits to Racine and the children. It got a little sticky with Jennifer in late November. She called Baxter at the office after Thanksgiving. "Joe, it's not fair that I've been stuck with the kids every weekend this Fall. I have a life of my own that I'm trying to rebuild. I want you to take the children on the weekends for the rest of the year. It's only fair." Baxter was in fundamental agreement with Jennifer. He had been remiss in his parental obligations to his children. He agreed to spend each weekend with them until the first of they year.

Baxter heard from Ed Ganski on the first Monday in December. The call came in conveniently timed after Baxter's Monday morning staff meeting.

"Joey! Ed here!" Ganski began the conversation "Did you get an invitation to Gordy's wedding?"

Baxter was dumbfounded! Gordy was getting married! His worthless, ex-con brother was getting married!

"There were a mess of invitations mailed around Thanksgiving. I just hope that you got yours. I know you're divorced and Diane wasn't sure as to the right address. Anyway, Joey, your brother, Gordy is getting married. We were afraid that your invitation was lost in the mail."

"It's the second Saturday in December, Joey and it's in Duluth," Ganski added.

"Ed, I haven't stayed in touch with things back in Iron Creek. How's Ma?"

"She's okay, Joe. The wedding thing is a little complicated and Rose Anne would really like to come, but she can't. Do you talk to your mother, Joe?"

"From time to time, Ed." Baxter had some people scheduled to come into his office in ten minutes. "Ed," he explained, "I haven't been close to my mother for a long time. I send her a card and a check at Easter, her birthday, and Christmas. That's it! I haven't talked to Rose Anne in about three years."

"Joey, this is kind of heavy duty stuff! Your Ma's not doing real well. She's retiring from the telephone company in December. Her legs are all swollen and she can barely get around. Maggie has been driving her to and from work, but it's getting harder and harder."

"Where's Gordy?"

"He's living in Duluth. He's kind of a right hand man to a fat Chinaman named Fong. Fong's got a bunch of businesses on Michigan Avenue, and a restaurant in West Duluth called the House of Fong. Gordy comes back once a month usually in mid-week to see Rose Anne."

"What does Gordy do for Mr. Fong?" Baxter asked.

"He does a little of this and a little of that. He collects rents, checks on things, visits the businesses."

"Gordy sounds like he's doing Executive Assistant work," Baxter commented.

"Whatever he's doing is steady and he's getting married. I'll get another invitation off, but time is getting short. Rose Anne really wants you to be at the wedding. She can't make it. To tell you the truth, Joey, Rose Anne hasn't been able to make it to the car to go to work this last week. Maggie's got her set up downstairs and has been getting groceries for her. You, being the older brother, Rose Anne thinks it's your duty to be at the wedding. It won't be a big deal, Joe. They're getting married in some chapel on Michigan Street and then there's a reception at the House of Fong. Diane and I figure we can be back in Iron Creek by 8 o'clock. I really didn't want to get in the middle of this and bother you with personal calls at work, but Diane is best friends with Maggie. Maggie's been working on Diane to get me to call you and make sure you show up."

"Ed, I've got a very busy schedule. How about if I send a very nice gift?"

"Joe, Rose Anne believes that Gordy needs family present at the wedding. Karl and Maggie are going to come, and they're bringing Lenore. There's also another agenda item. The Tweetmans are going to be here. Has Tommy called you yet?" Baxter sifted through his call slips. He had been out the week before. There were two calls from a "Mr. Tweetman" in the last week. Both indicated that the caller would call back.

"He's tried to call, Ed. But he didn't leave a number. Don't tell me that Tommy and Lucy are going to Gordy's wedding!"

"Tommy would only go if he thought he had a shot at selling Fong a computer. Lucy's back to close up Miss Marshalls. Francine ran it into the ground. Tommy decided to come out, and we thought we would begin to plan for a twenty-five reunion of Iron Creek High School class of 1953. Tommy said he could probably get a lot of the mailing stuff done through IBM. He's got permission from his District Manager and I figure we could hold it the first week in June."

"Ed, I would have to bring my kids. I have them every weekend through New Year's."

"They've never seen Iron Creek. Bring 'em! Tell them there will be a lot of Chinese food."

"Ed, who is Gordy marrying?" Baxter asked.

"The bride is a go-go dancer at a place called The Point. She's from Canada. She's supposed to have a great body. Also you should know this. She's a Negress!"

"Ed, is this a joke?" Baxter asked.

"No, Joe. It's for real! Rose Anne wants you to bring a camera and take lots of pictures."

"Ed, I've got to think about this and I have to go to a meeting. Let me call you back," Baxter begged off.

"Joe, Diane will kill me if I don't produce you for the wedding. I'm asking you to come for old times sake. It won't kill you and it will be something for all of us to talk about for the rest of our lives. Besides you can see Tommy and Lucy again and plan the reunion. Com'on Joey. Say you'll come!"

Baxter reluctantly agreed to attend his brother Gordy's wedding. He had no other choices than to bring the children and risk irritating Jennifer.

"He's the jailbird isn't he? You can't expose our children to his kind of people," Jennifer had protested.

"Jennifer, he's my brother and he's paid his debt to society. Gordy is now working as an Executive Assistant to a prominent Duluth businessman and is marrying a member of a well established dance group," Baxter countered.

"You're up to something, Joe. I have weekend plans every weekend through New Year's Day, and I have developed some important new relationships. But I don't want you to do anything irresponsible with these children." Jennifer broke off with what she believed was the last word on the matter.

Baxter drove into the driveway of the house on Palmer Street shortly after eight in the morning on Friday, December 16th. It was a grey morning with light rain and a temperature in the high thirties. The Racine streets were coated with dirty snow and he would have to drive through snow to reach Iron Creek. The drive could easily take eight or nine hours if there was snow. Why was he doing this? Baxter asked himself. Why not just drive the kids to a resort motel with a swimming pool and a movie theatre down the road? He really had no interest in attending Gordy's wedding.

The house on Palmer Street stood three stories high in its Victorian grandeur in need of a paint job. The house of Tom Washburn was beginning to appear dilapidated. It had been four years since Baxter had vacated his place at the house and it had slipped considerably. While Baxter had not been handy in maintaining the house, he had been scrupulous in calling in craftsmen to fix and mend the deterioration of the 75 year old house.

To the rear of the driveway was the garage with the carriage house where Agnes and Bill, Mr. Tom's driver, had lived in presumed celibacy in the upstairs rooms. The house held memories for Baxter. Outside Iron Creek, it was the longest he had lived any place in his life. It was a house that held the memories of a strange marriage and his legacy children. Joel was now eleven and Muffin was seven. The children had lived with a succession of au pairs after Baxter's departure and the death of Agnes. The au pairs were generally foreign exchange university students. They watched the children, dusted a little, prepared frozen TV dinners, and washed the dishes, but exhibited scant interest in the upkeep of the house.

Jennifer was gone most of the time. She had her work as curator of the Gellhorn Historical Institute and her graduate studies. These studies now spanned a half dozen academic disciplines, and Jennifer was done with the exception of her thesis in at least two of them. Jennifer also liked to travel to Europe, and was generally accompanied by men who were either on sabbaticals or who were performing research for important books. Jennifer's hey day had been the anti-war movement. It had lasted five or six years and provided her ample time to be outside the house making a statement. Jennifer was now examining environmental issues as her next crusade.

Baxter walked up the front steps against a chorus of creaks from the wooden steps, which appeared to be buckling slightly. The front door chimes were noisy. Jennifer liked noisy chimes. The house was large and when she was home, she spent a lot of time in the upstairs sitting room.

Jennifer answered the door. She wore a high-necked grey sweater, black stretch pants, high black boots, and black beret. Jennifer was well made up with blue eye shadow highlighting her saucer eyes, clean smooth skin, aristocratic cheekbones and the form of a twenty-four year old woman. Her breasts were medium rounded and Jennifer's waist and hips were narrow. If he were meeting her for the first time, Baxter might have fallen in love with her.

"Good morning, Joe. You're running ten minutes late," Jennifer greeted him.

"There was a long line at the car rental this morning," Baxter explained.

"Our agreement was that you would be here at eight sharp to pick up the children. It's ten after eight. Kenneth is picking me up at nine and I don't want to put him through the awkwardness of introducing him to my ex-husband," Jennifer complained.

Baxter was tempted to tell Jennifer how beautiful she was that morning. She was 38 years old and had moved into the late thirties fade of her beauty. Baxter knew that she was eager to recruit his replacement. He didn't know the name Kenneth. It was a new name. Baxter wished him luck.

"Well come in," Jennifer continued. "The children have been up since a quarter to seven. I had them pack last night, and they're very excited to be with their father. I want you out of the driveway no later than 8:45. Kenneth tends to be early." Baxter was allowed into the front hall and dutifully removed his rubbers. At the head of the landing was the oil painting of Mr. Tom which had once hung in the Washburn Manufacturing conference room. The old man was staring off into space posed in a black three piece suit.

"You've got Tom's picture back," Baxter observed.

"That Englishman, Basil, brought it out two weeks ago. I called him and asked for the painting. He said that Henry Wiggins Limited had acquired the painting along with the assets of the company. He told me that they like to bring in the sales representatives and have the picture on the wall to demonstrate continuity. I told him that Tom Washburn was my grandfather and that I lived in his house and that was where the painting belonged. If he wanted to show the picture of Tom to the sales representatives, he should bring them by the house and I would serve them tea and show them his study. We had several conversations on this matter. He asked me out for dinner. I took Mr. Basil Crowley to the Deer Lake Country Club as my guest. We talked it out and he agreed to drop off the painting after Thanksgiving. He came out here last week and I poured him a drink. It was a good thing, my friend, Kenneth stopped by. Basil finally took the hint to leave. Your friend, Basil, is a sleazy customer, and certainly not a British University man. I believe that he came to the house with the anticipation of taking advantage of me."

"When your friend, Kenneth came," Baxter asked, "Did Basil shout, 'Curses! Foiled again!'"

"You're not funny, Joe. You think you're funny, but you're not funny. Children!" Jennifer bellowed up the staircase. "Your father is here! Hurry!"

Jennifer led Baxter to the kitchen where he had spent so many hours with Agnes listening to classical music. She poured him coffee from the Mister Coffee. "Joel is in seventh grade at Marple Prep and he doesn't like it. Martha is in second grade at Montessori School and she loves it. You should try to spend some time with Joel this weekend. I have had some problems in communicating with him. Martha is fine. I'm worried about Joel. He seems so moody these days." There was the sound of thumps from the stairway and Baxter knew that the children were about to descend on them and he was relieved. He couldn't wait to be free of Jennifer and the house memories.

"Daddy!" Muffin ran to him. She was a little golden girl in a green dress with green shoes. Joel lingered behind her wearing a blue blazer, grey slacks, and loafers and sporting his mother's saucer eyes. He shook hands with Baxter. It was a limp handshake displaying a sweaty palm. "Good to see you, Dad," he greeted Baxter solemnly.

"We carried our bags downstairs," Muffin beamed. "We can go!"

"Then we should," Baxter led them out of the house on Palmer Street

He exchanged good-byes with Jennifer with a glance and had them out the driveway at 8:27. They bubbled after the car cleared the driveway. Baxter placed them both in the back seat to avoid the argument on who was going to sit with him in the front seat.

"Mother's boyfriend is coming," Muffin offered. "She didn't want you to meet him."

"It would be awkward for Kenneth," Joel commented authoritatively.

"It's always awkward in broken marriages for the suitor to meet the former husband."

"Is your brother a criminal?" Muffin asked as they cleared the driveway. "Mother said that he had been in prison."

"Look guys," Baxter explained. "My brother, Gordy, made a few mistakes, but paid for them by serving time in correctional institutions. He has been living outside correctional facilities for a long time now. You really don't have to go to the wedding. You can stay in Iron Creek. I will just be gone for four or five hours and I'll have someone sit with you."

"No!" Muffin pleased. "We want to go to the wedding and see the Chinese restaurant. Please don't leave us with a sitter. Mother does that all the time."

"Mother says that your family is all trash. Will we have to stay with them?" Joel asked.

"They are not trash," Baxter corrected his son. "They are working class people who were unfortunate enough not to have successful grandfathers to build an estate for them."

"Mother said that you were an opportunist. What did she mean by that?" Joel asked when they were a block away from the house on Palmer Street.

"Your mother occasionally gets confused on the subject of opportunists. An opportunist is someone who takes advantage of another person without regard for moral or ethical principles. When I married your mother, I believed that we were in love. This had nothing to do with the Washburn Manufacturing Company and your grandfather's position as President. Washburn Manufacturing Company was a failing company, Joel. After your great grandfather got sick, the company was very poorly managed."

"Mother says that you and other people ran the company into the ground, and that's why they had to sell to the English."

"Your mother may not be well informed on the Washburn Manufacturing Company. If she's not happy about the way the company performed, she should talk to grandfather, Nelson," Baxter explained.

After the initial barrage of questions, the children settled down and were sleeping as Baxter aimed the car in a northwestern direction toward Duluth/Superior with an eventual Iron Creek destination.

They slept soundly after Madison and Baxter listened to the classical station and reassessed his life process. Here he was 42 years of age, driving a rental car to Iron Creek, Minnesota with his two children sleeping in the back seat.

The last months had been frantic for Baxter and Jennifer was right. He had been neglecting his parental responsibilities. He would try to get to know them better this weekend. Baxter favored Muffin. She was loving, open, and uncomplicated. Muffin seemed to accept the unusual series of relationships with her mother, her father who lived outside the house on Palmer Street, her mother's succession of lovers, the au pairs, and the lavish affections of the Washburn grandparents.

Joel was more complicated. He had his mother's cheekbones and saucer eyes. Joel had sprouted this year and now had a tall thin frame. He seemed intelligent, but did barely enough to get by in school. He had no interest in sports and threw and caught balls awkwardly. Joel's major interest was in the theater. Baxter had taken Joel and Muffin to Sonny's Supper Club that summer to see Caroursel. They purchased a tape in the lobby after the performance and Joel had the entire libretto committed to memory two weeks later. He wrote and acted in skits and appeared to have talent. Baxter could please him by bringing a tape of a Broadway musical, and Joel would light up when they talked about the New York theatre. He couldn't understand why Baxter didn't see a play every time he visited New York. Joel was pleasant enough when he wanted something from Baxter, but he was beginning to sense that his son didn't like him.

Baxter's plan was to take Highway 51 out of Madison north and cut at Wausau to catch Highway 53 which would take him directly to Iron Creek. There was a long stretch of two lane driving on the cutoff where the road was bounded by dairy farms and men with caps slowed traffic in their tractors. The classical station from Madison faded and Baxter found a substitute station that also featured religious music. In the backseat, the children were sound asleep.

In three months, Baxter would be putting 750 miles between the children and him. He remembered Agnes begging him to stay in the house and be with the children. Baxter had put his career with McKenzie Barber first. Now he was 42 years of age and his career was all he really had, other than the children. New York and the promise to be a Partner at McKenzie Barber was in front of him. He was going to be an Executive Compensation Partner in the most demanding and competitive marketplace in the world and was also expected to run around in airplanes as if they were taxicabs.

Executive Compensation was beginning to bore Baxter. The fun part of his job was selling the work and then selling the plans to the clients. In between there was a lot of financial analysis, number grinding, and behavioral modeling. Baxter had accumulated a broad knowledge of business practices, accounting conventions, tax law, and he could weave that information into a narrow practice specialty that was becoming more and more crowded with competitors each day. Now Baxter was returning to the place where he had started out.

He felt burned out after Dominique. She never really left Baxter's mind. He thought about her in the morning as he lay in bed after turning off the alarm, and she entered his thoughts as he drank nightcaps in lonely airport motels. Sometimes he would leaf through his week-at-a-glance book and refer back to the days they had spent together. He would relive each day from the moment Michael Stokes had introduced them in the Barber-Paris office. Sometimes he would calculate the time gap. Five months, two days, and three hours ago Baxter had climbed the stairs to Dominique's apartment for the first time. He was in the habit of making a number of calculations back to times they had been together and the time frames were growing

*Dwight E. Foster*

longer. Would Baxter one day sit in a rocking chair and calculate that it was forty-one years, one month, six days, and fifteen minutes ago that he had made love to Dominique in the taxi on the way to Charles De Gaulle?

Baxter felt no desire to develop new relationships with women in the months after Dominique. He would have drinks with Lorna once every ten days, but that was to talk shop and exchange gossip. Lorna continued to be very well informed on the inner workings of McKenzie Barber. Over time he told her about Dominique, and she took his hand and said, "Poor Joe!"

Alice Dungler would call from time to time and send Baxter strange contemporary cards. She came through Chicago once when Baxter was out of town, and left him a two page handwritten note. Alice wanted Baxter in California. He expected that her motives were not to talk shop or exchange gossip. Alice was obviously a woman of aggressive action. Baxter felt very empty as he drove slowly behind a pick-up truck up the two lane road that brought him closer and closer to Iron Creek.

Baxter couldn't be certain as to what the children had been told about Baxter's family. Jennifer liked to believe that the Washburns were and elite Eastern Wisconsin family, and that she had married beneath her station to please her grandfather. She had quit sending Christmas cards to Rose Anne after Baxter had moved out of the house. Baxter's mother sent cards on Easter, Christmas, and his birthday. Baxter send flowers to his mother on her birthday and a fruitbasket at Christmas. Lenore would write regularly, and include a biblical quotation in each letter. She had graduated from Nursing School and was now working at the Iron Creek Clinic.

In recent letters, Lenore discussed a possible missionary calling to an underdeveloped country. Baxter exchanged Christmas cards with the Ganski's and the Tweetmans, but Baxter rarely heard from his brother, Gordy. When he did, it had to do with a small loan. Baxter sent him a check once for fifty dollars which was not repaid, and thereafter ignored Gordy's occasional requests. From the back seat, Baxter heard Muffin shout, "Stop that! I'll tell Dad!" and he knew the children were awake.

In later years, Baxter had memories of four events that had made up the weekend. The first was Friday night with the Ganski's. Second was his poignant meeting with Rose Anne on Saturday morning. Third was the planning meeting with the Tweetmans relative to the twenty-fifth anniversary gathering of the Iron Creek High School class of 1953, and last was the featured event of the weekend, Gordy's wedding.

Joel had never seen a place before like Iron Creek. "That big hole in the ground is a mine? Mines aren't supposed to look like that!" Joel protested.

"Can we stop and look?" Muffin had asked. "Can we see the creek?"

"In the morning when it's light, Muff," Baxter explained.

"We'll walk over to see your grandmother in the morning. We're going to bring her a nice coffee cake from Basinski's Bakery." Baxter turned off Mine Street to Broadway. The overheard Christmas decorations had probably been up since Thanksgiving and looked ratty. The Welcome to Iron Creek, Christmas USA sign had easily one third of its lights out. Baxter drove the car slowly down the street. There were empty store fronts and some leases had changed owners. The Polar Theatre was closed and there was a Going-Out-Of-Business sale sign at Miss Marshalls. The Greek restaurant was now called the Broadway Diner. At the end of the Broadway Avenue business district stood the Pennsylvania Hotel, a six story brick building with a sign that stated parking was in the rear.

"I thought we were going to stay at a Holiday Inn with a swimming pool. The billboard sign said that there was a Holiday Inn with a heated pool six miles ahead in Iron Creek. I want to stay at the Holiday Inn and swim in the pool!" Joel protested.

"The Pennsylvania Hotel is where your mother and I stayed the weekend when I proposed to her thirteen years ago. She would be heartbroken if we stayed any other place," Baxter said as he turned the engine off. "Besides we have a suite reserved. It will be much better than an old cinder block Holiday Inn. This hotel was built to house the great men of mining. Just you wait and see. You'll feel like you're part of Iron Range history." Baxter led them in the back door past a saloon called the Gentlemen Miner which he could not remember seeing before. He went to the front desk where Baxter was confronted by a middle aged bearded desk clerk who wore a blue tie with a blue flannel shirt.

"Baxter, party of three," Baxter greeted the desk clerk. The clerk shuffled through a file. "Says here you got the suite," he commented. "You'll be the only ones up on sixth floor. You sure you want to go up there?"

"We reserved the suite. I assume it's clean."

"Should be," the clerk said.

"Better be," Baxter replied. "We'll stay in the suite," Baxter said with his most fearsome glare.

"6D, at the end of the hall. Some of the hall lights have been reported out, but I'll have housekeeping get up there in the morning."

"Don't the visiting Penn-Mine people stay in the suite anymore?" Baxter asked.

"Nah," the clerk replied. "They generally stay at the Holiday Inn. They like the pool."

Muffin stopped Baxter in front of the elevator and pulled on his arm. "I have something to tell you Daddy," she whispered in his ear. "I'm scared, Daddy. Will we be safe?"

Joel had a strange smirk on his face, and Baxter could sense that he would spend the weekend terrorizing his sister if he had half the chance. The hallway on sixth floor was dim, but the suite turned out to be magnificent. It had been built to host the dignitaries of Pennsylvania Steel who visited Iron Creek for extended periods back in the glory days. There was a large living room with a fireplace, high ceilings, floor to ceiling bookcases lined with leather-bound books, a long leather couch, and three stuffed chairs. It reminded the children of the house on Palmer Street. There were paintings of the great men of mining, and a large drawing of the open pit when it had been half its present size.

"This is better than a Holiday Inn," Joel agreed.

"Can I sleep in your bed, tonight?" Muffin asked.

They parked in front of the Ganski home shortly after seven o'clock. It had been stuccoed since Baxter's last visit at the time of Mort's funeral.

Diane Ganski answered the door. Baxter observed the candies on the dining room table which had eight places set on a white table cloth. The little girl from Oklahoma still wore her hair long and Diane's face had weathered slightly over her twenty-two years of marriage.

"Joe, how good to see you. Welcome back, stranger. And you've brought your children. Come in. We have a surprise for you. Lenore's here."

Baxter led the children across the threshold and saw the child of his marriage with Maggie.

"Hello, father," she greeted him. Lenore was very tall and thin. Her red hair was tied in a pony tail and she wore a white blouse decorated with a blue cross necklace, a long dark skirt that reached half way down her calves, and black flat shoes. Baxter noted that she had inherited his big feet.

"Joel, Martha," Baxter said. "This is Lenore, your half sister."

Joel seemed to look past Lenore and bowed his head slightly in acknowledgment. He said something that sounded like, "How do you do." Muffin ran across the room and gripped both of Lenore's hands in hello. "I've always wanted a sister. Can we bring her back to Palmer Street, Daddy?"

Introductions were made all around. Ganski had a beer in his hand.

"How are you, buddy," he greeted Baxter. "It's been a while."

Two Ganski sons were in the room, including the oldest boy, Joe, whom Baxter quickly calculated at age 21 or 22 and a second son named Mortimer, who had to be nineteen. "Ronnie has a game tonight. He's playing for the Cougars," Ganski announced. His sons were square shouldered young men with their mother's eyes and their father's short torsoed bodies. They shook hands all the way around.

"Shouldn't we be at the game, Ed, if your son's playing?" Baxter asked.

"He hasn't gotten off the bench in two games. I told Coach Minchek how I felt, and he reminded me that he was the coach. I'm boycotting the Cougars until after the holidays. Joe and Mort played for the Cougars, and I think that Ronnie's the best one yet. Let me get you a beer, Joey."

"We're serving wine with dinner," Diane reminded her husband.

"Joey's had beer and wine on the same night before, Diane. He's a world traveler."

"Father," Lenore said when they were seated in the Ganski living room. "I would like to come with you tomorrow to Duluth for your brother's wedding. I have spent a good deal of time with Grandma since she has been sick. She's told me what a good person your brother, Gordy is and how he has turned around his life. I understand that he has become very successful in business now and what an example he must be for men who have made some mistakes when they were very young."

"What mistakes did your brother make?" Joel asked.

Baxter wanted to say that Gordy had tried to steal anything that wasn't nailed down, but he caught himself. Instead he said, "It's all in the past now, Joel, and really isn't important. The main thing is that he's found meaningful work and a wife." Ganski winked at Baxter when he brought him his beer.

"What church do you attend, Joel?" Lenore asked.

"We've been going to the Unitarian Church. Mother's been going out with the pastor. His name is Kenneth and sometimes he comes for dinner and plays the guitar."

"He plays the banjo too," Muffin added.

"Mother met him in the anti-war movement," Joel qualified the relationship.

"He was just divorced. He's like Daddy," Muffin said. "He has two children, our age, who live with him. We see them in Sunday School. She's off on a ski weekend with Kenneth."

"Muffin!" Joel protested. "You shouldn't go telling everyone about Mother's private life."

"How would you like to go to church with me on Sunday morning?" Lenore offered. "I have my own Sunday School class. You can meet a lot of fine little Christian boys and girls."

"Is your church Unitarian?" Joel asked.

"It's called Calvary Baptist Church," Lenore answered.

"We just go to Unitarian Church. Muffin and I aren't interested in going to Baptist churches."

Muffin nodded her head in agreement. "Just Unitarian. That's where we go."

Baxter took a long pull from his beer can. The Ganski boys each sat dutifully in their chairs with their arms folded and studied Joel and Muffin as if they were space children.

"Are you a ballplayer, Joel? Like your Dad?" Ganski asked.

"I don't like sports, Mr. Ganski. I'm interested in the theatre," Joel replied.

"Your Dad was a good ballplayer," Ganski commented.

"You were captain of the basketball team, weren't you, Mr. Baxter?" Joe Ganski, the oldest son offered, is an obvious effort to reposition the conversation.

"Yes, and I understand that you were captain your senior year, Joe," Baxter replied on cue. "What kind of year did you have?"

"We were eleven and eleven. Nothing like the 1953 Cougars." The conversation turned and Lenore went out to the kitchen to help Diane. The Ganski boys started to talk about themselves. Baxter learned that Joe Ganski had graduated from the community college with an AA degree in Engineering Technology and was now working in the Penn-Mine Taconite plant. Mort Ganski was working in construction during the days and taking a Civil Engineering Course in evening school at the community college. Ed Ganski has been elected to the City Council for two terms and was up for election next fall. Their talk was about Iron Creek as if it were the only community in the world that counted. Duluth and Superior were regarded as foreign big cities to be entered only on special occasions for specific purposes. They had discussed Coach Minchek and his feud with Ronnie Ganski.

"He's all plays. There's no freelancing. Ron's a shooter. He's like Tweetman in some ways. He took a couple of shots that coach didn't like, and now he's on the bench. Ron is almost as good a shot as Tweetman. Tommy Tweetman would have rode the bench for this guy, Minchek. Which reminds, Joey. You're supposed to call Tweetman and get together with him about the reunion."

"Aren't we supposed to meet for brunch tomorrow?"

"The Ganski's don't run in the same social circles as the Tweetmans. Tommy suggested that the three of us meet for a drink after dinner," Ganski said.

"We'll meet in our suite at the Pennsylvania Hotel. I've got a jug of Canadian Club if that's okay?" Baxter used the hall telephone, and dialed the Albright number. Lucy Albright answered.

Baxter identified himself and Lucy responded warmly. "Joe, how wonderful to hear your voice. Tommy's downstairs and I'll get him in a minute. Some of our plans have changed, but Tommy and I would like you to bring your family out to the Iron Creek Country Club for lunch tomorrow.

We have our children and we can arrange a children's table and the three of us can have a long talk. You and Ed and Tommy can get together and plan the reunion. We're closing up the stores and then the house is going up for sale. I'll give you all the details tomorrow. And do me a favor, Joe. Watch Tommy's drinking tonight." Baxter heard Lucy's voice call for Tommy.

"Hey, Joe. How are you——," Tommy's voice greeted Baxter.

Baxter explained that he had a suite at the Pennsylvania Hotel and asked if Canadian Club would be appropriate. They agreed to meet at 9:30.

Dinner was labored, but passed quickly. Lenore led the table in prayer. Carl and Maggie were continuing to prosper and their children were growing. Ed Ganski expected a local GOP challenge for his Councilman seat. Penn-Mine was hiring selectively. "Now, what about you Joey? How are you doing?" Ganski finally asked.

"I'm moving to New York in April," Baxter announced.

"New York City?" Their faces looked as though he had said that he was moving to Transylvania.

"Why are you doing that?" Ganski asked.

"Because the firm wants me there. I expect to be elected a partner next fall," he explained what his new job would be and they looked at him with blank stares.

"Now, Joe," Lenore asked, "What is it that you do again? Is it some kind of payroll work?"

Dinner was concluded at nine o'clock with the understanding that they would pick up Lenore at the clinic the next day and that Ganski would follow Baxter back to the Pennsylvania Hotel. Both Joel and Muffin were pleased to leave the Ganski house.

"Daddy," Muffin said in a tired voice from the backseat. "Don't make us go to church with Lenore."

Baxter secured two ice buckets from the bar, ordered cokes for the children, and returned to the suite. He managed to open the fireplace flue and fueled a small fire from a woodbox near the door. "Jesus!" Ganski said as he looked around the suite. "This is the good life up here!"

Baxter poured Canadian Club, instructed the children to change into pajamas, and watched the fire develop. They were joined five minutes later by Tom Tweetman. Tommy wore a crew neck sweater, wash pants, and a wind breaker. Baxter poured him three inches of Canadian Club in a glass full of ice.

"This meeting of the 1953 Iron Creek Cougars should commence," Ganski ruled.

Joel and Muffin reappeared and were introduced to Tommy Tweetman. "Are you another basketball player, Mr. Tweetman?" Muffin asked.

"I was a better than average basketball player, Muffin. But I am one hell of a computer salesman."

"Do we really want to hold a reunion?" Baxter asked.

"I'm for it." Tommy opened a zippered brief case. "I have a plan, complete with a GANT chart."

"What the hell's a GANT chart?" Ganski asked.

"The chart will explain itself." Tommy produced three copies of a program plan. It was of McKenzie Barber quality. The reunion was reduced to an objective, tasks, responsibilities, and critical action dates.

"I've got it organized so that Ed and I will take most of the load, Joe. I've tracked down most of the class and they seem to want a reunion, but most of them have moved far away. They're all over the country. We had 231 in our class and about 50 are still on the range," Ganski asked.

"Where did they go? Duluth?" Ganski asked.

"They went far beyond Duluth, Ed. They went where the opportunities were. There aren't many in Iron Creek unless you want to work in some dead end job with Penn-Mine. Pennsylvania Steel is in deep trouble. They may get out of the mining business one day."

Ed Ganski's face looked as if someone had told him that a meteor from outer space was going to hit in the next month.

"Tommy! Pennsylvania Steel will always be in the mining business. Penn-Mine is very important!"

"Ed, the headquarters has been moved from Iron Creek to Duluth to Pittsburgh. The handwriting's on the wall," Tommy said authoritatively. "Iron Creek is dying."

"We'll bring in new industry to replace Penn-Mine," Ganski protested.

"Not with your tax base and militant labor unions. This area's only hope is to attract tourists in the summer who like to fish."

Ganski looked to Baxter. "Do you agree with that, Joe?"

"I believe Tommy's pretty much on the mark, Ed."

Joel and Muffin were now sitting Indian style in front of the fire silently sipping their cokes.

"Then maybe we shouldn't have a reunion. What we ought to have is a close-the-town-party. I think both of you guys are full of bullshit. You don't know what you're talking about. Iron Creek's got a lot of life in it. My boys are settled in to spend their lives here. This is a damned good place to live! The reunion will be good for Iron Creek. Iron Creek will be around a long time after you guys are gone."

"Then let's have the reunion and get on with it!" Baxter declared. "I'm moving to New York in April, Tommy. My life is a little confused now."

"The Big Apple! That's great, Joe. That must be Mecca for McKenzie Barber!"

"I've been led to believe that I will be elected a Partner in October," Baxter explained.

"That's fantastic, Joe!" Tommy said enthusiastically. "You'll be in the big money with them. McKenzie Barber Partners live the good life. I'm excited for you."

Ganski looked at the two of them quizzically. "Will you be some kind of a big deal, Joe?"

"Let me explain, Ed," Tommy offered. "McKenzie Barber is the IBM of management consulting. They are the biggest and the best. They are owned by their partners and they have told Joe that he would be a Partner in October of next year. That is a very big deal. It's as good as being made a vice president of Pennsylvania Steel. They are bringing Joe into the biggest marketplace in the world. If IBM asked me to go to New York in a senior management role, I would be on the next plane."

"But you would have to sell your house and put your kids into new schools," Ganski objected.

"That's done all the time, Ed. If you want to get ahead at the senior level of any large scale organization, you have got to transfer when they want you to. We have moved six times since I joined IBM."

Ganski shook his head. "I don't understand you guys. The most important things in anyone's life should be their family and their community. A company is where you go to work. You give them a good eight hours every day and they pay you twice a month. If they want you to work longer than eight hours, they should pay you overtime. If you don't like what you're doing, you find another job. If they're not paying you enough, you talk at the union meeting, and maybe you go out. I left the union when they made me a supervisor and I'm damned sorry now that I did it."

Ganski drained his glass and rattled the ice cubes in silence for a minute as he stared into the fire. "Joey, I'm disappointed. I thought you'd go back to the union after college. The union's been gobbled up by these guys in Pittsburgh and they don't give a damn about the ore workers. They just like the dues coming in so they can print magazines with the union leaders pictures on it. They don't have enough smart guys. You could have been a leader in the union. But look at you. You're working on the pay of the big boys. The guys who used to hang out in this room and figure out how much productivity they could squeeze out of the miners at the lowest pay. Now you're staying in their old lair where they probably plotted to kill your father."

Ganski stood up from his chair. "I've had too much to drink and said too much." He folded Tommy's reunion plan and placed it in his jacket pocket.

"This reunion will be good for Iron Creek. I need to study your plan. I'll call you on it, Tommy. How long are you going to be in town?"

"Till after Christmas, Ed," Tommy said refilling his glass.

"I'll call you, Joey. I really appreciate your coming back for Gordy's wedding. Rose Anne is probably dying and Maggie didn't want to call you. So she got Diane to work on me to get you out here. Sam Fong is probably the shadiest guy in Duluth, and your brother is now one of his key henchmen. I don't envy you going to that wedding, Joe. If you want to leave the kids with us, we'll look after them. I wouldn't want to bring my kids into that crowd. I'm sorry if I said anything out of line just now. Look in on me before you leave town on Sunday." Ganski stooped down to say good night to Joel and Muffin. "You're good looking kids. Take care of your Dad." Joel shook hands with him and Muffin kissed him on the cheek.

Joel was animated with excitement when Baxter returned from seeing Ganski to the door. "Are we really going to see some criminals, Dad? Will it be dangerous?"

"Maybe I'll just take Lenore to the wedding and you can stay with the Ganski's," Baxter suggested.

"Lucy and I can take them," Tommy volunteered.

"I want to go to the Chinese restaurant," Muffin protested.

"I want to see the gangsters," Joel insisted. "Will you carry a gun, Dad?"

"We'll have Lenore and her Bible. That will be quite enough protection. Time to go to bed, gang. It's time for a tooth brushing contest."

Tommy Tweetman stayed until after midnight. "This is one of my last visits to Iron Creek," Tommy announced when Baxter returned from bedding down the children. "We'll be back for the reunion. Lucy wants the reunion. Her sister Francine ran the businesses into the ground, with some help from the local economy and the new mall on the edge of town. My Dad is retiring in March, and they're moving to Coral Gables. We're selling the house on Pine Hill and I've been transferred to Indianapolis. Mrs. Albright will be moving in with us, wheel chair and all. After that's all done, there's no reason for me ever to come back here, Joe. This is an ugly dying town. My Dad got stuck here and never got out. He interviewed for other jobs as Administrator for larger clinics in bigger cities, but always finished second or third, and somebody else was picked over him."

"I didn't know that, Tom," Baxter said sympathetically.

"Twenty-five years ago, Joe. I came here twenty-five years. I was a senior and co-captain of my team and my Dad moved us to Iron Creek so he could get an Administrator's job."

"The range was booming then, Tommy. It probably looked like a great opportunity."

"I remember that first time we played in the gym. I thought if this Baxter is the best that they've got, we're going to have a sorry team. As it turned out, we had a pretty good team. A dumb coach, but a pretty good team."

"I shouldn't have tried to bank that last shot, Tom," Baxter's memory was clear. He had the rebound, took the ball up, and went for the bank. The ball spun around, came out, and the 1953 Cougars were history."

That was the worst game I ever played, Joe."

"Why didn't you stay at Kentucky, Tom?"

"I should have stayed, Joe. I was spooked by the competition. I wanted to be the star and we had fourteen or fifteen guys on scholarship who were just as good as I was. I transferred up to a school where I could be a star. Then I decided when I graduated that I would go with the best company in the United States, work hard, and go right up to the top. That hasn't worked out either. I'm trapped in the middle as a Branch Manager. I turned down a move to Armonk because Lucy thought it would be too far from her mother. Now I'm not getting anywhere. Indianapolis is a bigger branch than Grand Rapids. But it's not a big pop upward. My kids are about the same age as yours. Now we are faced with the prospect of Grandmother Albright as a permanent part of our household. Joe, I've been thinking about leaving IBM. I don't want to sell for a competitor! But I would love to take one of those Vice President, Management Information Systems jobs with a customer. I don't know how to get one. Joe, McKenzie Barber has a lot of big clients and access to the top. Do you hear about those kinds of jobs?"

Baxter stared into the fire as if he were thinking about Tommy's problem. In reality he was wondering what his life would have been like if Tommy Tweetman's father had not taken the Administrator's job at the clinic. He would have Mrs. Albright on his hands. What would he have been doing other than going to New York as a Director level executive compensation specialist with McKenzie Barber? There would be no memory of Dominique Beaufort burnt into his memory.

"I can talk to our Information Technology guys and arrange for you to meet with them. I'm more concerned with how people are paid than how and why they're hired."

"Tommy nodded his head. "Anything you can do, Joe."

Baxter remembered Lucy's warning. Watch Tommy's drinking! Baxter started a campaign of yawns and Tommy Tweetman was out the suite door around twelve-thirty. Would Saturday be as bad as Friday, Baxter wondered?

Baxter regarded the visit of 926 Mine Street on Saturday morning with a sense of trepidation. He took the children to breakfast at the Pennsylvania Hotel Coffee Shop. They were seated in the window where they could look out on a cold Broadway Avenue. The time and temperature clock on the Range National Bank stated alternatively that it was 8:49 and the temperature was 6 degrees. They looked out onto the street and saw the residents with earlapped caps and hats with earmuffs. Scarves and mufflers abounded and breath turned into vapor.

Baxter instructed them to order a light breakfast and save room for a piece of the coffee cake that they would purchase at Basinski's Bakery. He nibbled on a piece of toast while Joel and Muffin devoured blueberry pancakes.

"Why haven't you taken us to meet our grandmother before?" Joel asked pointedly.

"Because she lives so far away," Baxter answered.

"And you grew up in a poor home?"

"Who told you that? Your mother?" He paused to take a sip from his coffee. "My parents were immigrants more or less. My mother was second generation Norwegian, and my father came from England. He was a miner by profession. They both worked very hard, but didn't get along very well. My father moved out of the house and my mother raised Gordy and me. We always had food in the house, clothes on our back, and we listened to the radio a lot. That was enough. In America, Joel, it's what you are, not what your parents were. My mother did all right by me."

Muffin reached over to pat Baxter's hands. "You're a good Daddy!"

"The Ganski's where we ate last night, are they a mining family?" Joel continued with his questioning.

"Mr. Ganski works for Penn-Mine, which is the Mining Company of Pennsylvania Steel. He doesn't dig ore. Rather he's the Supervisor of the Drafting Section. There is a great deal of engineering involved in the way ore is mined. It's transported from the pit, processed through a series of screens, and formed into pellets. That requires different skills than when my father worked in the mines. Mr. Ganski's sons have been, or are being trained, to work in the taconite plant. The jobs they will hold, my father couldn't have done. He was all muscle. Now, thinking and reasoning are required."

Joel was silent for a minute as if he were processing what Baxter had said. "I think I understand. Mother has always said that you were very smart, but very lower class."

Baxter signaled the waitress for the check. Joel was clearly his mother's son. "Let's get on with the day, gang," Baxter announced standing up from the table.

Basinski's Bakery was crowded with Saturday morning customers. He took number 29 from the rack at the counter and patiently waited in the rear of room for his turn. Some of the customers looked Baxter over. He appeared to be a familiar face that they couldn't place. One man with thinning hair, glasses, and wearing an open parka, studied Baxter with furtive glances.

"Are you Red Baxter?" he asked finally.

"I'm Joe Baxter."

"You played center for the Cougars the year they won the league?"

"The 1953 Cougars," Baxter qualified his team.

"That was the last time we had a basketball team worth a shit around here. My name's Paul Dolchek. I was two years behind you. I loved that '53 Cougars team. Ed Ganski always talks about you."

"What are you doing now, Paul?" Baxter asked.

"I'm a Foreman at the Taconite plant. Did you go and play college ball like Tweetman, Joe?"

"No, I went in the Army. I work in Chicago now," Baxter explained.

"These your kids?" Dolchek asked.

"Joel and Martha, this is Mr. Dolchek."

"Your Dad was a good ball player. They almost went to the State Tournament their senior year."

"I know," Muffins said. "Daddy missed the last shot. He should have shot for the rim."

"29!" The counter lady called out. Baxter held up 29.

They drove slowly down Broadway to Truck Street to 926 Mine Street. The house hadn't changed. There was a 1976 Chevrolet parked along side the sidewalk, and Baxter instinctively concluded that it belonged to Maggie.

"Now look, kids," Baxter spoke to them very seriously from the wheel of the parked car. "We're going inside to talk to my mother for a while. I want you to be polite and very careful of what you say to her. I think my first wife, Maggie, will be there. She's Lenore's mother and very close to my mother."

"This is like a soap opera, Dad," Joel said authoritatively.

"Mind your mouth, young man. Daddy's been known to be violent with smart ass kids. This is something that is expected of us and I won't let it last longer than an hour."

They walked up the steps to 926 Mine Street hand in hand and Baxter remembered the days when he had galloped down those very steps at the beginning and end of his morning run.

Maggie answered the door on the second ring. She was wearing a dark pants suit with a red scarf. Full breasted and bulky, she smiled a greeting to Baxter. "Good morning, Joe. You've brought your children. That's good!" She stood framed in the doorway and lowered her voice. "Rose Anne has her good days and she has her bad days. This is a bad day and she's in a lot of pain. You shouldn't stay more than an hour. She can't dress herself anymore. Either Lenore or me get over here in the morning to get her started, and one of us helps her get to bed each night. She's got a lot of things wrong with her. Her heart's weak and she's got pleurisy bad. She can barely walk. Rose Anne can still hear real good, so you can keep your voices down. Be sure to wipe off your feet."

They followed Maggie through the front hallway into the living room. The rug was as threadbare as Baxter remembered. The big Emerson radio had long since been replaced by a 22 inch color TV set. There was a tape cassette/radio/record player module with a multi-speaker sound system that was new.

Christmas carols were softly playing from the cassette player and there was a small Christmas tree decorated with family ornaments and bubble lights.

Rose Anne sat propped up in a chair between the sound system and the Christmas tree. Rose Anne was covered with an Indian blanket up to her neck and appeared to Baxter to be posed as a reigning Queen.

"Look who's here, Rose," Maggie announced them. "Joe and his kids, Joe Jr. and Martha."

"Joel!" Baxter's son corrected Maggie.

"And we brought you an Apple/Butter Pecan coffeecake from Basinski's," Baxter greeted his mother.

"And we've made coffee," Maggie said.

"Do you have any tea?" Joel asked. "I prefer tea."

"You're so young to be drinking tea," Rose Anne said. She was beginning to remind Baxter of one of the Chinese Dowager Empresses he had seen in the movies at the Polar Theatre.

"My mother started serving me tea when I was nine," Joel announced.

"She's training him to be an English Gentleman. Only the tea part is taking," Baxter added.

"Hello, Grandmother! I'm so glad to see you!" Muffin greeted her grandmother.

"What beautiful yellow hair! Come give your grandmother a kiss, Martha," Rose Anne commanded her.

Muffin climbed up on Rose Anne's chair and planted a kiss on her cheek. "I'm so happy to meet you at last, grandmother!" Maggie busied herself with serving the coffee cake, making tea, and pouring coffee. Rose Anne, still playing the queen, looked Joel over critically. "You're going to be tall like your father, but you must have your mother's eyes. I have never seen such big eyes."

"My mother is regarded as quite beautiful," Joel replied defensively.

"I met her once, and she sure was then," Maggie said serving Joel his tea.

"I haven't met Gordy's fiancé," Rose Anne said. "He doesn't come back to Iron Creek very often. Mr. Fong needs him during the week, and on Saturdays especially. I think he has some bad memories here about the way he was treated. If he comes, it's on Sunday night. I want Maggie to take a lot of pictures. Lenore is bringing a camera too. I want lots of pictures from the wedding and the reception. I have been waiting a long time for Gordy to get married, and now I'm not well enough to be at his wedding. I am in this room for most of the day now, and my friends visit me. Maggie is here one morning and Lenore the next. Maggie puts me to bed at night. They are very good to me. They take the place of my sons." There was a silence after Rose Anne finished talking. Baxter had never really liked his mother. He knew that he reminded her of his father and had remained close to his father. Rose Anne had always favored Gordy as her special baby.

Baxter looked around the room. "I'll always remember this room, Ma. We used to listen to the radio in this room. We listened to Fibber McGee and Molly, the Pennsylvania Steel Hour, Lux Radio Theatre, First Nighter, and Grand Central Station. There was no TV then, Joel."

"That must have been boring," Joel commented.

"I'm moving to New York in the Spring, Ma," Baxter blurted out the news of his move.

Rose Anne blinked. "You have become a wanderer. You wandered off to join the Army and you will probably wander all of your life. You would be better off staying put someplace. You could then become successful. I'm glad that Gordy has decided to stay close to his mother. Are you taking these children with you to New York?"

"They will stay with their mother in Racine and visit me periodically in New York," Baxter answered.

"Your father at least stayed in Iron Creek so that he could be with his sons. The way you're doing it is wrong."

"Dad has a big promotion. It's important for his work to be in New York," Joel surprisingly defended his father.

"Do you still type well? Your father was best typist in Iron Creek High School. I had hoped he would get a job in the order department of Penn-Mine and maybe become a supervisor one day. The union wanted him to go work for them. I didn't always trust the union. I didn't trust your father's friend, Spike. Spike was out in New York during the war and came back with a lot of sneaky ways."

"Father's with McKenzie Barber. That's a very famous firm," Joel protested.

"I don't know that Kinsey Barber. It's not famous in Iron Creek," Rose Anne said firmly.

293

"And that's what counts around here, Joel!" Baxter said. "Now Ma, what message do you want me to take to Gordy tonight?"

"Tell him I want to meet his wife as soon as possible. I know her name is Honey. That's an unusual name. I have never known anyone named Honey."

"It's a popular name in the South, Ma," Baxter said. "We may leave a little early this morning to go by the K-Mart and buy a camera. I'll have Joel and Muffin take pictures of the bride and groom just for you."

"What gift did you buy for Gordy and Honey?" Rose Anne asked.

"I have a check for them. A check will provide them the flexibility to buy something they really want," Baxter said. Rose Anne was silent for a moment. "You have changed, Joe. You have always been your father's son. Gordy has always been my son. Maggie has been like a daughter to me. Lenore has been a wonderful granddaughter. You don't belong here anymore. They do! They are my gifts to Iron Creek. You will be my gift to the world."

They labored through another fifteen minutes of small talk, each saying nothing in varying streams of words. Baxter rose promptly after one full hour in the company of his mother.

"Well this has been fun. We've got to get out to the K-Mart and on to a luncheon. We'll send you a bunch of pictures from the wedding." The children quickly followed Baxter's lead and ten minutes later, they were outside in the morning air. Maggie followed Baxter on the porch.

"I don't know how we're going to break it to Rose Anne that Gordy is marrying a colored girl, but let's talk about it first before one of us tells her."

"Maggie," Baxter replied. "Gordy has done a number of things that have been against the law. Let us rejoice that his marriage is within the law."

They were two blocks from the house before the children began to talk. "Who does your mother think she is?" Joel protested.

"She's got bad breath," Muffin concluded.

They arrived at the Iron Creek Country Club shortly after noon. They had purchased a Polaroid Camera. Following the purchase, Joel and Muffin had taken turns photographing each other. They were well prepared for the wedding.

The Iron Creek Country Club was much the same club that Baxter remembered from Tommy and Lucy's wedding reception. The dining room was half filled, and the bright mid-day sunshine was melting the morning frost from the windows. Lucy and Tommy Tweetman were already seated at one table near the window with their children seated two tables down against the wall.

"Hey, big guy!" Tommy Tweetman greeted Baxter. Lucy stood up from their table in a blue midi top, white skirt, and blue high heels. Her hair was cut in a pixie, and she was more full breasted than he remembered, but had maintained her waistline. This was an older version of the Lucy Albright who had sung the Arkansas Traveler in seventh grade.

"Joe! How wonderful to see you!" It was Lucy! Baxter's Lucy Albright! There were no noticeable lines in her face. Her body appeared firm and her manner confident. "What lovely children you have."

There were introductions and children were introduced to children. There were some fencing and positioning, but the children's communications were established.

Baxter seated himself with Tommy and Lucy and ordered a Canadian Club. They were back together again, but they had become different people. The people from Christmas 1952 had changed. They were twenty-five years older and their horizons had been altered.

"Your children are lovely, Joe," Lucy repeated when they were seated.

"Yours are too," Baxter replied. "And it's remarkable that they're the same age."

"I lost one child," Lucy said with her face frozen in a solemn expression. "Tommy and I were going to wait and then when we started trying, we had problems. As a result, we have younger children than our contemporaries. Are you divorced from Jennifer?"

"It's final now. There were some problems," Baxter responded limply.

"We came to your wedding, Joe. We were at the reception when they announced that Jennifer's grandfather had died," Lucy reported.

"Jennifer was very close to her grandfather. She had a nervous breakdown on the day after the wedding and really wasn't herself for a long time after. There were a number of problems. We became estranged and now we're divorced. There's really not a lot to say about it, Lucy," Baxter said.

"I told Lucy about your moving to New York next spring, Joe," Tommy offered.

"Joe, I understand from Tommy that it's a big promotion for you. He told me that you were likely to become a Partner with McKenzie Barber. We're very excited for you," Lucy offered. "Tommy and I are moving to Indianapolis from Grand Rapids and we're closing Miss Marshall's. It's more or less the end of an era. That's why we were so glad that we could get together for lunch. When will you go back?"

"First thing Sunday, Lucy," Baxter replied. "I'm Gordy's only brother and I got a little pressure to attend."

"That's what Tommy told me." Lucy took a sip of white wine. "I understand that Gordy is working for a man named Fong in Duluth who is regarded as a local gangster."

"His reputation is so bad in Duluth that we don't call on him. The Duluth Branch waits for Fong to call them," Tommy commented.

"Do you sell him?" Baxter asked.

"Of course we do. We sell damned everybody in order to make plan. But we don't court him as a customer."

"Are you sure that you don't want to leave your children with us?"

"Nothing could stop them from attending that wedding, Lucy," Baxter replied.

"Who else from your family is going?" Lucy asked.

"My mother can't make it. She's an invalid. I'm taking my daughter, Lenore, and Maggie and Karl will be driving down. Maggie and my mother have grown very close over the years," Baxter explained.

"Maggie. I think I saw her in the National Tea a couple of days ago. She's as big as a house."

"Previously the hottest body in the 1953 class of Iron Creek High School," Tommy commented.

"Tommy!" Lucy scolded. "The children might hear you. Well, let's bring each other up to date," Lucy commanded. "It's been twenty-five years since that Christmas of 1952 when we were all seniors at Iron Creek, and now we're going to organize a reunion. Do you remember what a good time we had that Christmas? Beth came up from Duluth and the four of us did things together and we went to the dance here? That's when I really fell in love with Tommy." Lucy held her hand out on the table and Tommy patted it.

Lucy began to recite a class history. It was centered on the kids who had lived on Pine Hill, as opposed to the kids on the other side of Broadway Avenue. There weren't a lot of surprises on the Pine Hill kids. A lot of them were back in Pittsburgh around their families.

"And you've heard, of course, about Beth?"

"Beth?" Baxter questioned.

"Beth Gold? Do you remember? It was twenty-five years ago. She came down to visit me over Christmas and you two were paired off."

Now Baxter remembered Beth Gold. He had heard echoes about a novelist named Beth Gold and some letters had arrived in the early 1960's, but Baxter hadn't thought about Beth Gold in a long time. She had bought him his first suit at the Glass Block Department Store in 1952. A little known fact!

"What about Beth Gold?" Baxter asked.

"She's become a famous novelist. She's on TV talk shows, and they made some of her books into a made-for-TV movies. One was a mini-series last spring. It was called Early August and it was about a French architect who fell in love with this American woman in early August of 1939 before the war and it followed their lives over twenty-five years. Beth is really quite famous now. She was published heavily and then dropped out to be part of the Anti-War movement. Now she's back with a vengeance."

"We get an annual Christmas card from Beth, Joe," Tommy interjected. "She updates us in three illegible lines and Lucy spends a month trying to figure out what Beth wrote on the card. Beth Gold is hot stuff right now! She's married and living in New York. I saw a picture of her in *Time Magazine* at the same party with Andy Warhol."

"Well that's what she wanted back in 1952. I'm pleased that she got it," Baxter observed.

"Now, Joe," Lucy asked. "Is there anyone important in your life now?"

At 4 PM Baxter picked up Lenore at the clinic to begin their trip to Duluth and Gordy's wedding. Lenore brought a gift wrapped in white paper with a red bow and sat in the front seat with her father. It had been a long day for Baxter. Meeting with Tommy and Lucy hadn't been much more fun than meeting with his mother. Lucy's purpose appeared to be to acquire information through pointed questions. Baxter didn't perceive himself to be in the information-giving business. Tommy looked to be on the hen-pecked side. The children got along famously.

Now they were moving down Highway 53 at an average speed of 68 miles per hour on their way to Duluth. Baxter would have to repeat the journey back to Iron Creek after the wedding. He concluded that he had done a number of dumb things over his life and this, certainly, was one of them.

Baxter realized when he was within six blocks of the Mission that he was in the derelict/skid row section of Duluth on Michigan Avenue. Gordy was true to form. The chapel was also called the Michigan Avenue Mission and there was a neon sign with a cross.

They arrived early at 6:15. The evening supper had been served and the Mission had been cleared out for Gordy's wedding. Baxter instructed Joel and Muffin to make several shots of the exterior of the chapel for their Grandmother.

Maggie and Karl arrived about six thirty. Maggie had changed into a full dress and looked to Baxter to be a medium large. Karl cordially shook hands with Baxter and they milled around the entrance until 6:45 when a man in a dark suit began to play the organ. They moved into the Chapel seats and by 6:55, the mission was, by Baxter's count, half-filled. Baxter wasn't certain as to where these people had come from, but they were quiet and respectful as they took their place among the white pews.

"Abide With Me" was played at 6:57 and a large man with a clerical collar appeared at the pulpit at 7:00 on the button. He smiled out at the audience and the Wedding March began to play. From a side door appeared three men in blue suits. The first out was Gordy with sallow features, long black hair, and a thin figure. He was followed by two heavyset men, who swaggered to their places behind Gordy at 75 degrees angle from the altar.

At the entrance of the chapel moving forward in time to the Wedding March were two fair skinned women dressed in blue dresses. One was blonde while the other was a redhead. Their dress hemlines were three inches above their knees. They were followed by a tall statuesque black woman dressed in a light blue bridal dress on the arm of an ageless Chinese man clad in a dark suit. She advanced down the aisle with the confidence of a royal princess.

The wedding went quickly. The man in the clerical collar possessed a sonorous seaman's voice and dispatched the couple quickly into matrimony. They marched down the aisle and were whisked away into waiting automobiles. It was obvious to Baxter that the real festivities would take place at Fong's restaurant. Baxter had failed to make eye contact with his brother, Gordy, either before or immediately after the wedding ceremony.

Fong's was a successful Chinese restaurant in Duluth. It was booked full on a Saturday night near Christmas. A party room had been reserved upstairs over the main restaurant floor and a sign announced;

Wedding Reception
Gordon and Honey Baxter

The reception line was formed in front of a long table just beyond the coat check. Lenore held hands with Joel and Muffin. Muffin periodically pulled Lenore down to whisper observations in the room. Karl and Maggie were three couples behind them on the stairway. The first bridesmaid was the red head. Her face was hard up close and she was chewing gum.

"I'm Joe Baxter, Gordy's brother," Baxter introduced himself. "And these are my daughters, Lenore and Martha, and my son Joel."

The bridesmaid clasped Baxter's extended hand and said, "I'm Flame. I didn't know Gordy had a brother."

Next was a heavy set man in a blue suit wearing a white flower in his lapel. Baxter again introduced himself as Gordy's brother and was greeted with a "Nice to see you, pal."

The blonde bridesmaid was more friendly. "A brother! Hey, Honey!" she called up the reception line. "I got a brother and a bunch of kids down here." She had well developed décolletage only partially concealed beneath the V on her blue dress.

"My name's Dagmar. You're got nice looking kids."

The last groomsman was an American Indian with a scar on his cheek. He did not take Baxter's extended hand and said a name that sounded like Johnny. Baxter hurried Lenore and the children past him to meet Mr. Fong.

"Oh," he beamed a smile. "You're the older brother from Chicago. And what a lovely grown-up daughter!" Mr. Fong said greeting Lenore. Joel looked Mr. Fong over very carefully before shaking hands. Mr. Fong represented the first underworld character he would meet over his life. Muffin was very serious. "I've never been in a Chinese restaurant. My mother says that you cook up dogs and cats."

Mr. Fong shook his head. "No missy, just beef, chicken, shrimp, and lobster. No collie dogs or Siamese cats," Mr. Fong replied with a cold smile.

Baxter's new sister-in-law was frowning when he drew up next to her. "Honey, I'm Joe Baxter, Gordy's brother, and these are my children," Baxter repeated his previous greeting. "Best wishes."

"Oh, you're the one from Chicago." Her face relaxed and formed a smile that showed a lot of white pointed teeth. "Gordy didn't think you'd be coming." Honey clasped Baxter's hand. Honey was a tall woman who stood nearly six feet in her high heels. She wore her hair in a short French haircut with large gold hoops in each ear. Her skin was the color of cocoa and there was an aura of strength about her. This was not a woman to tangle with. Baxter concluded quickly.

"You look like your father," Honey said after greeting Lenore.

Honey picked up Muffin from the floor and gave her a broad smile and a peck on her cheek. "You're a little sweetheart."

"Thank you," Muffin replied when she was back on the floor.

Finally came Gordy. He had to be in his late thirties now and his black hair was worn long like a mane. There were some grey streaks. Gordy had retained his sallow look.

"Well, if it isn't my long lost brother," he greeted Baxter. "Ma must have made you come."

"Best wishes of the day, Gordy." Baxter produced the envelope that contained his check from his suit pocket. "This is a little remembrance from us."

Gordy opened up the envelope in front of Baxter. The check was for $500. "Not bad, Joe," Gordy said and placed the envelope in his suitcoat pocket. "Glad you could come."

"He didn't seem very glad to see you," Joel commented when they had settled in a corner with soft drinks and Baxter's Canadian Club.

"He was glad to see our check," Baxter said.

Baxter unleashed Lenore, Joel, and Muffin to take pictures of the bridal party and began to circulate around the room. The reception attendees appeared to be a mixture of musicians, cocktail waitresses, and the people who hung around in the area south of Superior Street in Duluth. There were a number of blacks, but outside of the bartenders and serving people, there was only one Chinaman and that was Fong.

The reception line had dispersed and the room was filled with milling people. Mr. Fong paused to talk to Baxter, and Joel asked if he could take their picture together.

"I understand that Gordy's in your employ," Baxter addressed Fong. "What exactly does he do for you?"

"Gordy started as one of my drivers. He's a good smart young man who can be trusted and now I have him watching over a number of my business interests. I have some restaurants, night clubs, motels, and rental real estate. I need reliable people who can oversee things for me. Honey is a dancer at the Alley Cat Saloon. Have you ever visited the Alley Cat, Mr. Baxter?"

"I rarely come to Duluth, Mr. Fong," Baxter replied.

"The Alley Cat has been open ten years now. I opened it as a place for the sailors to visit when their docked ships at the end of Lake Superior. It is generally very busy. Tonight is a slow night. No ships in port."

"And Honey performs at the Alley Cat?" Baxter asked.

"She's been with us for nearly a year. That's a long time for a dancer. They tend to come and go, and sometimes come back. Flame has worked for us on and off for three or four years. The customers like to see new dancers. Honey has been a favorite. She goes by the name, Honey Lee Congo. But her real name is Mary Anne Jackson," Fong continued. "And you, Mr. Baxter, what do you do in Chicago?" Fong asked.

"I'm with the Internal Revenue Service," Baxter answered.

Mr. Fong slipped away and Baxter found his way over to Maggie and Karl. Joel and Muffin were now on their second roll of film with Lenore refilling the film cartridge.

"They sure are having fun with that camera," Maggie said with a beer stein in her hand.

Karl's hair was thinning and he seemed as bulky as his wife. He wore a dark shirt with a white tie under his plaid sport coat. "What do you think, Joe?" he asked.

"I think the kids will have taken enough pictures pretty soon to provide irrefutable evidence that I was here. Then I am going to get the hell out of here," Baxter responded.

"I mean, have you talked with Gordy and Honey?" Karl continued.

"I went through the reception line and I will say good night. That will be quite enough," Baxter said.

"Then you're just going to leave us alone with this problem? Just like you've walked away from every responsibility you've ever had?" Karl seemed angry and Maggie put her hand on his shoulder as if to calm him.

"Karl, I have met every obligation I've had back in Iron Creek. Should my mother become a financial burden, I'll help there. My brother is my brother. Give this thing a chance."

Baxter moved away from Maggie and Karl and began to work his way across the room to a table where the bridal party was seated. Flame, the red head, saw Baxter approaching the table. "Hey, Gordy. Here comes your brother."

Gordy and Honey stood up from the table. Honey smiled broadly displaying her sharp white teeth. "That was a very generous check," she said and kissed Baxter on the cheek. One of the groomsmen stood up and a chair was emptied for Baxter next to Honey.

"There are a lot of things to buy when you set up housekeeping. I thought a check would be handy," Baxter said. He seated himself between Honey and Gordy and was poured a glass of champagne.

"We set up housekeeping a lot time ago, Mister," Honey confessed.

"We're probably going to have a baby," Gordy added.

"Probably?" Baxter questioned.

"I got time to do otherwise, but I just might have this one," Honey said. "That sure is a nice little girl, you got. She told me she was taking pictures of me for her Grandmother Baxter, but that she was also going to show my picture to her Grandmother Washburn."

"So, Joe," Gordy began, "You still living in Chicago?"

"I'm moving to New York in April. When was the last time you saw Ma?"

"A month ago."

"You should get down there soon and bring Honey."

"Is Gordy's mother going to like me?" Honey asked.

"She likes very few people, but over time she'll tolerate you. I don't think she's got a lot of time left and Gordy has always been her favorite. It's important that you get down to see her soon."

Gordy nodded his head. Baxter took Honey's hand. "She's an old woman who has had her share of disappointments. Gordy has been very important to her."

One of the groomsmen tapped Gordy on the shoulder and announced that "Fong wanted to see him for a minute." Baxter suddenly found himself alone with Honey. Food had been served and there was a line forming in the direction of the buffet. The people in the line didn't seem to be concerned with the bride and groom leading the line.

"He talks about you, Joe," Honey said. "Gordy told me all about his older brother who was captain of the basketball team, went into the Army, finished at the university, went to work for a famous company and now travels all over the country. He really works hard for Fong. He used to come in and watch me dance. I used to see him standing at the bar watching me. Finally I got him to talk to me. Sometimes he's more like a boy than a man, but he's ready to watch out for me. I ain't never had that before."

"Where are you from?" Baxter asked.

"All over. I was born and lived in Winnipeg until I left high school. I have been down here ten years as an illegal alien. Where I've been working, people aren't fussy about work permits. Now I'm legal and a married lady."

"And my sister-in-law," Baxter agreed.

"How you feel about your brother marrying a black lady?"

"It's your business. You should get down to see our mother very soon. Where are you honeymooning?" Baxter asked.

"I'm going back to work at the Alley Cat Monday night. I'm working through New Year's. And that's it for a while."

Baxter rose up from the table. "I'm going to gather up my children and leave."

"Will I see you again?" Honey asked.

"Probably not," Baxter squeezed her hand and kissed Honey on the forehead.

Joel and Muffin were seated on the floor eating from heaping plates of Chinese food while Lenore watched over them.

"Want to go in a few minutes, guys? It's getting late."

"We want to have dessert," Joel demanded.

Baxter gave them a half-hour. He was on his last Canadian Club when Gordy approached him anxiously. "Did you tell Fong you were an IRS agent?" he demanded.

Joel and Muffin slept soundly in the back seat while Lenore rode with Baxter in the front seat animated and wired.

"What can I tell Rose Anne tomorrow, Dad? She expects me to come over after Church and tell her all about the wedding."

"Tell her that Gordy has married a nice girl from Canada and that he plans to bring her by to meet her very soon. That's all you should say."

Lenore shook her head. "It's just a hopeless situation. I know that Uncle Gordy has been in trouble and this woman is a nightclub dancer who takes off her clothes in front of men for money. Karl told me that Mr. Fong is a racketeer."

"You don't know that, Lenore. I talked with Honey and she impressed me as a straight forward logical person. Give them a chance, Lenore and stop being so judgmental," Baxter instructed his daughter.

Baxter drove in silence for five minutes before Lenore spoke again. It was a cold, crisp Northern Minnesota night and Highway 53 was dry.

"I just expressed myself in a very unChristian manner and I'm embarrassed. Please forgive me! You're right. I was being very judgmental about Gordy and Honey. I've got to help Mother and Rose Anne understand." Lenore's hand came to rest on her father's arm. "I do wish I lived close to you so that I could see you regularly. You're a very wise man, Dad. I found Jesus Christ and his influence on my life has been my guiding light. I found Jesus because you weren't here with me. You were someone who always sent nice gifts and checks, and I'm grateful for you helping me through Nursing School. I have loved being with you and the children tonight. Can I come out and see you when you're in New York?"

"Of course," Baxter replied and Lenore began to sob softly.

"I love you, Daddy."

Baxter rousted the children early in the morning and they were checked out from the Pennsylvania Hotel and on the road by 9:15. The children were wide awake for the trip back to Racine.

"I had a long talk with Mr. Fong, Dad," Joel said. "He seemed to think that you collected taxes from people. I told him you worked for McKenzie Barber, the most respected management consulting firm in the world, were very high up, and that you were moving to New York City. He seemed very happy to know what you did for a living."

Baxter drove the car over the Interstate Bridge into Wisconsin. Minnesota was behind him, as was Gordy's wedding, as was Iron Creek. He decided he would not be present at the 25th anniversary of the 1953 Cougars.

Christmas 1977 was a sad lonely time for Baxter. He had the children for company. The work activity pace slowed for the holidays and Baxter continued to live in his cramped studio apartment in Rosemont. He took the children to Sonny's for a production of *Man of LaMancha* and spent a couple of evenings drinking in the front bar while Buddy played the piano. Lorna and Baxter had Christmas drinks at Sage's East. She was usually good for insights into what was going on at McKenzie Barber.

Lorna was dressed smartly in a red suit with gold buttons and her hair was pinned tightly on top of her head. She did not look like anyone who had sung in the front bar of Sonny's. As in past conversations, Lorna opened up after her second martini.

"Burke is the one to watch. He seems to have accumulated a lot of power in this Partner-in-Charge of Strategic Planning job. He spends more time with Ernie Grey than anyone else including Clyde Nickerson. I shouldn't tell you this, but I will. They are about to close on an Employee Benefits consulting firm. It's called Frederick Partners Ltd and it's headed by a man named Walker Frederick, who is very well regarded. It's scheduled to be closed January 2nd."

"Where will Frederick report?" Baxter asked.

"To Bruce Dinsmore."

"Where will Alvardi report?"

"To Dirks."

"Then the Benefits practice will report one organizational level higher than Executive Compensation."

"Dinsmore will announce his retirement in August and a successor will be picked," Lorna reported.

"Who's going to succeed Dinsmore?" Baxter asked.

"Paul Brimmer. He's been promised the job by Ernie. The rumor is Burke might get Chicago. This means that Paul Brimmer will probably succeed Harvey and Dirks will get New York. Brimmer will succeed Ernie when he retires and Burke will become Deputy Chairman under Paul."

It rolled off Lorna's tongue as she sipped from her martini.

Would the boxes shift as fluidly in reality, Baxter wondered? Or would there be friction?

Baxter spent New Year's Eve, 1977, alone in his apartment, drinking Canadian Club, listening to Sondheim music, and reading his Christmas cards. His life in Chicago was coming to an end and in January he would look for an apartment in New York. At this time the previous year, Baxter had been unaware that Dominique Beaufort existed. He felt empty emotionally. Baxter was 42 years of age and outside his children, was quite alone. He began to sift through his Christmas cards.

From Jennifer:

Joe!

I was shocked to learn from the children that you had taken them back to Minnesota. They now reel off tales of Chinese gangsters and nightclub dancers and have pictures as evidence. You are not fit to be a parent and it's best that you're moving East. Your judgment is atrocious!

Yours in disappointment,
Jennifer

From Alice Dungler:

Merry Christmas! When the hell are you coming out to California again? There are some things I want to talk about with you. Give me an evening, dammit!

Alice

From Diane and Ed Ganski:

Good to see you, Joey. Looking forward to having you here this summer for the 25th.
Diane and Ed

From Lenore Baxter:

Daddy,
Good luck in the coming year. I will pray each day for you to Jesus Christ, our savior. I miss you and I love you.
Lenore

From Mr. and Mrs. Gordon Baxter

Thank you for coming to our wedding. We look forward to seeing you in the coming year.
Mr. and Mrs. Gordon Baxter

From Mr. and Mrs. Thomas Tweetman:

Joe,
How good to see you and meet your children! Try to visit us in our new home in Indianapolis during the coming year.
Tommy and Lucy

From Hamilton Burke III

Joe,
Looking forward to working with you in New York. Call me after the first of the year.
Ham

From Harley Dimon:

Best wishes for a joyous and wonderful holiday season for you and your family.
Harley

From Clyde and Mavis Nickerson:

Joe:
Yours in Christ for 1978.
Clyde

From Robert Friedman:

Looking forward to working closely with you in 1978.
The "Redeye" builds character.
Bob

From Teri:

Joe,
I think of you fondly and I'm not angry with you for
being such a shit to me when I moved out. I'm appearing in
a Dallas Dinner Theatre in *A Little Night Music*. Soon I'll be
old enough to play Madame Armfeldt. I miss your big body.
Merry Christmas.
Teri

From Lee Heller:

Joe,
I've heard the news about your coming to New York.
I'm very excited for you and offer my help in getting you
settled.
Lee
P.S. Andy Bourke says Hi!

From Andrea Bourke:

Joe,
I'm very excited about you moving to New York. At
last we'll have the opportunity to spend some "quality time"
together.
Andy
P.S. Natalie is now the mother of three!

From John Grunwaldyt:

Hi Joe,
Remember me? I hear you're moving to New York. Good luck and look me up.
Jon

From Jeff Long:

Merry Christmas, Cap'un,
I'm married now to a nice Atlanta girl and have an offspring on the way. I am now a Vice President with a venture capital company called Southwest Technological Services. A card is enclosed. McKenzie Barber is well into my past, but I still remember the day you and I went into the barrel in front of Chairman Grey. I also remember other events rather clearly like the night in the Sherry Netherland.
Jeff

From Bridgette Morgan:

So Joe,
You seem to have disappeared on me. My sister asks about you each day. She wants to meet you and will go roller skating with you at the drop of a hat. I described you as just another one of those men who kisses and flies away. I'd catch my sister quick. She's beginning to attract attention and the only Morgan girl left will be me. Merry Christmas!
Bridgette

PS I'm doing very well at Incognito. You might try writing. My sister thinks I made you up.

Baxter received one hundred cards without notes but nothing came from Dominique.

The period between the second day of January and the thirty-first day of March 1978 was another one of the great blurs in Baxter's professional life. He was on planes four days a week, and in the office two days a week. On Sundays he stayed in his studio apartment, drank coffee, read the *New York Times* Sunday edition, and read books about New York. He wrote a brief note to Bridgette Morgan about moving to New York and one week later received a large package of paper back books and maps showing how and where to live in New York City and its environs. She called Baxter twice in Chicago and he had been traveling. He, in turn, called her three or four times only to have a hard-bitten voice with a Bronx accent inform Baxter that Miss Morgan was traveling and interrogate him on why he was calling her.

A postcard arrived at the office with a view of the Hong Kong harbor on one side and the following message:

> Joe,
>
> What good news about you coming to New York. My sister was thrilled! I went down to the Barnes & Noble and picked out a mess of stuff for you to look over. I'm in the Far East for three weeks of work and one week of vacation. Do not move to Queens or the 300 block on 37th Street because that's where I live. 232 6C to be exact. Will be back in late Feb! Jesus! I've run out of space.
>
> Bridgette

Baxter located an unfurnished studio apartment on 78th Street between First Avenue and York. The building was a yellow brick eight story building with a single creaking elevator. The living room looked out on 78th Street and the kitchen window had an excellent view of an air shaft. Baxter took occupancy on March 1st with a one year lease, bought a sofa bed at Jennifer Convertibles and a lamp at the Second Avenue Bazaar. He would ship the rest of his things from Rosemont the last week in March.

He was set up to be a New Yorker effective April 3rd 1978.

Baxter finally had his fifteen minutes with Bruce Dinsmore during the first week of March. He was a tall, courtly, silver haired man in a blue three piece pin stripe suit, red tie, and gleaming black shoes.

"So you're Joe," he greeted Baxter after Miss Bunker, his secretary, had ushered Baxter into a large corner office. There was a massive desk with only an empty blotter and a pen set. It was a desk without paper or In and Out baskets. Dinsmore directed Baxter over to his couch and seated himself in a chair adjacent to the couch. A silver coffee service was on the coffee table and there were china cups similar to the ones Baxter had seen in Leon Harwell's offices.

"How about some coffee?"

"Please," Baxter said. "Black is fine."

His secretary poured two cups and looked to Dinsmore for further instructions. "That will be all for now, Charlotte. Hold my calls until Joe and I have finished our talk." Dinsmore waited until Mrs. Bunker left the office before he spoke.

"I've seen your personnel file and some very flattering recommendations about you. It looks like you're going to be a real addition to the New York office."

"Thank you, Mr. Dinsmore," Baxter responded cautiously. The man had been described as a figurehead and a shelf sitter, but Baxter recognized he was entering a new country with a temporary visa.

"Now what promises were made to you relative to your transfer?"

"The conditions and understanding of my transfer were committed in writing and you signed the document, sir." Dinsmore's eyebrows arched slightly. "Refresh me on what the memorandum said. I'll have Mrs. Bunker locate a copy later."

"I'm to relocate to the New York office effective April 3rd, 1978 as a Director in the Executive Compensation practice. I will report to Mr. Alvardi and provide oversight to the other practices around the country while assisting Frank in providing service to New York office clients. I have been nominated by the Chicago office for the Partnership and it is expected that I will be on the August ballot for partnership."

"We put that in writing?" Dinsmore asked.

"It was contingent on sustained performance and achievement of my goals."

"And how are you coming on your goals."

"I'm ahead of plan."

"Has anyone mentioned the acquisition of Frederick Partners to you?"

"I've heard bits and pieces, Mr. Dinsmore," Baxter responded.

"Well, Frederick Partners is a major step forward for McKenzie Barber to enter the Human Resources consulting market. We looked at the major benefits firms and really couldn't find a match culturally. Frederick Partners is one of the fastest growing, most highly respected Pension Consulting firms in the country. Walker Frederick will prove to be one of the most able direct admission partners the firm has ever attracted. He will bring with him a firm of fifty professionals with revenues of $8 million to McKenzie Barber. It will be a wonderful boost for the New York office. Frederick Partners can bridge the way into new client bases and segments. In our negotiations, Walker insisted on reporting to me directly. Now, Joe, you're wondering what all this has to do with your partnership nomination, aren't you?"

Baxter nodded and said "yes". He was beginning to smell a rat."

"Originally, in our negotiations, we anticipated that Walker would bring all of his senior people in as McKenzie Barber Partners. The remainder of his senior people would join McKenzie Barber at the Director level with the anticipation that they would be nominated for Partnership either next year or the year after. But then, over the last three weeks, we've had discussions with Walker's senior people. They hadn't shared in the buy-out revenues and were concerned with their chances of achieving Partnership after the merger. While intensely loyal to Walker, these senior people were ready to consider other career opportunities unless they joined McKenzie Barber as Partners. They are people with advanced technical skills, who according to Clyde Nickerson, would be very difficult to duplicate in the marketplace. We then put our heads together and decided to accept three additional Partners with the Fredericks' acquisition. However, with the addition of these three Partners, Joe, I'm afraid there will be no room for you in the New York office this year as an October 1st admission. Unfortunately, we have no other recourse than to defer you this year and place you in nomination for October 1, 1979. A year won't be so long and it will give you time to be accustomed to the New York office. We will see that you're not hurt financially," Dinsmore smiled warmly. "What do you say, Joe?"

Baxter stared straight ahead at Bruce Dinsmore's polished clean desk. He had been promised and the promise has been committed in writing. Now Dinsmore was proposing that Baxter accept a deferral.

"I'm having some difficulty with your arithmetic, Bruce," Baxter said staring at the desk and onto the Manhattan skyline. "You're proposing seven Partners from Frederick Partners for a $8 million practice. That's revenues per Partner of less than $1.5 million. I have a plan of $2.3 million this year. That would make me twice as productive as each one of those Frederick Partner admissions."

"You can't very well count Walker Frederick any more than you would include Ernie Grey in the McKenzie Barber Partner headcount," Dinsmore cautioned with a short nervous laugh.

"Take Mr. Frederick out and those admissions soar up to $1.33 million," Baxter computed. "That's below firm average and it's way behind my level of productivity."

"They're going to grow rapidly with us. I would expect then to be up to $10 or $11 million by FY 1979."

"I don't believe they can hire people fast enough to sustain that kind of growth the first year. You're suggesting that this new practice will grow in the 25 to 37% range during their first year as a McKenzie Barber practice. I personally doubt whether that kind of growth can be achieved. If it is, the average Partner will be up to $1.8 million and change excluding Mr. Frederick. You're going to be over-partnered in the Employee Benefit practice, Bruce."

"Joe," Dinsmore was shaking his head. "If Benefits were a mature practice, I would agree with your thinking. But it is new for McKenzie Barber and its client base and we must invest in the growth of this new practice area. Mature practices must support the growth practices. One of the reassurances that I had to provide Walker is that he would report directly to me. The second is that I would defer my retirement until 1982. It will mean some sacrifices for Mrs. Dinsmore, because she believes I've given too much of my life already to McKenzie Barber. I like to point out that Mr. Mac stayed until 75. The only way I'd step down now would be if Ernie Grey would ask me personally to do so in order to plan his own succession. I suspect that Ernie will stay until he's 65. I'll tell you this in confidence. Walker Frederick could well be my successor and he could be the chairman of this firm one day, Joe."

Baxter, who had been on the edge of the couch, settled back. Here was a man, who was either ahead of the pack or whom the pack had left behind. "I would like to meet Mr. Frederick on my next visit. In light of our discussion this afternoon, I may amend my decision to move to New York. I will either stay in Chicago or pursue a transfer discussion with Bob Friedman in Los Angeles."

"But, Joe. It's agreed that you are coming to New York. It's too late now really to reverse that decision. Frank Alvardi is counting on you, and the Operating Committee has approved your transfer. All I have asked you to do is to defer your partnership nomination for one year. I will be the New York Office Managing Partner through September 30th, 1981, and I assume that you will be a two year Partner at the time of my retirement. This will provide me the opportunity to increase your units of interest substantially in 1980 and 1981. I will guarantee you that you won't lose a penny by allowing us to defer you this year."

"But I wasn't planning to be deferred this year, Bruce," Baxter stated.

Bruce Dinsmore's door opened and Mrs. Bunker stood framed in the doorway in a black suit. "Mr. Dinsmore, your four o'clock appointment has been waiting nine minutes."

"Oh dear, Charlotte. Joe and I were in the midst of a most interesting discussion and I lost track of time. I would like you to arrange for Joe to meet Walker. Would you take care of that?"

"Yes, Mr. Dinsmore. Won't you come this way, Mr. Baxter." Baxter rose and Bruce Dinsmore gripped his hand in both of his hands. "Joe, I'm so glad we could have this talk. I like your sense of 'give and take'. I'm looking forward to having you as part of my New York office." The audience was over.

Baxter tried to call Dirks, Burke, and Alvardi in rank order from a lobby payphone in the Waldorf. They were all out of the office. Miraculously he found Dwyer in.

"Bill, Joe here," he greeted the voice that answered. "Dwyer".

"What kind of guy is Bruce Dinsmore?"

"He was the finest Industrial Engineering Consultant who ever lived in 1952. The poor old boy hasn't had an insight since. He is clearly a cork that floated to the top. I keep him far away from clients and anyone we want to impress who's likely to ask questions. He's a bit of a silver fox politically."

"How much power does he have?" Baxter asked.

"He had a great deal of power at one time, but now he seems to lose twenty watts a day. Everyone is waiting for Ernie to pull the circuit breaker on him," Dwyer responded.

"Can he block anything? Does he have any monkey wrenches left?"

"Joe, I doubt whether he really knows which end of the wrench to pick up these days. He's slipping fast, but not fast enough for some. What's bothering you, lad?"

"Should I take him seriously?"

"I would, but not a day after July 30th, because that's the day Ernie is going to ask him to step down."

"How can you be sure of that?" Baxter asked.

"Part of being in the New York office, lad, is having sound sources of information from Executive Office. Mr. Dinsmore will retire this year and go off into the happy Industrial Engineering land and eventually do methods work for the Lord. Take him seriously until the end of July and be damned careful of his successor. It's a matter of the devil you know versus the devil you don't know. There will be old scores to be settled. I have to run, lad. Looking forward to having you out here. We'll have to have a glass together."

Dwyer clicked off and Baxter stared at the Waldorf wall for a minute. The hell with it! It was too late to turn back!

Packing made the move a reality. Baxter packed the things he had accumulated over his five years in the Rosemont apartment into five large boxes and two clothes hampers. In addition, there was a couch, a sound system, a chest, three lamps, two bookcases, and a bed. Other than his bank account and his career at McKenzie Barber, he was asset-less. Jennifer was adamant that the children spend a minimum of one month in the summer with their father. This would free her up to travel with her latest lover. Baxter sipped his coffee in silence and waited for the movers to arrive.

He had slept his last night in the lonely white walled apartment and now he was moving across the country where he would move into another lonely apartment which was slightly smaller. After the movers came to collect his belongings, Baxter would take a taxi to the airport and board a plane to Los Angeles. There he would meet with Bob Friedman and Floyd Piper to establish Executive Compensation practice plans and goals for the remainder of FY 1978 and FY 1979. Baxter expected to spend Wednesday, March 29th in LA and catch the morning flight on Thursday, March 30th to

New York. He would arrive around six o'clock on Thursday and would have a three day weekend to settle into New York City.

The Chicago office had held a party for Baxter the evening before. Around thirty five people had turned out. Brimmer made a short speech and Baxter was given an expensive leather brief case with his initials embossed on it. Lorna had kissed him lightly on the mouth while Brimmer was on the other side of the room with his back to them. "I'll miss you," she said sadly.

"Are you going to come out and see me in New York?" Baxter asked.

"I hate New York, Joe," she answered.

Baxter felt very hollow. He had felt that way on the bus back to Fort Gately from Iron Creek and the time before Captain Dubak had rescued him from the Northeast Minneapolis rooming house. New York City was ahead for Baxter. Behind him was Iron Creek, Washburn Manufacturing, Jennifer, Joel and Muffin, the house on Palmer Street, and the burning memory of five days of love in Paris with a woman Baxter was unlikely to ever see again. There was a loud knock on the door and Baxter knew that the movers had arrived. Good-bye Chicago!

Baxter was scheduled to meet with Bob Friedman and Floyd Piper at 2 o'clock. Alice Dungler had left word with the receptionist and Friedman's secretary to route Baxter to her office when he arrived.

Alice had a window office a floor below the main reception area. It was cluttered with computer tapes, print-outs, ring binders, and file folders. It was the messiest office Baxter had ever seen at McKenzie Barber. On top of a file cabinet was a Mister Coffee with the coffee pot burned dry.

Alice was at an easel with a felt tip pen while two young men sat in side chairs reverently following the flow chart she was developing.

"Hi," Baxter said from the doorway of Alice's office. "I hear you're looking for me."

"Mr. Baxter!" Alice grinned. She wore a long sleeved white blouse, clip-on earrings, dark skirt, and black suede pumps. Baxter had never seen Alice in high heels before. Alice Dungler would never be pretty, but today she appeared to be attractive. She introduced her audience as Aaron and Paul. They were Information Technology Associates and the discussion was centered around computer hardware selection.

"Let's take a break guys. Mr. Baxter is in from Chicago to meet with Bob and Floyd this afternoon and then he's off to New York. I need some time with him. Let's pick this up around 2:30."

There were some limp handshakes and Baxter was alone with Alice. They ordered lunch in and Alice cleared off a spot on the corner of her desk for Baxter's sandwich and her salad.

"So, you're going through with it," Alice commented.

"It's the right thing to do," Baxter said.

Alice's door was closed and Baxter could see the outline of the Atlantic Richfield Building from her window.

"I think you're making a mistake. You should come out here and you should start working on it when you're in there this afternoon with Bob and Floyd. When do you leave?"

"In the morning."

"Do you have a hotel?"

"I have reservations at the Sheraton Grand," Baxter answered.

"Have dinner with me tonight. I'm north of the airport. I'll get you a room out by me and cancel you out of the Sheraton. Okay?"

"Just get me on the plane to New York when it's time to go," Baxter responded. He had sought Alice out because she was a well informed resource on the Western Region. He had intentionally arranged to meet with her before the session with Friedman and Piper. "Alice, tell me about Floyd Piper."

"He's everybody's golden boy. The only thing he loves more than the sound of his own voice is looking at himself in the mirror. He made Partner when he was in his twenties, married a socially well connected lady, and is very visible in the right circles. No one can ever remember Floyd distinguishing himself as a consultant. He's very good getting people in at the right levels of organizations. I see him as a highly skilled maitre'd who can barely remember the specials. The San Francisco office is very profitable and Floyd's got Ernie Grey and the Operating Committee convinced that it's that way because he knows what he's doing. He probably wanted to have the meeting with you in San Francisco. He regards Friedman as a junior Managing Partner who requires mentoring."

"And how's Friedman doing?" Baxter asked.

"Someone gave him a bottle of Managing Partner pills. I think he's on three a day. He's very serious and all of his discussions one on one with Partners and Directors when he can remember their names, are very strategic, tactical, fiscal and antiseptic. He's trying to be a serious leader. He has a new picture of his wife and kids in his office and I think he even took one of the Jewish Holidays off. I'm up early in the morning and caught him one morning having breakfast with a little number at an oceanside place up in Santa Barbara. She looked a little tousled. I suspect that he's cleaned up his act a little, but our boy, Bob, still thinks he's got the best gun in the West. He sucked Floyd Piper into a Managing Partners tennis match a month ago and cleaned his clock in public. Floyd is starting to get a little wary of our Bobby."

It was a quarter of two. Baxter got up from his side of the desk. "I better get going."

"Count your money before you go in the room with those two," Alice counseled. "I'm canceling your hotel and you're staying out by me tonight, Joe. I may even cook."

Baxter met with Bob Friedman and Floyd Piper in the small conference room adjoining Friedman's large corner office. They sat around an oval shaped table and three was a silver coffee service, an ice cub bowl and soft drinks atop of a small cabin in the corner of the room.

Floyd Piper was wearing a grey Armani vented suit with a red tie. Friedman wore a dark blue three piece suit. Floyd smiled a warm greeting to Baxter, while Friedman appeared to be in a very serious mood. He gave Baxter a wisp of a cold smile with a handshake. Baxter seated himself with Piper on his left and Friedman on his right.

"Well, Joe," Friedman began. "Floyd and I concluded that a personal meeting with you would be appropriate and critical before you got settled in New York. We have both been very displeased with the level of support we have received from the Executive Compensation practice leadership. We have been informed that your new role in New York will be to support the operating offices. We have also been advised that effective April 3rd, part of your New York office cost of service will be debited back to the Los Angeles and San Francisco offices."

"Joe, Bob and I wanted to have this meeting with you to establish some ground rules and objectives," Floyd added with a benign smile. "This debit note scheme looks like the brain child of Hamilton Burke, the Partner in Charge of Strategic Planning. Burke was over at Barber Europe for eight or nine years. He really doesn't have a feel for the way we work in the U.S. They have a lot of inter-office charging over there and they're always fighting with each other."

"We work in great harmony out here on the west coast, Joe," Friedman stated.

Baxter had two weeks to prepared for the meeting and had prepared a flip-chart passout organized into three sections. The dividers were labeled:

- Past Client Service
- Market Opportunities 1978-1980
- Longer Term Initiatives & Goals

"Let me take you through what I've observed. Then let me get your input on this retrospective. We'll get agreement on what has to be done and how to measure progress. Then we'll get it done," Baxter said.

He treated Friedman and Piper like clients. The meeting lasted two hours while they debated, nit-picked, and inflated the goals. In the end there was controlled enthusiasm. Floyd Piper said over and over again how much he liked Baxter's approach and format. "I'd like to have every one of my practice units go through this process," Floyd said enthusiastically.

"We've had a similar process in place in Los Angeles for two years now, Floyd," Friedman commented.

Floyd Piper excused himself to make some calls and Friedman invited Baxter into his private office.

"So you're New York bound, Joe. I really had hoped that you would transfer out here," Friedmans said. He was opening the door for the Los Angeles transfer again. "There's potentially a bigger market on the west coast than there is on the east coast and far less cluttered with competition. When you get tired of that dirty New York City life, Joe, there will always be a place for you in sunny California."

"What do you know about Walker Frederick and Frederick Partners?" Baxter asked.

"We've just acquired them. I was on the review team. He has a good little business that Burke overpaid for. Now they're making a bunch of them Partners. He's coming out to see me next week. Walker wants to hire about 100 people during FY 1978 and FY 1979 and set up practices in every major office of the firm. The firm has bumbled around for three years trying to acquire a major Employee Benefits Consulting firm. Burke took over the responsibility last summer and he got it done. Frederick Partners is probably as good as we're going to do. Ernie has placed Burke on the Operating Committee. You can bet that got everybody's attention. I understand that you know Burke pretty well, Joe."

"I knew him from Washburn Manufacturing Company. That was ten years ago. He was the consultant and I was the client liaison representative. I lost track of him when he went to Europe."

"I spent some time with him on the Frederick Partners review. He seemed to know you pretty well. He was out here a month ago and spoke very highly of you again. You weren't in the Army with him were you? Clyde Nickerson told me once that you were in some kind of tactical commando outfit."

Baxter was tempted to correct Friedman and explain about his time as a clerk for Sergeant Wilson, but decided to let it ride. Baxter simply shook his head and said that they had been in different wars.

"When do you go back, Joe?" Friedman asked.

"Tomorrow morning. I'm having dinner tonight with Alice Dungler," Baxter said.

"Alice Dungler?" Friedman looked at Baxter in shock. "How did you ever get acquainted with Alice Dungler?"

316

"I met her at the Train-the-Trainers conference that Nickerson put on last June. I find her very outgoing and able. I dropped by to see her before our meeting this afternoon," Baxter explained.

"Alice Dungler was here? In this office during the day?" Friedman questioned.

"She's a floor below. Keeps a full office," Baxter commented.

"Alice Dungler is our phantom Information Technology Director. One day soon, I expect that she will become our Phantom Partner. She rarely comes to the office during the day. She tends to come at night in her sweats. Alice has never attended a management group meeting. She always gets work and does it to the client's expectations. She sells, bills, collects, and gets her time sheets in one time. I do wish she could write more often. Even a card would be nice. She's a bit of an Amazon as I remember her. I would think that you would have other alternatives for this evening. I'm beginning to suspect that you're a rather unorthodox person, Joe. You may be some kind of pervert if you're having dinner with Alice Dungler. Most of the men, and a good deal of the women in the LA office, fear her. There have been some instances of male consultants who went out for dinner with Alice and were never heard from again. It's been rumored that she fucked them and then ate them."

Baxter looked across the desk at Friedman and concluded that it was time for him to take another Managing Partner pill.

Baxter awoke for the first time at five in the morning. He could feel the sea breeze from the window against his naked body which was only partially covered by a bed sheet. Where the hell was he? Baxter looked around and identified a snoring Alice Dungler beside him. Her muscular body was hoarding the single sheet. They were sleeping on a king size water bed in front of the window. Baxter's body was still on Central Standard time. He had a terrible headache and was very thirsty.

Baxter boasted himself up from bed and peered out at the 5AM darkness. The waves were rolling in against the sand and a light rain was coming down. Alice Dungler lived in an apartment without walls. The floors were bare with some furry scatter rugs and the long loft-like room was divided into sections. The mattress was in the rear of the two story duplex building facing the ocean. There was a kitchen area at the far end of the room marked by a table and four chairs. A conversational area was centered around Alice's sound system, an athletic area where the weights Alice lifted and the exercise machines were grouped, and finally there was an area with personal computers, printers, and a mini-computer. Without walls, the room was an enormous hall with a series of interest areas.

At the far end of the room was the bathroom. Baxter carefully padded his way across the room in bare feet to the bathroom at the far end of the enormous room. There was a large digital scale on the floor and the room was littered with skin creams and body oils. It took Baxter the better part of five minutes to locate the aspirins. He took two with a glass of water, relieved himself, and padded his way back to the bed. How had he gotten there?

Alice had driven Baxter north of Los Angeles and they were slightly beyond Ventura. Alice had insisted on cooking and they drank two bottles of wine while Alice prepared salmon on the grill.

"You don't have any walls?" Baxter commented after he was inside the apartment.

"Had them all knocked out," Alice explained. "I need open space."

"How far am I away from the motel?" Baxter had asked.

"You're in the motel, Joe," Alice affirmed.

They started to drink Tequila after dinner and Alice provided Baxter a tutorial on personal computers and network systems. "I used to be hog fat," Alice said. "They called me Porky in high school. I discovered exercise in college. Now I'm all muscle." She took Baxter's hand. "Feel me!" Alice guided him to her arm and then down across her hips to her thighs down to her calves. "It's all muscle, Joe. Now let's see what you're all about." Alice unzipped Baxter's fly and began to fondle him. "You have possibilities. Let's take off some clothes."

Alice Dungler was a powerful, aggressive lover. Baxter hadn't been with a woman since Dominique and Alice proved to be overwhelming. She mounted Baxter and pounded on him for the better part of thirty minutes. Her skin had the quality of hard rubber and she kissed Baxter with long wet hungry kisses from her enormous mouth. Baxter thought of Friedman's theory. 'She fucks them and then she eats them!'. Alice tended to have short spurting kinds of orgasms. Baxter counted twelve before she dozed off in his arms. Somewhere in the haze of white wine, Tequila, personal computers, weight lifting and exercise equipment. Alice had talked about a software development company she had formed. Baxter had agreed to visit it with her and take a later flight to New York. He could remember producing his ticket for Alice and a call being made to American Airlines.

"You've got the last seat in the front of the plane. 5B. Remember that!"

Now it was the next morning and all Baxter could remember was 5B. He hoped it would be a mid-day flight.

Baxter stared out at the water in the early morning darkness before he realized that the sun would be coming up behind him. Alice was brilliant, energetic, and physically powerful. She was potentially the most intimidating woman he had ever met.

Alice stirred and then brought herself upright moving a wave from the waterbed to Baxter's side of the mattress.

"5:20. Morning begins at 6 AM for this lady. Come on over here for a while, big boy." Baxter slid back on to the mattress and was greeted with a flurry of aggressive kisses about his body. "You're as good as I always thought you'd be, Joe."

They showered together after the six o'clock alarm went off and Baxter breakfasted on orange juice, coffee, and toast while Alice spooned away on oat based concoction with bananas and goat's milk. She dressed in a sweatshirt, shorts, and tennis shoes.

"I understand that you changed my flight last night," Baxter said.

"You agreed to see my company. It's north of here and we have a drive of about an hour or so. I'm just north of San Luis Opispo. You're on the "red eye". Leaves LAX at 10 PM arrives at JFK 6:03 AM on Friday. You won't miss a thing."

"Alice, what kind of a business are you operating? Isn't there a line in the Consultant's agreement that you devote full efforts to the interests of McKenzie Barber?"

"Oh, fuck that gobbledygook! I give the boys at McKenzie Barber as much of Alice Dungler as they're entitled. I make a lot of money for McKenzie Barber. But I'm at a time when I want to make a little money for Alice Dungler. Now that we've gotten sex out of the way, I want to make you a business proposition."

"What kind of proposition?" Baxter questioned.

"All in good time, handsome Joe. Take a cup of coffee for the car and don't put a necktie on. We might as well go to work. It will be the better part of the day before you'll be good for anything more than work."

They drove up Highway 101 in Alice's blue Volvo to the outskirts of San Luis Opispo and turned off into a small office park. The office park was a two story building fronted by a large parking lot and populated by an insurance brokerage, two law offices, an accounting firm, a sales office for a scientific instrument company, a title insurance branch office, a mortgage banking office, and an office supply store. Pacific Technologies was located in a rear office at the end of the hall.

"How long has Pacific Technologies been in existence?" Baxter asked as they drew up to a blonde wood door with black lettering.

"About eighteen months. I started up with my own money and then got some venture capital people to pop for some seed money." Alice punched a combination on the door, a buzzer sounded, and a red light over the keyboard turned green. Baxter followed Alice into a room full of Asians and East Indians. There were long benches with personal computers, computer tapes, floppy discs, displays, and printers. Alice was greeted by "good mornings" and "Hi Alice's". She escorted Baxter to the rear of the room where there was a small cubicle stacked with papers.

"This is the President's office, Joe. Pretty splashy, huh?" The door to the office was glass and there was a glass window on the wall outside that allowed Alice to view the entire room. There was a knock at the door and a Chinese girl in tee shirt, shorts, and sandals appeared with a pile of checks in her arms.

"Stick 'em there, Mary," Alice instructed the girl to leave the checks on a cleared corner of the right hand corner of her desk. "Say hello to Mr. Baxter. Joe, this is Mary Chin, our Controller. Mary, this is Joe Baxter. He's from McKenzie Barber and he works in New York."

Mary brightened and extended her hand timidly. "I'm glad to meet you, Mr. Baxter."

"Mary's been with me from the beginning, Joe. She's got an undergraduate degree in Accounting and is working on a MS in Computer Science at Cal Poly. She's very good at stretching out payables and collecting receivables. She and I represent the business brains of this outfit."

Mary Chin smiled self-consciously. "Not at all. Alice is the brains and I do what she wants me to. We are going to have a very successful company one day, Mr. Baxter."

"Mary, the checks I sign may be mailed on Friday at the last pick-up. The ones I don't sign, you should save for a week from tomorrow. Call each supplier and tell them that our Payables file has been misplaced and ask them to send a new bill. Promise that they will be paid within seven days after we receive their duplicate invoice."

"Yes, Alice." Mary Chin smiled a gentle compliant smile. "Nice to have met you, Mr. Baxter. I hope that I will see you again."

The glass door closed behind Mary. "You won't believe this, Joe, but Mary is one tough, cunning little bitch. She knows the game we're playing and recognizes the upside. Let me tell you about Pacific Technologies——."

They drank coffee from styrofoam cups, and Alice talked for about an hour with only limited interruptions. Alice signed checks as she talked. The checks that she did not sign were placed in a neat pile on the right hand side of the desk. Baxter noted that at the completion of Alice's soliloquy, the pile on the right hand side on her desk was twice as high as the pile of signed checks.

Alice Dungler was convinced that the personal computer was going to change the world. "Everyone will own a personal computer by the early 80's and PCs will move into the commodity stage of their life cycle. It will be similar to pocket calculators. The big money is to be made in software development. All those PCs are going to need software. That's what we're developing here. Plain vanilla software for the common man. Later we're going to move into other flavors for more discriminating tastes. Picture the model T Ford with the option of only one or two highways that take you

320

way out of your way. We're building the new highways that will provide the direction to take the computer user where he wants to go———."

Alice tended to be technical, but she verbalized concepts with clarity. Pacific Technologies software was now in the field and sales were beginning to build. The venture capitalists were ready to come in with more money to finance the growth of the company. Their stipulation for financing was that Alice leave McKenzie Barber and come in as a full time CEO of the company. "They want me to step away from my hobby and play for keeps. I'm going to do it, Joe."

"Leave McKenzie Barber, Alice? That sounds high risk," Baxter commented.

"Staying with McKenzie Barber in their Information Technology practice is high risk, Joe," Alice corrected Baxter. "They fall further behind each day, thanks to their numskull leadership. They are going to be marginally competitive in Information Technology by the early 1980's, but won't have caught on that they're marginally competitive until the mid-1980's. If I run this company correctly, guess right on the market demand, and mange the costs properly, I can make some serious money when I take the company public. I'm talking millions. Let me take you through the pro-formas, Joe."

"The five year pro-formas showed a $45 million revenue business that would made 15% pre-tax. Those are junk numbers. Venture capitalists like to see numbers and 15% pre-tax is one of their favorite percentages. They prefer 30%, but will accept 15%. These guys are well dressed car salesmen who have access to capital. They don't know a lot about internal combustion, but will fall in love with hood ornaments and believe they know all about cars. I believe we can do one hell of a lot better than that, Joe, if I can bring in the right EXP & COO. I need someone to pick up the business side. You know Finance, Sales and Marketing, and Administration. I'll run the software engineering and operations sided of the business. I need a partner, Joe."

"Do you have any prospects?" Baxter asked.

"One! You!"

"Jesus, Alice, I'm moving to New York and starting Monday. I know nothing about the computer software business and have a very primitive knowledge of computers. I have a child support obligation to my ex-wife, and I expect to be elected a Partner of McKenzie Barber in October."

"What sorry logic, Joe! Let me explain why you should jump at this opportunity! First, I think you and I would be something special together. We had our first run physically last night and I feel pretty good about it. Second, I can teach you the software business. You will never be a techy, but you would be a super business manager. You know financial reporting and finance, and you're good with people. I've seen you in action. You're a leader! You're probably better fit to run a company than I am because you're more patient. You're also good on the platform, which would help us with our shareholders and analysts and help us with our PE multiple. When the new money comes in, I'll pay as much as I can, more than me if it's necessary. Your kids would be better off in California than out in Wisconsin. There's no comparison in quality of life or life style. Take it from me, I used to live in Pittsburgh. Now let's talk about McKenzie Barber. Ten years from now, the firm is going to be a real loser. It's falling behind in every discipline to Robson Allen and there are a number of consulting firms started by ex-McKenzie Barber and Robson Allen trained people who are closing in behind them. The only competitive advantage McKenzie Barber has now is Europe. They were there first and they're hanging on. The US firm is irretrievably behind in Information Technology and every other practice is in jeopardy in terms of market erosion. You've been promised to be elected a Partner in October! Watch your head! They promise people things like that and they defer you! You know why they have to defer new Partners? Because the firm isn't growing fast enough in profits to support new Partners and they can't get the old time coasting Partners to retire because they're making too much money. They just bought this Employee Benefits Consulting firm, Frederick's & something. They are making a bunch of Partners to accommodate these Frederick's people. Ernie Grey doesn't think the firm has enough women Partners. So I get a call from Floyd Piper asking to meet with me for breakfast. I get myself dollied up and drive way the hell up to San Jose for breakfast with Floyd. He proceeds to give me a song and dance about McKenzie Barber needing women Partners. I suspect that he was just out of an Operating Committee meeting with Ernie Grey and our Chairman demanded to know where all the firm's women Partner candidates were."

"Floyd, baby, said that if I were to request an immediate transfer to San Francisco, he would see that I was on the Partner admission list they would vote on after Labor Day. Then he went on to say that Bob Friedman was new as a Managing Partner and that he may not be as aggressive as he should in nominating Partner candidates his first year. But if I did what he suggested, Floyd was confident that he could nominate and elect me this Fall. In reality he wanted to bribe me to come up there and bail out his Information Technology practice. I asked him about all the names that were proposed in January. He told me that 50% of those names were deferred one to two years. So nothing is in the bag, Joe. McKenzie Barber likes to play games with people's lives and ambitions. I want to get out into the real world, and I want you to come with me. How about it?"

"Alice I'm very flattered that you would consider me, but I'm on my way to New York tonight."

Alice opened up a bottom drawer of the desk and produced a thick 9" by 14" McKenzie Barber envelope sealed with masking tape. A Pacific Technologies label said in large letters:

JOE BAXTER—-PRIVATE

"This is some reading material for the plane. I'll have the next stage of my financing by July. Then I'm going in to resign effective October 1st, so I'll get my bonus. That's when I want you ready to come, Joe. I'll want you to come out again in late May to meet with the venture capital people. Then we can tidy up a contract for you which will include moving expenses."

Baxter looked into Alice Dungler's hard blue eyes set into her full face. She was trying to pull Baxter into her entrepreneurial company much in the same manner that she had pulled him into her water bed the night before. Alice Dungler was a woman who went through life overwhelming people.

"I've got to think about this, Alice. If I were to come out here and be a part of this business, we couldn't very well be sleeping together. It would look like hell to the investors, the customers, and the employees. By the way, that Employee Benefits consulting firm McKenzie Barber acquired is called Frederick Partners. You're correct about the number of Partners. They are allowing them seven and there's talk of deferring me after making it a condition of transfer. I really don't know what I'm walking into out in New York."

Alice looked at her watch. "I don't know if I want you out here celibate. It's a beautiful day and I feel like playing hooky. What do you say we get some sandwiches, a couple of bottles of wine, sit on a blanket, and have a picnic?"

With Alice Dungler, Baxter concluded, there really weren't a lot of options.

They picnicked in Santa Barbara on a thick blanket under a large tree on a grassy stretch overlooking the ocean. Baxter purchased a transistor radio and they drank three bottles of Chardonnay while dining on French bread, brie, munster, pate, and ham. Baxter located the classical station and settled in for the afternoon.

"Now I'm blowing my diet for today. You're a corrupting influence. I had better get a good screwing before you get on that airplane," Alice said between chomps on French bread and brie. "You know what I think about you, Baxter? You're in control of most things, but I think women take advantage of you. You need someone who will look out for you. I know I can make a go out of Pacific Technologies. You could find a real home with me."

"Why won't becoming a Partner with McKenzie Barber do it for you? Why do you want to risk what you have in a start-up company?" Baxter questioned.

"Joe, I didn't come to McKenzie Barber as a graduate business school virgin. There are a lot of smart attractive people at McKenzie Barber, but the ones who run the firm are the political consultants. They seem to rise right up to the top. So what if I make Partner? They'll pay more money, give me more to do, expect more, and keep me in my place. I want something of my own. If I fall on my ass, I'll go back to work for somebody else. That's the way you should feel, Joe Baxter, victim of women! Right now, Joe, you're a nice person. You go out to New York and stay and you're going to be just like the rest of them. Cynical, slippery, self-centered, and mean spirited. You come to Mama! We'll build something really good together."

They spent the afternoon on the blanket. Alice wanted to kiss once or twice, but Baxter didn't find her the kind of woman he wanted to kiss. He felt about Alice in the same way he felt about Ganski and Mort Himmelman in the old days in Iron Creek. She was fun, stimulating to talk and drink with, and was like one of the guys.

They told each other their life histories that afternoon. Baxter talked about his father, Spike, the great strike of 1950, the 1952-53 Cougars, and marrying Maggie. Then he took her through Washburn Manufacturing, Jennifer Washburn, and his introduction to McKenzie Barber.

"You have been victimized by women," Alice commented and then took her turn to tell about her life. "I grew up in Pittsburgh. My father ran a butcher shop and I was well fed. The kids used to call me Fatty, and I didn't have a date until I was well into college. Next door to the butcher shop was a Chinaman, who ran a gift shop. I used to hang around there during my breaks. Mr. Han, his name was. He showed me how to operate his abacus and suddenly I was into math. Later at the University, I got into weight lifting and dieting. I decided that I would never be fat again. I also found that I like to drink and fuck, but I scared the shit out of most men. I started humping with the Associate Professors and moved up to the Full Professors. That's how I got into the Doctorate thing. It's amazing how much scholarship money is around if you do the right things with the right people. I was heavy into mathematics, computers, and recreational screwing with academics. Pretty soon I found out that I was smarter than most of the men I worked with. I was working for this think tank Research Group when McKenzie Barber recruited me. They wanted me for FSO and I told them no dice. McKenzie Barber was good for me. The Research Lab wanted me to be leading edge, but they weren't into making money. I saw how McKenzie

Barber made money and I told myself, 'Hell, I can make money as easily as they can'. I bitch about the firm a lot, but Jesus, it has discipline and professionalism! But then I asked myself, do you want this big, bad McKenzie Barber outfit to take charge of your life? My answer is no. I have learned a lot and I have a vision, Joe. I believe I can build an important software company. Joe, you knocked my socks off at that training conference. I started asking around about you. I found out that you are a folk hero to the women consultants because of the way you handled that FSO job. Everyone knew that your marriage was screwed up. There is also a story going around about you having an affair with one of the consultants who was on that FSO job. She was supposed to have been engaged and ready to drop her fiancé for you. She told one girlfriend in strict confidence who promptly told three other best friends, who told the story to only a few of their closest friends. That's how you became a legend, Joe."

"It's all fiction," Baxter said. "My real love is Andy Bourke."

"Shit! They haven't made enough KY to make that woman interesting to a man!" Alice ruled.

Baxter had a long shower around seven o'clock in Alice's apartment. He viewed it as a cleansing shower. He had done everything that had been expected of him, and it was time to go to New York and put California behind him.

Baxter boarded the "red eye" flight to New York at first call around 9:40 PM. Alice had offered to park and wait with Baxter at the Admiral's Club, but he left her at the curb with a short kiss and a promise to think hard about Pacific Technologies. It had been a full two days for Baxter and he was tired of people. He decided he would have two Canadian Clubs, listen to classical music on the headset, and try to sleep as much as possible.

Baxter was seated in 5B, an aisle seat in the smoking section of first class. The section was filled with the exception of 5A, the window seat to Baxter. It appeared that he would be traveling alone to New York. He welcomed the solitude. His original plan was to be in his New York apartment at this moment. Now he was subjecting himself to another "red eye" flight in order to spend a day with Alice Dungler. He decided to review the material she had provided him in the envelope, call Alice next week, tell her that while he was flattered, he simply could not consider it at this time.

Baxter listened with one ear while the senior flight attendant recited the safety instructions and the plane began to pull away from the ramp. Then the plan stopped suddenly and returned to the ramp. A bell rang and one of the flight attendants scurried to the door. The door was released and a tall thin figure wearing dark slacks, dark glasses, and a broad brimmed hat over a mink coat entered the plane with a hanging bag. "Please do something with this, young lady," a woman's authoritative voice instructed the flight attendant. Then she removed the fur coat and handed it to a second flight attendant. The figure started quickly down the aisle and came to rest at 5B, Baxter's seat.

"Good evening," she said. "I'm 5A."

Baxter rose up from his seat. The woman removed her hat placing it in the storage compartment and revealed lengthy black hair tied at the nape of her neck by a silk cord. She was clad in a black pants suit with a cropped jacket. Under the jacket, she wore a white blouse and a gold locket. Her long legs were capped by tall high heeled black boots. She had high cheekbones and wore aviator glasses.

"So glad you could join me," Baxter greeted his seating companion.

"They closed the door forty-five Goddam seconds early," she replied. "I was on an important call. Young lady!" The flight attendant was commanded firmly. "As soon as we're up, I'd like a Remy and some coffee."

The plane pulled away form the gate again. "I prefer the aisle seat. Would you care to exchange?" the woman proposed.

"No," Baxter answered. "I prefer the aisle."

Then the plane was airborne, the central lights returned and the first class section flight attendant began their procedures of confirming names and collecting beverage orders. She leaned forward over Baxter to address his seatmate. "Your name, please?"

"Gold!" was the response. "I asked the other young lady to bring me a Remy and coffee, please."

"Baxter, Joseph Jr." Baxter added. "And I'll have another Canadian Club on the rocks."

"Joseph Baxter Jr.," the woman repeated. "That name has a familiar ring! Who are you?"

"I'm just a country boy from the Midwest returning from the lush corruption of Southern California to the quiet orderly disciplines of my newly claimed home, New York City," Baxter answered with the objective of closing off conversation after his Canadian Club had been consumed.

"Baxter!" the woman repeated. "It's a familiar name. Why?"

"You're probably confusing me with Warner Baxter who used to play in the Crime Doctor series of films. His films, of course included *Call of the Crime Doctor*, *The Crime Doctor's Revenge*, and *The Crime Doctor's Last Case*. I saw them all at the Polar Theatre in Iron Creek, Minnesota."

The woman pushed her aviator glasses up on her forehead and revealed dark eyes with slight circles appearing from under her make-up.

"Crime Doctor indeed! Iron Creek, Minnesota! You're Joe Baxter, the red-headed boy I spent Christmas with twenty years ago," she offered Baxter a well lacquered hand.

"I'm Beth Gold. Do you remember me?"

The flight attendant brought their drinks and looked to the woman. "Miss Gold, I'm reading The Seaside Lady. It's only a paperback, but could you autograph it later?"

"Of course, my dear," Beth responded. "Are you enjoying the book?"

"I just started it. But it seems very good. I've read just about all of your books?

"Good. Mr. Baxter, traveling with me, is a famous movie star of the 1930s. Perhaps you've seen him in one of his Crime Doctor films?" The flight attendant looked at Baxter strangely.

"The Crime Doctor's Duluth Adventure was always my personal favorite," Baxter added.

"Somehow, you're more believable as the son of the Crime Doctor," Beth said emptying her brandy into her coffee. "Now do you remember me? Because I certainly remember you. You provided me some valuable material for stories. I can remember that Christmas party we spent with that wonderful black sergeant and his wife. My goodness," she patted Baxter on the hand. "I'm all wound up and wide awake. Now I've got someone to talk to. I'm also dry on material. Now tell me, Joe what have you been doing with yourself over the past twenty years?"

Baxter, having told his life story to Alice Dungler that very afternoon had little interest in reciting it again to Beth Gold. He decided to use an old consultant's trick. He persuaded Beth to talk about herself. She acceded without a struggle. Beth went on to cover the years from that last night in Fort Gately up to the moment she got on the airplane that evening. Her story lasted three Remy's and was interrupted only by fresh drink orders and flight attendants bringing copies of books for Beth to autograph. Baxter started Beth's flow of words by asking her where she had gone after she departed the motel room in Georgia.

She stated this part of her story by carefully whispering into Baxter's ear in a soft clear voice. "I was embarrassed and angry. I had to get away from the whole bunch of you. I was very confused about my sexual orientation in those days. I thought I preferred women to men. Laura was a beautiful, open minded girl I met in Paris. We more or less took to one another. But she was always chattering abou her Yerfdog. Well she married him, put on about forty pounds over five years and he's some kind of a schoolmaster at a prep school after probably placing himself in the Guinness Book of Records for most failures of the New York Bar Exam."

"Godfrey was a good friend and a nice person," Baxter commented.

"They're both losers living off family trusts while Godfrey goes through his "Mr. Chips" routine," Beth said closing off the subject of Bwana and Laura. "I came out of that weekend with one great gain and that was the evening with the Wilsons. I wrote a wonderful story called *A Sergeant's Tale* that was published by Gotham Magazine. It established my reputation and a television production company wanted to buy the story rights from me. It was then that I figured out I had to have a first class agent. I signed up with Mitchell Starr. He looked like Tom Conway in the old Falcon television series. Black salt and pepper hair with a blow dry look before there were blow dryers, neat little mustache, English accent, and Brooks Brother suits when they were still in style. I though Mitch was the most sophisticated man in the world. I found out later that he was an English major from Brooklyn College and his real name was Mitch Goldblum. But that's New York City. Everyone reinvents himself every five years and does their best to wipe the traces of his old identities. You'll catch on to it, Joe. Anyway, Mitchell was the key strategist in building my reputation as a writer. The man has good taste, contacts, and he opened doors for me. I held some writing jobs for trade magazines, but worked my ass off writing fiction at night and on weekends. I wrote a book called *Scarlet Autumn* full of sex and intrigue about a woman whose lover had been murdered thirty years earlier. It became a great unsolved crime that haunted her life and then on the last page of her death bed, she admits the killing. I changed the ending five times before Mitchell talked me into going with my first ending. It was the hot book of 1960. Did you read it?" Beth asked.

"No," Baxter shook his head.

"Well, after Scarlet Autumn, I quit my day jobs and became a hot stuff novelist. Suddenly there were a series of Beth Gold novels. They weren't belles letters, but they sold well and I discovered what they call marketing. I was writing for a woman's audience, age 21 to 55, who wanted to read about beautiful people living on the edge of the fast track of life. I became a hot formula writer with Mitchell as my merchandiser and negotiator. I made a lot of money and Mitchell took his cut. Then Vietnam reared it's ugly head. Lyndon Johnson's bunch was sending a lot of sweet boys over to die to defend a corrupt government. The only cause I ever had before in my life was Beth Gold. Now I had the greatest cause of my life. Stop the war! Were you in the Peace Movement, Joe?"

"No. I had to work," Baxter explained.

"I was in it from 1966 to 1975. Nine years of protests and fighting. Mitchell lost a son in Vietnam during Tet. He was very proud of his son and bitter about the anti-war movement after that. He told me to get another agent after I led a protest rally at the 1968 Democratic National Convention in Chicago. There I was agentless, fighting injustices, trying to humble an evil, unlawful federal government. I didn't hang around with the Weathermen and blow up buildings. I wasn't a communist agent. I was quite comfortable with the capitalist system. I just didn't like the idea of drafting young men and sending them off to Vietnam to get their asses shot off in order to defend a bunch of corrupt, unelected officials in Southeast Asia. I became controversial and discovered what negative cash flow could do for a girl's complexion."

"I met my husband, Lester, in the Peace Movement. He was a young, good looking, blonde man from Cal-Berkely Law. Lester is a few years my junior and was very good at getting people out of jail. He was a great Habeas Corpus man and I fell in love with him. We lived together for about three years and got married in 1972. I lost about five years income, thanks to that Goddam war. I found a new agent, the Cromwell Group, and became the lead property of Louise Cromwell, the proprietor. Louise is Wellesley, book publishing editor, and now an agent. She's far more professional and strategic than Mitchell and I'm hot stuff again at last. I've been working on a screen adaptation with some Hollywood assholes for three days and now I'm heading back to real work. So there it is, Baxter. I'm 43 years old, married,—-and, oh yes. Lester and I adopted these kids from Vietnam. I believe we have two of them, but we may have more. I'm not certain of that! When they have their friends over, I'm not certain as to which ones to send home. Lester plays the mother role and we have a Nanny/housekeeper who looks after them in between smoking my cigarettes. Lester even knows their names. I suspect that Lester is not a very skilled lawyer. I have set him up in the Disco business. We have a place on west 65th Street called Lester's. It's a Sub S Corporation and loses money despite being packed every night. I suspect that the bartenders are stealing him blind. We live on Fifth Avenue in the 60's and we have a weekend place on the Cape. I have a godawful big nut to crack and—-," Beth said clinking glasses. "It's good to see you again, my man. You are, of course older. But you seem more polished and self confident. Who do you work for in New York?"

"I word for a management consulting firm called McKenzie Barber," Baxter replied assuming that he would now have to explain what McKenzie Barber was.

"I know McKenzie Barber. That's where Ernie Grey is the Chairman," Beth responded crisply. "Are you a Partner?"

"I expect to be this Fall. I'm just transferring out from Chicago. My official first day in the New York office is Monday. How much do you know about McKenzie Barber?"

"A reasonable amount. I did a story on McKenzie Barber and Robson Allen Harbridge for *Gotham Magazine*. It was called the "Management Consulting Giants" and ran about two years ago. I'll send you a reprint if you're interested. I didn't like the lead much and both firms wanted a review of the draft before publishing. Gotham wouldn't do it. The two firms hate each other!"

"Did you meet Ernie Grey?" Baxter asked incredulously.

"I had two sessions with him. I also met his wife, Millie, when we sat next to each other on the dias for a fund-raiser. She's read some of my books. I liked Ernie. He's very energetic and dynamic. I didn't like the Robson Allen bunch. They're very smart, quite elite, and they made a lot of catty remarks about stodgy old McKenzie Barber. I liked McKenzie Barber and Ernie Grey much better. His wife, Millie, is absolutely terrific. Now what do you do there?"

Baxter went on to explain about executive compensation only to have Beth interrupt him. "Frank Alvardi. I've met him. He looks like Joe DiMaggio. You work for Frank Alvardi! He's a very sexy man. He comes to Lester's every now and then."

"Beth, are you into business?"

"I'm quite into business, Joe. I believe that sexy business novels will be the market opportunity of the 1980s. It was Louie Cromwell who got me a lot of business writing assignments a few years back when I was trying to reposition myself from my Peacenik image. I took on a bunch of business profile stories for Gotham. The woman MBA market will be an important segment for me to address in future novels, although, as you can see, I'm very big with stewardesses. Now Joe, talk to me about yourself. You're still amusing. Are you married?"

"Divorced."

"Seeing someone regularly?"

"No. I know very few people in New York. For years I've just gone in and out."

"Where are you living?"

"78th and York."

"Not bad, but hardly distinguished. Do you have children?"

"They're back in Wisconsin living with their mother. They'll be visiting regularly though."

"You're a retread. A first quality retread and you'll be very much in demand."

"Demand for what?" Baxter asked.

"Companionship and sex. What do you think the market's like for professional women in their thirties and forties? It's retreads. A desirable retread profile is an attractive man with a good job in his late thirties to late forties. The single never-been-married men out here in that age bracket are all gay. The retread usually is bruised with guilt for kids from a busted marriage, and dropped into New York in a new job that usually is bigger than the job he held before. Does that describe you?"

"That's relatively accurate and a little disarming."

"I have someone for you to meet. I think you would be very well matched for her. Her name's Stephany Hart and she's a Securities Analyst. You know what a Securities Analyst does. She's attractive, very bright, and quite tall. Stephany's probably in her early thirties. She intimidates a lot of men. I think you two would get along very well. She would love your humor. You must give me your telephone number. I'll have a little dinner party and then you're on your own."

"I appreciate the attention, but I don't know how to react."

"It's simple, Joe. I'll arrange a dinner and you show up. Stephany has been very helpful in providing information on some of my writing projects. I owe her one and I'd like to offer you up. Fruit you've sampled is better to recommend to friends that fruit you don't know."

"The tree was a lot younger then," Baxter pointed out. "You make New York sound like a small town."

"It is, Joe. Lester and I reduced New York to 321 separate cultural and geographical networks one night. I drafted a story idea for *Gotham Magazine* on the subject. It bounced all way up to the Editor who took it to the Publisher. The Publisher didn't like it. So I dropped it. I don't write anything these days unless I know I'm absolutely sure I'll get paid for it. Do you read Gotham, Joe?"

"I've looked at the covers and the cartoons. They seem to sell a lot of advertising."

"Gotham is New York celebrating itself for the people out in Omaha and Kansas City who think of themselves as sophisticates. Gotham is what's happening in New York for the ladies in Darien and Greenwich. Anyway— I've lost my point haven't I?" Baxter had grown very drowsy. If only Beth had a button someplace that would switch her off.

"Miss! More Remy and coffee, please. Now where was I? Oh, yes, the network theory. I'm going to smoke. This is the smoking section and I assume that you were prepared to share seats with a smoker."

Baxter nodded his head. If Beth smoked, he reasoned, it might make it more difficult to continue talking. She produced a long cigarette holder from her purse, placed and lit a cigarette and stared at the ceiling. "Now here's your theory on New York's 321 networks———."

Baxter was asleep shortly. "Excuse me Beth. It's shuteye time," he announced and closed his eyes. Baxter dreamed about New York and all the women who would be after him. Maybe he'd even find one he liked.

There was a coffee service about five o'clock. Baxter pulled himself up to brush his teeth and shave a little. Beth was still drinking brandy and coffee with her cigarette holder in her mouth. Her tray was covered with newspaper clipping inside an open manila file folder. Baxter exited the lavatory to find Beth waiting to get in. "Good morning, Joe. I've got to make repairs for landing."

Baxter returned to the seat and looked across at Beth's tray. The clippings were all *New York Times* obituaries. Some were over a year old. He leafed quickly through them. All of the lives sounded interesting. They ranged from explorers to movie stars and included college presidents, dog trainers, radio singers, acrobats, war heroes, and ventriloquists.

"What's all this about, Beth?" Baxter asked after Beth returned with a new face.

"Naughty Joe. You've been peeking at my trade research secrets."

"The *New York Times* obituaries?"

"That's where I get a lot of character and plot ideas. You should read the obits religiously every day. There's a lot of charm, color, and history in people's lives being chronicled in two paragraphs. I was working on a new story concept while you were sleeping. I may work for an hour or so on the word processor when I get home. I have a late lunch with my agent Louise. God I need the weekend!" Beth placed her dark aviator glasses over her eyes and began to pack up when the flight attendant announced the landing instructions.

"Are you going to your apartment now?" Beth asked. "Would you like a lift? I have a car and driver picking me up. I can drop you."

"Really Beth," Baxter protested. "I can just grab a cab."

"I will have none of it, Joe. You're riding with me."

They left Kennedy in a stretch limousine. Beth had been greeted by a black uniformed driver holding a large card that said GOLD.

"It can be a godawful long drive in from Kennedy and I'm glad to have the company." Beth lit another cigarette and leaned back in the seat. "So my old pal, Joe Baxter from Iron Creek, Minnesota, is coming to New York with McKenzie Barber. Are you excited?"

"I'm tired."

"I'll have my secretary call you on Monday at the office with some dates when I can have Stephany over to meet you. You've put on a little weight, but you're still quite good looking. I hope that you and I will be good friends. I'll try to introduce you to some business writers. Your friend Alvardi plays them like a fiddle. Executive Pay is a hot subject in New York. Everybody is concerned about how much they should make and how to avoid paying taxes. Can you guess how much money I made last year?"

"Net personal service income?"

"Gross. Only my accountant knows how much I net."

"One million five," Baxter guessed.

"I'm twice that, Joe. I'd be in the poorhouse at one million five. This is New York, Joe Baxter. The streets are paved with precious metals. You are going to be very successful here. Beth Gold predicts it!"

Beth was dropped first at her Fifth Avenue apartment. It was an impressive stone building of a dozen stories that looked out into Central Park. There was an awning out in front and a uniformed doorman scurried to the limousine. "Welcome back, Miss Gold," he greeted Beth.

Baxter stepped out of the limousine into the damp raw morning air.

"That's us!" Beth pointed with a gloved hand. "We're in the north penthouse. PHA. Got it? Loved seeing you again, Joe." The doorman took the bag and Beth went up the carpet in long strides to the front door. She waved to Baxter and disappeared in the front door.

"421 East 78th Street, please," Baxter instructed the limo driver. It was 6:47 AM on Friday, March 31st, 1978. Baxter was now a New Yorker! A retread on the prowl! He would have to immediately re-invent himself. He had come East like Nick Carroway in the Great Gatsby. Baxter sensed he was there to stay.

(THE END)

# THE CONSULTANT
# BOOK III OF SHATTERED COVENANTS

The Consultant is the third book in a novel entitled SHATTERED COVENANTS. It is comprised of seven books which record the history of McKenzie Barber & Co., a twentieth century management consulting firm. SHATTERED COVENANTS is organized into seven books. The concluding books in the cycle are
- THE CHAIRMAN
- THE PARTNERS
- THE HOUSE OF HARWELL
- TWILIGHT & ENDGAME

Previously published book in the cycle include
- PRESENT & PAST IMPERFECT
- THE ROAD TO MCKENZIE BARBER

SHATTERED COVENANTS spans a time period beginning in1921 and concluding in 1992. It narrates the founding, rise and ultimate dissolution of a great American business enterprise.

# ABOUT THE AUTHOR

Dwight Foster, the author of *Shattered Covenants*, is a native of Minnesota who was transferred to New York City in 1980. He retired as a consulting partner from an international public accounting firm in January 1990 to form an executive search firm.

*Shattered Covenants* is a first novel, which represents an eight year project dealing with the passing of leadership in a professional services firm. *Present & Past Imperfect.* The consultant is Book III of a series of free standing novels relating to the formation of a major management consulting firm, its rise, zenith, decline, and ultimate compliant merger with a principal competitor. *Shattered Covenants* deals with the passing of CEOs (i.e. kings) and their ultimate effect on the careers and lives of the courtiers and rank and file professionals who follow the leadership of the CEO.

The author has spent his business career in the consulting industry and, for the past eleven years, has headed up a well-recognized executive search firm. Dwight Foster has published previously in management studies and magazine articles and is quoted from time to time in the national press. His experience in the practice of executive search and familiarity with organization and business models over the past thirty years provided the motivation to write a sweeping novel. The primary narrator of *Shattered Covenants*, Joseph Baxter, Jr., is the son of a labor martyr from Minnesota's Iron Range who rises to a Board Room, world traveling executive compensation consultant. Baxter is a modern day Candide who develops the cunning to survive in a ruthlessly competitive business world.

Dwight Foster is a University of Minnesota Alumnus, the father of two adult children, and is married to Dorothy Choitz Foster, a well-known consultant to the cosmetics and fragrance industry. The Fosters maintain an apartment in New York City and a permanent home in the Pocono Mountains of Pennsylvania.